"It might be about money, sweet-heart."

Her chest puffed out, pushing the front of the sleeveless blouse she wore. "I am not your sweetheart. And don't think I don't remember you, Detective Krolikowski. I know you and your partner picked up my brother before he was arrested. That case is closed."

"Maybe, but your fiancé's murder isn't. And we think you and your brother know something about it."

"This is about Richard?" Her eyes widened. But when he thought she'd start that reticent eye contact thing again, she surprised him by actually taking a step closer to the edge of the porch. "Now we're finally getting to the point, aren't we? Are you accusing me again of poisoning him? So I'm a suspect, not a victim. And here I thought you'd shown up because—"

"Because what?" He pulled the toy with a noose around its neck from behind his back and watched her sink back into the chair. "You want to tell us what the hell is going on with you

KANSAS CITY SECRETS

BY
JULIE MILLER

Published in Great Britain 2015
by Mills & Boon, an imprint of Harlequin (UK) Limited,
Eton House, 18-24 Paradise Road, Richmond, Surrey, TW9 1SR

© 2015 Julie Miller

ISBN: 978-0-263-25314-6

46-0815

Harlequin (UK) Limited's policy is to use papers that are natural, renewable and recyclable products and made from wood grown in sustainable forests. The logging and manufacturing processes conform to the legal environmental regulations of the country of origin.

Printed and bound in Spain
by CPI, Barcelona

Julie Miller is an award-winning *USA TODAY* best-selling author of breathtaking romantic suspense—with a National Readers' Choice Award and a Daphne du Maurier Award, among other prizes. She has also earned an *RT Book Reviews* Career Achievement Award. For a complete list of her books, monthly newsletter and more, go to www.juliemiller.org.

For my mom. It was challenging to write this book amongst unforeseen events that demanded my attention. But I wouldn't have traded your wonderful visit and recovery time for anything. I'm glad you're feeling better. I love you.

Chapter One

"Why did you kill that woman, Stephen?" Rosemary March asked, looking across the scarred-up table at her younger brother. "And don't tell me it was to rob her for drug money. I know that isn't who you are."

Rosemary studied the twenty-eight-year-old man she'd done her best to raise after a small plane crash several years earlier had left them orphans. She tried to pretend there weren't a dozen pairs of eyes on her, watching through the observation windows around them. It was easier than pretending the Missouri State Penitentiary's tiny visitation room with its locked steel doors wasn't making her claustrophobic.

But it was impossible to ignore the clinking of the chains and cuffs that bound Stephen March's wrists and ankles together. "You ask me that every time you come to see me, Rosemary."

"Because I'm not satisfied with the answers you've given me." She ran her fingers beneath the collar of her floral-print blouse, telling herself it was the heat of the Missouri summer, and not any discomfiting leer from another prisoner or the unsettling mystery of why her brother would kill a woman he didn't know, that made beads of perspiration gather against her skin. "I hate seeing you in here."

"You need to let it go. This is where I deserve to be. Trust me, sis. I was never going to amount to much on the outside."

"That's not true. With your artistic talent you could have—"

"But I didn't." He drummed his scarred fingers together at the edge of the table. For as long as she'd known him, he'd been hyper like that—always moving, always full of energy. Their father had gotten him into running cross-country and track; their mother had put a drawing pencil in his hand. Ultimately, though, neither outlet could compete with the meth addiction that had sent his life spiraling out of control. "Losing Mom and Dad was no excuse for me going off the deep end and not helping out. Especially when your fiancé…" The drumming stopped abruptly. "Just know, I was really there for you when you needed me."

"Needed you for what? If you had anything to do with Richard's murder, please tell me. You know I'll forgive you. We never used to keep secrets like this from each other. Please help me understand."

"I kept you safe. That's the one thing I got right, the one thing I'm proud of. Even the Colonel would have finally been proud of me," he added, referring to their father.

"Dad loved you," Rosemary insisted.

"Maybe. But he wasn't real thrilled having a drug addict for a son, was he? But I took action. The way he would have." His gaze darted around the room, as if checking for eavesdroppers, before his light brown eyes focused on her and he dropped his voice to a whisper. "For the last time, I killed that lady reporter to protect you."

Understanding far more about tragedy and violence

and not being able to protect herself and her loved ones more than she'd ever wanted to, Rosemary brushed aside the escaping wisps of her copper-red hair and leaned forward, pressing the argument. "Dad wouldn't have wanted you to commit murder. I didn't even know that woman. That's what doesn't make any sense. What kind of threat was she to me?"

Stephen groaned at her repeated demands for a straightforward explanation. He slumped back in his chair and nodded toward the family's current attorney standing outside the window behind her. "Why did you bring him?"

Fine. She'd let him change the topic. Although it was good to see Stephen clean and sober, he looked exhausted. Her younger brother had aged considerably in the months since he'd pleaded guilty to second-degree murder and been incarcerated, and she didn't want to add to his stress. She glanced over her shoulder to the brown-haired man in the suit and tie and returned his smile before facing her brother again. "Howard insisted on coming with me. He didn't want me driving back to Kansas City at night by myself. It was a kind offer."

The drumming started again. "He reminds me too much of his brother. Are you sure he's treating you right?"

She flinched at the remembered shock of Richard Bratcher's open hand across her mouth putting an end to an argument they'd had over a memorial scholarship she'd wanted to set up in her parents' names. Seven years later, she could still taste the metallic tang of blood in her mouth that reminded her she'd made a colossal mistake in inviting the attorney into their lives, falling in love with him, trusting him. Rosemary inhaled a quiet breath and lifted her chin. Richard was dead and she'd become a pro at setting aside those horrible memories and pasting a facade of cool serenity on her face.

"They may look alike, but Howard isn't like his brother. Howard's never laid a hand on me. In fact, I think he feels so guilty about how Richard treated us when I was engaged to him that he goes out of his way to be helpful."

"He's just keeping you close so you won't sue his law firm."

"Maybe." Initially, she'd been leery of Howard's offer to take over as the family's attorney. But he knew more than anyone else about the wrongful death and injury suit Richard Bratcher had filed against the aerospace manufacturer that built the faulty plane her father had flown on that fateful trip, and she couldn't stand to drag the suit out any longer than it had already lasted. Plus, he'd been nothing but a gentleman and rock-solid support through the continuing upheavals in her life. "Howard makes it easier to get in to see you. And he's responsible for keeping you in the infirmary wing to do your rehab instead of you being sent back to general lockup with the other prisoners."

"Don't stick with him because of me. I can handle myself in here. I don't trust him, sis."

Rosemary's smile became genuine. "You don't trust anybody."

Stephen sat up straight and reached for her. At the last second, he remembered the guard at door and raised both hands to show they were empty. Rosemary held up her hands, as well, and got a nod of approval before reaching over the battered tabletop to hold her brother's hands. "I trust you. I'm okay being in here because I know you're safe now. You *are* safe, right?"

Stephen's grip tightened, as if somehow sensing that

all was not well in her life. But Rosemary clenched her jaw and continued to smile. The last thing he needed was to worry about her on the outside, when he couldn't do a thing about it. "I am."

She was right now, at any rate.

The assurance seemed to ease his concern. He eased his grip but didn't let go. "That bastard Richard is dead. But it'd kill me if I thought his brother or anyone else was hurting you."

"I'm fine." What were a few obscene phone calls, anyway, after all they'd been through? Her hope had been to find a few answers for herself, not raise doubts in her brother's mind. "As much as we both wanted Richard out of our lives, I know you didn't kill him." Stephen had been in a rehab facility in the middle of a forty-eight-hour lockdown the morning she'd discovered her fiancé dead in bed at his condo, poisoned sometime during the night. She, however, had had no alibi and had spent several months as KCPD's number one suspect until the trail of clues went cold and Richard Bratcher's murder had been relegated to the cold-case files. Rosemary squeezed her brother's hands. "Whoever poisoned him did us a favor. But if you're protecting someone who wanted that reporter dead, or you're taking the blame for her murder because you wished you'd been the one to kill Richard… Please, Stephen. Talk to me."

His eyes darkened for a split second before he shook his head and pulled away. "I was using that night. I pulled the trigger. Now I'm done talking about it. You should be, too."

"Why?"

"Rosemary—" He bit down on a curse and folded his hands together, his finger tracing the marks he'd left in his own skin back in the days when he'd been too stressed-out to cope or on a manic high.

"It's okay, Stephen," she quickly assured him, alarmed by the frantic, self-destructive habit he'd worked so hard to overcome. "I won't mention it again."

This visit, at any rate.

Reluctantly, she acquiesced to his demand and sat back in her chair. She knew there had to be more to Stephen's motive for killing an innocent reporter than simply being high as a kite and not knowing what he was doing, as he'd stated in court. The monster in their own home had been the real threat, and, in her heart, she believed there was a connection between the two murders—a logical reason her brother was going to spend half his adult life in prison and she was going to be alone. But if Stephen wouldn't talk, she wasn't certain how else she could get to the truth about the two murders and finally put the nightmares of the past behind her.

Yet, until that revelation, Rosemary stuck to the role she'd learned to play so well, dutifully taking care of others. "Is there anything you need? I brought the books you asked for, and two cartons of cigarettes." She curled her fingers into a fist, fighting the instinctive urge to reach for the neckline of her dress and the scars underneath. Instead, she arched an eyebrow in teasing reprimand. "I wish you'd give those up. You know they're not good for you."

That earned her half a grin from her brother. "Let me kick one addiction at a time, okay?"

"Okay." A high sign from the guard warned her their time was nearly up. Rosemary blinked back the tears that made her eyes gritty and smiled for Stephen's sake as he stood and waited for the guard to escort him back to his cell. "I wish I could give you a hug."

"Me, too." But that kind of contact wasn't allowed. "I love you, sis. Stay strong."

As if she had any choice. She fought to keep her smile fixed in place. "I love you. I'll keep writing. And it wouldn't hurt you to pick up a pencil every now and then, either. Be safe."

He nodded as he shuffled to the door in front of the guard. "You, too."

Rosemary was alone for only a few seconds before another guard came to the door to walk her out to the visitors' desk. But it was long enough for the smile to fade, her shoulders to sag and her heart to grow heavy. How was one woman supposed to endure so much and still keep going on with her life? She followed the rules. She'd done everything that was expected of her and more. Why wasn't it good enough? Why wasn't *she* good enough?

"Ma'am?"

With a quick swipe at the hot moisture in her eyes, Rosemary nodded and got up to accompany the guard out that door into an antechamber and then out the next one into the visitors' waiting area. She jumped at the slam of each heavy door behind her, which closed her off farther from the only family she had left. With every slam, her shoulders straightened, her heart locked up and she braced herself to meet the concern that etched frown lines beside Howard Bratcher's eyes when he greeted her. "How are you holding up?"

"I'm fine."

While she waited in line to retrieve the purse she'd checked in at the front desk, Rosemary became aware of other eyes watching her. Not quite the lecherous leer she'd imagined tracking her from the shadows each night she got one of those creepy phone calls. Certainly not the solicitous concern in Howard's hazel eyes.

When the holes boring into her back became too much to ignore, she turned.

"Rosemary?"

But she didn't see Howard standing beside her. She looked beyond him to the rows of chairs near the far wall. The girlfriends, wives and mothers waiting to see their loved ones barely acknowledged her curiosity as her gaze swept down the line. There were a couple of men in T-shirts and jeans. A few more in dress slacks and polo shirts or wearing a jacket and tie like Howard. They were reading papers, chatting with their neighbors, using their phones.

But no one was watching.

No one was interested in her at all.

She was just a skittish, paranoid woman afraid of her own shadow these days.

Hating that any sense of self-confidence and security had once again been stolen from her, she turned back to the guard at the front desk and grabbed her purse. "Thank you."

But when she fell into step beside Howard and headed toward the main doors, the hackles beneath her bun went on alert again. She was suddenly aware of the young-ish man sitting at the end of the row against the wall. He wore a loose tie at the front of the linen jacket that remained curiously unwrinkled, and he was texting on his phone.

Was it that guy? Had he been following her movements with that more than casual curiosity she'd felt? Although it was hard to tell if he was making eye contact through the glasses he wore, he seemed to be holding his phone at an oddly upright angle, tapping the screen. He lifted his attention from his work and briefly smiled at her before returning to whatever he found so fascinating on the tiny screen.

Like an image of her?

"Rosemary?" She felt Howard's touch at her elbow and quickly shifted her gaze back to the door he held open for her. "Is something wrong?"

"I don't know." Stepping outside, the wall of heat and humidity momentarily robbed her of breath. But her suspicion lingered. "Did you see that guy?"

"What guy?"

They were halfway across the parking lot now. "The one who was staring at me?"

Howard glanced over his shoulder and shrugged. "They probably don't see a lot of pretty women here."

Pretty? Rosemary groaned inwardly at the sly compliment. She caught a few frizzy waves that curled against her neck and tucked them into the bun at the back of her head. After Richard's abuse, the last thing she wanted was to attract a man's attention. But the curiosity of that man in the waiting room had felt like something different. She shuddered in the heat as she waited for Howard to open the door of his car for her. "I think he took a picture of me with his phone."

"So you don't mean one of the prisoners?"

"No. He was one of the attorney-looking guys out in the waiting area."

"Attorney-looking?" Howard laughed as he closed the door behind her and walked around to his side of the car. He shed his suit jacket and tossed it into the backseat before getting in. "So we're a type?"

"Sorry. I didn't mean anything negative by that. I was just describing him. Suit. Tie. Maybe more on the ball than some of the others waiting to visit friends and family here. He looked like an educated professional."

"No offense taken." He pushed the button, and the engine of the luxury car hummed to life. "Could be a reporter, getting the scoop on Kansas City's newest millionaire visiting the state penitentiary."

Right, as if hearing her picture might be in the paper again was a whole lot better than thinking someone was spying on her. "I wish you wouldn't say that."

He pushed another button to turn on the air-conditioning. "What do you want me to call it? Your brother's in the state pen. It's public record."

"No. 'Kansas City's newest millionaire.'" She supposed the soap opera of her life made her recent wealth big news in a summer where most of the local stories seemed to be about the weather. "I'd give anything if that headline had never hit the papers. I hate being the center of attention."

"Yet you handle it all with grace and decorum." Howard reached for her hand across the seat, but Rosemary pulled away before he made contact, busying herself with buckling up and adjusting the air-conditioning vents. Even as the evening hour approached, the temperature across Missouri was still in the nineties. Seeking relief from the heat was as legitimate an excuse to avoid his touch as her innate aversion to letting a man who looked so much like his late younger brother—or maybe any man, at all—get that close to her again.

With a sigh he made no effort to mask, Howard settled back behind the wheel and pulled out onto the road leading away from the prison. "Hungry for an early dinner? My treat. Jefferson City's got this great new restaurant on top of one of the hotels downtown. You can see the Capitol Building and almost all the riverfront. Day or night, it's a spectacular view."

The answering rumble in her stomach negated the

easy excuse to say she wasn't hungry. Instead, she opted for an honest compromise. "Dinner would be great. But, could we just drive through and eat it in the car? I need to get home and let the dogs out. And we still have a two-and-a-half-hour drive to Kansas City ahead of us."

Howard had seen the wrongful death and manufacturer's negligence lawsuit his brother had started for her through to its conclusion. And though she'd trade the 9.2-million-dollar settlement for her parents in a heartbeat, she was grateful to the Bratcher, Austin & Cole law firm that they'd gotten the company to admit its guilt in their construction of the faulty wing struts on the small airplane that had crashed, killing her parents instantly.

And though Howard's interest might have as much to do with the generous percentage his firm had received from the settlement, Rosemary appreciated his attempts to be kind. However, her gratitude didn't go so far as to want to encourage a more personal connection between them. She'd thought Richard Bratcher was her hero, rescuing her from the dutiful drudgery of her life, and she'd fallen hard and fast. Richard had been her first love…and her biggest mistake—one she never intended to make again. But her business relationship and friendship with his older brother, Howard, shouldn't suffer because of it. She glanced across the seat and smiled. "Is that okay?"

Knowing her history with his brother, Howard was probably relieved she hadn't given him a flat-out no. He nodded his agreement, willing, once again, to please her. "Fast food, it is."

Almost three hours later, Howard pulled off the interstate and turned toward her home on the eastern edge of Kansas City. Although it was nearly eight o'clock, the sun was still a rosy orange ball in the western sky when he walked her up onto the front porch that ran clear across the front of her ninety-year-old bungalow.

From the moment the car doors had shut and she'd stepped out, she could hear the high and low pitches of her two dogs barking, and was eager to get inside to see them. She had her keys out and her purse looped over her shoulder when she realized Howard had followed her to the top of the stairs, waiting to take his leave or maybe hoping to be invited in for coffee.

What one woman might see as polite, Rosemary saw as suffocating, maybe even dangerous. As much as she loathed going out in public, she hated the idea of being trapped inside the house with a man even more. No way was she reliving that nightmare. With the dogs scratching at the other side of the door now, anxious for her arrival, Rosemary turned and lifted her gaze to Howard's patient expression. "Thank you for going with me to Jefferson City."

"My pleasure."

"Do I owe you some gas money?"

He chuckled. "Not a penny."

Finally getting the hint that this was goodbye, he leaned in to kiss her cheek. But Rosemary extended her hand instead, forcing some space between them. "Good night, Howard."

He gently took her hand and raised it to his lips to kiss the back of her knuckles instead. "Good night. I'll pick you up tomorrow?" he asked, releasing her from the gallant gesture and pulling away.

Right. More papers to sign. "I can drive, you know."

"But the drive will give me a chance to explain the trust fund and scholarship you'll be setting up before you sign anything." There'd already been plenty of explanation and she'd made her decisions.

"Howard—"

"That way you won't have to spend any longer than a few minutes at the office."

Now *that* was a selling point. Rosemary nodded her acquiescence. "I'll be ready. See you then."

She waited until he was backing out of the driveway and waved before turning around to unlock the door. She typed in the security code to release the alarm, but her hand stopped with her key in the lock. She wasn't alone.

Was *he* watching her? Would there be another vile message waiting on her answering machine?

I see you, Rosemary. Thinking your money can buy you security. Thinking those dogs will keep you safe. One of these days it'll be just you and me. I'll show you how justice is done. I'll take you apart piece by piece.

With her shaking hand still on the key, she glanced up and down the street at the peaceful normalcy of a summer evening in the older suburban neighborhood. There was an impromptu ball game in the Johannesens' front yard across the street. Mrs. Keith was out trimming her shrubs while her husband washed the car in their driveway.

Squinting against the reflection of the sunset in her next-door neighbors' living room window, Rosemary caught the shadowy silhouette of Otis or Arlene Dinkle. The brief ripple of alarm that had put her on guard a moment earlier eased. The Dinkles had lived next door for years, and had been friends with her parents long before Rosemary had moved back home to care for her teenage brother.

Unable to get a good look at which of the couple was eyeing her, Rosemary exhaled a sigh of relief and waved. They'd watched over her for a long time, including that night Richard had attacked her and she'd run to their house to call the police, fearing he'd come back after he'd stormed out. Her wave must have been all the reassurance the Dinkles needed to know she'd arrived home safely. The shadow disappeared and the blinds closed.

Breathing easier now, Rosemary unlocked the door and went inside. "Hey, ladies. Mama's home."

Her smile was genuine as she locked the door behind her and dropped to her knees to accept the enthusiastic greeting from the German shepherd with the excited whine and the miniature poodle leaping up and down around her.

"Hey, Duchess. Hey, Trixie. I missed you guys, too." She spared a few moments to rub their tummies and accept some eager licks before rising to her feet and doing a quick walk through the house with the dogs trailing behind her.

She really should have no worries about an intruder, especially with the yappy apricot poodle and the former K-9 Corps dog who'd been dismissed from the program because of an eye injury on hand to guard the place. If the dogs weren't alarmed, she shouldn't be, either. Still, she checked all the rooms, including the guest suite upstairs, before she set her purse down beside the answering machine on the kitchen counter.

No blinking red light.

"Thank goodness."

Her day had already been long and troubling enough without having to deal with another message from the unwanted admirer she'd picked up the night after news of her settlement being finalized had appeared in the *Kansas City Journal*. And she was certain the police department was tired of her calling in to report the disturbing calls. She knew she was tired of hearing the subtle changes in their tone once she identified herself. The officers were sympathetic when they saw her name in the system as a victim of domestic violence, but seemed to think she was some kind of crank caller when they read her abuser was dead and that she had once been a suspect in his murder. They probably thought she was some sort of paranoid crazy lady—or a woman desperately seeking attention when, in reality, she'd be far more content to fade into the woodwork.

The advice from the officer she'd finally been connected with had been to keep a log of the calls and let her know if she thought they were escalating into something more serious. If she'd known when Richard Bratcher's controlling demands were going to escalate into violence, she might have been spared a split lip, a broken arm and… She ran her fingers beneath the collar of her blouse, resting her palm over the old scars there. Talk about a sudden and unexpected escalation. But when images from that horrific time tried to surface, Rosemary pulled her hand away and stooped down to busy her fingers and brain with the much more enjoyable task of petting the dogs and rubbing their bellies.

After a happy competition for her affection, Rosemary kicked off her sandals and relished the cool tile under her toes. With both dogs dancing around her, she unbolted the back door and opened the screen door to let them out into the fenced-in yard to run around.

The warm breeze wrapped her eyelet skirt around her knees and caught the wispy curls escaping from her bun and stuck them to the warm skin of her cheeks and neck. With the nubby concrete of the patio still warm beneath her feet, she glanced up at the sky and tried to gauge how long they had before nightfall. While Trixie sniffed the perimeter of the yard and the big German shepherd loped along behind her little buddy, Rosemary walked to the edge of her in-ground pool and dipped her toes into the water. As tempting as it might be to cool off in the pool, she hated to be out after dark. Besides, Duchess and Trixie had been on their own for most of the day and deserved a little one-on-one attention. A few games of fetch and tug-of-war before bedtime would do just as much to help her forget these restless urges to prod the truth from her brother, rail against the fear and loneliness that plagued nearly every waking moment and live her life like a normal person again.

Laughing as Duchess barked at a rabbit in the Dinkles' backyard garden, startling Trixie with her deep woof and setting off a not-to-be-messed-with barking from the smaller dog, Rosemary opened the storage unit at the edge of the patio where she kept pool and outdoor pet supplies. One of the shelves was dedicated to a sack of birdseed, grooming brushes and a stash of dog toys.

She pulled out the tennis ball Duchess loved to chase and gave it a good toss, watching the dogs trip over each other in their eagerness to retrieve the faded yellow orb. Then she reached inside for one of Trixie's squeaky toys and gasped.

The last rays of sunlight hitting the nape of her neck could have been shards of wintry ice as she snatched her hand away from the gruesome display inside.

"I don't understand why this is happening," she whispered through her tight throat.

But she couldn't pull her eyes away from the tiny stuffed animal—tan and curly coated like her sweet little Trixie—hanging from a noose fashioned out of twine from the cabinet's top shelf. Nor could she ignore the typed message pinned to the polyester material.

I know what you did.

You don't deserve to be rewarded.

You can't escape justice.

Who would…? Why would…?

Duchess dropped the slobbery ball at her feet, and the dogs buffeted her back and forth, eager for her to throw it again. When she didn't immediately respond, the German shepherd rose up on her hind legs to help herself to another toy inside the cabinet, and Rosemary snapped out of her shock.

"Down, girl. Get down." Rosemary pushed the black-and-tan dog aside and closed the cabinet doors. Then she latched onto Duchess's collar and swung her gaze around the yard.

Was someone watching her right now? Was some sicko out there getting off on just how terrified he could make her feel?

She led the dogs to the side gate with her to check the front of the house. No doubt picking up on her alarm, Trixie barked at nothing in particular. At least, nothing Rosemary could make out. She saw regular, light evening traffic out on the street, with all the cars driving slowly past because of the kids playing nearby. The Keiths had gone inside. There was no visible movement in the Dinkle house next door.

Rosemary's breath burned in her throat. This had gone beyond excusing those calls as some drunk who'd read her name in the paper. Somebody wanted her scared? He'd succeeded.

"Duchess, heel. Trixie?" The German shepherd fell into step beside Rosemary as she scooped up the poodle. "No one's going to hurt you, baby."

She checked the separate entrance that led to the

basement apartment where Stephen had lived when he'd gotten older. Good. Bolted tight. Then she took the dogs inside the kitchen and locked both the screen and steel doors behind her before punching in the code to reset the alarm. She flipped on the patio light, gave the dogs each her own rawhide chew and walked straight through to the front door, turning on every light inside and out.

Verifying for a second time that every room of the house was empty, Rosemary returned to the kitchen to brew a pot of green tea and fill a glass of ice to pour it over.

Her hands were shaking too hard to hold on to the frosty glass by the time she'd curled up on the library sofa with the dogs at her feet and the lights blazing. She should turn on the TV, read a book, sort through another box of papers and family mementos that had become her summer project, or get ready for bed and pretend she had any shot at sleeping now.

Rosemary deliberated each option for several moments before springing to her feet and circling around behind the large walnut desk that had been her father's. She opened the bottom drawer and pushed aside a box of photographs to unlock her father's old Army pistol from its metal box. It had been years since he'd taken her and Stephen target shooting out at a cousin's farm in the country, so she couldn't even be sure the thing still worked, much less remember exactly how to clean and load it. Still, it offered some measure of protection besides Duchess and Trixie. She pulled out the gun, magazine and a box of bullets and set them on top of the desk.

Then, even if they thought she was some sad, lonely spinster desperate for attention, she took a long swallow of her iced tea, picked up the phone and called KCPD to report the latest threat.

Chapter Two

Detective Max Krolikowski was a soldier by training. He was mission oriented. Dinkin' around on a wild-goose chase to see if some woman had talked to some guy about a crime that had occurred ages ago, just in case somebody somewhere could shed some new light on the unsolved case he and his partner from KCPD's Cold Case Squad were investigating, was not his idea of a good time.

Especially not today.

Max stepped on the accelerator of his '72 Chevy Chevelle, fisting his hand around the steering wheel in an effort to squeeze out the images of bits and pieces of fallen comrades in a remote desert village. He fought off the more troubling memory of prying a pistol out of a good man's dead hand.

He should be in a bar someplace getting drunk, or at Mount Washington Cemetery, allowing himself to weep over the grave of Army Captain James Stecher. Max and his team had rescued Jimmy from the insurgents' camp where he and two other NCOs been held hostage and tortured for seven days, but a part of Jimmy had never truly made it home. Eight years ago today, he'd put his gun in his mouth and ended the nightmares and survivor's guilt that had haunted him since their homecoming.

Max had found the body, left the Army and gone back to school to become a cop all within a year. Getting bad guys off the streets went a ways toward making his world right again. Following up on some remote, random possibility of a lead on the anniversary of Jimmy's senseless suicide did not.

"Whoa, brother." The voice of his partner, Trent Dixon, sitting in the passenger seat across from him, thankfully interrupted his dark thoughts. "We're not on a high-speed chase here. Slow it down before some uniform pulls us over."

Max rolled his eyes behind his wraparound sunglasses but lifted his foot. A little. He snickered around the unlit cigar clenched between his teeth. "Tell me again why we're drivin' out to visit this whack job Rosie March? She's hardly a reliable witness. Murder suspects generally aren't."

Tall, Dark and Hard to Rile chuckled. "Because her brother—a convicted killer with motive for killing Richard Bratcher—is our best lead to solving Bratcher's murder, and he's not talking to us. But he is talking to his sister. At least, she's the only person who visits him regularly. Maybe we can get her to tell us what he knows. Besides, you know one of the best ways to investigate a cold case like this one is to reinterview anyone associated with the original investigation. Rosemary March had motive for wanting her abusive boyfriend dead and has no alibi for the time of the murder. She'd be any smart detective's first call on this investigation. It's called doing our job."

Max shook his head at the annoyingly sensible explanation. "I had to ask."

Trent laughed outright. "Maybe you'd better let me do the talking when we get to the March house. Somehow, I doubt that calling her a *whack job* will encourage her to share any inside information she or her brother might have on our case."

"I get it. I'm the eyes and the muscle, and you're the pretty boy front man." Max plucked the cigar from his lips as he pulled off the highway on the eastern edge of Kansas City. "I'm not in the mood to make nice with some shriveled old prune of a woman, anyway."

"Rosemary March is thirty-three years old. We've got her driver's license photo in our records, and it looks as normal as any DMV pic can. What logic are you basing this I'd-rather-date-my-sister description on?"

Max could quote the file on their person of interest, too. "Over the years she's called in as many false alarms to 9-1-1 as she has legit actionable offenses, which makes her a flake in my book. Trespassing. Vandalism. Harassing phone calls. Either she's got a thing for cops, she has some kind of paranoia complex or it's the only way she can get any attention. Whatever her deal is, I'm not in the mood to play games today."

"Some of those calls were legit," Trent pointed out. "What about the abusive fiancé?"

"Our murder victim?"

"Yeah. Those complaints against Bratcher were substantiated. Even though someone scrubbed the photos and domestic violence complaints from his file after his death, the medical reports of Miss March's broken arm, bruises and other injuries were included as part of the initial murder investigation."

"But the woman's never married. She's only had the one boyfriend we can verify." Okay, so a fiancé who'd hurt her qualified as low-life devil scum, not boyfriend, in his book. But Rosemary March had money. A lot of it. Even if she had three warts on the end of her nose and looked like a gorilla, there should be a dozen men hitting on her. She should be on the social register donating to charities. She should be traveling the world or building a mansion or driving a luxury car or doing something that would make her show up on somebody's radar in Kansas City. "The woman's practically a recluse. She has her groceries delivered. She's got a teaching degree, but hasn't worked in a school since that plane wreck her parents were in. She's probably a hoarder. Her idea of a social outing is visiting her brother in prison. If that doesn't smack of crazy cat lady, I don't know what does."

"It's a wonder you've never been able to keep a woman."

Max forced a laugh, although the sound fell flat on his eardrums. Somehow, subjecting a good woman to his mood swings and bullheaded indifference to most social graces didn't seem very fair. But there were times, like today, when he regretted not having the sweet smells of a woman and the soft warmth of a welcoming body to lose himself in. Looked as though another long run or hour of lifting weights in the gym tonight would be his only escape from the sorrows of the day. "I make no claims on being a catch."

"Good, 'cause you'd lose that bet."

He wasn't the only cop in this car with relationship issues. "Give it a rest, junior. I don't see you asking me to stand up as best man anytime soon. When are you going to quit making goo-goo eyes at Katie Rinaldi and ask her out?"

"There's her son to consider. There's too much history between us." Trent muttered one of Max's favorite curses. "It's complicated."

"Women usually are."

This time, the laughter between them was genuine.

When Max and Trent both got assigned to the Cold Case Squad, their superior officer must have paired the two of them together as some kind of yin and yang thing—blond, brunette; older, younger; a veteran of a hard knocks life and an optimistic young man who'd grown up in a suburban neighborhood much like this one, with a mom and a dad and 2.5 siblings or whatever the average was these days; an enlisted soldier who'd gone into the Army right out of high school and a football-scholarship winner who'd graduated cum laude and skipped a career in the pros because of one concussion too many. Max and Trent were a textbook example of the good cop/bad cop metaphor.

And no one had ever asked Max to play the good-cop role.

But their strengths balanced each other. He had survival instincts honed on the field of battle and in the dark shadows of city streets. He was one of the few detectives in KCPD with marksman status who wasn't on a SWAT team. And if it was mechanical, he could probably get it started or keep it running with little more than the toolbox in his trunk. As for their weaknesses? Hell, Detective Goody Two-shoes over there probably didn't have any weakness. Trent wasn't just an athlete. He was book smart. Patient. Always two or three steps ahead of anybody else in the room. He was the only cop in the department who'd ever taken Max down in hand-to-hand combat training—and that was because of some brainiac trick he'd used against him. And he was one of the few people left on the planet Max trusted without question. Trent Dixon reminded Max of a certain captain he'd served under during his Army stint in the Middle East. He would have followed Jimmy Stecher to the ends of the earth and back, and, in some ways, he had.

Only Jimmy had never made it back from that last door-to-door skirmish where he and the others had been taken prisoner. Not really. Oh, Max had led the rescue and they'd shipped home on the evac plane together after that last do-or-die firefight to get him out of that desert village. They'd been in Walter Reed hospital for a few weeks together, too. The two men he'd been captured with had been shot to death in front of him. Jimmy hadn't cracked and revealed troop positions or battle strategies, and he'd never let them film him reading their latest manifesto to use him as propaganda. But part of Jimmy had died inside on that nightmarish campaign—the part that could survive in the real, normal world. And Max should have seen it coming. He'd been responsible for retrieving their dead and getting their commander out of there. But he hadn't saved Jimmy. Not really. He hadn't realized there was one more soldier who'd still needed him.

He'd failed his mission. His friend was dead.

Despite the bright summer sunshine burning through the windshield of his classic car, Max felt the darkness creeping into his thoughts. The image of what a bullet to the brain could do to a man's head was tattooed on his memories as surely as the ink marking his left shoulder. He'd known today would be a tough one—the anniversary of Jimmy's suicide.

Trent knew it, too.

"Stay with me, brother." His partner's deeply pitched voice echoed through the car, drawing Max out of his annual funk. "Not everybody's the enemy today. I need you focused on this interview."

Max nodded, slamming the door on his ugly past. He rolled the unlit cigar between his fingers and chomped down on it again. "This is busywork, and you know it."

Probably why Trent had volunteered the two of them to make this trip to the suburbs instead of sitting in the precinct office reading through files with the other detectives on the team. Max didn't blame him. Teaming with him, especially on days like this, was probably a pretty thankless job. He should be glad Trent was looking out for him. He *was* glad. Still didn't make this trip to the March house any less of a wild-goose chase when he was more in the mood to do something concrete like make an arrest or run down a perp. "Rosemary March isn't about to confess or tell us anything her brother said. If she knows something about Bratcher's murder, she's kept quiet for six years. Don't know why she'd start gettin' chatty about it now."

Trent relaxed back in his seat, maybe assured that Max was with him in the here and now. "I think she's worth checking out. Other than her brother's attorney, she's the only person who visits Stephen March down in Jeff City. If he's going to confide anything to anyone, it'll be to his sister."

"What's he gonna confide that'll do our case any good?" Max stepped on the accelerator to zip through a yellow light and turn into the suburban neighborhood. Hearing the engine hum with the power he relished beneath the hood, he pulled off his sunglasses and rubbed the dashboard. "That's my girl."

"I swear you talk sweeter to this car than any woman I've ever seen you with," Trent teased. "But seriously, we aren't running a race."

"Beats pokin' along in your pickup truck."

Besides, today of all days, he needed to be driving the Chevelle. The car had been a junker when Jimmy had bequeathed it to him. Now it was a testament to his lost commander, a link to the past, a reminder of the better man Max should have been. Restoring this car that had once belonged to Jimmy wasn't just a hobby. It was therapy for the long, lonely nights and empty days when the job and a couple of beers weren't enough to keep the memories at bay. Or when he just needed some time to think.

Right now, though, he needed to stop *thinking* and get on with the job at hand.

Max put the sunglasses back on his face and cruised another block before plucking the cigar from his lips. "Just because the team is working on some theory that this cold-case murder is related to the death of the reporter Stephen March killed, it doesn't mean they are. We've got no facts to back up the idea that March had anything to do with Bratcher's death. March used a gun. Bratcher was poisoned. March's victim was doing a story on Leland Asher and his criminal organization, and there's no evidence that Richard Bratcher was connected to Asher or the reporter. And Stephen March sure isn't part of any organized crime setup. If Liv and Lieutenant Rafferty-Taylor want to connect the two murders, I think we ought to be digging into Asher and his cronies. The mob could have any number of reasons to want to eliminate a lawyer."

"But poison?" Trent shrugged his massive shoulders. "That hardly sounds like a mob-style hit to me."

"What if Asher hired a hit *lady*? Women are more likely to kill someone using poison than a man is. And dead is dead." Max tapped his fingers with the cigar on the console between them to emphasize his point. "Facts make a case. We should be investigating any women associated with Asher and his business dealings."

But Trent was big enough and stubborn enough not to be intimidated by Max's grousing. "Even if she turns out to be a *shriveled old prune*, Rosemary March is a woman. Therefore, she meets your criteria as a potential suspect. Doesn't sound like such a wild-goose chase now, does it?"

Growling a curse at Trent's dead-on, smart-aleck logic, Max stuffed the cigar back between his teeth. It was a habit he'd picked up during his stint in the Army before college and joining the police force. And though the docs at Walter Reed had convinced him to quit lighting up so his body could heal and he could stay in fighting shape, it was a tension-relieving habit he had no intention of denying himself. Especially on stressful days like this one.

Feeling a touch of the melancholy rage that sometimes fueled his moods, Max shut down the memories that tried to creep in and nudged the accelerator to zip through another yellow light.

"You know…" Trent started, "you take better care of this car than you do yourself. Maybe you ought to rethink your priorities."

"And maybe you ought to mind your own business."

"You're my partner. You are my business."

Max glanced over at his dark-haired nemesis. Conversations like this made him feel like Trent's pop or Dutch uncle, as if life had aged him far beyond the twelve years that separated them in age. Still, Trent was the closest thing he had to a friend here in KC. The younger detective dealt with his moods and attitude better than anybody since Jimmy. Nope. He wasn't going there.

"Bite me, junior." Max pulled up to the curb in front of the white house with blue shutters and red rosebushes blooming along the front of the porch.

"I know today is a rough one for you." Trent pulled his notebook from beneath the seat before he clapped a hand on Max's shoulder. "But seriously, brother. Did you get that shirt out of the laundry? You know you're supposed to fold them or hang them up when you take them out of the dryer, right? Did you even shave this morning?"

"You are not my mama." Although part of him appreciated the concern behind Trent's teasing, Max shrugged his hand away and killed the engine. "Get out of my car. And don't scratch anything on your way out."

Max set his cigar in the ashtray and checked the rearview mirror, scrubbing his fingers over the gold-and-tan stubble that he probably should have attended to before leaving for work this morning. Although the crew cut was the same as it had been back in basic training, the wrinkled chambray of his short-sleeved shirt would have earned him a demerit and a lecture from Jimmy. What a mess. One beer too many and a sketchy night's sleep had left him ill-equipped to deal with today.

Swearing at the demons staring back at him, Max climbed out, tucking in the tails of his shirt and adjusting the badge and gun at the waist of his jeans as he surveyed up and down the street. Looked like a pretty ordinary summer morning here in middle-class America. Dogs barking out back. Flowers blooming. Kids playing in the yard. Royals baseball banners flying proudly. Didn't look like the hoity-toity neighborhood where he expected a millionaire crackpot to live. Didn't look much like a place where they could track down clues to a six-year-old murder, either.

But he had to give Trent credit for dragging him out on this fool's errand. Driving the Chevy and breathing in the fresh air beat being cooped up in the office with a bunch of paperwork and his gloomy thoughts. Max tipped his face to the sunshine for a few moments, locking down the bad memories before he took the steps two at a time and followed Trent up to the Marches' front porch.

"What is this? Fort Knox?" he drawled, eyeing the high-tech gadgetry of the alarm on the front door, along with the knob lock and dead bolt. "My grandma lives in a brand-new apartment complex and doesn't have this kind of security."

"The woman does live alone," Trent reminded him.

Max peered in through the front bay window while Trent rang the doorbell. The front room was neat as a pin, if stacks of boxes and piles of papers on nearly every flat surface counted. But not a cat in sight. He refused to believe that the noise of dogs barking out back might in any way disprove his theory about crazy Rosemary March.

"Yes?" Several seconds passed before the red steel door opened halfway. He could barely hear the woman's soft voice through the glass storm door. "May I help you?"

Trent flashed his badge and identified them. "KCPD, ma'am. I'm Detective Dixon and this is my partner, Max Krolikowski. We're here to ask some questions. Are you Rosemary March?" She must have nodded. "Could you open the outside door, too?"

"If you step back, I will. I'll disable the alarm and come out."

Max moved to one side while Trent retreated to the requested distance between them.

Max had expected that shriveled-up prune from his imagination to appear. He at least expected to see a homely plain Jane with pop-bottle glasses. He wasn't expecting the generously built woman with flawless alabaster skin, dressed neck to knee in a gauzy white dress, exposing only her arms and calves to the summer heat. Although her hair, the color of a shiny copper penny, was drawn back into a bun so tight that words like *spinster* and *schoolmarm* danced on his tongue, he hadn't expected Rosemary March to be so…feminine. So curvy. He wasn't expecting to see signs of pretty.

He wasn't expecting the Colt automatic she held down in the folds of her skirt, either.

Chapter Three

Max's fingers immediately went to his holster. "Gun!"

The redhead nudged open the glass storm door and slipped the pistol behind her back as though they wouldn't notice it. "I asked you to step—"

"Damn it, lady. Keep that thing where we can see it." Max put up one hand to swing the door open wide and folded the other hand around her arm, sliding it down over her wrist until he had the barrel of her weapon in his grasp.

"Get out of my house—" The redhead gasped and recoiled, tugging against his grip. "Let go of me."

No way. Even if she didn't mean them any harm, he wasn't trusting that a fruitcake like her wouldn't accidentally fire off a round. "Damn it, lady, relax. We're just here to talk."

She curled both hands around the butt of the weapon now. If her finger reached that trigger... "Please don't swear like that. It isn't polite."

"And pointing a gun at us is?" Two of her hands against one of his was no contest. She stumbled out the door, uselessly trying to hold on while he pried the weapon from her grip. A rush that was more anger than relief fired through his veins when he realized how light it was. "Oh, hell, no." He turned aside, dropping the empty magazine from the handle and opening the firing chamber. "This thing isn't even loaded."

Her gaze was as icy cool as her skin. "May I please have it back?"

Max turned the gun over in his hands. "This thing is Army issue. About twenty years old." He reset the magazine and thrust the Colt back at her, butt first. If she recoiled half a step at his abrupt action and loud voice, he didn't care. "It isn't yours."

"It was my father's."

"Didn't he ever tell you that you damn sure never point an empty weapon at a guy whose gun can really shoot? Hell, what if I'd pulled my sidearm instead of grabbing yours?"

Her eyes were the silvery color of twilight as she angled them up to him, searching for the intent behind his mirrored glasses. She finally took the gun from him and hugged it near her waist. "You're swearing again."

"Looking down the barrel of a gun does that to me."

"I didn't point it at you," she snapped. "You had no reason to—" And then she inhaled a calming breath and turned to Trent, as though raising her voice to Max violated some code of conduct she wouldn't allow. "I was putting away my father's pistol when the doorbell rang. If I had known you were the police, I would have locked it up first. But I thought it was my friend here to give me a ride into the city, and he would understand. He knows I don't keep it loaded."

Jimmy's hand had held an Army pistol that fateful day, too. Max's mind went hazy for a split second as the gruesome image tried to take hold. But he ruthlessly shoved it aside. Of all the stupid, fool stunts for this woman to pull today. "You don't carry a gun around unless you're prepared to use it."

"And you don't just grab a person because you—" Her chin jerked up to give him a straight-on look at the pink stains dotting her pale cheeks before she clamped her mouth shut and dropped her gaze. Well, what do you know? Crazy Dog Lady had a temper.

"Ease up, Max," Trent warned.

Those gray eyes flashed in Max's direction although she turned her body toward his partner, rightly suspecting that Trent would be the one more apt to listen to a reasonable explanation. "You should have called first. I have an appointment this morning with my attorney. I wasn't expecting anyone else to come to the house."

"Maybe we should start this conversation again." Trent raised his notebook between them and intervened, leaving Max wondering if it was his partner's presence or some snobby code of behavior that made her check her tongue when she clearly wanted to lambaste him for putting his hands on her. She turned her full focus on the taller man, dismissing Max. Trent pulled off his sunglasses and tucked them into his chest pocket. "I apologize for my partner here. His PR skills might be a little rusty, but believe me, he's a good cop. You're perfectly safe with him. There's no one else I trust to have my back more. Are you Rosemary March?"

"You already know that or you wouldn't be here."

Trent managed to keep the patient tone Max hadn't been able to muster. "First of all, is everything all right, ma'am? It tends to put us on alert to see someone carrying a weapon. I assure you, Max was only trying to prevent an accident from happening."

Her gaze darted up to his. "Is that true?"

Max shrugged. "I don't like to get shot."

"But that's why you touched me? You thought I was

going to...?" Her voice trailed away and her focus dropped to the middle of his chest. "Sarcasm, right?"

"Oh, yeah." With a clear lack of appreciation for his cynical humor, her gaze bounced across the width of Max's shoulders, up to the scruff on his chin, over to the large bay window and finally down to the brass badge clipped to his belt. Prim and proper Miss Rosemary March was hiding something, buying herself time to come up with the right thing to say. Why? Something had her spooked. Was it the badge? His very real, very loaded gun? Was it him? Six feet, two inches of growly first sergeant in need of a shave could be intimidating. Was it Trent? Max's partner was even taller, still built like the defensive lineman he'd once been. And she had to be, what, all of five-five?

A chill pricked the back of his neck. That instant wariness, much like the split-second warnings he'd gotten over in the desert before all hell broke loose, put him on alert. Maybe he and Trent weren't the reason she was carrying that gun. Thinking he ought to be worried about more than that empty weapon, Max rested his hand on his holster and looked beyond her into the foyer. "Is someone in the house with you?"

"No." Too fast an answer.

When he reached for the door, she sidestepped to block his path. She put her hand up to stop him from opening the door. Max put on the brakes, but with his momentum he swayed toward her, breathing in a whiff of her flowery soap or shampoo. He heard her suck in her breath and felt her fingers push against him before she curled them into a fist and pulled back almost as soon as they made contact with his chest.

"Lady, I'm trying to help—"

"I said no." Although the firm tone drew him up

short, the warning was directed to the button on the wrinkled point of his collar.

And she was shivering. In this ninety-degree heat, he could see the fine tremors in the fist clutched to her chest.

Max huffed out a frustrated breath that she turned her face from. He scrubbed his hand over the stubble on his jaw and wisely backed away before he muttered the curse on the tip of his tongue. He wasn't able to read this chick at all. She wasn't wrinkled. She wasn't old. And the only thing prunish about her was the snooty tone that attempted to put him in his place time and again. And, hell, he had to admire anyone who dared to stand up to him on a day like today.

First, she'd been an imposition on his time. Then she was a threat. Now he could smell the fear on her, but she refused to admit to it.

And how could he still feel the imprint of five fingers that had barely brushed against him?

He splayed his hands at his waist and demanded that she start making some sense. "Are you hiding something? Is that why you don't want us inside?"

"No, I just don't like having anyone…" She pressed her pink lips together in a thin line, stopping that explanation. "It's a mess."

The boxes and piles of papers stacked in the room indicated she was telling the truth. Still, there was something off about this woman—about this whole situation. "Nobody comes to the door with a gun because she's embarrassed about her housekeeping. That thing is an accident waiting to happen."

"I'll explain it again." Oh, right. In case the dumb cop couldn't figure it out. "The gun was still out from last night. I've been going through my parents' things for months now and found it in my father's desk. I was putting it away before my ride comes to pick me up this morning. The doorbell rang while I was straightening up. I thought it was my attorney. I didn't want to keep him waiting." Despite the even, articulate tone, her soft gray eyes kept glancing up to him but wouldn't lock on to his questioning gaze. Probably because he wasn't letting her see it. She drifted a step closer to Trent. "I wasn't expecting anyone to come to the house. The officer took a report over the phone last night. I thought someone would come over then. But no one ever did so I assumed KCPD had dismissed my call."

Huh? That comment short-circuited his fuming suspicions. Max traded a look with Trent before asking, "What report?"

"The one I called the police about last night." Last night? He'd missed something here. Had she gone back to making spurious calls to 9-1-1? While Max was wondering if his communication skills had gone completely off the rails, Rosemary March's body language changed. Her free hand went to the stand-up collar of her dress and she puffed up like a banty hen trying to assert herself in the barnyard pecking order. "Would you mind taking off your sunglasses, Detective Krolikowski? It's rude not to let someone see your eyes when you're having a conversation with them."

"What?"

"Take off your glasses. I insist."

"You insist?" Max bristled at her bossy tone. "Boy, you've got to have everything just so, don't you."

"I don't think common courtesy is asking too much."

"Max." Trent nodded at him to do it.

Really? Max pulled off his glasses and hooked them on the back of his neck. She wanted the glasses off?

How about this, honey? He folded his arms across his chest and glared down into her searching gray eyes until they suddenly shuttered. She must have had her fill of cynicism and impatience because she retreated until her back was pressed against the glass door.

He didn't need to hear the breathy tone of her polite thank-you to recognize the sudden change in Miss Rosie's demeanor or feel like a heel knowing he was the cause of it. What had he done? Most people got in his face or blew him off when he got in a mood like this. But Rosemary March was different. So what if this conversation wasn't making any sense to him. He knew better than to let anybody's odd behavior get under his skin. His presence here clearly agitated her. She breathed harder, faster, and Max topped off his jackassery by noticing her full, round breasts pushing against the gauzy white cotton of that dress.

That little seed of attraction he hadn't expected to feel was clearly agitating him. "Ah, hell. Ma'am, I didn't mean... I wish I could explain where my head is today, but it's too long a story. Are you sure you're okay?"

She nodded, but he'd feel a lot less like a scary bastard if she'd get some color in those pale cheeks or lecture him again. Putting his hand on her and crowding her probably hadn't been the smartest moves. Something about the gun must have drummed up memories of Jimmy and put him on his worst behavior.

But that was a lousy excuse for a man sworn to protect and serve. This was about more than a soldier's or a cop's hardwired reaction to giving anybody a chance to get the drop on him or his men. And he could hardly explain his skepticism regarding her usefulness as a witness on this anniversary of Jimmy's senseless death.

He owed her some kind of apology for scaring her. For being a jerk. But the words weren't coming. Not today.

When had words ever been his strong suit?

Thank God, he was part of a team and could rely on Trent's handsome face and friendly smile to salvage this interview. Max cleared his throat and backed toward the front steps. "I'll, uh, just do a quick walk around the place if that's okay with you."

Miss Rosemary gave him a jerky nod, her gaze breezing past his chin again. "I left the message in the cabinet on my patio out back." Message? Trent glanced over his shoulder and traded a confused look, but Max wasn't about to ask. "The dogs will bark, but they don't bite." And then her twilight gaze landed on his. A fine, coppery brow arched in what might be arrogance. Or a warning. "At least, they haven't bitten anyone yet."

Nope. Didn't have to hit him over the head more than once. He had no business trying to make nice with anybody today.

"I'll look." He nodded to Trent. "You talk."

Max trotted down the steps and breathed a lungful of humid summer air into his tight chest while he made another cursory scan of the well-kept front yard. When he realized the lady of the house wasn't answering any of Trent's questions with him still in sight, he muttered a curse and followed the driveway around the side of the house.

Message in a cabinet? Was that code for something? Like *Scram, Krolikowski*? And that thing about the dogs not biting anyone *yet*—was that an attempt at humor to ease the friction between them, or her demure version of a threat?

He peeked through the window of the separate garage to see her sedan parked inside, along with a neatly arranged array of storage boxes and lawn equipment. She was right about the dogs barking. As soon as he came into view, a deep-voiced German shepherd with a cloudy eye and a yappy little bundle of curly tan hair charged the chain-link fence and let him know they knew he was there.

A fond memory of Jax, the big German shepherd who'd served with his unit, made him smile. Jax had died in that Sector Six firefight where the captain had been captured. The victim of a hidden bomb. A single bark had given them their only warning before the blast. Jimmy had taken the dog's death as hard as the loss of his men. "Son of a…"

Really? Just like that, whatever positives he could summon today crashed and burned. Irritated with his inability to focus, Max fixed the friendliest look he could manage on his face and approached the fence.

"Hey, big girl. Do you sit? Sit. Good girl." When the shepherd instantly obeyed his command, he figured the poodle was the one he had to win over. He squatted down and held his fist against the chain-link fence to let the excited little dog sniff his hand. They certainly hadn't had a feisty little fuzz mop like this one with the unit. "Hey, there, killer."

When the poodle finally stopped dancing around long enough to lick his knuckles, Max figured it was safe to open the gate and go inside. Apparently, Rosie March had spent a bit of her newly acquired wealth on more than security. Though this was by no means a mansion, the old house had plenty of room for one woman, and was well taken care of. New roof and shutters. Freshly painted siding and trim. The pool in the middle of her backyard was long and narrow, meant for swimming laps instead of sunbathing beside. Yet there was still plenty of green space for the dogs to roam. He shrugged and petted the pooches, who were leading as much as following him on his stroll around the yard. Nothing looked out of place here, but then his real purpose for volunteering to do recon was so the lady of the house would take the panic level down a few notches and talk to Trent.

And he could get his head together and remember he was a cop. He needed to do better. So far, the only thing he knew for sure about this investigation was that Rosie March smelled like summer and her hesitant touch stayed with him like a brand against his skin.

Max rubbed at the spot on his chest. So what did that mean? He was lonesome enough or horny enough to think he was attracted to Miss Prim & Proper just because she'd touched him? Or was that a stamp of guilt because his big, brusque attitude had frightened the woman when he should have been calming her?

"Idiot!" Max punched the palm of his hand.

The German shepherd barked at the harsh reprimand and darted several paces away. "Easy, girl." He held out his hand and let the big dog cautiously sniff and make friends again. "I'm not mad at you. I'll bet your mama never raises her voice like that, does she." He cupped a palmful of warm fur and scratched around the dog's ears. Who was he to call Rosie the Redhead crazy? He wasn't exactly firing on all cylinders himself today. "Don't you be afraid of me, too."

While the shepherd forgave his harsh tone and pushed her head into the stroke of his hand, the poodle rolled on her back in the grass, completely comfortable with his presence there. Max chuckled. "At least somebody around here likes me."

And then he became aware of eyes on him. Not a shy

gray gaze worried about what uncouth thing he'd say or do next. But spying eyes. Suspicious eyes.

With his senses on alert, Max knelt down between the two dogs and wrestled with them both, giving himself a chance to locate the source of the curious perusal. There. East fence, hiding behind a stand of sweet corn and tomato plants. Nosy neighbor at nine o'clock. With a clap of his hands, the dogs barked and took off running at the new game.

Max pushed to his feet and zeroed in on the dark-haired woman wearing a white bandanna and gardening gloves. "Morning, ma'am."

Her eyes rounded as though startled to be discovered, and she tightened her grip on the spool of twine she'd been using to tie up the heavy-laden tomato plants. "Good morning. Are you the police?"

"Yes, ma'am." He tapped his badge on his belt. "Detective Krolikowski, KCPD. And you are…?"

"Arlene Dinkle. We've lived here going on thirty years now," she announced. "There's not going to be trouble with Rosemary again, is there?"

Again? The dogs returned and circled around his legs. Max sent them on their way again. "Trouble?"

Mrs. Dinkle parted the cornstalks that were as tall as she was and came to the fence. She lowered her voice to a conspiratorial tone. "There was a man who used to stay with her sometimes. Don't think the whole neighborhood didn't notice. Things haven't been right at this house for a long time."

Maybe he could pick up some useful information on this recon mission, after all—and make up for the interview he'd botched out on the front porch. Max strolled to the fence to join her. "You mean Miss March's fiancé? He stayed here?"

"A couple of times a week. When he was alive." The older woman clucked her tongue behind her teeth. "Some folks think she killed him, you know. Between those rumors and her juvenile delinquent brother, she definitely brought down the quality of this neighborhood."

That shy, spooked lady on the front porch brought down the neighborhood? That delicate, feminine facade could be the perfect cover for darker secrets. And if Bratcher had been here on a regular basis, she'd have had plenty of opportunity to slip him the poison that had killed him.

But he was having a hard time aligning the image of a calculated murderess with the skittish redhead who protected herself with an unloaded gun. She wasn't that good of an actress, was she? "You know anything about that murder?"

"I should say not." Unlike Rosemary March, Max could read this woman with his eyes closed. Arlene Dinkle liked to gossip. Although he found her holier-than-thou tone a little irritating, the cop in him was inclined to let her. Judging by the streaks of silver in her black hair, she'd been sticking her nose into other people's business for a long time. "Now there's all that publicity with that legal settlement or wherever her nine million dollars came from. Did you know there were reporters at her house two months ago? One of them even came to our home to find out what we knew about her."

"And you told this reporter about Miss March entertaining her fiancé overnight, what, six, seven, years ago? Did you ever see any indication that Mr. Bratcher was violent with Rosie?"

"Rosie? Oh. You mean Rosemary. Yes, there was that one time she came to our house to use our phone—said her lawyer friend who was getting her all that money after her parents' plane crash—oh, the Colonel and Meg were such good people—I don't understand how their children could turn out so—"

"What did Rosie say about her lawyer friend?" Max cut her off before she rambled away on a useless tangent.

She snorted a laugh that scraped against his eardrums. "*Rosemary* said he'd trapped her inside the house until she agreed to sign some prenuptial agreement and marry him. Made no sense at all. They were already engaged. She pounded on our door in the middle of the night, woke Otis and me both out of a sound sleep. Blubbering about how we needed to call the police." The dogs were circling again. Disapproval seeped into Arlene's tone and she pulled back from the fence. "That's when she got the big dog. Washed out of K-9 training. But I swear that dog would still take a bite out of you if you look at her crosswise. The little one digs in the topsoil of my garden, too. Reaches right under the fence. Rosemary ought to put up a privacy fence. She certainly can afford to do it."

Really? Then how would you spy on her? Max kept his sarcasm to himself and followed up on the one key word that might actually prove useful in an investigation. "You said *trapped.* Was Rosie—Miss March— injured in any way that night? Did you believe her when she told you that her fiancé hurt her? Threatened her?"

"Oh, she had some blood on her blouse and she was cradling her arm. I thought maybe she'd been in a car accident or had fallen down the stairs. We let her use the phone right away, of course, and sat with her until the ambulance and police arrived. But we saw her fiancé drive away, so I wondered why she just wouldn't use her own phone."

"If Bratcher hurt her, she was probably afraid he'd come back. Getting out of the house would be a smart survival tactic."

Arlene straightened, as though insulted that he would doubt her word against Rosie's. "Richard Bratcher was an upstanding member of the community. Why on earth a handsome, charming man like that would ever have to resort to anything so—"

"Arlene." Max caught a glimpse of movement at the sliding glass door on the Dinkles' patio before another man's voice interrupted the tale. "I'm sure the detective isn't here to chat with you. You let him be."

Arlene whirled around on the man with salt-and-pepper hair who must be her husband. "He asked me questions. We were having a conversation."

"Uh-huh." The lanky older man extended his hand over the fence. "I'm Otis Dinkle. We've lived next door to Rosemary and her family since she was a little girl. Is everything okay?"

At least Arlene had the grace to look a little ashamed that she hadn't asked that. Max lightly clasped the older man's hand, assuming that his presence meant he wasn't getting any more facts or nonsense from his wife. "Max Krolikowski, KCPD. I'm not sure, sir. My partner and I are looking into an old case." Maybe this was as good a time as any to test the veracity of Rosie's claims about receiving threats. "But I understand there may have been a disturbance here yesterday?"

"You mean like a break-in?"

Max nodded. "Or a trespasser on the property?"

"Not that I've seen." Otis tucked his fingers into the pockets of his Bermuda shorts and shrugged. "She was gone all day yesterday. I didn't see any activity after she took the dogs out for their morning walk."

"Her new attorney dropped her off last night," Arlene added. "Her dead fiancé's brother. I knew there was something funny going on. The two of them probably—"

Otis put up a hand, silencing his wife's opinion. "She didn't even let him into the house, Arlene. I don't think it's anything serious."

Max arched a curious brow. So the gossipy missus wasn't the only one watching the March house. "You saw her come home last night?"

Otis nodded. "We keep an eye on each other's place. Maybe chat in the front yard or across the fence when we're both out mowing. Other than that, though, Rosemary keeps pretty much to herself. We used to do stuff with her parents, but now that they're gone, she's just not that social."

"You didn't see anyone lurking around the house who shouldn't be?"

"Her dogs would have raised a ruckus. I didn't hear anything like that."

"They were locked up inside, Otis," Arlene reminded him.

"So, no intruders?" Max clarified. "Nothing you saw that seemed...off to you?"

Otis scratched at his bald spot, considering the question. "No, sir. Other than she didn't go for her regular swim this morning. It's been pretty quiet around here since her brother got put in jail. But then, we're retired. We don't keep late hours."

Yet he spied over the fence often enough to know Rosie's morning routine and when she came home at night. Curious.

"Well, if you do see anything suspicious, give us a

call, would you?" Max reached into his back pocket and handed the man a business card with his contact information.

Arlene clutched the ball of twine against her chest. "Are we in any danger?"

"I don't think so, ma'am."

Otis held the card out at arm's length and read it. "I'll be. Cold Case Squad? This isn't about a break-in. Are you investigating her fiancé's murder, Detective Kro-likowski? You think she did it?"

If poison wasn't such a premeditated means of mur-der, he might have been willing to dismiss his suspicions about Rosie as a justified case of self-defense. "Do you?"

"If you'd said Stephen, yes—that kid always was the rebellious sort. Good thing he was in rehab that week or you cops would have come down really hard on him. But honestly, I can't see Rosemary raising a hand to anybody. But what do I know? Like I said, she keeps to herself." He winked as a grin spread across his face. "It's those quiet ones you can't trust, right?"

With Arlene's snort of derisive agreement, Max reached down to pet the German shepherd, dismissing the Dinkles. He'd stomached about all he could of po-lite conversation today. "Remember to give me a call if you see or hear anything suspicious."

"Will do."

Max clapped his hands and played one more game of try-to-catch-me with the dogs while the couple went back to their back porch, arguing about people breaking in next door and whether or not the neighborhood was safe anymore. As he watched the two dogs run a wide circle around the perimeter of the yard, Max shook his head. If the Dinkles were his neighbors, he'd probably avoid socializing, too.

So what, exactly, would make a healthy woman of means isolate herself the way Rosie March had? Keeping a low profile was generally rule number one for someone who'd committed a crime. Was it the publicity surrounding the lawsuit and sudden fortune she'd won? There were probably friends and family coming out of the woodwork, trying to get a piece of that nine million dollars. He'd hate that kind of spotlight, too. Was she ashamed because her brother had killed a woman, robbing her for a fix? Nobody knew better than him what it felt like to miss the signs of a loved one spiraling out of control. Or was Miss Rosie March just plain ol' afraid of her own shadow because life had dealt her a raw hand? That could explain the frequent 9-1-1 calls and why she'd unpack her daddy's Army pistol.

Max had a feeling there were a whole lot of secrets that woman was keeping. Ferreting them out would require a degree of insight and patience he lacked. KCPD had better send out someone else from the team, like Olivia Watson, so they could talk woman to woman, or cool and unflappable Jim Parker, or even nice guy Trent—without his bad-cop partner tagging along to make a mess of things.

Max watched the Dinkles settle into patio chairs, shaking his head as Otis plugged in earbuds while Arlene peeled off her gloves and prattled on about too many cops and dogs and reporters for her liking. Max tuned her out, too, and whistled for the dogs to return. "Come here, girls!"

He finally conceded that this outing hadn't been a total waste of his time. He'd done some decent police work, confirming that Rosie had a motive for killing Richard Bratcher. Although Arlene had dismissed the violent details that had soured Max's stomach, a woman who'd been held hostage by her abuser might feel she had no other way out of the relationship than to murder the man who terrorized her.

He liked the dogs, too. As much as the dogs he'd served with overseas had detected bombs and alerted his unit to insurgents sneaking past the camp perimeter or lying in wait out on a patrol, they'd been the unofficial morale officers. There was little that a game of fetch or a furry body snuggled up in the bunk beside him couldn't take his mind off of for a few minutes, at least.

The muscles in his face relaxed with an unfamiliar smile as the shepherd and poodle charged toward him. But the dogs ran right past, abandoning the game. Abandoning him.

Tension gripped him again, just as quickly as it had ebbed, when he heard the clanking of the gate opening behind him. The mutts were showing their true allegiance to their copper-haired mistress by trotting up to greet her. Rosemary March followed Trent through the gate and latched it behind her, stopping on the opposite edge of the narrow pool. She knelt down in that starchy dress to accept the enthusiastic welcome of her pets, and Max's cranky, used-up heart did a funny little flip-flop at the unexpected sight of that uptight, upper-crust woman getting licked in the face and not complaining one whit about muddy, grass-stained paws on her white dress.

Great. That was the last thing he needed today, thinking he had the hots for the most viable suspect in their murder investigation—a good girl, no less, who seemed to push every bad-behavior button in his arsenal, a woman who was all kinds of wrong for him and his crass, worldly ways. She was a suspect, not an opportunity. He needed to get his head back in the game.

"Miss March was visiting her brother yesterday," Trent began, giving Max a heads-up nod across the narrow width of the pool, indicating that he'd gotten her to open up to him. Max raised a surrendering hand, promising to watch his mouth and not blow any progress Trent had made in his absence, and started a slow stroll around the pool to join them. "She thinks she spotted a man paying undue attention to her down at the prison, and that he may have taken a picture of her—"

"I don't think." Rosie glanced up at Trent, then pushed to her feet. "I know. He didn't have to stare at me. He was watching me on his phone."

So, still no news about the Bratcher murder. Max played along. Getting her to talk, period, was the first step in getting her to talk about their investigation. "Did you know this guy?"

"I'd recognize him if I saw him again, but I've never seen him before." She backed up onto the patio, keeping both men in sight as Max closed the distance between them. "You don't believe me." She looked across the yard to her neighbors, probably guessing how he'd spent his time back here. Her chin came up as she glanced over at the tall, plastic cabinet, then trained those accusing gray eyes on him. "You never even read the threat, did you? What did Otis and Arlene say to you? You think I'm making this all up."

"I don't know what I think," he answered honestly.

Apparently, that wasn't a good enough answer. With a frustrated huff that might be her interpretation of a curse, she walked past him and opened the cabinet doors. She backed away, picking up the poodle and hugging the dog to her chest, averting her eyes from the shelves inside. "Look for yourself. This is why I called the police."

Max muttered a real expletive when he saw the message and noose hanging inside. He glanced back and scratched around the ears of the little dog who bore an unmistakable resemblance to the toy on display. "Looks a lot like you, killer."

Miss Rosie's eyes widened along with his when his fingertips accidentally brushed against her arm. A split second later she jerked away, pulling herself and the dog beyond his outstretched fingers. "Her name is Trixie. Is someone going to hurt my dogs? Is someone going to hurt me?"

"You don't know who sent this?"

She shook her head and backed another step away.

Right. Not his dog. Not his anything. *Do your job already.* Max busied his hands by snapping a couple of pictures with his phone before pulling out his pocketknife. Trent had come up beside him to inspect the cryptic message. Max asked, "You got a bag in that notebook?"

Trent pulled out a small plastic evidence bag and held it open while Max cut down the threat. The sisal looped around the toy's neck reminded him of the spool of twine Mrs. Dinkle had been using in her garden. He peeked around the cabinet door and caught Arlene watching from her back porch. Otis remained oblivious as she quickly glanced away. Could it be that simple? "Any reason why your neighbors might want to scare you?"

"Because Arlene hates dogs as much as she loves the sound of her own voice?" Max almost grinned at the spunky dig of sarcasm. But Rosie clapped a hand over her mouth. "I'm sorry. That wasn't very polite." She was reining her emotions in again, a skill Max envied, especially today. "The Dinkles aren't responsible for this. And they certainly weren't in Jefferson City snapping pictures of me yesterday. I'm guessing the money from the settlement is the reward that creep is talking about.

Believe me, it doesn't feel like any kind of compensation with all the hassle that has come with it. I'd rather have Mom and Dad and my old teaching job over millions of dollars any day."

I know what you did.

So, who was close enough to Rosemary March, besides her brother locked away in prison, to know or even suspect that she'd murdered Richard Bratcher? Who else cared that she might be guilty?

He plucked the sealed bag from Trent's grasp and dangled it like a pendulum in front of her face. "Can you prove you didn't put this note out here yourself, Rosie?"

Her face went utterly pale. "What?"

"What are you doing, Max?" Trent cautioned.

"Testing a theory." He closed the cabinet doors and moved a step closer. "Have you gotten other threats, Rosie?"

"Yes. Wait. Rosie?" Instead of recoiling from him, she planted her feet, her hand fisting in the dog's curly hair. "We are not friends, Mr. Krolikowski, so you have no right to be so familiar. Or condescending. Especially when it sounds as though you're calling me a liar."

"*Are* you lying, Rosie?"

"Stop calling me that."

"It's a pretty good diversion to make us think someone's after you."

"Diversion from what?" Her chest puffed out, and a blush crept up her neck as understanding dawned. "I'm such an idiot. This is about Richard, isn't it?"

"It's a reasonable question, considering your history. You're kind of like the lady who cries wolf with all your phone calls to 9-1-1."

"My history?" Her cheeks were as rosy as his new nickname for her now. "We're finally getting to the

point, aren't we? Is KCPD accusing me of killing him
again? Are you accusing Stephen? And here I thought
the police had shown up because…" She stared at the
evidence bag in his hand for a moment, her chin trembling against the tight clench of her mouth. Then her
lips buzzed with an escaping breath and she walked to
the gate. "Duchess, heel. Sit." The German shepherd
settled onto her haunches beside her mistress, staying
put as Rosie opened the gate. Rosie shifted the poodle to
one arm and pointed down the driveway with the other.
"I'd like you two to leave my home. Now. And please
don't gun your engine on your way out of the neighborhood. There's already enough gossip about me without
hearing complaints about loud cars leaving my house."

"There's not a damn thing wrong with the way I
drive, lady. You and your brother had more motive than
anybody to kill Richard Bratcher. I think you'd be less
worried about my car and more worried about talking
to us and trying to prove your innocence."

She shook her head, probably biting down on some
unladylike crack about being innocent until proven
guilty. But all he got was a succinct dismissal. "If you
won't help me, I'm not helping you. If you gentlemen
have any further questions about Richard's murder, you
may call my attorney."

Man, that woman was the definition of control. No
blowing her stack or shedding a tear or slapping his face.
No answers. No freaking reason he should be so per-
plexed or fascinated by her. He walked up to her, letting
his six feet two inches lean in close enough to steal a
breath of her summery scent. "Gentlemen? Honey, I'm
as far from being—"

"Max, shut up." His partner pushed him on out the gate.

"You, too?" Max patted his chest pocket, but there

was no cigar there. Damn it. The stress, the suspicion, the guilt—too many emotions were hitting him way too fast to deal with them properly. He shook his head and strode toward the Chevelle. "I should have called in sick. I don't need this kind of convoluted drama. Not today." He spun and pointed a finger at the redhead whose cool eyes had locked onto him. "You really need the cops someday, lady, you come and find me. But you'd better be willing to talk and you'd better make sense." He turned and resumed his march toward the car. "I need a drink before I screw anything else up today."

"Excuse us, Miss March. Thank you for your time." Trent hurried to catch up and fall into step beside him. "You know we're not going to get anything out of her now, right?"

"I know."

"You really think she's making up these threats to make her read like a victim instead of a suspect?"

"She's smart enough to do it. Ah, I don't know what I think."

"Hey, Max." A strong hand on his arm stopped him. "I'm on your side, remember?" The tone of Trent's voice was as full of reprimand as it was concern. "It's a little early for the Shamrock, isn't it?"

"Not today, it isn't." He shrugged out of Trent's grip and circled around the car. It was probably best for everybody here—that frightened, pissed-off woman; his best friend; this case; this job; Jimmy's memory; him— if he just walked away.

But something drew his gaze over the roof of the car back to Rosemary March. She'd followed them along the driveway toward the porch, catching the end of their conversation. But she froze as soon as his eyes locked on to hers, one arm hooked around the poodle, the other clinging to the shepherd's collar. From this distance she looked smaller, fragile and as painfully alone as he'd ever been. She'd needed someone to make her feel safe, and he'd chosen to play his bad-cop role to the hilt. He deserved the truckload of regret that dumped on top of the guilt already weighing him down.

Max swung open the car door and climbed inside to start the engine. "Not today."

Chapter Four

Rosemary squeezed her fists around the long straps of her shoulder bag, staring at the steel doors of the elevator while Howard Bratcher rattled on about the trust fund and investment portfolio he and his accountant had put together for her on Stephen's behalf. She'd understood the benefits and restrictions and attorney fees clearly the first time they'd discussed splitting up and managing the settlement money, but it was easier to let him repeat himself than to explain the troubling turn of her thoughts.

Two detectives had come to her home this morning. As if her encounter with that grizzled, grabby, surly Detective Krolikowski and his bigger, quieter partner wasn't upsetting enough, it was dismaying to learn that KCPD had reopened the investigation into her fiancé's murder and considered her and Stephen suspects again. Even six years after she'd found his dead body in his condo, blue faced and frozen midconvulsion, it seemed Richard still had the power to destroy any sense of security and self-worth she'd ever had.

The disturbing phone messages and threat in her own backyard left her as on edge and unsure of the world around her as those last few months with Richard had been. Her morning visit from Detectives Dixon and

Krolikowski had only intensified her feelings of losing control over her own life.

Trent Dixon might have looked like a Mack truck, but he'd been businesslike, pseudofriendly. He'd kept his words polite and had respected her personal space. But Max Krolikowski made no bones about their reason for being there. And despite the military haircut that reminded her so of her father, he'd been coarse, forthright, unapologetically male—not a kindly paternal figure in any way, shape or form.

The broad-shouldered detective with the stubbled jaw and wrinkled shirt was as different from Richard's suit and tie and courtly charm as a man could be. He was right to keep his eyes hidden behind the mask of those sunglasses. On first glimpse, those deep blue irises had been full of ghosts and despair. But upon a closer look, a quick shift in attitude revealed a frightening sort of defiance—as though some great pain was crushing in on him before he summoned his considerable strength or pure cussedness or both and crushed it, instead.

He'd grabbed her, sworn his frustration with a vast vocabulary of objectionable words, accused her of lying, gossiped with the neighbors about her, made friends with her dogs and then invaded her personal space and gone vulgar and insulting again. He couldn't be more unsuited to her guarded sensibilities.

But it wasn't the lack of manners or even the not-so-subtle doubts about her innocence that stuck with her an hour after he'd driven away.

She'd forgotten how warm a man could be.

The heat of the summer sun on his skin mixed with temper and muscle—Max Krolikowski didn't have to touch her for her to be aware of the furnace of heat that man could generate. Yet he *had* touched her, singeing her skin with his abundant warmth. Rosemary wiggled her fingers around the strap of her purse, remembering the shock of his rough hand sliding over her arm. No man who wasn't her brother—she sneaked a glance up at Howard—or a brotherly type, had touched her since long before Richard's death. Frissons of white-hot electricity had danced across her skin beneath the sweep of the detective's hand. She'd reacted to his touch.

And then she'd touched him. Her hand had encountered a wall of warm, immovable muscle when she'd pushed against his chest. For a split second, her fear and fortitude had given way to a reaction that was purely female. Surprisingly aware. Completely out of character for her now.

She remembered closeness. Wanting. She remembered she was a woman.

Rosemary twisted her neck from side to side in discomfort, feeling as if the cold steel walls of this elevator were closing in on her. Why would her hormones suddenly awaken and respond to an ill-mannered beast like Max Krolikowski? Did she have no sense when it came to men? She'd never had a thing for bad boys before. Of course, she hadn't had the chance to have much of a thing for any man. But wasn't rule one that she needed to feel safe? Could it be that six years of isolating herself in order to recapture control over her own life had left her so lonely that any man barging past those meticulously erected barriers was bound to trigger a reaction?

It was all very unsettling. Max Krolikowski was unsettling. Knowing she was still thinking about him, wary of him, curious about him, wondering why Trixie and Duchess had taken to him so readily, was messing with her carefully structured, predictable world.

"We're here." The elevator dipped as it came to a

stop, startling her from her thoughts as much as Howard's interruption had. But by the time the doors slid open, Rosemary had her chin and armor back in place. She arched her back away from the brush of Howard's hand there, hugged her purse to her side and hurried on out the door.

Rosemary stepped out into the cold, modern decor of the Raynard Building's top floor into the Bratcher, Austin & Cole, Attorneys-at-Law, reception area. Before she reached the granite-topped reception counter, Howard wrapped his fingers around her elbow and pulled her to a stop so he could whisper against her ear. "I thought, perhaps, you'd let me take you to lunch afterward."

She didn't immediately process that he'd asked her out on another date, because her mind was too busy comparing the light, cool clasp of his fingers to the purposeful heat of Max Krolikowski's grasp.

Really? She groaned inwardly. Although she couldn't say if her dismay stemmed from her unwanted obsession with the bullying detective or Howard's puppylike determination to turn their relationship into something more than a friendship. How many ways could she say no without hurting his feelings?

Pulling away, she offered him a wry smile. "I don't think that will work today. I've got so much to do at home. There's still a ton of Mom and Dad's stuff to go through."

Howard's smile dimmed. "I understand. Rain check?"

An office door clicked shut at the north end of the hallway and a woman's shrill voice bounced off the sterile walls. "What's she doing here?"

Rosemary's day went from bad to rotten as she turned to face Charleen Grimes. It was impossible not to feel like a frump in the face of the blonde woman's artful makeup and thoroughbred legs. It was impossible not to feel the resentment licking through her veins, either. "Howard is my attorney. Why are *you* here?"

"You don't have to engage her, Rosemary." Howard put his arm around her shoulders and pulled her to his side. This time, she didn't pull away. Nothing like a run-in with her dead fiancé's mistress to sap her strength. "Charleen, what are you doing here?" he demanded with courtroom-like authority. "I thought I made it clear you needed to find different representation."

"You mean besides your brother? I did. I just had an appointment with Mr. Austin." Charleen sauntered across the gray carpet, bringing a cloud of expensive perfume and vitriol Rosemary's way. "You're the one who's got a lot of nerve, showing your face here. I loved Richard. Why couldn't you just let him go?"

After his first attack, Rosemary had been in shock. But after the second time, when he'd twisted her arm so violently it snapped, she'd been more than willing to push Richard Bratcher out of her life. "I told Richard it was over between us. The two of you could have been together. With my blessing."

"Liar."

Rosemary's shoulders pushed against Howard's arm as indignation kicked in. How many people were going to accuse her of that today?

"He pitied you. He said you needed him too much to ever leave you."

What he hadn't wanted to leave was her money. He'd made it clear that he would continue to have Charleen or whomever he pleased in his bed after their marriage because no uptight, inexperienced, overworked mouse like her would ever be able to satisfy a man's appetite. And if Richard's words weren't cruel enough, the slap across the face had been. She'd pulled off his ring and held it out to him. But he'd twisted her arm and the nightmare started.

Rosemary gritted her teeth, blanking the memory of running for her life yet not being able to escape her own home or Richard's torture until he'd run out of cigarettes and had gone for more. "I don't know what to say, Ms. Grimes. Clearly, you're still grieving."

"Grieving? I'm mad because he's dead, and it's your fault."

Apparently, Richard hadn't treated his mistresses like the punching bag she'd been. Rosemary's love for him had died long ago. Why hadn't Charleen's? "It's been six years."

"Feels like yesterday to me. Maybe because two detectives—Watson and Parker—came to my boutique this morning and asked me questions about Richard's death. That's why I'm here—to alert my attorney." Charleen towered over Rosemary with her three-inch heels and movie-star figure. She used that height to her advantage to sneer down her nose at Rosemary. "But I told them who I suspected."

"That's enough, Charleen." Howard removed his arm to clasp Rosemary's shoulders with both hands and turn her to face him. "Is that true? Has KCPD started a new investigation?"

Rosemary shrugged out of his grip. "Why are you asking me?"

The tall blonde laughed. "Because he thinks you did it, too."

"Suzy." Howard snapped his fingers at the receptionist gaping behind her desk. "Escort Ms. Grimes back into Mr. Austin's office."

"But Mr. Austin has a client with—"

"Get her out of here!"

"Yes, sir." The dark-haired receptionist hurried around the stainless counter. "Ms. Grimes, may I take you to the lounge and get you some tea or coffee?"

Rosemary had flinched at Howard's raised voice, but Charleen seemed amused by his anger. "Your brother would never speak to me like that."

"My little brother did a lot of things I didn't approve of." Howard moved his tall body in front of Rosemary, blocking her view of the other woman. "If you want to continue to be a client of this firm, I suggest you learn how to keep your mouth shut and behave like a lady."

"Like boring little Miss March?"

"Do you understand what slander charges are, Charleen? I won't have you accusing Rosemary of something she didn't do."

Rosemary heard a snort of derision. "How do you know she didn't kill Richard?"

Howard's shoulders lifted with a deep breath as Charleen followed the receptionist down the long hallway to the other attorney's office suite. With a hand at Rosemary's back, he escorted her in the opposite direction. Once he closed the door to his inner office behind him, he tried to take Rosemary into his arms. "I'm so sorry the two of you had to run into each other."

But comfort was the last thing she wanted, especially with her temper brewing in her veins. She pushed away from his hug and circled around his desk to look out at the Kansas City skyline. Maybe the world was more normal outside that window. "Six years. I thought…" She crossed her arms in front of her as a shiver ran down her spine. "It was foolish to hope the nightmare of your brother was all behind me. I guess people won't leave me alone until his murder is solved and the real killer is in prison."

Howard shrugged off his suit jacket and draped it over the back of his chair, coming up behind her. "Did the police question you about Richard?"

Rosemary nodded. "Two detectives came to see me this morning, too."

"You should have called me right away. I don't want you talking to the police without me present."

When his hands settled on her shoulders again, Rosemary moved away. "Why? I didn't kill him. I don't have anything to hide." Although she hadn't really answered any of Detective Krolikowski or Dixon's questions once she realized they weren't responding to her complaint about the harassing calls and ugly threat. She stopped her furious pacing and inhaled a calming breath. It was wrong to take her frustration out on her friend. "I'm sorry, Howard. This must all be difficult for you, too. Not knowing who's responsible. I'm guessing the police will be questioning you again, as well."

He waved off her apology and followed her around the desk, where he pushed aside some knickknacks and perched on the corner. "Let them come. My alibi's as solid now as it was six years ago. I'm not worried."

"Still, the memories of your brother—I know you loved him. Our reasons may be different, but you need closure as much as I do."

"I'm so sorry, Rosemary. So sorry for everything. I knew Richard had a temper, but I never knew he was hurting you. Maybe if I had known, I could have done something to stop him. But he was so ambitious, so greedy. He never wanted to put in the time and the hard work to pay his dues and get ahead. He always looked for the shortcut. I guess I thought he'd grow out of it one day. I thought you were a good influence on him, that your marriage would be a success." He glanced toward the door, indicating the confrontation with Charleen Grimes. "You were certainly a better class of woman than those floozies he was always taking to bed. As talented a litigator as he was, he was an embarrassment to the reputation of the firm. Cost us clients. Our father went to his grave thinking Richard was never going to amount to anything worth making him a full partner."

"I don't blame you for anything Richard did. You weren't your brother's keeper."

"Maybe I should have been." He reached for her hand, and she forced herself not to dodge his grasp this time. "I intend to take care of you, though, to make up in some small way for the grief he caused you."

Rosemary managed to drum up a smile of thanks before pulling away. "How about you show me those papers you worked so hard to prepare."

Fifteen minutes later, the papers were signed and she was ready to leave. "I'll drive you home," Howard offered.

But Rosemary slung her purse over her shoulder and urged him back to his chair. "I can call a taxi. I know you have work to do." Besides, she'd already spent most of the patience and socializing she had in her today and needed some time alone to decide how best to manage—or avoid—all this attention suddenly being thrust upon her. She needed to set her emotional armor back into place. "But thank you. And thanks for running interference with Charleen."

He raised her hand to his lips and kissed it. "My pleasure. If you say you didn't kill Richard, then I believe you. And I'll defend your innocence until my dying breath." He tugged her closer and Rosemary put a hand on his stomach to keep him from completing the embrace. Still, he lowered his head to rest his forehead against hers. "Even if you did kill that bastard brother of mine in self-defense or because he deserved it, I'll defend your innocence."

Um, thank you? Her chest tightened at his declaration of support that sounded vaguely as if it wasn't real support at all. Before he could dip his lips to hers, Rosemary pushed away. "I didn't kill Richard."

"Of course not." Why didn't that throwaway remark sound as convincing as it might have even an hour earlier? When Howard circled back to his chair, Rosemary hurried to the door. "I'll talk to you soon."

Not too soon, she hoped. But she kept the thought to herself and closed the office door behind her.

AFTER A WALK with the dogs to maintain their training and give them exercise, several laps in the pool to work her vexation with Howard out of her system, and chicken from her back patio grill for dinner to fill her stomach, Rosemary settled down in the library with a glass of wine to attack another box of family papers and photographs.

Sorting through items from her and Stephen's past, as well as those things that had belonged to her parents, served several purposes. From the most practical—the long-term project gave her something meaningful to do with her time since the suspicion of murder had made it practically impossible to find a teaching job at any certified school. The settlement gave her plenty to live on, but she was a grown woman with two college degrees and a fertile brain. If she couldn't occupy her thoughts and work toward goals, she'd go mad. One of those goals was to possibly sell this place, or at least clear out enough space so she could significantly remodel the interior. There were a lot of good memories here. But there were a lot of bad ones, too. And while the familiarity of her childhood home made it a little easier to cope with the grief, panic and uncertainty of these past few years, there were days like this one when the same-old, same-old felt more like a prison where she was destined to live out her days as the neighborhood pariah—the woman who'd benefited from her parents' deaths, the woman who'd gotten away with murder.

Instead of letting the loneliness and fear take hold, Rosemary plunged into the never-ending—sometimes sentimental, sometimes sad—task of sorting papers, mementoes and heirlooms into piles of things to treasure, items to store or sell and things to throw away.

And so, with the drawn shades and night outside her windows closing her into solitude, Rosemary sat on the thick braided rug in the middle of the library floor, with piles of letters and photographs spread out around her. Duchess stretched out on the cool wood at the edge of the rug while Trixie claimed the couch.

Humming along with the Aaron Copland ballet music playing softly in the background, Rosemary smiled at an image of her father in his Army pilot's uniform, taken a few years before her birth. He'd had that freckled, youthful look for as long as she'd known him, even when his hair had started to gray. Not that the silver strands were that noticeable with his hair cropped so closely to his head. He used to joke that it was time for a trip to the barber if a strand of hair so much as tickled his ear.

Memories of her father drifted to another man with the same broad shoulders and buzz cut. Max Krolikowski was taller than her dad, thick chested and muscular instead of lean and lanky, more tawny haired than strawberry blond. And he certainly lacked that boyish smile. But she could picture the gruff detective dressed in a similar uniform. She could picture him in a gritty, action-packed war movie. What was she thinking? There was nothing fake about Max Krolikowski. She could picture him marching across an asphalt tarmac, boarding a troop transport like the one her father had flown, heading off to fight in a real war.

Rosemary's blood rushed a warning signal to her brain. She shouldn't be picturing the surly detective at all.

With a guilty start, she tucked the tiny snapshot back into the envelope with the letter to her mother. Max Krolikowski was nothing like the quiet gentleman Colonel Stephen March had been. Why couldn't she let her fascination with that rude excuse for a cop go?

Focusing on happier times, she retied the ribbon around the bundle of letters her mother had kept from the correspondence she and her father had traded when he'd been away on his first post after graduating college on his ROTC scholarship. Remembering the love her parents had shared chased away her troublesome thoughts, and Rosemary rose up on her knees to reverently place the love letters in a box marked *Keep*.

She hiked up the wrinkled hem of her dress to crawl over to the box she was sorting and pull out another stack of bound envelopes. But as she sank back onto the rug, her smile faded. "What are these doing here?"

In the chaos surrounding Richard's ultimatums and his subsequent murder, she must have tossed these letters into the wrong box. They weren't correspondence between her mother and father, but a bundle of envelopes from Richard addressed to her.

With her neckline unbuttoned in deference to the

summer humidity, despite the house's air-conditioning, Rosemary mindlessly rubbed her knuckles over her collarbone and the neat dots of puckered scar tissue there. Once, she'd thought it romantic that Richard had sent her notes and poems and pictures, just as her father had sent them to her mother. But now she was wondering why she'd ever kept the tangible reminders of her own foolishness. He hadn't even written the first letter until she'd mentioned how her parents had made such an effort to stay connected when they'd been apart. Now she could see it had all been part of his master plan to make her fall in love and accept his proposal. Weighed down by responsibility and sadness, desperate for someone caring and positive in her life, she must have been an easy mark for a smooth operator like Richard.

"Idiot," she grumbled, reaching out to toss the entire stack into the trash can beside the desk. But then she realized that half of the envelopes hadn't even been opened. A check of the postmarks indicated he'd sent these in the weeks between her breaking off their engagement and filing a restraining order against him, courtesy of his older brother, and Richard's death.

Against her better judgment, she opened the first envelope and pulled out the familiar parchment with the letterhead from his father's law firm. Rosemary shook her head as she read his dramatic scrawl. "I'll end the affair with Charleen. I'll work on my weakness with other women. I love you. I still want to marry you."

There was no apology for the arm he'd put into a cast or the cigarette burns that marred her skin. Not even an acknowledgment of the cruel coercion he'd used to force her to sign the prenup guaranteeing him a share of her settlement money. Just a blithe pronouncement of love. Funny, if she'd been thinking clearly back then, she'd have seen that all the sentences were "I" statements. Maybe if she'd picked up on those egocentric clues when they were first dating, she could have spared herself the mistake of giving her heart to the wrong man.

Rosemary returned the letter to its envelope and reached for her wineglass to wash away the taste of disgust with a crisp pinot grigio. The trash was too good for these reminders of that sick relationship, so she dropped it and the rest of his letters into a box and set it aside. This winter, she'd burn them with the first fire in the fireplace. She smiled as she raised the goblet to her lips to take a sip.

But a flicker of shadow in the window behind her reflected off the glass.

Her stomach clenched. Wine sloshed over her hand as she spun around. Nothing. Just the blinds swaying with the current of air blowing from the AC vent. She inhaled a deep breath, willing her heart rate to slow down.

Probably just the headlights of a car driving past.

But then Duchess lifted her head, growling a low warning in her throat. Trixie jumped to her feet and barked, startling Rosemary. "What is it?"

She set down the wineglass with a trembling hand, running a quick mental check. Doors locked. Windows locked. Alarm system armed. Lights on. Dogs at her—

Rosemary screamed at the explosion of shattering glass outside. Trixie sprang from the couch as Duchess leaped to her feet. Both dogs dashed to the front door. A man-size shadow darted past the blinds. Someone was on her front porch. Why didn't the alarm go off?

The dogs' frantic barking nearly drowned out the second explosion of smashing glass. The translucent light filtering through the blinds suddenly went dark and she realized someone out there was breaking the lights. Pounding on the porch railing and furniture outside.

Avoiding the door. Avoiding the windows. Avoiding doing any damage that would trigger a siren and flashing lights.

Shrinking away from the assault on her house, Rosie screamed again at the crunch of metal on metal. "Stop it." She hugged her arms around her waist. "Stop it!"

But a crystal-clear moment of clarity fired through her brain, snapping her out of her chilled stupor. What if the intruder smashed through the door next and turned whatever weapon he was using on her dogs?

Or on her?

A wailing alarm couldn't help her then.

Rosemary lowered her hands into fists. "Duchess! Trixie!"

The barking paused for a second, then started up again, warning away the intruder at their door. Rosemary snatched her cell phone off the desk and ran into the hallway, grabbing their leashes off a foyer chair and joining the canine alarm. "I'm calling the police!" she shouted. "Get out of here! Now!"

Footsteps pounded across the slats of her porch and faded into silence. The man was running away. "Duchess, sit. Come here, Trix."

As silence fell outside, Rosemary regained control of the dogs. Kneeling between them, she hooked them up to their leashes and pulled them back from the door. Did she dare unlock it to see what was going on? Trixie, especially, was ready to charge whatever danger was on the other side of that door, and Duchess's low-pitched growl indicated that no one here felt entirely safe. She almost wished it was a random act of vandalism or attempted burglary. But she'd dealt with too many threats these past few days to believe she was anything but the intended target. She transferred both leashes to her left hand and pulled out her cell, her thumb hovering above the 9 on her screen.

But was calling KCPD again really an option for her? Was there any cop out there willing to help a murder suspect?

Rosemary pocketed her phone and waited a good two minutes, until the growling subsided and she got Trixie to sit beside the bigger dog. That meant whoever had been on her porch was long gone. It was safe to open the door, right?

Ignoring the thumping pound of her heart inside her chest, Rosemary typed in the disarm code, unhooked the chain and dead bolt and twisted the doorknob. Still in her bare feet, she stayed inside the locked storm door to survey the damage. There was shattered glass everywhere. A broken table. The intruder had taken a bat or crowbar or some other heavy object to the lights on either side of her door, plunging her porch into darkness. But there was enough light shining out from the foyer to see the dented black metal mailbox hanging by a screw from the siding beside the door.

Once she was certain the intruder had left, she pulled the leashes taut and nudged open the storm door.

"Oh, my God."

There was enough light to read the note hanging from the flap of her mailbox, too.

Murdering whore.
Justice will be done.

She swayed on her feet, shock making her lightheaded for a moment. Her landline rang in the house behind her and she jerked in surprise, sending the dogs into another barking frenzy.

Avoiding the broken glass beneath bare feet and dog paws, she pulled Duchess and Trixie back into the house and locked the storm door. After the fourth ring, the machine in the kitchen picked up, and a man's garbled voice echoed like a creepy whisper throughout the house. "I can see you, Rosemary. I know you're alone. Those dogs can't protect you. I know you're afraid."

The shiver that shook her body nearly robbed her of breath. She didn't remember slamming the front door or releasing the dogs or pulling her cell from the pocket of her dress.

But some shred of a memory stopped her from completing the 9-1-1 call.

KCPD had blown off her last report of a threat. She didn't need anyone patronizing her fears—she needed to feel safe. She wanted to prove to the police she wasn't lying—that she was the victim now, just as she'd been six years ago. With the dogs at her heels, Rosemary ran to the answering machine at the back of the house. But she had no intention of picking up the phone or even erasing that sick message. She had no intention of dealing with Dispatch and being put on hold or winding up as a footnote on some report.

Instead, she pulled the phone book from beneath the machine and looked up an address.

She knew where she could find at least one cop tonight.

Chapter Five

Max swallowed a drink of beer that had lost its chill and set the mug down on the rim of the pool table at the Shamrock Bar. He leaned over, blinking his bleary eyes and lining up the shot, tuning out the drone of conversations around the room and the jingle of the bell over the bar's front door. "Six in the corner pocket."

He tapped the cue ball and grinned as the pink ball caromed off the rail and rolled into its target. Finally, something was going right today.

He'd circled to the end of the table to assess his best angle for dropping the seven ball before realizing the noise level of the thinning crowd had paused in a momentary hush. Even his opponent on the opposite side of the pool table seemed to have frozen for a split second in time.

"She's new." Hudson Kramer, a young cop with a shiny promotion and the subsequent pay hike burning a hole in his pocket, lay down his cue stick and combed his fingers through his hair as glasses clinked and conversations started up again. Was the game over? Hud's mouth widened with a lopsided grin as his eyes tracked movement behind Max. "Wonder if she's lost. Maybe she needs a friend to help her find her way."

With Kramer's grumble of protest at having his shot

at winning back the money he'd lost tonight interrupted, Max turned and saw the last person he'd ever expect to see in a bar. "I'll be damned."

Rosemary March's copper-red hair was pulled back in a bun that wasn't anywhere as neat and tidy and screaming *old maid* as it had been this morning. *Fire and ice.* The unexpected metaphor buzzed through his head at the sight of several loose, wavy red strands bouncing against her pale cheeks and neck as she moved. The idea of her letting all that hair flow freely around her shoulders and tunneling his fingers into a handful of it hit him like a sucker punch to the gut. Max sat back on the edge of the table, propping his cue stick against the floor to hold himself upright as she approached.

He must have had too much to drink and was conjuring up hallucinations. He closed his eyes and muttered a curse, wondering why he wasn't conjuring up images of babes on swimsuit calendars instead of Miss Priss with the sharp tongue and crazy ideas.

He opened his eyes again. Nope. She was real. And she was excusing her way past a couple of tables and a cocktail waitress, heading straight toward him and the pool tables. She'd exchanged the dressy sandals for a pair of flip-flops, but she still wore that white, high-necked dress from this morning, looking as virginal and out of place in a bar at this hour as he'd felt at her house this morning. Didn't mean she didn't look all kinds of pretty to a half drunk, half horny bastard like him.

"Ah, hell," he muttered again, wishing he'd said no to that last beer so he could control that little rush of misplaced excitement at realizing she'd come to see him.

"Detective Krolikowski?" She stopped a couple of feet in front of him, her fingers tightening around the strap of the purse she hugged in front of her. Mistaking his dumbfounded silence for a lack of recognition, she tilted those dove-gray eyes to his and introduced herself. "Rosemary March? We met this morning? I'm not armed, I promise."

"I know who you are, Rosie. You here for a drink?" When the waitress slid between the redhead and the nearest table, Max automatically reached out. Rosie pried at his hand when he tugged on the strap of her purse to pull her out of the other woman's path. Her hips jostled between the vee of his legs and his thigh muscles bunched in a helpless response to her unintentionally intimate touch there. Max instantly popped his grip open and let her scoot around his leg into the space beside him. Ignoring his body's traitorous response to a warm, curvy woman, he held up two fingers to capture the waitress's attention. "Wait. You probably want something fancier than a beer. Wine? One of those girly things with an umbrella?"

"Nothing, thank you."

Oh, he was in a bad way today. After waving off the drink order, he turned on the edge of the pool table and pulled a long, copper-red wave away from the dewy perspiration on Rosie's neck. Warm from her skin, he rubbed the silky strand between his thumb and fingers. "So is this you lettin' your hair down? You go to a bar, but you don't drink? Or is this a temperance lecture for me? Couldn't get enough of puttin' me in my place this morning, eh?"

"No, I... What are you doing?" She jerked away, snatching her hair from his fingertips and tucking it behind her ear. "This was a dumb idea."

Max pushed to his feet and thumped the tip of his cue stick on the table in front of her, blocking her escape. "Hold on, Rosie Posy. What *are* you doing here?"

Her shoulders lifted with a deep breath and she turned, staring at the collar of his shirt before tilting her wary eyes up to his. "I overheard you and your partner talk about coming here. The Shamrock Bar. I looked up the address in the phone book."

"Do you ever give a straight answer to a question?" He hunched down to look her right in the eye. "That's how you found me. Now tell me what you want. Let me guess—you're a pool hustler, and you're here to win ten bucks off me to spite me for being such a jerk this morning."

Hud Kramer walked up behind her before the shocked O of her mouth could spit out an answer. "I bet she could take you, Max."

Max bristled at the interruption. Why was that kid grinning? "Shut up."

Rosie turned to include both men in her answer. Sort of. If looking from one chin to the other counted. What was that woman's aversion to making direct eye contact? With that tart tongue of hers, he couldn't really call her shy. But something had to be going on to make her subvert that red-haired temper and any other emotion she might be feeling. "I haven't played for a long time. I used to be pretty decent back in college when I'd go out with friends, but I don't think I'd win."

"I'd be happy to give you a few tips, Red." The younger cop seemed to take any answer as encouragement to his lame flirtations. "Aren't you going to introduce us, Max?"

But when Hud leaned in, Rosie flinched back, maybe sidling closer to what was familiar, if not necessarily what she considered friendly. Max shifted in an instinctively protective response, and her hair tangled with the scruff of beard on his chin, releasing her warm summer scent. His pulse leaped and he was inhaling a deep breath before he could stop himself. Rosie March might be a baffling mix of mystery and frustration, but she exuded a wholesome, flowery fragrance that was far more intoxicating than the beer he'd been drinking.

Max growled, irritated by how much he noticed about this woman. And he was even more irritated that the younger detective had noticed it, too. "Get out of here, Kramer."

A soft nudge to the chest with Max's pool cue backed Hud up a step, but the young hotshot was still smiling. Yes, the woman had rebuffed him in favor of the older detective who needed a shave and an attitude adjustment. But Hud wasn't about to lose to him twice in one night. "Our game isn't finished, Krolikowski. I have a feeling I'm about to make a comeback."

Groaning at the taunt, Max set his cue stick on the table and pulled out his wallet. He reached around Rosie to hand a ten-dollar bill to the young officer. "Here. Take it."

"You're conceding defeat?"

"I'm conceding that you annoy the hell out of me and I'm tired of puttin' up with you. Now scram."

"Yes, sir." Kramer took the sawbuck with a wink and a mock salute and headed straight to a green vinyl seat in front of the polished walnut bar to order a refill.

With more room to avoid him now, Rosie quickly stepped away and moved around the corner of the table. "I'm sorry you lost your money. That wasn't my intention." She pulled open the flap on her purse and pulled out her wallet. "I only wanted to talk to a police officer."

Now she wanted to answer questions? Max scanned the booths and tables around the bar. "Take your pick.

The majority of the men and women here work in some kind of law enforcement."

"Could I talk to *you*?"

He looked down to see her holding out a ten-dollar bill. Muttering a curse, he pushed the money back into her purse. At this late hour, every young stud in the place was looking for any unattached females who might be interested in one last drink and a chance to get lucky. They wouldn't know that Rosie was a person of interest in a murder investigation. They wouldn't care about her eccentricities or that she could rub a man wrong in every possible way. Like Kramer, they were noticing the outward appearance of innocence and vulnerability. They were seeing the promise of passion in the red flag of Rosemary March's hair. Maybe they were picturing what it would look like down and loose about her bare shoulders, too.

Even in his hazy brain, Max knew she didn't belong here.

"Let's get out of here. Robbie?" He looked to the Shamrock's bearded owner at the bar, and tossed some bills on the table to pay for his tab. "Come on."

Grabbing Rosie by the arm, he turned her toward the door. Whatever she wanted from him, he wasn't about to go toe-to-toe with some young buck who wanted to pick her up just for the privilege of finding out. Although she hurried her steps beside him to keep up, she tried to shuck off his grip. But Max tightened his fingers around her surprisingly firm upper arm muscles and didn't let go until he'd ushered her out the front door into the muggy haze of the hot summer night.

He took her past the green neon sign in the front window so that curious eyes inside wouldn't get the idea that she might be coming back before he released her. He plucked a fresh cigar from his shirt pocket and leaned back against the warm bricks. "Now talk to me."

Once he released her, she took a couple more steps and turned. "You smoke?"

"Not exactly." He tore off the wrapper and stuffed the plastic into his pocket. Then he held the stogie up to his nose, breathing in the rich tobacco scent until he could rid the distracting memory of fresh summer sunshine from his senses. Light from the street lamps and green neon sign in the window reflected off the oily asphalt of the street behind her, making her seem even more out of place in the dingy surroundings. At least he didn't have to deal with Kramer or anybody else hittin' on her out here. Max set the cigar between his teeth and chomped down on it. "Make sense, and make it fast, okay?"

He watched the reprimand on her lips start and die. Good. He wasn't in the mood for one of her lectures on the evils of swearing and smoking—one of which he hadn't done for years. She seemed to consider his request for brevity and nodded. "Actually, I want you to come to my house. I had a trespasser tonight. I don't know how long he was there before he started vandalizing my front porch. He broke the lights and left a message in my mailbox. It's…disturbing, to say the least." She reached into her purse and pulled out a folded sheet of white paper with just her thumb and forefinger and held it out to him. "It's typed like the one I found on the back patio. No signature to say who it's from."

Straightening from the wall, Max snatched the paper from her fingers and unfolded it. "Somebody threaten your dogs again?"

Her chin shot up and her cheeks dotted with color. "He's not after my dogs. He just knows they're a way to get to me. To scare me."

"You keep saying *he*."

"Or she. I don't know who it was. All I saw was the shadow on my porch and the damage after the dogs' barking scared him away."

Max squinted the words on the note into focus. "Murdering whore. Justice will be done." Anger surged through his veins and he swore around the cigar. "You should have reported this ASAP to 9-1-1 instead of taking the time to track me down."

"I don't want to be brushed off with another phone call, and I certainly don't want to be accused of making it up again."

"What makes you think I'm gonna believe you?"

Her tongue darted out to moisten her lips, and his pulse leaped with a response that told him he was already far too interested in this woman to remain objective. Probably why he was such a growly butt around her. He didn't want to like her. It didn't make sense to like her. And yet, she was doing all kinds of crazy things to his brain and libido.

"To look at you, and listen to the way you talk… You're military, aren't you? Or you used to be? Not just the haircut. But, the way you stand. The way you move. You recognized Dad's gun as Army issue, and you remind me of him when he was young. Except, he was shorter. More patient. And he didn't smoke."

Hell. Where was she going with this? Suspicion tried to move past the fog of alcohol and put him on alert.

"Dad was in the Army. A career man who retired as a colonel. Isn't there some band of brothers code I can call on for you to help me? Without treating me like a suspect in a murder case?"

Max tilted his face to the canopy of cloudy haze reflecting the city lights overhead. He'd spent the day mourning his fallen band of brothers, cursing his inability to save them all—to save his best friend. He couldn't do this. He couldn't call on that part of him to do his duty and fail again. Not for this woman. Not for a comrade in arms or superior officer he'd never even met. With a self-preserving resolve, he lowered his gaze to hers and handed back the note. "You should have called Trent. He's the reasonable one."

"No one will listen to reason." Her hands fisted in frustration. "I need someone who'll help me out of blind faith in my innocence…or out of a sense of duty. Or honor. Besides, I don't know where your partner is. But I remembered you said you were coming here for a drink."

"That was this morning. What made you think I'd still be here?" A little frown dimple appeared between her eyebrows when she wrinkled up her nose in an unspoken apology. Oh. Her opinion of him was that low, huh? He supposed he'd earned it. And yet she'd sought him out instead of Trent or one of the other off-duty detectives and uniforms inside the cop bar. Maybe he shouldn't alter her opinion of him by telling her he'd gone back to his desk at the precinct and put in his full shift before grabbing a burger and heading to the Shamrock. "How will me going to your place prove you didn't put this note there, too?"

The soft gaze that had held his for so long dropped to his chin. Her skin blanched to a shade of alabaster that absorbed the harsh green color of the neon sign. He didn't like that unnatural color on her. He didn't like feeling like a first-class rat for blanking the color from her skin.

"Hey, I…" Max pulled his cigar from his mouth with one hand and reached for a red tendril with the other. Although she startled at his touch, she didn't immediately pull away this time. Instead, she watched his hand as he sifted the silky copper through his fingers. "I'm sorry, Rosie. I'm having a really sucky day. It's hard to see the good in anything or anybody tonight."

"You're not always like this?"

He chuckled at the doubtful face she made. "Some say I am. But on this one day every year, I'm an extra sorry SOB."

"I wish you wouldn't swear like that. I get that you're angry, already."

Oh, he was angry, all right. At himself. At friends who died. At failing to save them.

"I get that you're hurting. Did something bad happen?"

"Yeah. Something very bad happened. To a friend of mine." She'd tilted her eyes up to his, bravely held his gaze. Maybe it was a trick of the lights and shadows, but from this angle, standing this close, her eyes filled with compassion, maybe even a little of that same odd awareness he'd been feeling about her. A man could lose himself in the deep, soft shadows of her eyes if he wasn't careful. As uncomfortable with her intuition about him as he was with the male interest stirring deep inside him, he pulled his fingers from her hair and retreated. "You said your daddy served?"

She nodded, retreating a step herself. "He flew troop transports and cargo planes until he retired from active duty. Later, he commanded a local unit in the National Guard."

Max thought of the unseen pilots and navigators who'd flown him, Jimmy and the rest of their battered squad from the Middle East into Germany. Another transport had finally brought them and the caskets of their fallen friends stateside. The world was a mighty small place in some ways. "He flew soldiers home?"

"Sometimes. Is that important?"

Those pretty, intuitive eyes snuck right past his survival armor. An image of Jimmy's frozen dark eyes blipped through his thoughts. *Never leave a man behind.* He crushed the memory that left him reeling and grabbed her arm, pulling her into step beside him and striding down the sidewalk. "Where's your car? I'll walk you to it and then follow you back to your house."

But when he stepped off the curb he stumbled. His momentum pulled her against his chest for a split second, imprinting his body from neck to thigh with her warm curves, filling his head with that damnable clean scent he wanted to bury himself in.

"On second thought, maybe you'd better drive."

She was the one who grabbed a fistful of shirt and his shoulder to steady him and guide him back to the sidewalk. "You're drunk, aren't you?"

There was that snappy, righteous tone again. Her eyes had gone cold. "That was my goal, honey. It helps me forget."

Rosie didn't waste any time pushing away. "This was a mistake. I thought you were different."

"You are the most confounding woman…" With his emotions off the chart, his hormones twisted up in a mix of lustful curiosity and a craving for the peaceful solace he'd read in her eyes—not to mention the four beers he'd drunk since dinner—Max tossed his unlit cigar into the gutter and stopped her from walking away. "Did something scare you tonight or not?"

He spun her around and pulled her up onto her toes, bringing her lips close enough to steal a kiss if he wanted to. And, by hell, he wanted to.

Shifting his hands to the copper bounty of her hair, Max tunneled his fingers into the silky waves and pulled her mouth to his. With a gasp of surprise, her lips parted and Max took advantage of the sudden softening of that preachy mouth by capturing her lower lip between his. He drew his tongue along the supple curve, tasting something tart and lemony there. Her lip trembled at his hungry exploration. He felt the tiny tremor like a timid caress and throttled back on his blind need. Another breath whispered across his cheek, and he waited for the shove against his chest. But her fingers tightened in the front of his shirt, instead, pressing little fingerprints into the muscles of his chest, and she pushed her lips softly against his mouth, returning the kiss.

Something twisted and hard, full of rage and regret, unknotted inside him at her unexpected acceptance of his desire. Frustration faded. Anger disappeared. The wounds of guilt and grief that had been festering inside him all day calmed beneath her tender response. He threaded his fingers into the loose twist of her bun, pushing aside pins and easing the taut style until her hair was sifting between his fingers and his palms were cupping the gentle curve of her head. "Your hair's too pretty to keep it tied up the way you do, Rosie. Too sexy."

"Detective Krol—" He kissed her temple, her forehead, reclaimed her lips once more. He'd reached for her in a haze of frustration and desire, but she was holding on with a gentle grasp and angling her mouth beneath his. It wasn't a passionate kiss. It wasn't seductive or stylized. It was an honest kiss. It was the kind of kiss a man was lucky to get once or twice in his life. It was a perfect kiss. Beauty was taming the beast.

Or merely distracting him?

Detective?

Ah, hell. He quickly released her and backed away, his hands raised in apology. "Did something scare you tonight...besides me?"

"You didn't scare me," she lied. Her fingers hovered in the air for a few seconds before she clasped them around the strap of her purse.

Max scraped his palm over the top of his head, willing his thoughts to clear. "Just answer the damn question."

She nodded.

She wasn't here for the man. She was here for the cop. He'd like to blame the booze that had lowered his inhibitions and done away with his common sense, but fuzzy headed or sober, he knew he'd crossed too many lines with Rosie March today. "I think this is where you slap my face and call me some rotten name."

Her eyes opened wide. "I wouldn't do that."

"No, I don't suppose a lady like you would."

Her lips were pink and slightly swollen from his beard stubble. Her hair was a sexy muss, and part of him wanted nothing more than to kiss her again, to bury his nose in her scent and see if she would wind her arms around his neck and align her body to his as neatly as their mouths had fit together. But she was hugging her arms around her waist instead of him, pressing that pretty mouth back into its tightly controlled line. When had he ever hauled off and kissed a woman like that? With her history, she'd probably been frightened by his behavior and had given him what she thought he wanted in hopes of appeasing him, counting the seconds until he let her slip away. She had to be terrified, desperate, to come to him after this morning's encounter. The fact that she wasn't running away from him right now had to be a testament to her strength—or just how desperate she was to have someone from KCPD believe in her. And, for some reason, she'd chosen him to be her hero.

Max scrubbed his palm over his jaw. He hadn't played hero for anybody in a long time. He hadn't been any good at it since Jimmy's suicide. He did his job, period. He didn't care. He didn't get involved. This woman was waking impulses in him that were so rusty from lack of use that it caused him pain to feel himself wanting to respond to her request. "What do you need from me?"

She tucked that glorious fall of hair behind her ears and tried to smooth it back into submission. "I think I'm in real trouble. And I don't know what to do. KCPD thinks I might be a killer, so they're not taking me seriously and won't look into these threats. But I thought that you…maybe you'd set aside your suspicions and do it for my dad. I know it's an imposition, and I know you'd rather be investigating me for murder than deal with some unknown stalker you think I made up, but—"

"You're right, Rosie. I was a soldier. Sergeant First Class, US Army. A man like your dad brought me and my buddies home from a hell of a fight where we lost too many good men." For the first time in a lot of months, on that flight across the Atlantic, he'd been able to close his eyes and sleep eight hours straight, knowing he and his men were safe from the enemy as long as they were on that plane. "What was your daddy's name?"

"Colonel Stephen March."

"Maybe I don't owe the colonel personally. But I owe." She'd appealed to the soldier in him, tapped into that sense of duty he'd once answered without hesitation. She had him pegged a lot sooner than he was figuring her out. "And I owe you for putting up with me on my worst day."

"Is there something I can do to help? Besides…" She

ran her tongue around her lips, maybe still tasting some of the need he'd stamped there. "I'm a very good listener."

He grumbled a wry laugh. So, no offer to repeat that kiss, eh? "Just give me a chance to be a better man than the one you met today."

"You'll come look? You'll help me?"

Either he was the world's biggest sucker, or Rosie March was in real danger and she believed he was her best chance at staying safe. Whether he was doing this for her or her dad or to atone for all the mistakes he'd made today—all the mistakes he'd made in the past eight years—he was doing it. "Yes, ma'am." Wisely keeping his hands to himself this time, he gestured for her to lead the way to her car. "Let's go find this lowlife."

Chapter Six

"Why do you swear so much?" Rosemary glanced away from the stoplight to the big, looming silence sitting beside her in the passenger seat of her car. Although the beard stubble on his square jaw took on a burnished glow from the lights from the dashboard, Max Krolikowski's craggy face remained hidden in shadows. And while she normally appreciated the absence of any confrontation, ten miles without one word left her questioning the wisdom of this last-resort plan to seek him out as an ally.

"Like you said. I'm angry."

And hurting. He said something bad had happened to a friend. If there was one thing she understood about people, it was the stages of pain and grief a person went through when he or she lost someone or something very dear to them. She'd gone through them with her parents, her brother's drug use and murder conviction. Her relationship with Richard. Denial. Anger. Sadness. Acceptance. Only, Max Krolikowski seemed to be stuck in an endless loop of anger and pain.

The light changed and she drove through the intersection. His fingers drummed a silent rhythm on the armrest of the car door. Was that endless tapping an indication that his temper was still simmering beneath the surface? She remembered those strong fingers tangled in her hair, holding her mouth beneath his. He'd used words like *pretty* and *sexy*—and she'd believed him. For that moment, at least.

Richard had never used words like that with her. She'd looked nice. She'd do him proud at a family dinner or business luncheon. And Richard's embraces had never been so spontaneous, so unabashedly sensual.

When Max Krolikowski kissed her, she'd felt that knee-jerk instinct to flee from the unfamiliar, from the potential danger of the unknown. But she'd felt something else, too. She'd felt need. She'd felt heartache. She'd sensed a hopeless man discovering some shred of hope.

Or maybe she was the one who'd succumbed to the need to be held and wanted and important to someone— even for a few seconds outside a noisy bar. Because once he'd gentled his kiss, once she understood there was something besides anger driving his embrace, she'd become a willing participant. A shyly eager partner. Out of her depth, perhaps, but not afraid.

There was something bold, raw and honest about Max's emotions that was completely foreign in her experience with men. But she'd take that kind of blunt honesty, that disruptive force of nature, over Richard's cool charm any day. Richard's cruelty had been a blindside waiting to happen. At least with Detective Krolikowski, she knew to expect the unexpected.

Which brought her thoughts around to the question she'd really wanted to ask. "Why did you kiss me?"

"I saw the chance. I took it. It seemed like the right thing to do at the time."

And now? Did he still think she was…kissable? Rosemary's hands tightened around the steering wheel as the next question came out in a throaty whisper. "Is that what you want from me?"

The drumming stopped. "You mean like payment for helping you out?" He muttered a succinct curse.

"Language, Detective."

"Wow. Your opinion of me must be lower than I thought." His voice was deep and resonant and laced with contempt. "Don't lecture me on my mouth and insult me at the same time. If you're going to treat me like a degenerate, I might as well talk like one."

Rosemary's grip pulsed around the wheel as a defensive temper flared in her veins. "I wasn't insulting you. I'm just trying to understand what's happening between us. My experience with men is rather limited, and hasn't been entirely positive. I haven't had control over a lot that's happened in my life. And now some creep is trying to undermine what little sense of security I do have." She glanced across the seat and found deep blue eyes bearing down on her. She quickly turned her attention back to the neighborhood streets and took a deep breath to cool her outburst and resume an even tone. "I need to understand so I won't be caught off guard again. As for the swearing? If you need to use those words to get your emotions out, then go ahead, I'll get used to it. But they remind me of someone I'd rather not think of."

"Bratcher? Is that how he talked to you?"

The accuracy of his guess made the scars on her chest burn with remembered terror of her erudite fiancé transforming into Mr. Hyde. She rubbed at her collarbone through the linen dress she wore, willing the memories to subside before they could take hold. Max waited with surprising patience until she nodded. "Ninety percent of the time, Richard was the perfect gentleman. But sometimes, in private, he'd blow up."

"Probably when you had a difference of opinion or you tried to assert yourself?"

Rosemary exhaled a breath that buzzed her lips, her temper cooling to match the facade. Max was sounding more like a cop now. And with the finger of suspicion pointed elsewhere for a change, she found his questions easier to answer. "Once he put that ring on my finger, he changed. I knew then it was just about the money. He didn't love me. I didn't realize just how much he loved that settlement money, though."

"Rosie, I'm not aiming any of those words at you, and I don't mean to offend you. It's just I'm a bull in a china shop and you're a piece of china."

She had the scars, inside and out, to scoff at half of that idea. "I'm not fragile. It's just…I'd rather not hear them."

His disbelieving laugh was a deep, hearty tone from his barrel chest. "Yes, ma'am. I'll try to do better."

Despite the suspicion that he might be mocking her, Rosemary nodded her thanks. "That's all I ask."

They drove an entire block before he surprised her by continuing the conversation. "I wasn't thinking when I kissed you, either. I was just doing what felt right at that moment. Look, I admit, I've had a few drinks, and I'm not that great at filtering my thoughts and emotions in the first place. You smelled good."

She *smelled* good? How could such a simple phrase feel as flattering as being called *pretty* or *sexy*? Frankly, she thought she might need a shower after the stress and heat of the day. But his words made her lips tighten against the urge to grin.

He shrugged, his big shoulders seeming to fill the empty space inside her car as he searched for more of an explanation. She could feel the warmth emanating from his body when he turned in his seat to face her and gripped the wheel more tightly to keep from leaning toward it.

"Rosie, I didn't analyze it. I felt like kissing you. The opportunity was there, so I did."

After this morning's battle of wills, she'd been certain the rather earthy Max Krolikowski wouldn't give her a second look—unless he was throwing darts at her picture. "I didn't think I was your type."

"Neither did I." He sank back into his seat with a low exhale. His eyes drifted shut. "Don't worry. I won't let it happen again. I'm a cop, doing the job I should have done this morning. I'm not expecting any favors from you."

Now, why did that reassurance kill any urge to smile? Ignoring her uncalled-for disappointment, Rosemary turned her car into the driveway and shut off the engine. When she saw the dark expanse of her porch and heard the dogs barking inside, it was easy to remember that she'd asked him here to help with the threats, not the loneliness. "We're here. I didn't touch anything except for the note." She pointed to the street lamp behind them. "There's a little light from the street, but if you need a flashlight, there's one in the glove compartment."

He pulled out the flashlight and tested it before shutting the compartment and climbing out. When he hesitated outside his door, Rosemary did the same. He scrubbed his hand across his jaw, a habit that drew her attention to its firm, square shape and the intriguing mix of tawny, gold and brown stubble there. Richard had always been clean-shaven. But Max's day-old beard had been a sharp contrast against her softer skin. His beard had been ticklish, abrading, stimulating—his lips and tongue had been soothing in the aftermath.

Fortunately, he spoke before she succumbed to the silly urge to run her tongue across her lips, remembering what he'd felt like there.

"You know, if you get mad at me, I'm not going to hurt you like Bratcher did. I know I talk loud and need to clean up my act, but I would never lay a hand on you in anger." His gaze found hers when she didn't immediately respond. "I'm not going to leave, either. I said I'd help, and I promise to do what I can."

"For my dad."

He opened his mouth to say something, but changed his mind and circled around the hood of her car, ending the conversation and slipping into detective mode. "Yeah. For your dad. Hooah."

HUA. Heard. Understood. Acknowledged.

Nodding at the military acknowledgment she remembered her dad using, Rosemary followed him up onto the porch. When Max stumbled over the top step, she instinctively reached out to help him. But he caught her arm instead, urging her back behind him while he swept the beam of light over the upended rocking chair, splintered wood and shattered glass littering her porch. "Son of a—" He bit off the curse and released her. "Somebody was smart enough to avoid triggering the alarm—or else plain lucky. This is a lot of rage. Who blames you for your fiancé's death?"

"Who doesn't?" He swung the light over to her, hiding his opinion of her flippant remark in the shadows. Rosemary shook her head, not understanding how a dead man could still be wreaking so much havoc in her world. "I wasn't holding Richard to any promises. I broke off our engagement. I wanted him out of my life."

"Murder is a permanent way to do that."

She pushed the flashlight aside to look him in the

eye. "How many times do I have to say it? I did not kill Richard. The only reason I was at his condo that morning was to tell him to stop threatening Stephen with trumped-up charges. He thought blackmailing me would convince me to take him back, but Howard, my new attorney, helped me get a restraining order. I wanted to deliver it to him myself—prove that he couldn't intimidate me anymore."

"But you didn't get to say any of that. You found him dead?"

She nodded, squeezing her eyes shut against the horrible memory of Richard's dead, discolored body. But his puffy blue lips weren't the only detail she recalled. She hugged her arms around her waist before opening her eyes and looking up at Max again. "I could tell he'd been there with another woman. There were condoms on the nightstand and her perfume was still in the bedding."

"He cheated on you, threatened you, abused you. A jury would see that as a lot of motive to kill a man." At her wounded sigh, Max's big hand clamped around hers before she could storm away. "But I'll start working on the assumption that you didn't. Maybe we can track down this other woman. See what she knows."

She remembered her confrontation with Charleen Grimes that morning. Charleen had been so certain that Rosemary was responsible for ending her lover's life. Could that have been a show to hide her own culpability? There'd certainly been plenty of witnesses to her accusations. Still, why would Charleen want to kill the man she professed to love? Rosemary had a feeling the affair had been a tempestuous one. But poison wasn't exactly a spur-of-the moment weapon.

"Rosie?" Max's growly voice interrupted her thoughts. "If you know who the other woman was, I'm going to need that information. The best way to prove your innocence is to find out who really killed your ex."

Rosemary tugged her hand from his grasp and tried to gauge the sincerity of his words. "You believe me?"

"I promised to help."

Not exactly a rousing vote of confidence. But she was scared enough to take it. She gestured to the mess on her porch. "Do you at least believe I'm not doing this to myself?"

"I think I need a clearer head to make sense of what's going on here." He swung the flashlight toward the sound of the dogs barking behind the door. "Sounds like they need to get out and run around. You got coffee?"

"I can make a pot."

"Do it. Give the dogs a few minutes outside, then keep them in the house with you. Wait. We'll go in through the back. I want to get pictures of the damage before anything is moved. I want to bag that note of yours, too."

He made no attempt to touch her again but fell into step beside her to walk her down the driveway. With every passing second, he was becoming more cop, more man of duty, rather than the tipsy desperado who'd pulled her into his arms and kissed her because he thought it was a good idea at the time. She should be grateful for his professionalism, for the distance he put between them now. That would make it easier to keep her guard up and stay focused on the problems she needed to deal with.

"You got a toolbox somewhere?" he asked, waiting for her to unlock the back door.

"Yes. Dad's workbench is still out in the garage."

"Then I'll need it open, too." After she gave him the pass code, he waited for her to air the dogs, even tussling a little bit with Duchess and Trixie himself, before urging them all back into the house and telling her to lock the door.

Rosemary fed the dogs a treat, brewed a fresh pot of coffee and pulled the makings for a simple sandwich from her fridge.

An hour later, she carried the last of the coffee to the front door to refill Max's mug before she washed the dishes. She could do this. She could grab his plate and fill his mug and get back to the kitchen without getting herself into any uncomfortable conversation or unwanted physical contact with the man. Although the dogs were eager to spend more time with their new friend on the porch, she shooed them behind her before stepping out to find Max putting the finishing touches on replacing her mailbox.

"Want the last cup?" she offered.

"Sure. I'm going to have a whale of a headache in the morning, but the food and caffeine help." He nodded toward the empty mug and plate on the bench he'd moved beside the rocking chair to replace the broken table.

"Is that a thank-you?" she asked, wondering if there were any manners lurking under that tough hide of his.

"Yeah." He paused with his hand in her father's toolbox, then faced her. She'd like to think that was a blush of humility on his cheeks, but she suspected the flush of color in the shadows was due to the hard work and the temperature that had barely cooled at one in the morning. "You didn't have to go to the extra trouble, but I appreciate it."

"You're welcome." Relaxing enough to smile at the unexpected compliment, she nodded toward the twin glare of bare lightbulbs on either side of her front door. "You didn't have to go to all this trouble, either. I'm grateful. But that wasn't why I asked you here."

"I've always liked working with my hands. Keeps me out of trouble," he added without any elaboration, before plucking a screw from his pocket and going back to the job at hand. "You'll have to get new globes to cover the bulbs I replaced, but everything is cleaned up and secure. As soon as I finish this."

"Uh-huh." Rosemary didn't move. So much for keeping a polite distance and hurrying back into the house. Max's shirt had come untucked somewhere along the course of the long day. And as he raised his arms to drill in the last screw, his shirttails lifted up and his jeans slipped a tad, giving her a glimpse of his gun and badge and a set of abs that belied the beer he claimed to have consumed tonight. She knew he was brawny. She expected him to be fit working for the police department. But the holstered weapon and strong male body beneath the wrinkled clothes and antisocial attitude made her a little nervous.

Although she couldn't say if the suddenly wary tempo of her heart stemmed from the clear reminder that Max was a cop, and cops ultimately treated her as a suspect rather than a victim—no matter how nice they were being about fixing the vandalism on her front porch. Or maybe those tingles of awareness of a man were a real attraction, fed by the unanswered questions she still had about that kiss. When she realized her gaze was lingering on the thin strip of elastic waistband peeking above his belt, she snapped her gaping mouth shut and turned her attention to refilling his mug.

A relationship was the last thing she wanted, right? Richard had made it perfectly clear that she was too timid, too plain, too boring, to ever turn a man's head to thoughts of passion. She was far better suited to domesticity and duty than she was to warming a man's bed or heart. And though, logically, she knew his cruel words had been used to break her spirit and manipulate her, the sting of self-doubt reared its ugly head whenever she noticed a man as something other than a friend or acquaintance. Why set herself up for disappointment and humiliation when the most attractive quality she had, according to Richard, was the money in her bank account?

A relationship with Max Krolikowski could be especially problematic since he seemed to be even less refined, led more by his instincts and whatever he was feeling at any given moment than Richard had ever been, pushing her even more out of her comfort zone and making him a real enigma in her limited experience with the opposite sex.

Not that Max was offering any kind of a relationship. He wasn't interested in her money. He wasn't particularly interested in being here at all. Max was here because he'd been in the Army like her dad. He was a creature of duty as much as she was. A soldier would do for another soldier or his family.

And a military family would do for a soldier in need.

Rosemary put down the plate she'd retrieved, and set the coffeepot beside it. Far better to clear the air between them than to muddy the waters with some foolish fantasy that wasn't going to happen. Clinging to the rocking chair he'd righted, she faced him again. "What happened to your friend? Is it something that interferes with your work a lot?"

Max removed the bit and carefully laid the drill back in her father's toolbox and closed the lid. For a moment she didn't think he was going to answer. Then he crossed into the shadows near the porch railing and sat, crossing his arms in front of him, looking big and unassailable. "You're determined to talk about this, hmm?"

Rosemary withdrew behind the chair. "I believe, maybe, if we're going to be working together, we need to."

"You think this is going to be a team effort?"

"I know you have more questions for me. I don't expect you to help me for nothing—"

"Relax, Rosie." He dipped his face into the light, his sober blue eyes drilling straight into hers. "I'll help you—you help me. Just go easy on the lectures and the heart-to-hearts and remember—I'm giving you fair warning. You can't fix me."

"Are you broken?"

His eyes narrowed and his head jerked slightly, as if her question surprised him...or struck a nerve. Muttering one choice word, he sat back against the porch post. "You're not the only one who's lost people you care about. Eight years ago today, I lost my best friend. Captain James Stecher. We served together in the Middle East."

"He died in battle?"

"Nope. Stateside. Shot himself. Post-traumatic stress."

"Oh, Max." His blunt answer made her eyes gritty with tears. She reached out to squeeze his hand or hug away the pain she imagined hiding behind that matter-of-fact tone.

"I thought it was *detective*."

The growl of sarcasm and his stalwart posture made him seem impervious to pain—or at least unaffected by her compassion—so she curled her fingers around the back of the rocking chair instead. "I'm sorry."

"For what? I'm the one who screwed up. I should have been able to save him."

He rose and leaned across the chair to pick up his coffee. Rosemary managed not to jump when his body heat brushed past her. But when he straightened beside her—tall, broad, the sleeve of his cotton shirt brushing against her shoulder and raising goose bumps—she couldn't help retreating a step.

"I've decided I'm not going to make the same mistake with you," he said.

"What does that mean?"

"It means I need you to drive me to my car at the Shamrock. Then I'll follow you back here and sit out front the rest of the night." He turned and doffed a salute to the shadow in the Dinkles' window she hadn't noticed until that moment. She gasped as the shadow disappeared, and the blinds swayed with Otis or Arlene's hasty retreat. "You've already got the neighbors' attention by bringing me here. I'm guessing you don't entertain a lot of men."

She lifted her panicked gaze to his. She hadn't even noticed the Dinkles' curiosity, but Max had probably been aware of her nosy neighbor the entire time. "Do you think that's necessary? I just wanted a police officer to see what was happening to me and write a report."

"I intend to do more than that, Rosie."

Her blood ran cold at the ominous portent in his voice. "Do you think something else is going to happen?"

"I'm not going to give whoever this bastard is a chance to scare you again. Or do something worse. There's only so much guilt a man can live with." He continued to scan the neighborhood from her dark porch, even though the Dinkles' spying had been temporarily thwarted. He picked up the note he'd sealed in one of her plastic sandwich bags. "If Bratcher's killer is behind these threats, he or she could be doing it to divert suspicion onto you. Keeping an eye on you might ferret out the suspect."

"I see." Rosemary understood the logic, even if she didn't relish the idea of playing the part of bait for KCPD. Shivering now, she hugged her arms around her middle. "So watching over me and what happens here helps your investigation?"

"Possibly." He reached out and rubbed his hand up and down her bare arm, eliciting more goose bumps as her skin warmed beneath even that casual touch. "But that's not the only reason. If this guy is someone who blames you for Bratcher's murder and thinks they're meting out some kind of justice…?" He lifted his fingers to her hair, scowling at the lone tendril falling against her neck as if he didn't like that she'd pinned the rest of it up into a practical bun again. His palm settled along her jaw, and, instinctively, against her better judgment, she leaned into his warmth. "Look, the only thing you have to understand about me is this. I'm not losing anyone else on my watch. You're still my team's best shot at solving this case. If something happens to you, chances are, we'll never uncover the truth."

If something happens? Even the heat from his callous hand wasn't enough to erase the chill crawling over her body. So volunteering to watch over her wasn't personal at all. It was a practical move on his part. She should appreciate practicality. But the no-nonsense offer hurt, made her wish she hadn't gone to him for help, after all.

Pulling away, Rosemary crossed to the front railing and looked to the street, picturing Max's car parked beside the curb. A man with a gun and a baby blue muscle car should draw all kinds of attention to her quiet home. Attention she didn't want. "What exactly are you saying? You're going to stake out my house every night until you finish your investigation? You're just going to wait until this guy makes good on one of his threats?"

She felt his breath against her neck as he walked up behind her. Her eyes drifted shut at the unintentional caress. But it wasn't reassurance he was offering. "Actually, I was thinking more along the lines of moving into your basement apartment. Your neighbors, this stalker, and possibly the killer, are already going to question why I'm here. But they might drop their guard a little bit if they think I'm the new tenant."

Rosemary scooted away from the warmth she craved. "But that's Stephen's apartment."

"He's not going to be using it for a few years." He caught her by the wrist and turned her to face him, his stony expression telling her his idea wasn't really up for debate. "We're talking a matter of weeks, maybe even days, that I'd be here. I get that I overstepped some personal boundaries and made you uncomfortable earlier, but my plan makes sense. I'll clear it with my team leader tomorrow."

"What if I say no?"

"Why would you say no?" He leaned in, close enough for the moonlight to pick up the color of his eyes and make them glow like a predatory cat as he glared down at her. "I thought you wanted to uncover the truth as much as KCPD does."

"I do." She tugged her wrist free and folded her hands together, willing him to understand the inviolate need to maintain the one place of sanctuary she had left in the world. "But I'm not comfortable having a man in the house. Even with the separate entrance, it would feel like I'm locked in there with you and I wouldn't be free to come and go when I want to. You're laying down rules. You're taking over my life."

"You came to me for help. Do you want to catch a killer or not?" He pointed to the trash bag with the mess from the vandalism he'd cleaned up. "Do you want this sh—" He caught himself, held up a hand in impatient apology and changed the word. "Do you want this garbage to stop? I don't care how many locks you have on that door, if this guy escalates any further, you won't have time to wait for help to get here."

She dropped her gaze to the middle button on that broad chest and considered how helpless she would be against Max's strength if he ever decided to turn on her the way Richard had. She'd thought she could hide in the sanctuary of her own room, lock Richard out. But even without Max's muscular build and physical training, Richard had been able to kick down her door, destroy her phone before she could call for help and hold her hostage for several hours. Repeated threats against her brother had been enough to keep her from pressing charges later. She absently rubbed her palm over the scars on her chest, drifting back to that horrible night.

But two blunt-tipped fingers sneaked beneath Rosemary's chin and tipped her face up, forcing her back to the moment. Max's stern face hovered above hers. "Rosie, I'm not any good at guessing games or reading between the lines. You look me in the eye and tell me exactly what you want."

A dozen different wishes popped into her head. She wanted the memories of Richard's abuse erased from her mind and body. She wanted Max Krolikowski to kiss her again. No, she wanted the sober detective gently touching her skin to *want* to kiss her. She wanted the self-assurance that Richard had stolen from her so she could tell Max all the wishes running through her mind. She wanted her parents alive and her brother safely home from prison. Ultimately, though, there was only one thing that mattered.

"I want to feel safe."

With a firm nod, Max dismissed any further discussion. He picked up the toolbox and the trash bag and paused in front of her. "Then this guy won't get to you again. I'll need a key. I'll need you to do what I say, when I say it. And I'll need you to trust me."

"I know you mean that to be reassuring, but…" She trudged back into the house and locked the door when he indicated that he was heading around to the garage and she shouldn't remain outside by herself. She whispered against the door as she threw the dead bolt. "That's what Richard said, too."

Chapter Seven

Max recognized Olivia Watson's short, dark hair as she waited to get on the elevator at KCPD headquarters to report for their morning shift. Thank goodness. He hated running late.

Despite the throbbing in his temples left over from last night's trip to the Shamrock Bar, Max jogged across the foyer's marble tiles. "Hey, Liv. Hold the elevator."

"Good morning, Max." The brunette detective smiled a friendly greeting as he slipped in beside her and headed to the back railing. He leaned his hips against it, exhaling a deep breath. She pointed to the wraparound sunglasses he was still wearing. "The lights too bright in here for you?" she teased.

Great. Trent must have blabbed about him drowning his sorrows last night. And Liv here, like a mother hen to her boys on the Cold Case Squad, couldn't resist making sure he was all right. Max was a grown man, the oldest member of the team. He didn't need any mama or sister or busybody sticking her nose into his regrets. Time to play the old boyfriend/former-partner-who'd-nearly-ruined-her-career card. "Detective Cutie-Pie giving you any grief? Or do you still need me to punch him out for you?"

But Olivia refused the bait and punched the button for

the third floor. "I think I finally got it through Detective Brower's thick skull that I don't love him, nor does he even remotely turn my head anymore." She raised her left hand and wiggled her fingers in front of his face. "Of course, the engagement ring Gabe gave me makes a clear statement as to where my heart and loyalties lie."

Max grabbed her wrist to get a better look at the respectable rock on the plain gold band on her third finger. "Hey, congratulations, kiddo." He let her go and leaned in to kiss her cheek. "So that pesky reporter is finally going to make an honest woman out of you."

"Gabe is not pesky."

Max shrugged. "I suppose he did help us catch a killer and put Leland Asher in prison. But reporters who badmouth the department still aren't my favorite people."

She leaned against the back wall beside him and jabbed him with her elbow. "Hey. Gabe has printed some nice things about KCPD now, too. He's honest. Always tells it like it is—whether it's good press or not. It's why I trust him. It's one of the things I love best about him."

He nudged her back. "As long as he makes you happy."

"He does."

If Max had any family besides his grandma, he'd wish it included an annoying "sister" like Olivia. Of course, she already had three big brothers, a father and grandfather looking out for her. If Gabe Knight passed muster with her family and she was genuinely happy with this guy, then so was Max. "Then I guess I'll put up with him."

"Do you own a suit and tie?"

He let his head fall back and groaned. "Why?"

"Because I'm inviting you to the wedding."

"You ask a lot of a man, don't you?"

"Only the ones I care about and respect." She reached over and tapped his cheek. "I like the clean-shaven look this morning. Remember how to do that for the wedding. What's the occasion?"

He was glad the elevator had stopped and the door was opening. He'd shaved for work more than once this week. Or maybe that was last week. Had he spruced up in an effort to redeem himself in the eyes of a certain critical redhead? "Hell."

Olivia followed him out into the morning bustle of the third-floor detectives' division as the shifts changed from third watch to first watch. "So what makes you grouchy with an extra side of cranky this morning?"

Trent Dixon was there to meet them as they checked in at the sergeant's desk. "One too many beers last night, I'll bet." Before Max guessed the younger man's intent, Trent had snatched the sunglasses off his face. "Yep. I swung by your apartment this morning to make sure you got here. But nobody answered."

Max snatched the glasses back and hooked them behind his neck. "Did you break in to see my bed hadn't been slept in?" he groused.

"That's for amateurs." He patted the shield on his belt. "I've got one of these, remember? All I had to do was ask nicely. Your super let me in." Trent and Olivia both grinned as they led the way past their desks to the break room for a morning cup of joe.

But Max knew his partner's concern was real. "I left early. Had an errand to run. I dozed a couple hours in my car."

"In your car?" When Max stopped in the hallway outside the break room, Trent and Olivia did, too. Trent was serious when he came back and clapped a hand on Max's shoulder. "But today's a new day?"

Max nodded. His annual Jimmy funk was out of his system—or at least relegated to the backseat in the carful of sticky issues he had to deal with. He looked from one detective to the other, letting them know this wasn't the hangover talking. "I think I got us a lead on the Richard Bratcher murder case. Not from the source you might expect. I was following up on it. Remember our little interview gone south yesterday?"

Trent snickered. "Rosemary March? Is she suing us? Filing harassment charges against you?"

Max rubbed his knuckles over the unfamiliar smoothness of his jaw. She probably would if he tried to kiss her again. Not that he had any plans to do so. In the sane, sober light of day, he…was wondering if any part of Rosie's gentle response had been real. Man, he was going to have to keep his wits about him and his hormones in check on this mission. "I'm going to be spending a lot of time with her over the next few days."

"Come again?" Trent asked.

They were all in cop mode now, listening.

"Turns out her dad was military, and she's latched on to that aspect of me. She looked me up last night to help with a problem." He glibly skipped past the whole kissing, sparks flying, guilt trip gone sideways incident outside the Shamrock and filled them in on the vile message and rage-fueled destruction he'd tried to repair for her. "Rosie's stalker is legit. And he's escalating. She could turn out to be a good witness for us, but not if this guy gets to her first."

"Rosie?" Liv asked, looking to Trent for an explanation. "You mean Stephen March's sister?" Olivia had no love for Rosie's brother since his efforts to cover up the murder he'd committed had involved several attempts on Olivia and her new fiancé's life. "When did she become Rosie?"

With a shrug, Trent gestured to Max, indicating he had no clue why his partner would give a cutesy nickname to the person who'd been not only the prime suspect, but the only suspect, period, in the initial investigation of Richard Bratcher's murder six years ago.

"It's just what I call her, okay?" Max wasn't about to explain anything personal to either of them, especially since he couldn't pinpoint why *Rosemary* didn't seem to fit the woman who'd gotten so far under his skin yesterday. *Rosemary* was a murder suspect. A mission objective to be explored and dealt with.

Rosie was, well, he wasn't quite sure. And while part of him wanted to blame last night's kiss and desire to get involved with her problems on an unfortunate mix of beer, lust, loneliness and guilt, Max was afraid his connection to Rosie went a little deeper than a cop doing his duty. That whole band-of-brothers logic she'd used to justify seeking him out had only sealed the deal.

Whether he had his team's backing or not, he'd given his word that he would help Rosie unmask her stalker. But finding the bastard who terrorized a vulnerable woman would be a hell of a lot easier if he had the Cold Case Squad and resources of KCPD backing him up.

Ignoring the question, Max stuck with talking copspeak to Trent and Olivia. *That* he understood. "The timing of these threats is suspect. Either someone connected to the murder is trying to point the finger at her to keep us from looking at them, or someone who knew Bratcher blames her for his death, and is punishing her for it since we haven't arrested anyone for the crime yet. I documented the evidence last night at her house. Rosie couldn't have done that kind of damage herself unless she was doped up on something. With her brother's history of drug abuse and an aversion to drinking, smoking and swearing, I'm guessing she doesn't get high."

"Wait a minute," Trent interrupted, nudging Max and Liv to a private corner as the hallway filled with A-shift cops reporting to the conference room for Morning Roll Call. "You went back to her house?"

"Would you believe she picked me up at the Shamrock Bar?" Trent's expression indicated not. "Close your mouth, junior." Here was the really incredulous part. "Apparently, Rosie thinks I can be her hero. Watching her house, doing what I can to catch this guy who's terrorizing her, should get me close enough to get the answers we need from her. I think she knows more names linked to Bratcher we haven't found yet. I believe she can give us leads that'll make this cold case hot again. If she can't break open this investigation for us, then I have a feeling the guy who's after her will." Max braced his hands at his waist, looking up to Trent and down at Liv to include them both. "I don't think I can do this on my own, though. I have to sleep sometime. Plus, I'll need a liaison to Katie—" the team's information specialist "—and all her records when I'm out in the field. And somebody has to be with Rosie 24/7 while I'm following up some of those leads."

"Whatever you need, brother," Trent offered. "If Miss March turns out to be the linchpin to this investigation, I'm sure Lieutenant Rafferty-Taylor will want the whole team involved."

Olivia agreed. "I'll go brief Jim." Jim Parker was her partner, another member of KCPD's Cold Case Squad. "Are you sure we can trust her, Max?"

"I didn't think so at first, but yeah. I think she's being straight with me." Max's measurements of the dents in the mailbox and light sconces made him think the perp's weapon of choice had been a metal baseball bat. If he'd chosen to take a swing at Rosie or one of the dogs defending her, KCPD would have been investigating something far more serious than vandalism. "I'm hoping my word is enough for you guys to let me run with this."

Liv nodded. "You guys covered for Gabe and me when we needed backup. So you know I'm there for you." When she reached up to brush an unseen greeblie off the shoulder of his shirt, Max wondered if he'd really needed neatening up, or if—with all the other detectives and uniforms filing into the room across the hall—that was her professional version of a supportive hug. "See you two at the morning meeting."

Max grabbed a cup of coffee and followed Trent into the conference room. Weaving through men and women gathered in conversations between the long, narrow tables facing the captain's podium, they found two open chairs near the back of the room.

Max had barely raised the paper cup to his lips when Trent slapped his leather folder on the table and leaned over to ask, "You sure you can do this? Yesterday, Rosemary March was a whack job, and today the *old prune* you couldn't wait to get away from is *Rosie*, and you're going to be her knight in shining armor. Why the change of heart?"

Max raised his gaze to the curious officer eavesdropping on their conversation from the opposite side of the table. The young man with the nosy intent turned out to be Hudson Kramer from the Shamrock Bar. "Did you score with that redhead last night, Krolikowski?"

"Sit down, junior, and mind your own business."

"You struck out, huh?" Grinning like a schoolkid,

Kramer braced his hands on the table and leaned closer. "S'pose I could get her number?"

"No, I don't suppose you could." Raising his hands in mock surrender, the younger detective wisely turned away and took his seat before Max lowered his cup and glanced over at his partner. "You don't think I can handle this mission…er, assignment?"

"Max, you are the toughest SOB I know. You can make anything work if you set your mind to it." Trent rested an elbow on the table and thumped Max in the chest. "But I also know you're a pussycat in there. Your emotions get the better of you sometimes. Hell, if Kramer's razzing can rile you, then I've got to wonder just what Rosemary March means to you."

"She's a solid lead on our case. And somebody's got her in his sights." Max downed another sip of the hot brew. "I'm protecting a potential witness. I'm doing my job."

"Uh-huh. I can deal with the crazy guy once a year on the anniversary of Jimmy's death, and cover for you." The conversations around the room receded into background noise when Trent dropped his voice to a whisper. "But if you don't do some healing, if digging up Rosemary's secrets is going to keep you stressed around the clock and you start flipping out again, the lieutenant is going to order a mandatory psych eval on you. You could get suspended if you wig out on the job again, or you start hitting the Shamrock every night. You're too good a cop for that—too good a man. I don't want to see you lose it."

"That's mostly why I'm doin' it." Yeah, as if stepping up to be that pretty, prickly woman's bodyguard was some kind of therapy for him. More like penance. Still, it felt like the right thing to do. "I didn't save Jimmy."

Max sat up at attention, his posture reflecting his resolve. "But I'm damn straight going to save her. I'm gonna make things right in this world for once."

"And solve Bratcher's murder?"

Captain Hendricks took his place at the podium and the room instantly quieted. The black man swept his gaze across the room, greeting them all. "Good morning."

"Yeah. Sure," Max muttered beneath the other officers' responses. "That's the idea."

An hour later Max was on his second meeting of the day and his third cup of coffee, sitting through a Skype call between drug research expert and CEO Dr. Hillary Wells of Endicott Global, a drug company based in the KC area, and the other members of the Cold Case Squad.

The brunette woman with short hair and a white lab coat over the business suit she wore filled up the viewing screen in Ginny Rafferty-Taylor's office. Lieutenant Rafferty-Taylor was the veteran detective who headed up the Cold Case Squad. Dr. Wells and the lieutenant seemed to be about the same age, and both were successful professional women. That was probably why Dr. Wells's answers were all directed to the lieutenant. Everyone else in the room seemed to be beneath her time and interest.

"RUD-317 is a cancer-fighting drug," the woman on the screen explained. She seemed more interested in fiddling with the jar of hand cream on her desk than in the interview. "It's not for recreational use."

"Our victim wasn't a cancer patient, Doctor," the lieutenant clarified. "And if he used drugs recreationally, he kept it private. We have no arrests or complaints on record."

"His file says he was a smoker," Trent pointed out. "Is

it possible our guy got private treatment? A diagnosis in a foreign country not in his US records? He had money. Maybe the cure worked."

Dr. Wells barely spared a glance for Max's partner. "It's possible. RUD-317 is available in other countries." She glanced down at her notes on her office desk. "I'd have to double-check the status to see if that was true six years ago." She raised her dark eyes to Lieutenant Rafferty-Taylor again. "We've never seen side effects like you describe with RUD-317. I wonder if your victim had an allergic reaction to something in the formula. Or perhaps there was a bad combination of drugs in his system. We do have specific protocols in place for using the RUD products."

The lieutenant might be a petite little blonde, but she was tough as nails, and Max respected her for it. She wasn't going to let the other woman dismiss their case. "Dr. Wells, there are too many other circumstances related to the death of this particular victim for KCPD to readily dismiss it as an accidental drug overdose. We're looking at it as a homicide."

"I see." Dr. Wells jotted something on her notes. "If you fax me a copy of the medical examiner's report, I'd be happy to take a look at it to confirm her conclusions or add to it if any discrepancies jump out at me."

"We'll do that. Thank you, Dr. Wells."

The brunette woman leaned toward the camera, her face filling the screen. "I'd certainly hate for bad publicity surrounding one of Endicott Global's medical products to get out. Trust me, the board of directors is always on me about maintaining Endicott's public image. If one of our company's drugs was used to commit a murder, I want to know about it. Its misuse might require altering our product labeling and warnings so it doesn't happen again accidentally. We might even have to pull the drug off the market. You know how prevalent lawsuits are nowadays. People can make a fortune and ruin a company that does good work."

Max shifted uncomfortably in his seat at the mention of lawsuits. They were nothing but trouble. It didn't look as though Miss Rosie Posy's nine million dollars were doing her any good.

"I'll have one of my detectives get in touch with you to follow up."

The lieutenant ended the call and Max was back to justifying his plan to the other members of the Cold Case Squad. "Rosemary March wouldn't give us anything yesterday," he explained. "She's not that comfortable with cops."

Lieutenant Rafferty-Taylor arched a silvery-blond eyebrow at him. "So what's your *in*?"

He looked to the woman sitting at the head of the conference table and shrugged. "I remind her of her dad."

"Ouch." Jim Parker, Olivia's partner and the newest member of the team, made a face across the table. "You're not that much older than she is. That has to be hard on the ego."

Max skimmed his hand over the top of his jarhead haircut. "Former military."

Jim got serious and nodded his understanding. "She trusted her father, and so she trusts you."

"Something like that." Max set his cup down beside the stack of case files in front of him and pulled out a photograph of Richard Bratcher to set on top. "I believe she's as anxious to solve Bratcher's murder as we are. This guy made her life hell when he was alive. He's been dead six years and he's still doing the same."

Olivia Watson rested her elbows on the table and

leaned forward. "And she thinks finding the killer will make her stalker go away? Could whoever is after her be the real murderer, trying to frame her?"

"That's one idea I had," Max agreed. "Either that, or we've got an unsub who thinks she did it and got away with killing Bratcher."

"So, we need to be interviewing people who were close to Bratcher besides the Marches." Olivia sat back. "Do we have anyone on that list?"

"I'm working the stalker angle." Katie Rinaldi, the brunette information specialist assigned to the team, looked up from her laptop at the far end of the table. "I've been surfing social media sites, trying to track down the pictures Miss March alleges were taken of her when she visited her brother in Jeff City."

"Find anything?" Max asked, suspecting that Rosie was a private enough woman that she wouldn't willingly put herself out on the internet.

Katie's ponytail bobbed behind her as she shook her head. "Nothing yet except for some newspaper photos related to winning that settlement on her parents' behalf, Mr. Bratcher's death and her brother's sentencing for murder." She lifted her blue eyes to include everyone around the table. "But I'm just getting started. I've got some facial recognition software I'll plug in and run against other sites. If her stalker posted pics anywhere, I'll find them and forward the info to your phones and computers."

"Good idea," Jim said, his expression turning grim. "That's how those crooked cops down in Falls City where I worked undercover tracked down my wife. Through a simple picture from our first date she posted online. This guy ain't playin' if he's gotten that close to your witness."

Lieutenant Rafferty-Taylor agreed. "That's a good strategy, Katie. If there are unsanctioned pictures of Miss March online, I want to know who put them there."

"Yes, ma'am."

The lieutenant turned her attention to the big man sitting beside Max. "Trent, let's get those written threats and telephone messages Miss March has received in for analysis. See if any of them are traceable."

"Will do."

Max nodded, appreciating the team following his lead and treating Rosie as a threatened witness instead of a suspect. He tapped the case files on the table in front of him. "I talked her into coming in this morning to look at some photos from known associates of Leland Asher and the vic. Maybe she can ID the guy she saw that way."

Ginny Rafferty-Taylor was a sharp thinker who'd solved several homicide investigations before accepting the promotion to head up the Cold Case Squad. She allowed her team to run with their instincts but demanded their ideas be backed up with hard facts. "We're still working on the theory that several of KCPD's unsolved cases are related?"

They'd had this same discussion several months earlier, when Olivia had closed the six-year-old murder of Danielle Reese, the investigative reporter Stephen March had killed—the crime he was now serving time for in Jefferson City. Although Max's focus was on one woman and one case, he had to agree the idea of connected murders had merit. "It could have happened that way. The Marches had a strong motive for eliminating Richard Bratcher, yet Rosie lacked the means and Stephen lacked the opportunity. We've got Stephen March for murdering Ms. Reese even though Leland Asher and his organization are the ones with the motive for killing her. Asher had an alibi for the night of that murder."

The lieutenant tucked a short, silvery-blond lock behind her ear. "Does Asher have an alibi for the night of Bratcher's murder?"

"I'd love to ask him," Olivia volunteered. "I hate that he's serving a mere two years in prison. Maybe we can make his stay more permanent. If he's behind any of this, we should be able to get a list of contacts he's had recently. Jim and I can look at the prison's visitor logs."

Jim nodded. "We'll find out who he's close to on the inside, too."

Katie Rinaldi tapped her finger against her lips. "It's like that Hitchcock movie, *Strangers on a Train*—you kill the person I want dead and I'll kill yours, and no one will ever be able to prove a thing."

The possibility of the seemingly unrelated murders having a common link had been Olivia's idea to begin with. "There has to be a connection between Leland Asher and the Marches or Bratcher we can find."

Katie ran with the idea. "What if there's a third murder involved that connects everything? Or a fourth or a fifth?"

Trent rolled his chair away from the table and spun toward Katie. "Why don't we stay away from the movies and focus on reality. If we can get Rosemary March on board, I'm sure we can find facts to solve Bratcher's murder and make our case."

Bristling at the criticism, Katie put her hands back on the keyboard and typed a note. "I'll do the research in my spare time—start cross-checking all unsolved murders from the last decade or so. If I find something… *when* I find where those unsolved murders overlap, I'll let you know."

"When do you have spare time?" Trent grumbled. "You're either working or doing something with Tyler and your family or doing one of those stupid plays."

"It's a hobby." Katie's eyes flashed with temper, although her tone remained politely articulate. "And I've made some new friends by getting involved with the community theater. I'm allowed to have a hobby."

Not when it took time away from any possibility of Trent and the single mom spending time together rekindling their high school sweetheart relationship. Max turned away to hide the shaking of his head, happy to leave the soap opera of young love to those who had the energy and fortitude to deal with it. Cupid could just keep his arrows away from a confirmed ol' bachelor like him, and let him do his job and get from one day to the next without any more hassle than necessary.

And yet... Max looked through the window separating Lieutenant Rafferty-Taylor's office from the main floor and saw Rosie March and a tall guy in a fancy suit following one of the uniforms past the maze of detectives' desks toward a row of interview rooms. He was half-aware of other strategies being discussed around the table, of assignments being given. But he was more aware of how the bright flowers printed on Rosie's black dress warmed the pale perfection of her skin. Although the high neckline and modest hem of the sleeveless dress covered up all the interesting bits of her figure, and that old-lady bun at her nape made his fingers itch to free her hair again, there was a distinctive tightening behind his zipper that couldn't be blamed on the desire to drown his sorrows in alcohol or any willing woman this morning.

Stone-cold sober, the dutiful daughter of a colonel was still gettin' to him like an irritation beneath his skin. Could he be just as distracted by the undercurrents of tension between him and Rosie as those that had flared between Trent and Katie a few moments earlier?

Apparently so. Max's hand curled into a fist beneath the table when Rosie startled and drifted back a step, hugging that long shoulder bag to her chest as Hudson Kramer jumped up from his desk to greet her and the suit guy with the silver sideburns. The irritation running beneath Max's collar felt an awful lot like jealousy when he saw Kramer turning on the charm. What did that kid see in Rosie? Was Kramer into that cougar thing? Did he have a penchant for redheads? Or...

Nine million dollars?

The other hand fisted beneath the table. If Hud Kramer had recognized Rosie from the newspaper and thought he could sweet-talk his way into a few dates and a little payout—

"Brother." Trent clamped a hand down on the arm of Max's chair and shook him out of his glowering stare. His partner was kind enough to point toward Lieutenant Rafferty-Taylor, who'd also noticed his straying focus.

With a nod to Max, silently welcoming him back to the meeting, the petite lieutenant continued her summary. "Let's follow up on the toxin that killed Bratcher, too. Sooner rather than later. Endicott Global is big business. If they're worried about bad publicity that might come from being tied to Bratcher's murder, I don't want to give Hillary Wells or anyone else there a chance to scrub their records from six years ago." The lieutenant glanced at the notes on her computer screen. "And if they can give us new information that might not show up on the ME's report, I want to know that, too. With Jim and Liv on the road to Jefferson City, and Trent on forensic evidence detail, Max, I'll leave that to you?"

He jotted the directive in his notebook. "Yes, ma'am."

The lieutenant closed her laptop and stood. "Very well. You've got point on this, Max. Get whatever you can out of Miss March. Use Trent as your contact, and keep us in the loop for any kind of backup or research you need."

Max nodded, then pushed his chair back the moment they were dismissed, eager to get to Rosie to verify that the plan they'd agreed to last night was still in place. He scooped photos and reports and stuffed the files into his binder to sort out later.

He hadn't even made it around the corner of the table when he stopped in his tracks. But it wasn't the young stud wannabe chatting up Rosie that rankled this time. "Who does that guy who came in with Rosie look like to you?"

"An attorney?"

Max picked up the photo of Richard Bratcher and tossed it onto the table in front of Trent. "Look again."

Trent picked up the picture and whistled under his breath. "An older version of our vic. Now that's awkward." He rose to his feet beside Max. "They're looking pretty chummy. You think the two of them could have plotted together to kill Richard?"

Max didn't want to think that Rosie had plotted anything. But a partner in crime turning on her could certainly explain the stalker. A man who wanted revenge on the woman he thought killed his brother would, too. "I think I'd better go introduce myself."

Trent grinned as Max headed out the door. "Call me if she throws something at you or threatens a lawsuit."

Hud Kramer took the stack of mug shot books the uniformed officer had been carrying, and led Rosie and the other man to the closest interview room. Max dumped his binder on his desk, ignoring the papers that spilled out, and quickened his stride to catch up to the group when Rosie hesitated in the doorway and the ringer for their dead guy nudged her on inside.

"She's not going to like that little room," Max muttered, catching the door before it closed in his face. He pushed it open and stepped inside, looking first to those pretty gray eyes that zeroed in on him and widened before her gaze shuttered and she looked down at the table that cut the room in half. Hell. He'd agreed to help her, hadn't he? Why was she still shying away from him? More important, why did it bother him so much that she did? Max turned his attention to Kramer. "I've got this."

"I was just doing the heavy lifting." Seriously? The younger detective made a point of flexing his muscles when he set down the thick books. "I was keeping the lady occupied until you got out of your meeting."

Max pointed a thumb over his shoulder. "Get out of here and go do some real police work."

"Yes, sir. Bye, ma'am." He winked at Rosie on his way out, earning a soft smile.

"Thank you, Detective Kramer," she answered. Max's groan of annoyance faded when Rosie lifted her gaze to him again. Better. He liked it when he could see into the cool depths of those pretty eyes. But that look was far from a come-on, and her succinct tone reminded him of the reason she was here. "Good morning, Max."

"Morning. You want to introduce me to your friend?"

"Of course." She gestured to the man beside her. "Detective Krolikowski—this is my attorney, Howard Bratcher."

Max extended his hand but hesitated midintroduction. This guy was definitely going on the suspect list. "Bratcher?"

The attorney sealed the handshake. Firmer than Max

had expected. But Howard Bratcher quickly withdrew his hand to stand beside Rosie. "Yes. I'm Richard's brother. I know KCPD has reopened the investigation into his murder. Believe me, Detective, I'm as anxious as Rosemary to identify his killer and clear her name. Richard was an embarrassment to my father, and our law firm. There was no love lost between us. Rosemary's parents were clients of my father's, and she's been my friend and a client of the firm for several years. I'm here for her, not Richard."

Old family friends, hmm? Or something more? Howard slipped his arm behind Rosie's back, and her shoulders stiffened. Max's brewing suspicions edged into something more protective when she turned out of Bratcher's embrace and wound up facing the corner of the room. She reached out and brushed her fingertips across the back wall, and Max wondered if the word *trapped* was going through her mind again.

"Rosemary? I thought this might be a needlessly upsetting errand." Ah, hell. Was this guy thinking he could manipulate Rosie—and her money—the way his younger brother had? Despite his disclaimer, did Bratcher blame Rosie for his brother's murder and think she owed him some kind of payback? The solicitous attorney reached for her. "Would you like me to take you home?"

She wanted his protection? Max pulled out a chair and propped his foot on it, casually sitting back on the tabletop—purposefully blocking the attorney's path to Rosie. "She told you about the damage done to her house last night?"

The attorney pulled up short, his gaze dropping to the chair, then back up to Max. He was probably trying to figure out whether the lumbering detective was clueless, rude or smarter than he'd given him credit for. *That's right, buddy. It's the last one.* Howard Bratcher backed off a step and faced Max. "Yes. That's why I insisted on driving her here today."

Max's gaze went to the soft gray eyes that watched him from the corner of the room now. "Rosie's got her own car. She's perfectly capable of driving herself."

The attorney's eyes narrowed. "We've been close for several years, Detective. I'm concerned for her welfare."

How close? "Did you see the man who was taking pictures of her at the prison?"

"I didn't see anyone taking pictures."

Rosie stepped forward, grasping the back of the chair. "The man with the cell phone? I pointed him out to you. Described him as a lawyer-type guy?"

"I recall your amusing description, but—"

"You didn't stop to take a good look at the man who upset your close friend?" Max challenged.

"I don't remember."

Rosie's hopeful gaze crashed at Howard's noncommittal answer.

If this self-absorbed wise guy was her ally, no wonder she'd sought Max out for help. Even half-toasted, he'd paid attention to the details this bozo had missed. Unless Howie here had missed them on purpose. Could he be behind this terror campaign? Max's ability to read people might be on the fritz, but logic alone told him that a longtime friend would know best what kinds of things could frighten a woman the most.

For a split second, Max understood Rosie's aversion to being confined inside a small space. Especially with Mr. I'll-support-you-as-long-as-I'm-in-charge using up so much breathable air. With so-called friends like Bratcher here, Max wondered how much of Rosie's isolation had to do with her past, and how much had to do with her fear of getting *trapped* in another relationship with someone who, even without similar looks, had to remind her a lot of her dead ex-fiancé.

Following an instinct as ornery and strong as the urge to kiss her last night had been, Max snatched her hand, kicked the chair under the table and pulled her past the tailored suit. "Come with me, Rosie."

"Where are we going?"

He opened the door, picked up the mug shot books and tightened his grip around her protesting fingers as he led her into the familiar bustle of the main room.

Howard's snort of derision followed them out the door. "Shouldn't you address her as Miss March, Detective?"

Shouldn't you recuse yourself from serving as her attorney, Howie?

Max kept his snarky remark to himself and pulled Rosie around chairs and desks, colleagues and computer towers, suspects and complainants in for questioning and statements, until he reached the two desks pushed together where he and Trent worked. He dumped the notebooks on top of the blotter and pushed aside the mess of notes and files before pulling out his chair for her.

"It can get noisy out here, but you'll have plenty of space to spread out. Move anything you want that's in your way." She paused, tilting her face to his, no doubt questioning his sudden bout of chivalry—maybe even questioning if he was the same man she'd recruited for bodyguard duty last night. But the grief and guilt over Jimmy's death was firmly contained today. He hoped. Taking care of Rosie March—keeping her safe from stalkers and pompous attorneys and wannabe boyfriends—was his mission now. Flattening his hand at the small of her back, he urged her to sit. "I apologize for the clutter, but as you can see, there are no walls here. Those interview rooms are all tiny."

When her lips curved into a serene smile, Max nearly succumbed to the boyish urge to smile in return. "I can work here just fine. Thank you."

The crown of her hair brushed past his nose as she moved into the chair, and Max couldn't help but take a deep breath of her sweet, summery scent. A man could get addicted to Rosie's fragrance. Who was he kidding? Old maid bun and conservative clothes aside, Rosie March turned him on like some kind of crazy aphrodisiac. Maybe because he kept thinking of what she'd be like without the severe hairstyle and all that skin covered up.

Reminding himself that she was an assignment, and that she had more of a relationship with her dogs than she did with him, Max pulled the first mug shot book in front of her. "Here you go."

Her shoulders lifted with a resolute sigh and she flipped over the cover to look at the first six men. "So I just start turning pages to see if I recognize anyone who might have been watching me at the prison?"

"Or anywhere else. Unfortunately, we have even more photos you could look at, but I narrowed down the suspect pool to men with a history of harassment and other predatory crimes who fit the general description you gave." He left out the fact that pictures of Leland Asher and his known associates were scattered throughout the books, as well. If the crime boss was behind Richard Bratcher's murder or the threats against Rosie, she'd have to make the connection herself for any kind of case against him to stick. And if she recognized anyone who might be working for Howie here… Max tossed one of the books over to Trent's neat desk. "There, Howie. You can look through some of our pics, too. See if anyone there jogs your memory from the prison waiting room."

Not that he'd trust Bratcher's recognition, or lack thereof, of anyone in the book. But it would get the attorney farther out of Rosie's personal space.

Instead of taking the hint and moving to Trent's work space, Howard circled behind him to bookend the other side of Rosie's chair. "I don't like your tone, Detective Krolikowski. And I'd appreciate it if you'd show my client more respect."

"I've got nothing but respect for Miss March." Max leaned his hip against the edge of the desk, facing the woman between them. She was picking up the papers of an old report that had fanned across the desk and tucking them into a neat stack. "You got a key for me?" Max asked.

Howard put a hand on Rosie's shoulder. "What's he talking about?"

"This is between the lady and me." Although the dots of color on her cheeks made him wonder if she was going to renege on the deal they'd made. "Rosie? Do you remember my terms?"

Do what I say. When I say it. Trust me. If Jimmy had trusted him enough to share how bad things really were, then maybe Max could have gotten him help. He could have been there for his friend. He could have taken the gun away from him. He could have saved—

"I haven't forgotten." Rosie interrupted the guilty gloom of his thoughts and set aside the neat stack of papers before reaching into her purse. She pulled out a single key and laid it in his outstretched palm. Her fingers lingered a little longer, dotting his skin with warmth. Her upturned gaze locked on to his for a moment, as if she sensed that he'd checked out for a split second. "This was Stephen's. It will get you in the back entrance."

With Rosie unexpectedly pulling him back to the present, Max frowned, curling the key into his palm, catching her fingers in a quick squeeze before she drew away. "Not the main part of the house? Do I at least get access codes?"

The heat faded from her cheeks. "The apartment has a separate entrance. It's not hooked up to the alarm system. I didn't think you'd—"

"We'll make it work," Max interrupted when he saw Howard Bratcher leaning in to intervene. "I'll see you there on my lunch break."

"So soon?"

"I'm a soldier, remember? I travel light."

Howie's hand settled on her shoulder. "Rosemary, what is this detective talking about?"

Max stood to face him, squaring off over the top of Rosie's coppery bun. "Didn't she tell ya? We're moving in together."

"Excuse me?" Uh-huh. The touching? The temper? This guy thought he and Rosie were more than friends. He at least thought he could control her actions and influence her decisions.

Shrugging off her attorney's hand, Rosie went to work pulling items from beneath the three mug shot books and straightening the rest of his desk. "Max is moving into my downstairs apartment."

"That's right, Howie. I'm her new tenant." He had his story all worked out. "Good part of town. Use of a pool. My building is being renovated. Renting a couple of rooms costs less than staying in a hotel. And Rosie didn't seem to mind having a little extra security around the house."

"I see. Why didn't you tell me you were taking on a new tenant?"

Rosie's busy hands stopped. "Because it didn't concern you. My name has been in the papers, Howard. You said it yourself. *Kansas City's newest millionaire?* And now these threats?" She tilted her face up to her attorney. "Even with the security system you had me install, I've never really felt safe being there by myself. Duchess is getting older. Trixie makes a lot of noise but isn't a real threat to anyone. I really didn't think having a cop on the premises at night could hurt."

Howard knelt down beside the chair, pulling Rosie's hand into his. "You know I have connections to private security firms across the city. I could have hired someone if I'd known how truly frightened you were."

"I did tell you. I told Detective Krolikowski, too." She pulled her hand away and glanced over at Max before busying her hands again. "He listened."

Tell him, honey. Rosie March isn't alone and vulnerable anymore.

Howard pushed to his feet. That was not a friendly look. "You know I have only your best interests at heart, Rosemary."

"I know," Rosie answered. "And I'm grateful for all you've done for me. But I need to do this for myself. I need to do more to make decisions and handle my own problems."

"I see."

"Maybe you should go back to your office, Bratcher," Max suggested. "This may take a while. I can give Rosie a ride home. After all, we're heading to the same place."

"I'll be keeping an eye on you, Krolikowski. If you take advantage of Rosemary in any way, I will have your badge. And know I'll be asking around to find out what kind of cop you really are."

"Detective?" a quivering voice asked.

Max propped his hands at his waist, ready to take whatever threat this blowhard threw at him. "I intend to make sure no one takes advantage of her in any way."

"If you're using Rosemary as some kind of pawn in your investigation—"

"Max."

Rosie's sharp voice demanded his attention. "What is it?"

He braced a palm on the desk and leaned in to see what had alarmed her.

She held a picture that had fallen out of his file on Leland Asher. A picture of Asher and his entourage from a hoity-toity society event at the Nelson-Atkins Museum of Art. Only, Rosie wasn't pointing to the crime boss. She was pointing to the younger, shorter man with glasses standing on the other side of Asher's date.

"I know him. This is the man from the prison."

Chapter Eight

Rosemary wondered how she was ever going to survive the first night with Max Krolikowski living in her basement.

If she couldn't stop this restless pacing, flitting from one room to the next, she'd never get any sleep. She'd start a project in the library, leave it at the first unfamiliar noise and wind up in the kitchen, refreshing the dogs' water bowls. She'd hear the muffled voices of a television newscast through the floorboards, then head off to the front room to adjust the blinds. She'd peek out a window to look at the clouds gathering in the sky and covering the moon, but she'd hear the rumble of thunder in the distance and go back to the kitchen to make sure it was Mother Nature talking and not her new tenant grumbling about something downstairs. Then the dogs would woof at something outside and the whole anxious cycle would start over again.

Max's Cold Case Squad hadn't been able to immediately identify the man in the picture with Leland Asher, since he didn't have a record and wasn't in their criminal database. But she was certain the narrow-framed glasses and nondescript brown hair belonged to the man who'd smiled and taken her picture at the penitentiary. Knowing there was a mystery man out there somewhere, bent on terrorizing her, who might or might not have some connection to organized crime, was upsetting enough. But adding in the disruption of having a man on the premises once again, a man who seemed to occupy her thoughts the way Max did, left her unable to find any sense of calm or control. Routine, and the secure normalcy that went with it, had flown out the window.

Max had probably only needed a few minutes to put away the items he'd brought in his backpack and duffel bag and familiarize himself with the bedroom, bathroom and kitchenette, which he said would serve him just fine. And why wouldn't the man just go to bed already? One time she'd discovered Max out front, installing the new glass globes on her porch lights.

"The weatherman says we're having thunderstorms tonight," she warned.

"I know." He continued his work, sounding far too nonchalant about making himself at home here. "I want to make sure everything is secure before I head to bed." He nodded for her to go back inside. "But you go ahead."

Much later, she peeked out the door to find him reclining in her rocking chair, sitting in the dark with his big booted feet crossed on the porch railing. His shirt hung unbuttoned and loose from his shoulders, the tails flapping in the breeze that was picking up as lightning flashed in the clouds overhead. He still wore his gun and badge on his belt, and a stubby, unlit cigar that made him look like the gruff Army sergeant he'd once been was tucked into the corner of his mouth.

"Go to sleep, Rosie," he'd ordered, before removing the cigar and turning those watchful blue eyes to catch her spying on him. "You're safe."

Safe from her stalker, maybe. There'd been no phone call, no threat, no visit from anyone who wanted to hurt her for twenty-four hours now. But she wasn't so safe from the curious attraction she felt toward the unrefined yet inarguably masculine detective. And she certainly wasn't safe from the troubling memories of being alone with another man who'd turned her home into a prison where he'd inflicted pain and fear until fate alone had allowed her to escape.

"You won't bring that cigar into the house, will you?"

"No, ma'am."

Her fingers curled and uncurled around the edge of the door. "You need your sleep, too."

"Good night, Rosie."

Rosemary locked herself in her bedroom after that, counting down the hour until she heard the apartment door open and close at the back of the house. Duchess sat up from her cozy pillow beside Rosemary's bed, and Trixie yipped at the unfamiliar sound.

Lightning flashed and thunder rattled the window panes. A few seconds later the rain poured down, whipping through the trees and drumming on the new roof, finally drowning out the sounds of the house and the man in the room below hers.

"Settle down, girls," she whispered. "It's just a storm." The dogs curled into their respective beds and fell asleep long before Rosie turned out the bedside lamp and crawled beneath the sheet and quilt.

But it was hard to follow her own admonishment. Normally, the sounds of a summer storm lulled her into relaxing, but her sleep was disrupted by memories of the moonlight gleaming through the golden hair that dusted Max's muscular chest, and the desire to run her fingers there to discover the heat only hinted at when she'd touched him through his shirt. She remembered that kiss, too, and the way his hands had moved with such urgency through her hair. Maybe he'd put his hands in other places, skim them over her skin and pull her against all that brawny strength and heat. Maybe he'd kiss her again, and this time he wouldn't hold back. Maybe she wouldn't hold back, either.

Later, the bold wishes that filled her dreams and left her perspiring and uncomfortable in her crisp cotton sheets mutated into darker, more disturbing images.

Max's tawny jaw and imposing shoulders gave way to a shadow that was taller, slimmer, darker than the night. Rosemary squirmed in the tangle of covers as the shadow darted past her window. The black figure swirled around the walls of her bedroom, spinning closer, moving so fast that the sea of black miasma soon surrounded her bed. She moaned in her sleep as the blackness closed in all around her, stealing away the light, robbing her of warmth.

Her breathing quickened as the chill permeated her skin. But her arm was too weak to push it away. The darkness consumed her, reached right into her very heart and ripped it from her chest. Then she was burning, bleeding, begging for a reprieve.

A tiny circle of light flared in the darkness and a voice laughed. The tiny light was a fire, glowing brighter, hotter with every breath. She was powerless to move, powerless to do anything but anticipate the coming pain. Laughter rang through the darkness as the fire moved closer and closer, until the hot ember hissed against her cold skin, branding her.

Rosemary came awake screaming. She shot up in bed, her hand clutching at the scars on her collarbone, her heart pounding in her chest. In the instant she realized the torture had been a dream, the instant she realized the shadows were no more than one of the Dinkles' trees, silhouetted by lightning against her window shade, the instant she realized she was perfectly fine and lowered her hand, she realized the laughter was real. High-pitched. Distorted. Distant.

The threat was real.

Duchess was on her feet, growling at the window. Trixie jumped onto the bed and barked. The repetitive laughter, fading in and out like a clown running in circles, was coming from outside in the storm.

"Max?" Fear hammered her pulse in her ears. She needed Max.

A clap of thunder slammed like a door in the distance, and Rosemary jumped inside her skin. "Rosie?" She heard a rapid knocking, like gunshots at her back door. "Rosie!"

"Max?" Rosemary quickly kicked away the covers twisted around her legs and slid off the edge of the bed. She pulled her sleep shirt down to her thighs and crossed to the door. "I'm coming!" But the laughter started up again behind her and she froze. It grew louder, tinnier. The knocking at her back door stopped and a chill skittered down her spine.

Grabbing Duchess's collar as she walked past, Rosemary went to the window. With her heart in her throat, she pulled back the curtain and peeked between the shade and the sill. Lightning flashed and she jumped back from the faceless figure in a black hood standing there.

She screamed again.

A deeper voice shouted outside in the storm. "KCPD! Get on the ground!" The laughter stopped abruptly and when the next bolt of lightning flashed, her window was empty. She saw a blur of movement in the blowing rain as she dropped the curtain and backed away. She heard a familiar grumble of curses.

"Max!" she shouted. What was he doing? If the intruder could threaten her dogs and terrorize her, what would he do to Max? What if he bashed in Max's head with that baseball bat? Would he kill the detective guarding her? Then who would stop him from coming after her? Saving Max was imperative to saving herself. Saving Max was imperative, period. "Max?" Tripping over the excited barking dogs, Rosemary turned and ran. Her fingers fumbled with the stupid lock on her door before she finally opened the thing and slung it open. "Max!"

The wood floor was cold beneath her bare feet, the kitchen tile even colder. She ran through the darkened house but skidded to a stop and abruptly changed course at the furious sound of knocking at her front door now. "Rosie!" He was safe. She would be safe. "Open the damn door! Rosie! Answer me!"

"I'm here. Is he out there? Did you catch him?"

"Rosie!"

She punched in the alarm code, unhooked the chain and dead bolt, turned the knob. Max jerked the storm door from her grasp the moment she'd turned its lock. The blowing rain whooshed in sideways around him, splashing her face and shirt before he pushed her back inside the foyer.

"You've got too many damn locks. I couldn't get to you." While he griped away, she ran straight into his arms, pressing her cheek against the wet skin of his chest, sliding her hands beneath his soggy shirttails and linking them together at the back of his waist. He walked her back another couple of steps, shutting the steel door behind him. "I lost him. You have to answer me when I call you. You can't scream like that and not answer…

Okay." Once the adrenaline was out of his system, once he realized how she shuddered against him, clinging tightly to his strength and heat, he curled one arm behind her back and set his gun on the front hall table with the other. His growly tone softened. "Okay, honey." He reached behind him to throw the bolt yet never let go. Then he came back to wrap both arms around her and nestle his jaw at the crown of her hair. She willingly rocked back and forth as his chest expanded and contracted against her after the exertion of chasing a shadow through the storm. "I'm gettin' you all wet."

She shook her head against the strong beat of his heart. "I don't care."

He pulled her sleep-tossed hair from the neckline of her pink T-shirt, smoothing it down her back in gentle strokes. "You're okay. He's gone."

"Did he hurt you?" A crisp wet curl of chest hair tickled her lips. A muscle quivered beneath the unintended caress.

"Me? Nah, I'm too tough for that kind of thing. Are *you* hurt?" He sifted his fingers through her hair until his warm, callous palm cupped the nape of her neck. "Ah, hell, honey. Your skin's like ice." He shifted his stance then, curling his shoulders around her, rubbing his hands up and down her back. "I heard a noise and saw that guy outside your window, but I lost him in the rain once he jumped the Dinkles' hedge out front. And it's way too dark to be firing blindly into shadows. I didn't want to take the time away from you to do a search, in case he doubled back and broke in. I couldn't risk leaving you alone."

Rosemary's shirt and panties were slowly soaking up the moisture from his rain-soaked clothes. But the furnace of heat on the other side of those wet jeans and unbuttoned shirt that he must have hastily tossed on seeped right through the layers of damp material, warming her skin and easing her panic.

Once they were both breathing normally again, he pressed his lips against her temple before easing some space between them, although he continued rubbing his hands up and down her back and the arms she crossed between them. "Tell me what happened."

She watched the rain from his scalp run in rivulets down to his scruffy jaw, pooling at the tip of his chin before dripping onto her arm. "I had a nightmare."

His hands stopped their massage and squeezed her shoulders, demanding she meet his concerned gaze. "Uh-uh. That guy was real. Standard-issue hoodie and dark jeans. At least six feet tall. Wish I'd taken the time to grab my flashlight so I could have seen his face."

The cop was returning. The warmth was leaving. Rosemary hugged her arms more tightly around her waist, suddenly self-conscious to be standing toes to toes in a puddle in her foyer wearing little more than her long pink T-shirt. A wet T-shirt now. Not that she had any illusions about turning Max's head, but she didn't want to embarrass him, either. "I was dreaming of things Richard did to me. When I woke up, that man was at my window. For a split second, I thought…" She shrugged away from Max's touch and shivered. "It was the same man who vandalized my porch. I'm sure of it."

"Your scream woke me. When I got outside, I heard that crazy caterwauling." He picked up his gun and tucked it into the back of his jeans before scrubbing his fingers over his chin and wiping the moisture on the front of his shirt. Was she really still standing there, staring at the glistening wet skin of his chest? "Sorry," he apologized, mistaking her fascinated longing for some kind of effrontery. His big fingers fumbled to pull the soggy cotton together over the hills and hollows of muscle and hook a few buttons to the placket. "He's long gone. There were footprints beneath the sill. I went back to snap a picture, but they're washing away." Max reached into his shirt pocket and pulled out a little red plastic box. "I found this out there in the grass." He pushed a button, and a warped recording of laughter played.

Rosemary recoiled from the sound. "That's what I heard."

"It's cheap. A noisemaker from a party store. Sounds as though there's water in the mechanism. With the storm, there's no way we're getting fingerprints off this thing. Maybe on the inside, though. Looks like there's something wedged in there. Do you have a plastic bag?" Although she missed the warmth of his body pressed against hers, she knew this businesslike interchange was more important than her own foolish cravings for physical contact. Tucking her hair behind her ears, she nodded. The dogs fell into step beside her, joining their little parade to the kitchen. Max brought up the rear, stopping in each doorway along the hall, checking inside the rooms to make sure everything was still secure. "Sorry about your floor. I'm making a mess."

She stopped at the bathroom to pull her robe from behind the door and shrugged into it, adding another layer of warmth and modesty now that she was done throwing herself at her downstairs tenant. "It'll clean up. I believe you think I'm a prim-and-proper prude. A little mud and water don't bother me." Stepping into the kitchen, Rosemary flipped on the light and eyed the path of water and big muddy prints from Max's bare feet that marked her hallway. "The dogs have tracked in worse. I just like knowing the rules and what's expected of me—

and what to expect from other people." She crossed to the bank of drawers beside the oven but hesitated. "I hope I didn't put you in an awkward position before. I don't normally wrap myself around a man while I'm in my pajamas." The burn of embarrassment crept up her neck and into her cheeks at that rather suggestive description of seeking refuge in his arms. "I mean, I don't…not without asking first. But I was scared. And I was worried about you."

Rosemary glanced up as he leaned his hip against the countertop beside her. "Do you hear me complaining?"

She was relieved, and more disappointed than she should be, to see him dismissing her panicked indiscretion with a wry grin. She tried to match his easy smile. "You *are* very good at vocalizing what you're thinking and feeling, aren't you, Detective?"

His smile disappeared and he reached over to catch a tendril of hair that stuck to her damp cheek and tucked it behind her ear. "I thought I'd earned a Max from you by now."

Her gaze drifted to the front of his shirt and the three buttons that he'd fastened into the wrong holes. Rosemary couldn't stop the smile from curving her lips again. This man was a tornado blowing through her controlled, predictable world, upsetting her routine, ignoring her personal barriers, waking wants and needs she thought had died long ago. And yet he was growing more dear to her, more necessary as a protector, a friend and maybe something more, with each encounter. Even if all he ever wanted from her was a drunken kiss and the chance to solve Richard's murder, she was glad that he'd barged into her closed-off, humdrum life. She opened a drawer and pulled out a box of plastic storage bags for him. "Here. Max."

Nodding his approval, Max pulled a pocketknife from the front of his jeans to pry open the red box. "Looks like our perp took it apart to modify it somehow. Even with industrial glue, though, it didn't reseal completely. That's probably how the water got inside."

"That horrible sound reminded me of Richard. Of that night. He laughed when he…" The scars on her chest seem to throb and she tied the robe more snugly around her damp T-shirt.

"Who would know about him laughing that night?" Max asked, pulling out a chair at the table to tinker with the box. "Somebody had to know it would rattle you."

"I'm not sure. It's probably in the police report."

"That's public record if somebody looks hard enough. Who else?"

Rosemary considered herself a very private person, but after that night, she'd been desperate to find someone who could help her escape Richard's tyranny. "My brother, Stephen. A couple of friends."

"What friends?" Max glanced up from unscrewing the back of the box. "Crimes are solved in the details. I need you to tell them to me."

Rosemary wondered if the storm outside could somehow cool the air inside the house, as well. "Otis and Arlene, when I went to their house to call the police afterward. Howard."

"Your attorney?"

She nodded. "I told him everything when he was putting together the restraining order."

What about a statuesque blonde who blamed her for Richard's death?

"You got a suspect for me?" he prompted, sensing her thoughts turning.

Rosemary pulled out another chair and sat kitty-corner from him. "Richard could have told one of his mistresses. I ran into one of them at Howard's office the other day."

"*One* of…?" Max's curse was short and pungent. "Sorry. I know you hate that."

"Not as much as I hate not knowing who's doing this to me. Her name is Charleen Grimes. She said your friends Detectives Watson and Parker had shown up at her boutique to ask her questions. She was pretty ticked off." Rosemary remembered the hate and pain spewing from Charleen's perfectly painted lips that day. "She accused me of killing Richard."

"And getting away with it? Like that first note?"

Rosemary nodded. Charleen's verbal attack in Howard's office that day still rankled. But the memory of the blonde woman striding across Howard's office and towering over her was triggering a different memory. "Charleen is tall for a woman. Could she pass for a man at night, in the shadows?"

"It's possible. The guy I chased tonight was wearing clothes so baggy and nondescript I'd be hard-pressed to confirm a gender. I just assumed it was a guy." He wedged the tip of his pocketknife into the seam around the box. "I want to meet this Charleen… Finally." With one more twist of his knife, the box popped open and a soggy piece of paper fell out and plopped to the floor.

"What's that?"

He put out a hand to keep her from picking it up. "Don't touch it. I'll bag it for prints and have Trent take it to the lab tomorrow."

"You know it's not there by accident. I want to know what it says."

He used the plastic bag to retrieve it from the floor and gently shake it open. "Ah, hell."

It was a black-and-white photocopy of a picture. Of her.

Her thoughts instantly went to the mysterious photographer who'd snapped a picture of her in the visitors' room at the state prison. It was even more disturbing to see her wearing a different outfit than the flowered blouse she'd worn that day. She didn't have to move any closer to see the candid image of her climbing into a cab outside Howard's office building. "How long has he been watching me?"

When Max would have slipped the note into the bag and hidden it away, she grabbed his wrist and insisted on seeing every last gruesome detail.

Her eyes and heart had been x-ed out on the picture. Someone who was very angry with her had drawn a noose around her neck in black ink and typed a message neatly across the top.

I want to feel my hands around your throat, your pulse stopping beneath the pressure of my thumbs. You will burn for what you've done.
    There will be justice for Richard.
    Ha. Ha. Ha.

But the creepiest part was the five black marks dotting the top of the white dress she wore—five dots right across her collarbone where the burn scars Richard had inflicted upon her lay.

"How could he know? How could anyone know?"

Rosemary was only vaguely aware of Max moving as the room swirled around her. With her hand at her throat, she sank into the back of the chair and closed her eyes.

"Rosie?"

She heard the gruff voice calling to her in the distance. Someone knew her darkest secrets. Someone was using those secrets against her. To terrorize her. To punish her. To plunge her into a nightmare from which she could never escape.

"Rosie."

Rough hands grabbed her shoulders, shook her. She was cold. So cold.

Then the hands closed around either side of her head and she fell forward until her mouth ran into something firm, hot. Something warm and moist pressed between her lips, parting them. The world gradually took the shape and form of fingers tangled in her hair, tugging lightly at her scalp. The pressure on her mouth became pliant lips that tasted of salt and heat and toasty tobacco. The taste was familiar yet new. Potent, with a tickle of sandpapery stubble on the side. Max. Max was kissing her. His hands were holding her. His tongue was sliding against hers. In one moment, she was the stunned recipient of bold passion—in the next, her tongue darted out to catch his and she leaned into the kiss. Deepened it. Came alive with it. Her throat hummed with anticipation. She stretched to fit her mouth more fully against his.

But when her hands came to rest against his chest, he pulled away. The room was still swaying when her eyes fluttered open and she looked into the damp, craggy face of the man kneeling in front of her chair. "Max?"

He stroked his thumb across her tender lips, brushed her hair behind her ears. "You checked out on me there. Don't scare me like that, okay? Stay with me."

The disorienting fear and helplessness faded. Other emotions—confusion, hope, desire—grew stronger. She touched the lines of concern crinkling beside his eyes. She brushed her thumb across the masculine line of his bottom lip, absorbing the heat from his skin into hers.

She could hear her heart beating over the drumbeat of rain outside. "Another opportunity you couldn't pass up?" But there was no humor in her laugh, no answering humor in his eyes. "You shouldn't kiss me like that unless it means something to you."

Max's lip trembled beneath her thumb. A deep groan rose from his chest. And then he was pushing to his feet, pulling her with him. His mouth covered hers, hot and wet and full of a driving need she answered kiss for kiss.

He lifted her onto her toes and she wound her arms around his neck, leaning into his sheltering strength. There was little finesse to Max's kiss. But then, she had little to compare it to beyond Richard's smooth, practiced seduction that left her feeling unsatisfied and inadequate.

Rosemary liked this infinitely better. There was little to second-guess about a man sliding his hands down her back to squeeze her bottom and lift her off her feet into his hard thighs and the firm interest stirring in between. Max's cheek rasped against hers as his lips scudded across her jaw and pulled at her earlobe.

His words were basic. "Your skin's so soft. Your hair smells like summer and rain. It's the cleanest scent. I could breathe it in all night long."

When he reclaimed her lips, his tongue was bold, his hands were bolder. Rosemary gasped when she felt his palms branding her skin beneath her shirt. The tips of her breasts tingled, grew heavy and tight as they rubbed against the hard wall of his chest. She wanted his hands there, soothing their needy distress, exciting them more. This kiss was the wildest, most unexpected, most perfect embrace of her life. She was an equal partner, giving, taking. She slipped her hands up into the prickly crop of his military-short hair, turning his head to the angle of kiss she liked best.

"Rosie…honey…" His fingers dipped beneath the elastic of her panties. Yes. She wanted his touch there, too. She was forgetting the past. She was unafraid of the future. There was only Max and this moment and feeling safe and desired.

But when she curled her leg around Max's knee, instinctively opening herself to the need arcing between them, he pulled his lips away with a noisy moan. Her mouth chased after his to reclaim the connection, but his hands were on her shoulders now, pulling her arms from around his neck. Her toes touched the cold tile floor again, jarring her back to common sense. Suddenly, the water that had soaked through her clothes seemed just as cold. She rested her hands at his shoulders a moment to steady herself but curled her body away from his. One moment she was alive and on fire, the next, she was shivering and confused.

Rosemary grasped the back of the chair to keep herself standing as Max determinedly backed away. "That's not why I'm here. I've got a mission. I made a promise." His chest expanded with a deep, ragged breath. "Ah, hell. Quit looking at me like you either want to shoot me or eat me up. I'm trying to do the right thing here."

Max's rejection instantly sent her back to the times in her relationship with Richard when he'd rebuffed her advances. "I wasn't very good, was I? I'm sor—"

"Do *not* let that man come between us." Max swiped his hand over his mouth and jaw and spun away. Just as quickly he faced her again and grabbed her wrist. "You call me whatever crass SOB you want to." He pulled her hand to the front of his jeans and cupped it over the unmistakable warm bulge behind his zipper. "This is what you do to me. I don't know why you and me fit together this good. If I could take you to bed right now and finish this, I would." He released her and backed away, raising his hands in apology. "But that's not what I'm here for. Neither one of us needs that kind of complication in our lives. I have to keep the mission in mind. I'm a cop. I have to think like a cop, not a..."

"Not a what?" she asked, her voice barely a whisper.

But he didn't fill in the blank. "It's not your job to deal with me. I'm damaged goods, Rosie. You can do better than me."

"Now who's apologizing?"

With a shrug of his massive shoulders, he scooped up the noisemaker and message that had sent her into shock and slipped them into plastic bags. "I'm going back outside to give everything a once-over—make sure our friend hasn't come back. I need to call this in to my team, too. My description of the perp is pretty vague, but it's a place to start. I'll have a black-and-white swing through the neighborhood, just in case he's hiding out somewhere." He headed to the back door. "I'll be right downstairs. Just a scream away."

Rosemary shook off her stupor and ran after him, grabbing his arm. "You're leaving me?"

He looked down over the jut of his shoulder at her, his growly voice calming. "I don't want to push my luck by overstaying my welcome."

Right. He was being all noble, doing this for her, respecting the boundaries she'd forgotten herself. She released her desperate grasp and stepped away, rubbing her hands up and down her chilled arms. "You better go call your team. I'll be fine."

"You're gettin' pale again. I'll stay if you want me to."

Rosemary shook her head. "No. You have a job to do. I'll be fine. You're here for me to draw out Richard's killer, not to babysit me."

"You know that's not the only reason I'm here."

"For my dad? You said you owed something to a man like him."

Max exhaled a grumbling sigh. "I doubt your dad would make me ten kinds of crazy the way you do. Would you really be okay with me here in the house? Because, frankly, running up and down those basement stairs and breaking through all your locked doors makes me feel like I'm miles away. What if that guy wasn't content to stay outside your window? If he'd gotten inside the house I'd have had to shoot my way in to get to you."

She was so confused—coming to terms with the idea that she could have feelings and desire for a man again, wanting to solve Richard's murder as quickly as possible, evaluating the false boundaries of her reclusive life that had at least given her the illusion of being safe— what was she supposed to choose? "I don't think gunfire in the house would be safe for Duchess and Trixie."

"Or for you. Would you feel safer if I stayed tonight?"

"I don't know."

"Yeah, you do. Everything else aside, would you feel safer?" He tapped his cheek to ask her to look him in the eye and answer. "Up here, honey."

She did look up into those expectant blue eyes. Yes. In every way that mattered, she felt safe with Max. Rosemary nodded.

"Say it, Rosie. Don't make me think I'm bullying you into this."

"I'm not inviting you into my bed. But you are awfully warm, and I can't seem to shake this chill and…" She hugged her arms around her waist but bravely held his gaze. "I don't want to be alone tonight. Would you stay with me?"

The taut line of his mouth relaxed. "I like a clear set

of rules, too. So no hanky-panky, but you wouldn't be adverse to a little cuddling? You know, so I can keep an eye on you and you could borrow some body heat?"

"That would be enough for you?"

He brushed a copper tendril off her cheek and tucked it behind her ear. "That would be perfect."

Rosemary smiled. "Then I can live with those rules, too."

"You know the drill." He opened the door. The wind had shifted, blowing rain beneath the patio roof and through the screen, getting their damp clothes wet again. "Lock up. Keep the dogs with you."

"Yes, sir."

Max hurried over to the apartment entrance to make his phone calls and she locked the door behind him. Plucking the wet cotton knit away from the goose bumps on her skin, Rosemary whistled for the dogs. "Come on, girls."

She changed into a fresh sleep shirt and gathered a sponge and some towels, and dropped to her hands and knees to mop up the mud and water in the foyer and hallway. By the time Max returned, she had a load of soiled towels going in the laundry, the dogs settled in with rawhide treats and her quilt pulled off her bed to wrap around her shoulders as a makeshift robe until her own clothes dried.

Max toweled himself off and changed into a dry T-shirt and jeans he'd brought with him before wandering into the library to find her sitting on the rug, going through another box of her parents' things. He took a sip of the hot decaf coffee she'd fixed for him. "I'm willing to take the couch, but I've slept on enough hard bunks and sandy ground to want to avoid the floor if that's okay."

Rosemary grinned and pointed to the sofa where

Trixie had climbed on top of the pillow and blanket she'd set out for Max. "Just push her off. She's got plenty of rugs and pillows around the house to sleep on."

While she finished sorting through an envelope of photographs from a family vacation, tossing the blurry pictures and duplicates in the trash, Max sat. Instead of jumping down, Trixie climbed into his lap and lifted her paws for a thorough tummy rub. When Duchess abandoned her treat and came over to share a little bit of the action, Max reached down to rub the German shepherd's tummy, too.

But then he clapped his hands and shooed both dogs away to turn his full attention on Rosemary. "It's late. We have meetings tomorrow, a couple of leads I'd like to pursue. And in case you thought it was up for debate, it's not—you're coming with me."

When she reached for another envelope of photographs, Max cleared his throat. "Honey, you need some sleep. So do I. Either go to bed or come here."

The teasing command overrode any shyness or second thoughts she was feeling. Clutching the quilt around her shoulders, Rosemary turned off the desk lamp. Max turned off the lamp beside the sofa and set his gun and badge on the table beside his coffee mug. Rosemary sat down beside him, watching the diminishing lightning flicker through the blinds in the front window.

A voice, equally dark as the room now, spoke beside her. "The rules I agreed to included some cuddling." He draped his arm over the back of the couch behind her shoulders, reminding her of the body heat she craved. She curled her feet beneath the quilt beside her and leaned into him, resting her head against his shoulder. His arms folded around her and the quilt, tucking them both to his side. "That's better."

Without a visible clock to keep track of the time, she wasn't sure how long it was before the warmth of the quilt and man holding her seeped deep into her bones and she was drifting off to sleep. "Max?"

"Hmm?"

"You called me honey tonight. More than once."

"I guess it just slipped out. I wasn't trying to over-step—"

"I like it. I like that you call me Rosie, too. Nobody else calls me Rosie. It makes me feel…normal."

"Normal?"

"You know, not an unemployed millionaire murder suspect who talks to her dogs more than she does to people?" She rested her palm above the deep-pitched chuckle that vibrated his chest. "I'm sorry to be so much trouble. I'm glad you're here. But if I wig out on you at some point during the night, just know it's nothing personal."

"Uh-uh." Max slipped his fingers under her chin and tilted her face to his. "You don't apologize for anything. Whatever you have to say to me, don't be afraid to say it. I'm not Richard. What you see is what you get. You know what I'm thinking or feeling at almost any given moment. It isn't always pretty, but there are no surprises."

"I don't like surprises, anyway."

"You, lady, are the biggest surprise of all." He pressed a chaste kiss to her forehead before swinging his legs up onto the couch and stretching out beside her, pulling the quilt up over them both. "Now, go to sleep. That's an order."

Feeling toastier and more tired by the second, Rosie curled up against Max and drifted off to a deep, nightmare-free sleep.

MAX AWOKE TO sunlight streaming through the blinds, a dog licking his elbow and feeling incredibly hard.

He supposed a creamy thigh wedged between his legs did that to a man. And while there might have been a woman in his past he'd have undressed and gotten busy with to start the new day, this was Rosie March. And there were rules with Rosie. Keeping her safe, proving her innocence, earning her trust and fighting to make sure he was worthy of whatever affection she threw his way meant following those rules as surely as he'd follow an order from a superior officer. Still, while she snored softly on his chest, he raised his head and breathed in the sweet, clean scent of her copper-red hair that reminded him of coming home and leaving battlefields behind him. He wasn't a saint, after all.

But a bigger pair of deep brown eyes were staring at him now. Between Duchess's stoic plea and Trixie's eager tongue rasping along his arm, Max got the message. He reached down to scratch around the poodle's ears. "Need to go outside, girls?"

When Duchess jumped to her feet and the little dog started dancing around, Max tried to calm them. "Shh. Mama's sleeping. I'm coming. Give me a sec."

Sometime during the night, the quilt had ended up on the floor, and Trixie had claimed it for a bed, so there was nothing but the woman herself he needed to extricate himself from. Max palmed Rosie's hip and gently lifted her so he could pull his legs from beneath hers. Then he turned onto his side to pull his shoulder from beneath her head. But his efforts to carefully free himself from the woman draped on top of him without waking or embarrassing her halted when the neckline of her T-shirt gaped open and he shamelessly took a peek at the plump, heavy breasts that had pillowed against his side and chest most of the night.

But that little rush of lust quickly dissipated when he saw the puckery burn scars along her collarbone, marring Rosie's beautiful skin. He tucked his finger beneath the stretchy cotton and pulled the material aside to get a better look.

"Son of a…" Five perfect white circles the size of a cigarette tip. That explained the high necklines. He dropped his knees to the floor and pulled his arm away as his temper brewed. He vowed then and there to give up the cigars completely—not even a stress-relieving chomp for old times' sake. Nobody did that kind of damage to themselves. That was done to her. He'd have been tempted to pull the trigger on Richard Bratcher himself if he'd known that bastard had trapped her inside the house and tortured her like that.

Jimmy had been tortured. Physically, mentally, emotionally. Had Rosie endured the same?

Jimmy hadn't survived the aftermath of all that had been done to him, all he'd seen. In the end, he'd died alone. If there'd been anything in Max's power he could do to save his buddy, he would have.

Rosie was all alone in this house. But she wasn't going to cope with Bratcher and his cruelty by herself anymore. For Rosie, for her father, for his own sanity and redemption, Max intended to capture a killer and put a stop to anyone or anything that tried to hurt this woman again.

Perhaps sensing his unblinking stare and darkening mood, Rosie stirred on the couch. She smiled before opening her eyes. "Good morning."

Max didn't trust himself to speak. He curled his fingers into a fist and pulled it away from her.

Rosie's smile disappeared in an instant and she was wide-awake. When she saw the direction of his gaze, she sat up and scooted to the far end of the couch. "What are you doing?"

"Trying not to put a fist through your wall."

"Ugly, aren't they?" She pulled her oversize shirt back into its modest place and picked up the quilt, draping it over her shoulders and covering everything between her chin and her feet. "I suppose with nine million dollars, I could afford to get some plastic surgery and make them disappear. They're there to remind me that I've never really been safe, I've never really been free since that man entered my life. I can never drop my guard or give my heart again. Not until the rumors are put to rest and that crazy stalker—"

When she pushed to her feet, Max was there to stop her from bolting from the room. He caught her face between his hands and dipped his head to kiss her. It was brief, it was passionate, it was full of the unspoken promise he'd made to her moments earlier.

When he released her, she wasn't quite so set on running from him. "What was that for?"

"I saw the chance to do it, so I did."

Shaking off his show of support, his vow to protect her, she headed for the hall anyway. "I don't think I can do this, after all, Max. You need to go."

"Did Bratcher put those marks on you?"

She stopped, pulling the quilt more fully around her. Her huddled silence was answer enough. Hell. No wonder she'd checked out last night when she saw that sick, doctored-up picture. That kind of graphic accuracy about her past abuse had no other function but to remind her of her worst fears. To make her feel as powerless and alone now as she had back then.

He wasn't giving Rosie the chance to ever feel that way again. "Shower and get dressed and grab some breakfast—or whatever your morning routine is. You're coming with me today."

"But you have to work." Her shoulders lifted with a heavy sigh and she turned, gesturing to the boxes and books all around them. "And I'm still going through Mom and Dad's papers. You don't think I'm safe here during the day? I'll have Duchess and Trixie with me. Send one of your uniformed officers over to keep an eye on me." She shrugged the quilt higher onto her shoulders and hugged it tight around her neck, hiding even more of herself from him—as if his body hadn't already memorized the shape and weight of those generous hips and breasts. "Won't I just be in the way?"

"You aren't a prisoner in this house anymore, Rosie. We talked about this last night. Staying here by yourself isn't an option. I don't want to wait until Trent or someone else from the team gets done with morning roll call to take over the watch here—and I won't trust you with anyone else. We have secrets to uncover, a murder to solve."

"And you think I can help?"

"This morning I have a meeting at Endicott Global. I'd like you to come along on the off chance we see your guy from the picture, or anyone else you might recognize there. In fact, I want you to keep your eyes open anyplace we go, in case he's following you." KCPD still hadn't identified the young man yet. But Max had a feeling in his gut that the man was key to linking Bratcher's murder to Leland Asher's organization and a host of other crimes. "Before we do that, we're going next door. Your neighbors are always peeking at you and seem to have an opinion on everything. Maybe they saw something last night."

"Oh, joy."

Good. Sarcasm beat that self-conscious guilt and avoiding him. "You're the key to my investigation, Rosie. Maybe the key to my redemption over Jimmy's death, too."

"That wasn't your fault."

He put up a hand to stop that argument. "You fight your demons your way, and I'll deal with mine on my own terms. I want you in my sights 24/7 now. Okay? I promise to knock off at five when my shift is over, and I'll bring you back to do your paperwork thing here."

"You're not really giving me a choice, are you?"

"If you don't go, neither do I. And that means we'll never find Bratcher's killer."

A beat of silence passed before she nodded and turned. "Put the dogs in the backyard on your way out. I'll get ready."

Chapter Nine

"Brace yourself," Max warned, pressing the doorbell. "And remember, the idea is to keep them talking."

Rosemary inhaled a steadying breath and hugged her shoulder bag closer to the navy blue animal-print dress she wore. "That shouldn't be hard."

Arlene Dinkle wasn't smiling when she answered the front door. But then, neither was Max.

With a clean shave and a fresh shirt tucked into his jeans, there was little left of the man who'd held Rosemary so tenderly and securely through the night. This guy wore a gun and a badge and an attitude that outgrumped Arlene's early-morning mood.

"Good morning, Mrs. Dinkle." Max flashed his badge but not a smile. "You remember me, don't you?"

"Detective Krolikowski." Arlene carried pruning shears and a small bouquet of cut roses in her gloved hands. "I remember you. Did you catch that trespasser?"

"The department's working on it. I'm following up on what might be a related crime. There was an attempted break-in at Miss March's house last night, and I was wondering if you or your husband saw anything. May we come in?"

"Strange men at all hours, that old car parked in your driveway, and now this?" Arlene's dark gaze slid over to

Rosemary. "You draw a bad element to this neighbor-hood like a magnet, don't you?"

Bristling at the catty remark, Max's hand clenched at the small of Rosemary's back. But his tone remained good-ol'-boy professional. "Let's get one thing straight, Mrs. Dinkle. You do not get to speak to Miss March like that. She's a victim, not a criminal. You'll give her the same respect you would this badge."

The older woman's petite frame puffed up. "Well, I've never been spoken to—"

"Rosemary. Good morning." Otis strolled out of the kitchen in a pair of track pants and a muscle shirt, car-rying a ball cap and bottle of water. He reached around his wife to push open the screen door. "Detective. Please, come in."

There was no offer of a cup of coffee, not even an offer to sit. The fragrance from the roses Arlene had been trimming overwhelmed their small foyer and tick-led Rosemary's sinuses. But Otis's welcoming smile seemed genuine. "Trouble next door again?"

"I'm afraid so, sir."

"A man peeked in my window last night," Rosemary explained, trying to keep her tone as even and uncowed by Arlene's rudeness as Max's had been. "He left a threat that indicated he wanted to kill me."

"Oh, my. That's terrible." Otis's smile faded. He swung his gaze over to Max. "Did you catch him?"

"The police haven't caught anybody," Arlene groused. "Now we have Peeping Toms making death threats run-ning around our neighborhood? You know if they can't get into your house, Rosemary, they'll try to break into ours." She thumped her husband's arm. "We can't af-ford the same kind of high-tech security she has. I told you we should have sold this house and moved ten years ago." She swung her arms out, indicating the rest of the house, inadvertently drawing Rosemary's attention to at least five more vases of roses scattered across the living room. "You never listen."

"Is there a flower show coming up, Arlene?" Rosemary asked. The woman certainly loved her gardening, but the overwhelming smell of attar in the house was giving her a bit of a headache.

"I'm trying to save my prize roses," Arlene explained. "That storm last night nearly did them in. At least I can dry these and save the perfume for potpourri. Unless, of course, some gang person breaks in and robs us. Or kills us in our sleep."

"We're perfectly fine here, Arlene." Otis's quiet, almost monotonous voice was such a contrast to his wife's shrill tones. "Rosemary's the one who's been hurt, not you. It was probably some crackpot who wanted to see what a millionaire looks like."

"Or someone casing the homes in the neighborhood to rob us," she insisted. "I told you about that fancy truck I've seen cruising up and down the street at all hours of the night. And don't think I haven't asked. No one around here owns it."

Otis shrugged. "I would have heard anyone poking at our windows. The game was on until one in the morning." He scratched the bald spot on top of his head. "Now that I think of it, I did hear some shouting last night. I figured it was someone caught out in the storm."

Arlene clutched the roses to her chest. "They were probably sending signals, telling each other how to get in. Otis, you should have called the police."

"Why? I couldn't make out any words."

Max held up a hand to end the marital debate. "It was

probably me shouting. The perp never said a word. Could you tell me a little more about this 'fancy truck,' ma'am?"

The woman could certainly be counted on for details. "I don't know models and makes, but it was one of those extended cab trucks, with a backseat for passengers?" Max pulled a pen and notebook from his pocket and jotted the description. "It was dark green—almost looked black, but I saw it under the street lamp a couple of nights ago and it was definitely dark green. The trim around the wheel wells was black, though."

"Did you happen to get a license plate?"

She thought for a moment. "I don't think it had one. It had those stickers in the window—the ones the dealer puts on when you first buy a car?"

"That helps."

Arlene almost smiled at the morsel of praise.

But her sour frown returned when Otis reached out and patted Rosemary's shoulder. "Are you all right, dear?"

She nodded. "But understandably, seeing the man gave me a good scare. I'm lucky Max was there."

Arlene crossed her arms with a noisy harrumph. "Your parents would have been mortified to know you're alone in their house entertaining a man overnight."

Her parents would have been glad to know that Max had kept her safe. "Not that it's any of your business, Arlene, but Max is renting Stephen's old apartment downstairs."

"Oh." That seemed to deflate Arlene's judgmental superiority a bit. "I misunderstood. So the police are providing extra protection for dangerous neighborhoods like ours?"

The only danger zone on this block seemed to be Rosemary's house. But until she could prove her innocence, she supposed Arlene would continue to believe she lived next door to a murderess and a hive for illegal activities. "It's nice to have a cop living nearby, isn't it?" Rosemary choked out the polite words in the name of neighborhood peace and getting the Dinkles to answer Max's questions.

Max didn't waste time with making nice. "Did you see the green truck last night, ma'am?"

Arlene pursed her lips together, thinking. "No."

"When the truck was here before, did you happen to look at the driver?"

"Not really."

"Did either of you see or hear anything around midnight last night?" Max asked.

Otis crossed his arms and shrugged. "We had that big thunderstorm blow through about that time. Pretty noisy. I didn't hear anything."

"But you were awake watching the ball game?" Max clarified. "I pursued the suspect in the direction of your yard. He crashed through the hedge out front and took off between the houses. I lost him in the storm."

"My hawthorn bushes?" Arlene set the stinky roses on the nearby credenza and pushed between Rosemary and Max. "First my roses and now the hedge? I've been training those bushes for years now." When she hurried out the door and across the yard, Rosemary, Max and Otis followed. "If you arrest this Peeping Tom person, I'm suing him for property damage, too." The older woman stopped in front of the gap of crushed branches in her leafy green hedge. Her shoulders sank with dismay. She picked up one of the broken stems, still full of green leaves and long thorns. "This is ruined. I'll have to plant a whole new shrub and trim the others down to match."

"I'll pay for the new bush, Arlene," Rosemary offered.

"Of course you will. This is your fault. And it's not as though you can't afford it."

For a split second, when Max reached around Arlene, Rosemary thought he was shoving her out of the way for being such a witch. Instead, he pulled loose a scrap of soggy black sweatshirt material that had caught on one of the bush's long thorns. He showed the tatter to Rosemary before holding it up for the Dinkles. "The man I chased wore a black hoodie. Have you ever seen anyone like that around here? The driver of that truck, perhaps?"

"Don't be ridiculous," Arlene answered first. "It's too hot to wear a sweatshirt, even at night. Ours are all packed up until the fall."

Max closed the torn material in his hand and stuffed it into the pocket of his jeans. "I didn't ask if you owned a black sweatshirt, Mrs. Dinkle. I asked if you'd seen anybody wearing one."

The dark-haired woman glanced up at her husband. But was that a plea for help out of talking herself into an awkward corner or the remembrance of something familiar in her eyes?

Otis, oblivious to any underlying message, threw up his hands. "Don't look at me. I have no idea where my old hoodie is."

"I don't suppose you could produce that hoodie, could you, Mr. Dinkle? Let me check to see if there's a chunk of cloth torn out of it?"

"You think my husband is spying on Rosemary, Detective? That he would threaten her?"

"Like I said, ma'am. I'm just here looking for some answers." Max wrapped his fingers around Rosemary's arm, indicating the interview was over. "If you two find that hoodie, or spot anyone else wearing one in the area, give me a call. Let me know if you see that truck again, too. Thank you for your help."

Rosemary hurried her steps to keep up with Max's long strides around the end of the hedge and across her yard to climb inside his blue Chevelle and head to their next appointment. As she buckled herself in, she waited for him to finish texting on his phone and asked, "We didn't find out anything useful from them, did we?"

"I'm asking Trent to see if he can run down the owner of that truck. It's a long shot, but it could be significant." He tucked the phone into his pocket before starting the car's powerful engine and backing out of the driveway. "We also found out that Otis was awake when our unsub was running through his yard. I can't believe that neighbors as curious as they are didn't go to the window when they heard me shouting. Unless one or both of them are hiding something. And we found out he owns a black hoodie—even if he claims to not know where it is."

"We've been friends and neighbors for years. Why would Otis want to kill me?"

"I don't know. Maybe he doesn't. But I can't imagine he's a very happily married man. I'm guessing he's got all sorts of hobbies to distract him from that shrew. Listening to music, running."

"You think scaring me to death qualifies as a hobby?"

Max reached across the center console to squeeze her hand. "The Dinkles' information might not mean a thing except that you need to find better neighbors. I'm figuring out all the pieces to the puzzle right now. Pretty soon we'll be able to discard the ones that don't fit, and put the right ones together and find our answers. We'll get this guy. Whoever it is. We'll clear your name.

I promise." He released her to shift the car into Drive. "Want to have a little fun?"

"I thought we were focusing on finding those puzzle pieces."

He grinned. "Not all day long. Hold on."

He gunned the souped-up engine and spit out a cloud of exhaust right in front of the Dinkles' house before speeding away.

Rosemary laughed when she saw, in the side-view mirror, Arlene's hand fly up and the woman launch into a tirade that had no place to go except at her poor husband. But Otis didn't put up with it for long. Arlene was probably still complaining about ruined hedges and smelly exhausts and who knew what else when Otis plugged in his earbuds, pulled his cap over his head and took off on his morning jog.

She turned and relaxed in the car's bucket seat. "You're naughty, Detective Krolikowski."

Max slid his mirrored sunglasses on. "Yep. I kind of am."

But her smile quickly faded when she considered the idea that turning her life upside down and forcing her to live like a recluse might be someone's idea of a hobby.

ROSIE STROLLED THE grand hallway on the executive floor of the Endicott Global building, studying the oil paintings and watercolors displayed on the paneled walls. Max stood close by, studying her.

The drive to the industrial park area north of downtown Kansas City had given Max the chance to get the Cold Case Squad up to speed on events from the past twenty-four hours. He'd dropped off the party-store recording device and the sick threat buried inside it at the precinct with Trent to see if the lab could get anything useful off the water-soaked items. Liv and her fiancé, Gabe Knight, who thought he recognized the society event in the photo with the young man Rosie had ID'd, were using his connections at the *Kansas City Journal* to track down a name. Trent had given the information about the dark green truck cruising Rosie's neighborhood to the team's information guru, Katie Rinaldi. If anyone could track down the owner of a truck with no license plate or VIN number, it was Katie and her magic computer tricks.

Right now, Max was playing a waiting game—his least favorite part of police work. Waiting for information from his team, waiting for the appointment that was running late…waiting for these feelings he had for Rosie to start making sense.

He'd been with a few women most of the world would consider prettier, and certainly more outgoing and daring than Rosie. But this was more than a pickup in a bar—a one-night stand before he moved on in the bright light of day. This was more than repaying a debt he owed an Army pilot he'd never met, more than an assignment Lieutenant Rafferty-Taylor had given him. Whatever was happening inside him, it was even more than doing for her what he hadn't been able to do for Jimmy. Whatever was going on between him and Rosie Posy was complicated and messy, unlike any sort of relationship he'd toyed with before.

Sure, her needy grabs and shy kisses could turn him inside out. A man could lose himself in her cool eyes and the warm scent of her hair. They'd talked. She'd listened. *He'd* listened. When the hell had that ever happened? He was no lothario, but her responses to his touch, whether it was a drunken kiss or a platonic cuddle, made him feel powerful, male—as if he might just be a decent catch for the right woman, after all. But how could a woman who was so wrong for a guy like him ever be the right one?

And since when did he get so philosophical about a woman or wanting to understand his feelings, anyway?

He had a job to do. Period. HUA. He wasn't going to let any distracting emotions cloud his judgment or get in the way of solving this murder again.

In a few long strides, Max caught up to Rosie. She seemed to like these paintings of farms and fruit and people he didn't know, hanging in gaudy gold and heavy wood frames that seemed more about showing off how much money Endicott Global made in a year rather than the art itself. Or maybe Rosie was just more capable of being patient and feigning interest than he'd ever be.

She'd stopped in front of a life-size oil painting of a white-haired man with a wizened face, standing in front of a fancy marble mantel. The old geezer's posture was surprisingly straight, which made Max think the guy was former military. But with his pin-striped suit, and thumb tucked into the watch pocket of his paisley vest, Max got the idea that the guy was more of a politician or businessman than anybody who'd gotten his hands dirty down in the trenches.

"He looks important," Rosie said, staring up at the painting.

Nope, he wasn't any good at pretending to be interested in something he wasn't. He went for prettier works of art himself. Like the woman draped over his randy body when he'd woken up this morning. He reached over and brushed a curling copper tendril off her cheek. She shivered when his fingertip circled around her ear. Yep, this lady was more responsive to his touch than she probably ought to be. "Why do you wear your hair like this? Don't tell me it's in deference to the summer heat."

She shrugged and moved a step beyond his reach. "It keeps my naturally wavy hair under control."

"You'd turn more heads if you lost a little bit of that control."

"I'm not interested in turning heads. I've been in the spotlight far more than I ever wanted to be. I already have bright red hair and pasty white skin." Warm copper silk and unblemished alabaster that was finer than the marble in that pretentious painting was a more accurate description in his mind. "It's calmer, easier to get through life, to be more subdued or conservative—whatever you want to call it—and not draw attention to myself."

"That's Bratcher's doing, not yours."

Rosie swiveled her gaze up to him. "That makes you angry?"

"Yeah. He's been dead six years. It pisses me off that that man can still hurt you."

"Wearing my hair in a bun hurts me?"

"Thinking you've got to have a certain look or act a certain way or else somebody's going to hurt you. Being afraid like that isn't right." He tugged at the tendril that had sprung back onto her cheek. "Be yourself. Tell the world what you want and go for it. I think there's some fire hiding under that ladylike facade of yours. Wear your hair down and loose if that's the way you like it, or shave it off in a buzz cut—which I hope like hell isn't what you really want."

"Max. Your language," she chided in a whisper, glancing over at the receptionist at the main desk. "We're in a public place."

Instead of apologizing, he fingered the top button of her blue-and-white dress. "Unhook a few of these. Good grief, woman, it's ninety-three degrees out there and it isn't even noon yet."

She swatted his hand away. "No."

His resentment of Richard Bratcher quickly gave way to a lopsided grin. "Told you there was fire in there."

And then he thought of the real reason she wore those high-necked dresses and his mood shifted again, raising her concern. "What is it?"

"Those scars are badges of honor. You survived. That takes real strength." Jimmy Stecher's worst wounds were far less visible. "I'd bet money you've got some form of PTSD, just like Jimmy did. I think of all the pain and guilt and fear Jimmy kept locked up inside him. Maybe if he hadn't believed he was all alone...if he'd known he could rail at me or talk or whatever he needed, I'd have been there for him. He shouldn't have tried to control every little thing. Clearly, he couldn't handle the pressure. No one can."

"Max. I'm not going to kill myself." Her soft voice pierced the heavy thoughts that had blurred his vision. She brushed her fingers against his, down at his thigh. "I've seen a therapist. I'm coping. Besides, I'm not alone. You're with me."

He turned his hand and captured hers in a solid grip. "Good. You're growing on me, Rosie. I'd hate to finally figure you out one day and then lose..."

Ah, hell. Max's thoughts all rolled together in a jumble. Lose what? Her? After just a few days, he wouldn't do anything so dumb as...anything that felt so right as... He'd fallen for Rosie March.

Max pulled his hand away and stuffed it into the back pocket of his jeans. Well, of course he had. When had he ever done anything the easy way? This was sure to come back and bite him in the butt. Because Rosie

March probably had no plans to ever fall in love again, and certainly not with a boorish, potty-mouthed tough guy like him.

Perhaps mistaking the source of his uncomfortable silence, Rosie changed the conversation to a more neutral topic. She pointed to the white-haired man in the painting. "Who do you think this is?"

The tapping of high heels on the marble flooring thankfully interrupted them. Dr. Hillary Wells walked up. "That is Dr. Lloyd Endicott. The founder of our company." Although Max recognized the older woman from the computer screen at the Cold Case Squad meeting, she was taller than he'd imagined. Her short, dark hair and high cheekbones were even more striking in person. She wore a pricey skirt and blouse beneath her stark white lab coat and, as Max remembered the preferential treatment from the meeting, he wasn't surprised that she extended her hand to Rosie first. "Hi. I'm Dr. Hillary Wells. You're here for an appointment?"

"Yes," Rosie answered.

He flashed his badge before shaking her hand. "Max Krolikowski, KCPD. This is my associate, Miss March."

Hillary gestured to the double doors behind the receptionist's desk, and they fell into step beside her. "Come into my office. I apologize for running late. Even though I'm overseeing the entire company now, I still like to keep my hand in the lab where I started—before Dr. Endicott discovered my talents and promoted me. Keeps a girl humble, you know. I was following up on some experiment results. If I'm recommending to the board that they up funding for a new product line, I want to make sure I know what I'm talking about."

After ordering coffee from her assistant and showing Rosie and Max to two guest chairs, she hung up her lab coat and pulled on a jacket that matched her skirt, instantly switching from scientist to CEO. She came back to her desk and opened a tub of hand cream. As she rubbed the cream into her skin, she pointed to the door, indicating the portrait of the distinguished gentleman Rosemary had asked about. "Lloyd started his research in a small lab not far from our location. Brilliant man. He developed a viable oral chemotherapy treatment with minimal side effects. A dozen patents later, he had multiple labs doing the research for him, he was building production facilities around the world, and Endicott Global went public." She sat in her chair behind the desk, her tone growing wistful. "The man died a billionaire, but he was always happiest puttering around in the lab."

"He sounds like a father figure to you," Rosie suggested.

"Very much so," Hillary agreed. "He was certainly a mentor of mine. We worked closely together for a number of years. I suppose that's why he handpicked me to succeed him. He had no children of his own and had been a widower for some time."

"I was close to my father, too. You must miss him."

"I do. Lloyd was an elderly man, but he was always young at heart." Her assistant brought them each a coffee and slipped out as quietly as he'd come in. Dr. Wells took a few moments to drink a sip and compose herself. "He was taken from us far too soon. Terrible car accident."

Rosie cradled her mug in her lap, probably feeling real empathy for the other woman, or maybe just thinking about how much she missed her own dad. "I'm so sorry."

"Thank you." Hillary swallowed another sip, then set her mug aside. She grew more businesslike and turned her attention to Max. "Now. How may I help you, Detective? You're following up on the report KCPD sent me?"

"Yes, ma'am." Hopefully, he'd be able to uncover a more useful puzzle piece here. "The Richard Bratcher case? The ME found a toxic amount of RUD-317, a drug your company produces, in his system. Can you tell us about it?"

Dr. Wells picked up a pair of reading glasses and opened a folder on her desk to skim the file. "Ah, yes. After reading your ME's report, I asked my assistant to pull the pharmaceutical file. So what are your questions about the drug?"

Rosie moved to the edge of her seat and set her coffee mug on the desk. "You keep calling it a drug. But it poisoned Richard. Surely, it's not still on the market."

"RUD-317 is used for the treatment of certain cancers. It targets and reduces malignant tumor growth. In some applications it eradicates the cancerous growth completely. In others, it contains the malignancy." Dr. Wells thumbed through her file and pulled out a thick set of papers stapled together. "Six years ago it was brand-new on the market. These are the drug trials immediately preceding that time to tell us who had access to RUD-317 outside of the lab. Our staff, of course, is all bonded, with signed confidentiality agreements. It would be impossible for one of them to get the drug out of the lab. Every shift goes through a security check when they leave."

Max bit down on the urge to argue her point. Nothing was impossible if you knew the right person and had the right leverage.

"Richard was never sick a day in his life. If he had cancer, he never told me." Was that distress he heard in Rosie's voice? Did she really care that that monster might have been battling cancer?

"You knew Mr. Bratcher personally?"

"Yes."

"Not every patient chooses to share with his loved ones when he has a serious illness."

Rosie sank back in her chair, her confusion and unease with this conversation making her press her pretty mouth into a grim line and her eye focus drop to that self-conscious, don't-notice-me level she used as a defense mechanism.

Max reached across the space between their chairs to squeeze her hand. When that gray gaze darted over to meet his, he winked, silently encouraging her not to give up the fight. Then he released her and turned his attention back to Dr. Wells. "If you read the ME's report again, Doctor, you'll see he wasn't being treated with the drug. Bratcher wasn't sick." Not physically sick, at any rate. "Either he had access to the drug himself, or someone on your list there had a motive for killing him."

The dark-haired CEO sat up ramrod straight, clearly displeased with him questioning her authority. She held up the packet of paper. "All I can tell you is that there is a Bratcher in this study. He could have been part of the placebo group, or he could have been a legitimate patient who was cured and continued to use the drug against our advisement."

Dr. Wells set the packet down, rested her elbows on top of it and steepled her fingers. Here it came. The lecture telling Max that he, the Cold Case Squad and ME's office had to be wrong. Because Dr. High-and-Mighty there was always right.

"Our report, in conjunction with the ME's autopsy, indicates that your Mr. Bratcher had consumed a far bigger dose than recommended, or multiple doses over a short period of time. There was a huge quantity of RUD-317 in his system. More than enough to trigger the convulsions, aspiration of stomach contents and suffocation that led to his death." She sat back in her chair, blithely unaware or uncaring of how the gruesome details surrounding Bratcher's death made Rosie go pale. "If Mr. Bratcher was murdered, then you have to prove how all that medication got into his system. Someone could have opened the capsules and slipped the RUD-317 into his food or drink, or replaced some other medication he regularly took without his knowledge. But unless you can prove any of that, all you have is a drug overdose, and Endicott Global is not responsible."

Max pushed to his feet. This interview was done. Dr. Wells had gone CEO on them, more interested in protecting her company and its profits from a potential lawsuit than in helping them solve a murder.

Max thanked her for the coffee and little else. "I'll need a list of all the patients in that clinical trial, and any staff, researchers or salespeople who would have had access to the drug six years ago. Maybe one of them had a grudge against Bratcher. It could be a disgruntled client, or somebody he took for a lot of money."

Dr. Wells closed the file and stood, also. "I'll have my assistant forward the staff contacts later today. Patient names are confidential, however. You'll need a warrant for me to share that."

"My lieutenant's already working on it."

"Then as soon as my office receives it, I'll get you a list of everyone who had contact with the drug."

Max was ready to leave, but Rosie was a class act all the way. "Thank you for your time, Dr. Wells."

"Glad to help." The CEO followed Max and Rosie to the door. "Detective Krolikowski, I can't believe that anyone employed by Endicott Global or its affiliates would abuse our drugs and knowingly hurt someone.

We take too much pride in our work, in our mission to save lives."

"Nonetheless, I want that list."

"Very well." She caught the door before Max could close it behind them and extended her hand to Rosie again. "Rosemary? Perhaps I'll see you at one of the museum's upcoming fund-raisers. I sit on the city's cultural arts board. We're always looking for new donors to support the arts in Kansas City."

Rosie shook the doctor's hand and nodded her thanks to the invitation. But when he would have expected her to quickly pull away, Rosie continued to hold on for an awkward length of time. What was that redhead up to?

"Dr. Wells, did you have access to RUD-317 six years ago?"

The two women locked gazes. To her brave credit, Rosie wasn't the first one to look away. Hillary ended the handshake and gave the door a nudge, herding them out. "Of course I did. I helped Lloyd create it. But I never even met your Mr. Bratcher. Why on earth would I want to kill him?"

The door snapped firmly shut in their faces. Suddenly, Dr. Wells's assistant was there to walk them to the elevator. Max glanced down at Rosie. "I guess our meeting's over."

Once the elevator doors closed behind them and they were alone, Max sat back against the railing and asked, "What was that handshake thing about?"

"I can't be certain. Maybe it's a woman's intuition, or perhaps an old memory is trying to surface."

"I need a little more to follow what you're getting at."

She thrust her right hand at his face. "Smell that."

"Whoa." Max grinned and ducked to one side to avoid an accidental punch to the chin. But he caught a whiff of what Rosie was talking about. He laced his fingers together with hers and drew her hand to his nose again. He breathed in the floral scent of Hillary Wells's hand cream. "You said you smelled perfume on the sheets in Bratcher's hotel room that day."

Rosie nodded. "I just assumed it was Charleen Grimes who'd spent the night with Richard. But maybe there was someone else there, a different woman." She pulled her hand away and wrapped it around the strap of her purse. She leaned against the back wall beside him. "Six years is a long time to try to pinpoint an exact scent, and it's probably not anything that could help you make an arrest—"

"But it's another potential piece of the puzzle."

Chapter Ten

Rosemary followed Max off the elevator onto the top floor that housed the office suites of Howard's law firm. The day had been a long one. She was hungry for dinner. She'd love a long swim to ease the tension from her muscles. Duchess and Trixie were probably dancing around the house to be let out to do their business. She was done talking to people who wouldn't give her straight answers.

And ever since the idea of Otis Dinkle spying on her had been put into her head, she'd felt as though someone had been following her all day as Max carted her from interview to interview—keeping her in sight, keeping her safe. Max assured her they were gathering useful clues, expanding KCPD's list of suspects and crossing others off the list who either had an alibi or lacked a motive to kill Richard and threaten her.

More than anything, she wanted to go home to her quiet little house and be surrounded by her parents' things and her beloved pets. Maybe she and Max would get to talk. Maybe he'd see the chance to steal another kiss and take it. And maybe, if her scars and the self-confidence that sometimes failed her hadn't been too much of a turnoff, he'd offer another night in his sheltering arms and she'd know a second night of blissful sleep. He'd said she had to be bold and ask for what she wanted—that he was no good at reading between the lines and guessing. Well, what she wanted was to go home. With him.

But when she opened her mouth to say as much, Charleen Grimes unfolded her long legs from the couch in the center of the room and crossed the floor in her three-inch heels.

"That's Charleen Grimes," she whispered, instead.

"The mistress?" Max clarified. Rosemary would have turned around, gone back downstairs and walked home if Max's hand hadn't been at her back, drawing her forward beside him. He dipped his face beside her ear and whispered, "The woman needs some meat on her bones. Your ex must have had a thing for making love to sticks." He turned his fingers to pat the swell of Rosie's hip. "I'll take a real woman any day."

"Bless you, Max." Rosie's chin lifted a little higher at the praise. "Good evening, Charleen."

"Well, if it isn't the little murderess herself."

Howard stepped out of his office at the end of the hallway and hurried to join them. "Charleen, you are way out of line." He snapped his fingers to the receptionist for her to notify Mr. Austin that his client had arrived for her KCPD interview. "Remember our conversation about slandering my client."

"*I'm* out of line?" She ran her painted nails along the lapel of her blue silk jacket. "Which one of us is here to be questioned as a murder suspect?" Charleen's blue eyes narrowed. "You and your nine million dollars took Richard from me. I will never forgive you."

A sad realization washed over Rosemary. "You really loved him, didn't you?"

"A lot more than you ever did."

Most certainly. "Did you love him so much that you'd rather see him dead than with anybody else?"

"How dare you, you little mouse. I'm the only one who wants justice for Richard. All you're concerned about is saving your own skin."

"Justice?" Rosie's blood turned to ice in her veins. How many of those crude threats had mentioned justice for Richard? Were Charleen's words a horrid coincidence? A slip of the tongue? Or was there something much more ominous and far too familiar in the accusation?

Charleen took another step and Max's hand shot between them to keep the woman from coming any closer. "Stay with me, Rosie." His blue eyes met hers with a pinpoint focus, probably checking to make sure she didn't slip into another one of those trancelike states where she was paralyzed with fear. She blinked, nodded, silently reassured him she wasn't so upset by the other woman's words that she couldn't function. "Maybe I'd better handle this interview on my own," he suggested.

Howard was instantly at Rosemary's side. "Perhaps so, Detective. I don't know why you have her out doing your job."

Max's shoulders came back at the irritation in Howard's voice. Thankfully, he didn't take the bait and continue the argument. "Just get her someplace safe for twenty or thirty minutes, okay?"

"My pleasure." Howard's cool hand cupped her elbow, pulling her away from Max. "You're welcome to wait in my office while your friend conducts his business."

"Thanks." While Howard tucked Rosemary's hand into the crook of his elbow and led her to his back corner office, Max escorted Charleen in the opposite direction to Mr. Austin's suite at the end of the hallway.

"What's that perfume you're wearing?" he asked. "It's sexy as all get-out."

"Don't try to charm me, Detective Krolikowski. You haven't got the chops for it."

The man wasn't as clueless as he pretended to be. "So I can't buy that scent for my girlfriend?"

Charleen stopped and leveled a glare at Rosemary. "No."

Girlfriend? Was that part of his investigative bag of tricks to get a suspect talking—using her as the proverbial burr that could get Charleen agitated underneath her saddle? Or could there be a grain of truth in that one word? Rosemary's pulse did a funny little pitter-patter at the hope that he might be halfway serious about claiming her as his.

But Charleen's hateful gaze was a painful reminder that Rosemary needed this part of her life to be over. Charleen pouted her ruby-red lips into a smile and linked her arm through Max's, figuratively taking from Rosemary what Charleen claimed Rosemary had taken from her. The tall blonde sashayed her hip into Max's as their voices faded down the long hallway, and Rosie's nostrils flared with an emotion that was far closer to feeling possessive about Max than feeling inadequate lined up next to a woman whose beauty she couldn't match. "It's a personal scent, designed especially for me. Back in my modeling days—"

"Don't let her get to you. Charleen's a bitter, vindictive woman." Howard closed the outer office door and followed Rosemary into his private office, locking the door behind him. Was he that worried about the tall blonde causing a scene that would upset her? "In her own way, I think she truly loved Richard. But she didn't handle all the other women and one-night stands as well as you did."

Rosemary's laugh held little humor. "I don't think I handled his cheating well at all." She dropped her purse into one of the guest chairs and sat in the other, leaning back and closing her weary eyes. "It does devastating things to a woman's ego and ability to trust when she finds out she's not enough for her man."

"Are you enough for Krolikowski?"

Her eyes fluttered open at the unexpected question. "Excuse me?"

Howard shrugged and crossed to the wet bar in the corner. "I couldn't help but notice how chummy the two of you have gotten these past few days."

She sat up straighter. "We're working together. I finally have someone at KCPD treating me like the victim, not a prime suspect."

"Seemed friendlier than that to me." He held up a mug. "Coffee?"

"Please."

Friendlier? Certainly Max had become important to her these past few days. He'd been the only one to believe that the threats against her were real and not some scam to gain sympathy or divert attention onto another suspect in KCPD's Cold Case Squad investigation. Okay, so it had taken a little blackmail in the form of appealing to his military roots to finally get him to listen. But once he saw the damage to her front porch and read the notes, he believed. He protected. He upset her small, familiar world in frightening, exciting ways, and yet he made her feel safe. So, yes, they'd become friends—an opposites attracting, differences complementing each other kind of thing. But something in her heart wanted them to be much more.

Once this case was solved, however—assuming they could piece all the old secrets together to complete the puzzle and finally solve Richard's murder—would she be enough to interest a man like Max? Would there be other reasons he might want to remain a part of her life?

"Here you go." Howard handed her a mug of the steaming brew and took a seat on the corner of his desk, facing her. He swallowed a drink, then splayed his fingers and looked at his hand before rubbing his knuckles against the leg of his lightweight wool slacks. "Is he making any progress? Getting the job done?"

Rosemary cradled the warm mug between her hands. "You know how important it is to me to clear my name. It's the only way to convince Charleen and my neighbors and the rest of the world that I didn't get away with murder. Maybe I could get a job teaching again. Max is helping change people's opinion of me. He's expanded the list of suspects so that my name's not the only one on it for a change. He makes it more comfortable for me to interact with people." She shook her head. "I still can't claim that it's easy—my trust issues make it hard to socialize for long with big groups or certain people, of course—but he makes it easier to try."

"Good for him." Howard set his mug on the desk and scratched at a trio of welts on his left hand. "I made life easier for you, too, if you remember. I kept you from ever being formally charged for Richard's murder by reminding the police they didn't have enough evidence to take the case to the DA for prosecution."

"I appreciate that, Howard. I don't know how I would have gotten through the last six years without you. You were so helpful with Stephen's case, too." When she saw how badly the red marks were irritating him, she set her mug on the desk, too, and got up to cradle his big hand between hers. "Where did you get those nasty scratches? I think you need some hydrocortisone or calamine…"

Puncture wounds. A dermatitis reaction to a foreign substance, like leaf sap or pollen.

Rosemary released his hand and backed away as if his skin had burned her. He'd grappled with a hawthorn bush. "You?"

The dark eyes looking back at her were anything but friendly, patient or professional. That hard, cold, disappointed look was a lot like…his brother's.

"The canned laughter was a little theatrical, but that scream of yours was worth every penny."

Rosie glanced at the door. Did she need to run? Would he really hurt her? "I thought you were my friend."

Howard's voice was laced with contempt. "And I thought you were smart."

Rosie dropped her chin and shivered. So talking was out. Ingrained habits from an abusive relationship were hard to break. She felt herself tensing, bracing, preparing herself for whatever cruel words would spew from his mouth. She inched away as the dimensions of the locked room closed in on her.

He'd trapped her.

Just like his brother had.

Only, she wasn't alone in her house with a dangerously unpredictable man. She wasn't alone at all. Max was right down the hallway. Okay, about a hundred feet down that hallway. With at least three closed doors in between them.

Rosie's chin shot up as she shook off the crippling fears of the past. She grabbed her purse and dashed to the door.

But Howard beat her to it. Moving surprisingly fast for an older man, he planted himself between her and escape. She quickly circled behind his desk and leather chair, scanning the room for an available weapon if she needed to defend herself.

"I lost my brother because of you," Howard accused.

"I didn't kill him."

"I don't care who did. I'm just glad he's gone." He moved to the desk and Rosie backed up to the window. "He was blowing through the family fortune, ruining the firm with his indiscretions. That's why he latched on to you—for the money and respectability."

"You're not like him, Howard. Please. You were kind to Stephen. You took care of our legal and financial needs. You helped me get Richard out of my life."

"Damn right, I did. You owe me. I've been there for you every step of the way. I was patient with you and all your little idiosyncrasies." As he came around the desk, she countered his path, keeping as much distance as possible between them. The wary beat of her pulse nearly choked her. If he laid a hand on her the way Richard had… "You depend on me," he reminded her. "When you started getting those threats, when your mysterious stalker knew so many intimate details about you and Richard and said he wanted to kill you, I knew you were afraid."

"I was terrified. Why would you do that to me?"

He pounded his fist on the desk and she jumped. "So you would come to me for help. Not to some uncivilized thug of a cop. Good grief, I heard you picked him up in a bar. You're my class of people, Rosemary, not his."

"That uncivilized thug is right down the hall, Howard. I'll scream and he'll throw you in jail so fast—"

"He can't hear you through soundproofed walls. And I have a feeling Charleen won't be a very cooperative witness and that her interview will take a while. Long enough for you to come to your senses and remember who your real hero is."

Her gaze darted from the thick walls lined with books to the tenth-story window and locked door that offered her only means of escape. "I'm not that frightened mental invalid beaten down by grief and abuse anymore. The real me is coming back. Max!"

When she charged toward the door, Howard shifted direction and snatched her arm, pulling her against him and slapping his other hand over her mouth to silence her. "You won't scream, because I'll have his badge if you do."

Rosie froze in his painful grip and he moved his sweaty palm off her lips. "You'd do that? You'd ruin his career?"

Howard laughed. "It'd be easy enough. Krolikowski is already on thin ice with the department. Public drunkenness. Anger issues—"

"He's not like that—"

"—a blatant disregard for regulations and comportment. He'd probably come in here and beat me up if he could hear you. Imagine the mileage I'd get out of that with the commissioner."

She tugged against the hand on her arm. "I'd tell his superior officers the truth. You're crazy."

"Oh, *I'm* crazy? Says the thirty-something recluse who lives inside a fortress, dresses like an old maid and is afraid of her own shadow? You think they'd take the word of a murder suspect over a respected member of the court?" His moist breath spit against her ear. "Whatever you think you have with him is done. *I'm* the man you need. You're going to marry me."

Her hips butted against his desk. His thighs trapped her. "Never. You threatened to kill me, Howard."

"I would have married you and made the threats all go away. That was the plan. I wanted you so scared that you'd have to come out of that cave you hide in and turn to someone for help. And it was working until Krolikowski came along." He flattened his hand against his chest. "It was supposed to be me. For six years I've planned how we would be together. I showed you more patience than any normal man could. I set it up so that *I* was the man in your life."

"You were my friend."

"People have married for less."

"I don't love you."

"That doesn't matter. We could have a successful business partnership. I'm more mature than my brother ever was. I wouldn't make demands on you."

She lowered her chin and shook her head. "That damn money."

"Now that's hardly ladylike. Krolikowski's bad habits are rubbing off on you." He spoke to her cowed head. "I've earned you, you freak. I sided with you against my brother's memory. I was loyal to you. I did everything I could for your loser brother. Who else would have you?"

"If that's the deal you're offering, I'd rather be alone." When she zeroed in on his Italian loafers, she felt a flare of red-haired temper flooding through her. She was done being the Bratcher brothers' victim.

She brought her heel down hard on his instep and shoved her shoulder into his chest, freeing herself. Howard stumbled back into a bookshelf and she ran for the door. "Max!"

All she had to do was scream if she was in trouble, and he'd come running. No matter how many floors or doors were between them. He'd promised.

"Max!" Ignoring Howard's threat, she threw open the door.

"Your choice. His career is over. You will not leave me for him."

"I was never yours."

He cinched his hands around her waist and tossed her toward the desk. She bruised her hip against the corner, but he was there before she could scramble away, capturing her against the solid oak. "He's rough, exciting, animalistic, I bet."

"What is wrong with you?" Rosie clawed at his neck, beat at his chest. "Get your hands off me. He's going to arrest you."

Howard bent her back over the desk, his thigh sliding between hers. She slapped at the hand that skimmed her breast. "Is that how you like it? Rough? I don't have to be a gentleman. All these years I thought that was what you wanted. But I could send you a few more love notes if you want."

"Get. Off. Me." Her shoulder hit a coffee mug, sloshing the hot liquid onto her arm. Forget the Colonel's empty Army pistol. She reached up, closed her hand around the mug and tossed the hot liquid in his face. She wasn't the only one screaming when she ran for the door. "Max!"

But she'd only riled the beast. Before she made it to the door, Howard caught her and shoved her up against the bookshelf. He closed his hands around her neck in a choke hold that cut off her voice and her breath and stuck his red, scalded face near hers. "I always wondered what it was like when Richard got rough with you."

Rosie twisted, gouged, kicked. She tried to suck in a breath, but the sound gurgled in her throat. Her chest constricted. Ached. Howard had lost it. There was no reasoning with him now.

"Rosie!" A fist pounded on the locked door.

Maybe Howard hadn't heard the same angry shout she had. He tightened his grip around her neck. "There *is* a little rush to this, isn't there? I can feel the pulse points beneath my thumbs. Does it hurt? Do you feel like doing what I ask now?"

Pound. Pound. "Rosie!"

She scratched at his injured hand, but she was getting weak. She needed air. White dots floated across her vision and the room tilted.

"If you don't say yes to me, I'll make sure you go away for Richard's murder. I know enough details about your relationship to make you look guilty as sin. I'll even defend you…and, sadly, lose your case." He nuzzled her ear. "What will it be? Boyfriend or me? Prison? Or marri—"

The frame around the door splintered and the heavy oak swung open beside her. Max rammed Howard like a linebacker, tearing his grip off Rosie, freeing her. The two men flew across the desk and Rosie collapsed to her knees. She sucked in a deep breath that scratched her throat and filled her deprived lungs with precious oxygen. A chair toppled, another broke.

"Max." Her voice came out in a hoarse croak. His fist met Howard's jaw with a thud, and the attorney's head snapped back. "Max!"

"You keep your hands off her. Understand?"

Howard laughed in response, not putting up any fight. "Temper, temper, Officer. Oh, I am so reporting this. Cop Attacks Attorney."

"The attorney's a nut job." Max flipped Howard face-down on the carpet, put his knee in the man's back and cuffed him.

His grizzled jaw was tight when he reached over to touch Rosie's bruised neck and arm. "He hurt you."

"I'm okay. I'll be okay." Her voice was getting stronger. The room blossomed with color again after she'd nearly passed out. Max's blue eyes. The red blood at the corner of Howard's mouth. Rosie pushed to her feet, leaning on the shelves for support. "Howard sent those threats. It makes sense. He knew the details of my relationship with his brother. He wanted to scare me so I'd turn to him. Fall for him, maybe." Howard giggled like a child as Max helped him into a chair. She averted her gaze from those crazy cold eyes and looked to the man who had saved her. Again. "I turned to you, instead."

"You're sure you're okay?" He palmed the back of her neck and pulled her onto her toes for a quick, hard kiss that left her a little breathless again. His chest expanded in quick, deep inhales after the brief fight and sprint down the hallway. "Thank God you can scream, woman. I don't want to think about what could have happened if I'd been even a few seconds late. I had the receptionist call 9-1-1. Uniformed officers should be here any minute."

In the meantime, Rosie didn't complain when he hooked his arm around her shoulders and pulled her against him. She was quickly learning that this was where she felt the safest. "He was no better than Richard. How do I keep attracting these winners?" she added, the sarcasm clear, even in her husky tone.

Max went quiet for a few seconds, then covered the silence with a wry little laugh. "I'll throw his butt in jail for a very long time."

But Rosie tugged on his shirt, stopping him midreport. "Howard didn't kill Richard. He's hardly a perfume kind of guy. And how would he get his hands on RUD-317?"

"He could be the Bratcher in that pharmaceutical trial Dr. Wells is holding on to." He tapped the shoulder of the curiously subdued man sitting on his cuffed hands. "Hey. How about it, Bratcher?"

Howard grew more subdued as the manic thrill he'd discovered when he'd been choking her subsided. She could tell he was thinking more like a lawyer than the man with the violent obsession who'd brought a baseball bat and terror to her home. "I don't know what you're talking about."

"Can I at least book him for making terroristic threats to you?"

"Be my guest." Rosie nodded, wishing she felt more relief at finally identifying the man who'd preyed on her darkest fears.

Max didn't seem to think this was over yet, either. "We've got two perps—Howie here and the woman who killed his brother six years ago. Ah, hell." Max pulled her toward the broken door to look out into the lobby but stopped when he realized he'd be leaving Howard unguarded if he went any farther. "Charleen Grimes just left with her attorney." He pulled out his cell and punched in a number. "I'm calling the team. We're gonna end this thing."

MAX LEANED AGAINST the Chevelle's front fender while Rosie finished giving her statement to Olivia Watson. He nodded to Jim Parker, walking past with a large evidence bag holding the black sweatshirt hoodie with the torn sleeve he'd found in the trunk of Howard Bratcher's car.

A car. Why couldn't the attorney drive a fancy green

pickup truck like the one Arlene Dinkle had reported seeing in the neighborhood? Now that would make the puzzle come together all neat and pretty. But Bratcher didn't own a truck. Maybe it was nothing but coincidence that an unidentified vehicle would show up in the same time frame as each of Bratcher's visits to Rosie's house. But, like most of the cops he knew, Max didn't like coincidences. If a good cop looked hard enough, there was almost always a rational explanation out there somewhere. Did the green truck mean someone else was watching Rosie's house? Their killer, perhaps? Or had Arlene made the whole thing up?

The truck wasn't the only piece to the puzzle that was bothering him. The summer night was still plenty warm, but Rosie kept running her hands up and down her bare arms as she and Liv talked over by Liv's SUV, as though she had a chill she just couldn't shake. Max wanted to put his hands there and warm her up. No, what he really wanted was to get her out of here—away from the flashing lights and endless questions and Howard Bratcher locked in the back of Trent's SUV to someplace quiet where they could be alone. Where he could hold her long enough to chase away that chill.

"Did you send a unit to keep an eye on Charleen Grimes?"

Max pulled away from the car at the approach of his lieutenant, Ginny Rafferty-Taylor, straightening to a civilian version of attention as his team leader came up beside him. "Yes, ma'am. If she goes anywhere besides home or her shop, or does anything suspicious, we'll know about it."

"In the meantime, we got a copy of that list of drug test patients and research and production staff from Endicott Global. Katie's going over it with a fine-tooth comb to see if Charleen's name pops—or any other family or business associate who could have gotten her access to the drug." The lieutenant tucked her short, silvery-blond hair behind her ears and leaned her hips back against the car the way he had a moment earlier. "You did good work today, Max."

He slid his fingers into the back pockets of his jeans and shrugged his frustration. "I haven't solved our case yet."

"Take the compliment. We've been working this murder for six years now. This is the first forward progress we've made in almost that long." She nodded toward the conversation wrapping up near the building's front door. "Miss March filled me in on the threats Howard Bratcher made against your badge, too. Don't worry. I've got your back. I didn't settle for just anybody on my squad. You were all handpicked for your various expertise."

"I gave Bratcher a fat lip." He eyed the purple bruises already appearing on Rosie's pale skin as she paused beneath a streetlight before crossing the street to join them. He felt his fingers curling into fists again. Was that supposed to be his area of expertise? Laying a guy out flat for nearly squeezing the life out of a woman? "I suppose I have an anger management class in my future?"

"You were protecting someone you care about." The lieutenant leaned in and whispered, "Besides, didn't I ever tell you I have a soft spot for big guys who are good with their hands?"

"No."

She squeezed his arm before walking away to her car. "You should meet my husband sometime."

Max chuckled. "Yes, ma'am."

Rosie exchanged good-nights with the lieutenant before joining Max at the car.

"Cold?" Max brushed his hands over the goose bumps dotting her arms.

She shook her head and shivered anew. "Confused, maybe. Disappointed in my inability to function out in the real world."

"That's harsh."

"Tonight made me feel like I'm not meant to be anything more than a prize to be stolen or swindled. Howard was so angry. Just like Richard." She raised her gaze to his. "Why couldn't I see it? Why did I think Howard was my friend?"

"Because you've got a heart, Rosie March." He opened the car door and pulled his black leather jacket from the backseat to drape around her shoulders. "Here. I think it's human nature to trust people, to want to see the best in them. Especially if that's the way they want you to see them. Most people keep their deepest thoughts and insecurities and shortcomings hidden. Good people and bad." He freed a couple of tendrils from the collar of the jacket. "I'm glad the bad things in this world haven't warped you like me yet."

She linked her fingers with his and held on when he would have pulled away. "I'm always going to believe you're a good guy, Max. Thank you. I can never repay you for listening to me, believing me. Jimmy would have been proud of you for standing by me and helping me get Howard out of my life."

"Just promise me if you meet anyone else named Bratcher, you'll run the other way instead of making friends."

At last, she smiled. "I promise." She braced her free hand against his chest and stretched up to kiss his cheek. "You did great, Sergeant. Thank you."

"Why does that sound like goodbye?" He tugged on

her fingers and led her around to the passenger seat. "I live in your basement."

"But I thought—with Howard under arrest…"

This mission wasn't over yet, as far as he was concerned. "There's still a killer out there I'm looking for. And we've stirred up enough of a hornet's nest today that I'm not letting you out of my sight until we identify the woman who was in Bratcher's bedroom that night and I can close my case." He opened the car door for her to get in. "Buckle up."

Her smile eased his concern a fraction. "Yes, sir."

By the time he'd circled back to the driver's side, Trent was jogging up to meet him. "Hey, brother."

"What is it, junior?"

His partner handed him a DMV printout of Glasses Guy, the man Rosie had ID'd from the society page photo. "Meet Leland Asher's nephew, Matthew."

"Son of a gun." He handed the printout over to Rosie. "Look familiar?"

"That's him. Is he part of his uncle's organization?" She handed the paper back. "What's his connection to me?"

"It may not mean anything. We can't tie him to any criminal wrongdoing," Trent answered. "But he does visit his uncle in prison."

"So he could be a courier for getting his uncle's messages in or out of Jeff City." Max quickly skimmed the rest of the information on the page and muttered a curse. Matt Asher drove a Chrysler sedan, not a green pickup. "So he doesn't have a connection to the Bratchers, either."

Trent shook his head. "He's got an alibi for most of the nights the stalker was at Rosie's house."

"Which is?"

"Believe it or not—therapy. He sees a clinical psychologist. I'm guessin' he's got family issues. We'll keep an eye on him to see if any messages are passed between him and Uncle Leland when he visits him in prison. But right now, we've got nothing on him. We can't touch him. Plus, the kid's only twenty-two. He was barely old enough to drive when Bratcher was murdered."

Max looked up to his partner and thanked him.

"Not a problem. Anything else?"

"Yeah. Send somebody over to watch Rosie's house tonight. I need some solid shut-eye."

Trent waved to Rosie to reassure her, as well. "I'll be there myself as soon as I process Bratcher."

"I owe ya."

"Don't worry, brother. I'll collect."

MAX AND THE DOGS heard the quiet whimpering over the rainfall sounds of the shower coming through the bathroom door. He didn't know about Duchess and Trixie, but he wasn't sure how long he could stand that heartbreaking little mewl before he busted down another door to get inside and do something about it.

The house couldn't be locked up any tighter. He had his Glock strapped to his belt. The blinds throughout the house were drawn to dissuade the Dinkles' and anyone else's curiosity about the copper-haired recluse, and he knew Trent was parked in his truck out in the driveway tonight. So no way had anyone gotten past all those lines of defense to hurt her.

Still… He knocked softly at the door. "Rosie? Honey, are you okay?"

"Just a minute." Although he could easily jimmy the old door lock, he scrubbed his hand over his stubbled jaw, waiting impatiently through some sniffling and shuffling noises. Then the running water stopped.

A few seconds later, the latch turned and the door opened.

"You girls, stay," he ordered. Not waiting for an invitation, he slipped inside the white-and-black-tiled bathroom and closed the door behind him.

"What is it?" Rosie asked, clutching the lime-green towel that hung from the scalloped swells of her breasts down to the top of her thighs. His pulse rate kicked up in hungry awareness, so he wisely hung back by the door. "Is something wrong?"

"I hope not." Ignoring the long, wavy strands of wet copper that clung to her shoulders and sent tiny rivulets of water down her arms and into the shadowy cleft between her breasts, Max focused on the ugly marks marring the skin around her neck. He brushed his fingers across the blue-and-violet bruises there. "Are you in pain? Is your throat still sore? The paramedic said that gargling would help." He ran through the checklist of possible complications related to her assault. "Are you having any trouble breathing or swallowing? Maybe I should have run you to the ER instead of bringing you home."

She offered him an unconvincing smile. "I'm okay. I'm sore. But the hot water helps."

So, no physical pain. That would have been easier to deal with. With the pad of his thumb, he wiped away a tear that lingered on her cheek. "And this?"

She turned her head and pressed a kiss into his palm. "You once said that I could tell you anything, that you'd listen."

"That's right." He made a valiant effort to avert his gaze from all that creamy bare skin peeking out above and below the edges of the towel. But the burn scars and bruises at her neck were a sobering reminder to his traitorous body that she wanted to have a serious conversation here. "Is everything okay?"

"You said I should look you in the eye and ask for what I want." She tilted those soft gray eyes to his and he lost his heart to her a little more. "I want you to stay."

"I wasn't planning on going back to the basement."

"No. I'm not saying this right." Her gaze dropped to his chin, then bounced right back. "Stay here. With me."

The walls of restraint that were keeping his libido in check took a serious hit. But he didn't want to misunderstand. "Honey, don't tease a man. Are you asking me to take you to bed?"

She nodded and reached up to trace her fingers along the line of his jaw, waking dozens of very interested nerve endings there. "I want to do more than cuddle tonight, Sergeant. I want to feel like a normal, desirable woman. I want to feel good hands, safe hands...*your* hands on me. I want to erase—"

"I get the message." Max already had her in his arms. His mouth was on hers, his tongue driving inside to claim her taste for his own. He drove her back against the tile wall, imprinting her curves against his harder body. Her hands slid up to his face and hair and his slid down to grasp her hips and pull them into the cradle of his thighs.

His jeans felt thick. His shirt was an impediment. And that towel definitely had to go.

With their lips clinging to each other, their hands explored places that were tender and hard. Silky and soft. Cool and hot. He got his belt off and his holster safely set aside on the vanity before she reached for the zipper of his jeans.

"Not yet, honey." He caught her wrists and moved her hands to his chest, encouraging her to go after the buttons on his shirt while he shucked out of his boots and jeans.

By the time he was as naked as she was and he'd fished a condom out of his wallet, her lips had discovered the taut, eager nipples of his chest and a bundle of nerves behind his left ear. He'd feasted on her lips and filled his hands with the heavy weight of her breasts. He tongued his way from one curve to the next, stopping only to turn the shower back on and adjust the temperature to a soothing warmth before he palmed the back of her thighs and lifted her into the shower with him.

"Max," she gasped, her thighs clenching when the water first hit her skin.

"Easy, honey." He pulled her into the heat of his body and switched positions, taking the brunt of the spray on his back. "I want to make this as good for you as I can."

Then he grabbed the bar of soap and really went to work. She wanted to forget that Howard had touched her? That Richard had abused her? Max wanted to imprint himself all over her body. He put his hands every place he could touch—her feet, her legs, that sweet round bottom. He washed her stomach and back and arms and breasts, running the creamy soap over her beautiful skin. Then he moved the soap between her legs to wash her there.

Her thighs clenched around his hand. Her fingers dug into his shoulders. Her forehead fell against his chest. "Oh, Max. Max." She said his name, over and over, in breathless whispers against his skin. Soon, he set the soap aside. With the heat of the water and the heat of his hand pressing against her most tender flesh, he felt her tighten, quiver. And when he slipped a finger inside her, then two, she cried out his name and convulsed around his hand.

How could any man not think this brave, vibrant, responsive woman was anything but sexy and desirable?

But it wasn't enough. For either of them.

The shy siren with the beautiful body slipped her arms around his neck and pressed every decadent inch against his hot, primed body. Not even the water sluicing over his head and shoulders could come between them as she pulled her mouth down to his and asked for what she truly wanted.

"You, Max. I want you inside me. Now."

His fingers shaking with the need of his body, he reached around the shower curtain and ripped open the condom packet. All he remembered were her hands learning his body, her lips demanding kiss after kiss. He happily obliged her exploration until he could take no more.

"Now, honey."

"Yes."

He picked her up and her legs wrapped around his hips as he eased himself inside. He held his breath for a moment, filling her, expanding her warm sheath to accommodate his desire. With his strong hands holding her securely between the tile wall and his body, he began to move inside her. Slowly, at first. A thrust, a kiss. A thrust, a nibble of her ear. His lips moved lower with each thrust and she arched her back, offering him her body. He closed his mouth over the proud peak of her breast, swirled his tongue around her pearled nipple and she gasped.

His body demanded faster, harder, and hers accepted, welcomed, blossomed with his need.

The one glitch came when he pressed a kiss to the

scar on her collarbone. Her fingers tried to push his lips away. "Don't," she whispered. "They're ugly."

But Max insisted on gently kissing each mark. "Every inch of you is beautiful to me."

And then the need became too great. The rhythm between their bodies synced and moved together. The water ran, the heat consumed him. And with a final thrust that blinded him to all but the crazy, inexplicable love he had for this woman, Max poured himself out inside her.

A few minutes later, after catching their breaths and another quick rinse in the cooling shower, Rosie turned off the water. He wrapped a towel around his waist and another around her, then lifted her into his arms and carried her to bed.

He shoved a pair of bed-hog dogs onto the floor and laid her down. Max climbed in beside her, pulled the covers up over them both. Spooning his damp, spent body next to hers, he pulled Rosie to his chest, buried his nose in the sweet scent of her hair, and they drifted off into a deep, healing sleep together.

Chapter Eleven

Max awoke to a dog licking his ear and an empty pillow beside him.

A brief moment of panic—that Rosie had somehow been taken from him while he slept, with that dreadful sense of finality he'd felt the morning Jimmy hadn't shown up for their fishing weekend—roused him completely. But the panic quickly ebbed when he smelled the coffee brewing in the kitchen and heard the strains of an orchestra playing softly from another part of the house. Rosie was fine. Just an early riser, eager to get a start on a new day. Hopefully, not a woman who was having regrets about the night before.

And then there was the poodle who'd taken such a shine to him. Pushing aside Trixie's tongue, Max sat up. She switched the licking to his hand until he spared a minute to give her a tummy rub. "Really? Is this going to be a thing with you?"

He set the fuzzy morning greeter on the floor and got up to use the bathroom, retrieving his shorts and jeans and pulling them on. He tucked his holster into the back of his belt and pulled out his phone to put in a quick call to Trent to get a status report.

"Morning, sunshine," Trent teased. "How'd you sleep?"

"Better than you, I'm guessin'. Anything I need to know about?"

"Everything's quiet out here. I got a call five minutes ago from Jim. He said Charleen Grimes left her condo, drove through a coffee shop, then went to work. Apparently, they're having a big summer clearance sale at her boutique if you're lookin' for a new dress."

"No, thanks." Max shook his head and went to the kitchen to pour himself a mug of coffee. Even after a stakeout, the younger detective was too chipper in the morning for his tastes. "Anything else?"

"You need to call Katie. She's got some information you'll want to hear."

"Got it. I've got my coffee now, so you can leave. Thanks for keeping an eye on things."

"Not a problem."

Max drank half his coffee and ate a cinnamon roll that he hoped Rosie had left out for him before dialing Katie's number.

"Good morning, Max." Was everyone he knew a morning person?

"Morning, kiddo. Trent said you had something for me?"

"You bet. I tracked down a short list of dark green, extended cab pickup trucks with black trim—sold in the KC area in the past month, so it would still have dealer stickers and not a registered license plate yet."

"How short is the list?"

"Three trucks. Here's where it gets interesting."

Normally he was amused by Katie's flair for drama, but this morning he just wanted to get the info and get back to Rosie. "Tell me, sunshine."

"All three were purchased as fleet vehicles for Endicott Global."

Max opened his mouth to swear but decided Katie didn't need to hear him any more than Rosie did. But that Wells woman had lied to them with a straight face. The CEO fit two of the three puzzle pieces—she had access to the drug that killed Richard Bratcher, and a company vehicle had been spotted near Rosie's house. "You did good, kiddo. Thanks."

More awake and on guard and ready to face whatever reaction Rosie had to that steamy shower they'd shared, he sought her out and found her sitting on the braided rug in the library. He needn't have worried about her having regrets or feeling self-conscious about her beautiful body or feeling pressured to turn one night into a full-blown relationship. She jumped up from the boxes and papers she'd been sorting and hurried across the room, smiling.

The jeans she wore kind of caught him off guard. He wouldn't have thought she even owned a pair with that wardrobe of dresses she usually wore. But he couldn't help but smile back—or cling to the kiss she rose up on tiptoe to give him. "Morning, Rosie Posy."

"Max, look what I found." She hadn't pinned her hair up yet, either, which distracted him from the stationery and envelopes she juggled in her hand. "I was going through some old letters Richard had written me. I felt like I was starting a new life today so I wanted to get rid of my past. I mean I'm thinking of myself as Rosie instead of Rosemary now. I'm not afraid some creep will come to my house every night anymore. I was going to throw away all these old letters he sent me."

He put a hand up to stop the philosophical discussion he wanted to hear more about—later—and urged her to get to the point. "What did you find, Rosie?"

"This." She tossed most of the letters she held into a box, then unfolded one stamped with the Bratcher law firm name at the top. A rock settled in Max's gut. This couldn't be good. "Richard must have stuck this letter in the wrong envelope. It's to his mistress, not me."

He took the letter. "You know, for a man I've never met, I sure do dislike him."

Rosie pointed to the salutation at the top of the paper. "Look who it's written to."

Max drew in a satisfied breath as the third piece of the puzzle fell into place.

Charleen Grimes wasn't the only woman Richard had cheated with.

"We've been looking for the wrong mistress."

It was a love letter to Hillary Wells.

"I'M TIRED OF WAITING."

"Sir, I told you she was on a conference call… Sir?"

Rosie nodded to the sputtering assistant at the front desk as Max flashed his badge and marched right past him into Hillary Wells's office at the Endicott Global building.

She plowed into Max's back when he suddenly stopped. He spun around to catch her hand and keep her from tumbling, but she could see what had stopped him. The office was empty.

"Is there a back door to this room?" Max asked. "She's not here."

The assistant stepped into the office and looked around, too. He threw up his hands as if surprised to see his boss had left.

Max clapped him on the shoulder and pushed him out of his path. "Nice stall, kid. You hear from the boss lady, tell her KCPD wants to have a conversation with her."

"Yes, sir."

While they were driving down the highway, Max

alerted the Cold Case Squad that Hillary Wells was in the wind. She'd skipped out on her appointment with Max and Rosie and hadn't left her contact information with her assistant. She wasn't answering any of her phones, and, according to Katie, who'd tried to locate her via GPS, Dr. Wells's cell phone had been turned off.

"Wait a minute." Katie hesitated, probably reading something off one of her computer screens. Rosie had put Max's cell on speaker and held it up for him to speak and hear while he drove the Chevelle.

"What is it, kiddo?" Max prompted.

"It looks like she has a cabin down by Truman Lake. I've got a ping off her vehicle's smart system there."

"Give me a twenty." Once Katie gave them the cabin's location and directions to get to it, Max made his way to the south end of the city and drove over to one of Missouri's most popular recreation areas.

An hour later, after a scenic drive through the northern edge of the Missouri Ozarks, they pulled into a gravel driveway behind a dark green pickup truck.

"Son of a gun." Katie's research was right on the money. "She's here," Max announced, nodding toward the windows along the front of the cabin that had been opened to let in the warm summer breeze. He took Rosie's hand and pulled her into step beside him and they walked to the front door. "Today, maybe you'd better let me do the talking. I have a feeling the good doctor won't be such a cooperative witness this time." He knocked on the door. "KCPD. It's Detective Krolikowski, Dr. Wells. I'd like to ask you a few more questions."

When the woman didn't immediately answer, Rosie asked, "How does this work, exactly—you ask her if she killed Richard?"

Max grinned. "Well, the direct approach doesn't usually work for most suspects."

"It worked for me."

He reached over and sifted his fingers through the ponytail hanging down the back of her T-shirt. "You, Rosie March, are the exception to most rules."

After more than a minute with no response, Max knocked again. "KCPD." He motioned Rosie to stand back to the side as he pulled his weapon.

His wary posture put her on guard, too. "Do you think something's wrong?"

His shoulders lifted with a deep breath. "I hope she hasn't done anything stupid like take some of her own drugs to get out of doing prison time."

"Suicide?"

Max's jaw trembled before he knocked on the door one last time. He was thinking of his friend Jimmy. "I'm comin' in, Dr. Wells."

Rosie clung to the safety of the wall while Max turned the knob and pushed open the door.

A gunshot exploded close to Rosie's ear and Max went flying back off the front step. "Max!"

He hit the ground with a horrible thud and pulled his knees up, groaning, rolling from side to side as the front of his shirt turned red with blood.

Hillary Wells marched out of the cabin, shifted the aim of her gun at Rosie and warned her, "Don't move."

Rosie clung to the cedar planking of the cabin while Hillary picked up Max's weapon, which had been jarred from his hand when he'd landed.

She unloaded the magazine of bullets from his gun and tossed the weapon one direction into the woods surrounding the house, and the magazine into the trees in the opposite direction.

Hillary turned back to Rosie, using her gun to give succinct directions. "Now handcuff his wrists together. Then get his keys and load him into the backseat of his car. You're driving."

ROSIE SWIPED AWAY the tears the spilled from the corner of her eye, not sure if they were tears of fear that Max's head kept lolling from one side to the other as he bled out into the backseat, or pure, white-hot anger for the woman sitting in the passenger seat, calmly giving driving directions while training her gun at Rosie to ensure her cooperation. She suspected it was a little of both. Hillary Wells had killed one man Rosie had thought she loved, and now the woman was going to kill Max. And that would be a loss from which Rosie was certain she'd never recover.

Rosie glanced down at the typed suicide note Hillary had forced her to sign by threatening to shoot Max again. The Endicott Global CEO had written an essay of pure fiction, where Rosie confessed to murdering her abusive ex-fiancé by filling a bottle of champagne with RUD-317, seducing him in his condo and sneaking out after he'd overdosed on the drug. When the Cold Case Squad detective unmasked her as the killer several years later, she shot him before her secret could be revealed. But she'd fallen in love with the detective and, regretting her rash action, killed herself.

Rosie shifted her grip on the wheel and tried to think of a way she could escape and get Max to an ER for medical treatment. He kept sliding in and out of consciousness. His breathing was labored and his skin was far too pale.

"No one who knows me will ever believe that note."

Hillary smirked. "They won't believe you're a strong enough woman to commit cold-blooded murder?"

"No. They won't believe I'd ever want to seduce Richard."

The deep-pitched chuckle from the backseat infused her with renewed strength and determination. "That's my girl," Max rasped.

But Hillary didn't appreciate the humor. "I knew you were going to be trouble. You couldn't be content, could you? Nobody could prove you murdered Richard, but as long as you were the police's prime suspect, no one was looking at me, either." She indicated a narrow side road and ordered Rosie to turn. "Richard was a scumbag—greedy, self-centered, violent—the world is better without him. It was a win-win situation. You weren't in jail and he was out of your life. But you had to know the truth, didn't you?"

"He's never been out of my life since I met him. Clearing my name is the only way I can finally say goodbye to his influence over me."

Sheer will seemed to fuel the grumbling voice from the backseat. "Why did you kill him, Doc? You didn't like that he cheated on you, too? Or are you just a man hater?"

"It was purely business." She pointed to a gravel road among the trees. "Turn here." Rosie obeyed, following Dr. Wells's directions deeper into the forested recreational area dotted with remote cabins around the dam and creeks that fed them. "Richard was a two-night stand. I picked him up in a hotel bar."

Rosie glanced in the rearview mirror. Max opened his eyes and nodded. He remembered it, too. Rosie had picked him up in a bar and recruited him into helping her. She hadn't regretted a moment of their time together since.

"How is murder a business deal?" Rosie asked, concentrating on the narrowing road. They were dropping in altitude, too. They were approaching a remote cove off the main lake.

"I needed someone else dead and out of my way before he cheated me out of my life's work and rightful position at the company."

"Lloyd Endicott?" Max guessed.

"Yes." The woman was completely unapologetic about the death of her so-called friend and mentor. "I knew I'd be the first person the police would look at if it was proved Lloyd's death was anything but accidental. So I made a deal with a colleague to arrange for his death, and in exchange, I was asked to eliminate Richard."

"Strangers on a Train," Max muttered.

"What?"

"Nothing. I have a couple of friends who like old movies."

Turning up her nose as if polite chitchat was beneath her, Hillary used the gun to give Rosie the next direction. "Pull up over there at the old boat ramp. Leave the engine running."

"Who wanted Richard dead?"

"I'm not allowed to say. A deal's a deal."

"Killing us can't be part of the deal. Isn't the trick to getting away with murder that you have an airtight alibi while someone else does the dirty work for you?"

"Hence, the signed confession. When your bodies are found, they'll find the letter and file your deaths away as a murder-suicide."

Rosie's heart squeezed in her chest at the pained

expression on Max's face. She knew it wasn't just the bullet hole in his gut, but the memory of his best friend's suicide that was tearing him up.

Forcing Max to suffer like this, taking away the man who'd given her a few days of happiness simply wasn't fair. Not after everything else she'd been through. She wasn't exactly sure what that feverish sensation flowing through her veins was, but Rosie was thinking that Max had been right about her. She wasn't that quiet, demure, fragile woman by nature—that was a persona she'd taken on to survive her life with Richard and the terrible years that followed. Rosie had a redheaded temper firing through her blood.

She shifted the Chevy into Park and looked straight ahead at the gray-green water and whitecaps below. "Dr. Wells, I think you should know that I would never commit suicide. I've fought too hard to survive and to find happiness. No one will believe the story. There'll be an investigation."

She found Max's questioning gaze in the mirror and darted her eyes twice to the right. *I've got a plan. It's a crazy one. But I'm not giving up without a fight.*

Max nodded. "Hooah." HUA.

Heard. Understood. Acknowledged.

Clutching his stomach, he sat up a little straighter. "I love you, Rosie."

"I love you."

"Isn't that just sickeningly sweet," Hillary sneered. "You know what to do. As soon as I get out, shift the car into Drive. I'll make your boyfriend's death as painless as possible—a shot to the head. Then you drive the car into the lake. Unless you'd rather me wait to put the gun in your hand after I shoot you, too?" The dark-haired woman laughed. "Personally, I'd choose drowning in this deep part of the lake. That way, at least, I'm giving you a sporting chance at surviving."

Rosie took a deep breath and shifted the car while Hillary unbuckled her safety belt and reached for the door handle. "I know you love this car, Sergeant."

His expression turned as grim as she'd ever seen it. "Do it!"

Rosie stomped on the accelerator as Hillary turned to shoot Max. The car jerked forward, toppling the woman off balance. When she tumbled back against the seat, Max surged forward with a feral roar, looping his handcuffs around Hillary's neck as the gun fired.

"Max!" She heard his grunt of pain, saw the red circle appear on his shoulder and stain the front of his shirt.

His stranglehold on Dr. Wells went slack. "What are you doing? Stop!" she cried, struggling to free herself from the noose of Max's arms.

There was nothing Rosie could do but hold on and pray as the Chevy leaped the top of the boat ramp and hit the old concrete and rocks farther down. The car bottomed out, threw its passengers up to the ceiling. The gun bounced out of Hillary's hand and skittered along the floorboards. The other woman screamed as the car hit the water and plunged, nose first, in a slow-motion dive to the bottom of the lake.

The bruising wrench of the seat belt stunning Rosie quickly gave way to panic as the gray-green water rushed in. She was ankle-deep in the cool water before her brain kicked in. She quickly unhooked her seat belt and climbed up onto her knees to help Max escape.

"Max?" No answer. "Sergeant, can you hear me?" she shouted in a firmer voice. When his groggy eyes blinked open, she softened her command. "Can you unhook your seat belt?" She unlooped his arms from the headrest where he'd caught Hillary, then scrambled over the seat when the water rushed over his lap and his bound hands made it impossible to find the release.

Rosie spared a brief glance for the woman who'd tried to kill them, but at some point of impact, Hillary had struck her head and she was floating, unconscious, off her seat. Worrying more about the man she wanted desperately to save, Rosie took a breath and sank below the water that was pouring over the seat to release Max. When he, too, started to float, she pushed his body up to the ceiling where there was still air. "Breathe, honey. Take a deep breath."

She took several breaths herself, filling her lungs as deeply as she could before the translucent water hit the corner of her mouth and she sputtered.

She tipped her mouth to the ceiling. "Let me do the work, okay? Just don't fight me. You saved me, and now I'm going to save you."

He nodded his understanding before his eyes closed and the water rushed over his head. After snatching one last breath from a pocket of air, Rosie dove beneath the water to unlock Max's door and push it open. The changing water pressure made the car sink faster, but sucked them both out of the car when she grabbed onto his shirt and pulled him with her.

Then it was a series of kicks, a pull of her arm and ignoring the panicked need to breathe before she broke the surface of the water. Refilling her lungs with reviving air, she pulled Max's heavy body onto her hip and held his head above water as best she could while she fought the wind-tossed waves and swam in a side-stroke to shore. She was near exhaustion by the time she reached a shallow enough depth that she could stand.

"Stay with me, Max," she urged, wiping the water from his face and hair and dragging him to shore.

She slipped a couple of times trying to push him up onto the dry ground between the rushes, grass and rocks. He was conscious, at least, thank God, because once he could get his legs beneath him, he helped push himself higher onto the bank. But then she lost her footing on the slick, mossy rocks and fell into the water again, swallowing a mouthful as she sank beneath the surface. When she pushed herself back up, a hand latched onto hers. Relief swept through her as she surfaced.

"Max…" Stunned, she would have fallen again, but the man who pulled her from the water didn't release his grip. "You."

When the young man with the glasses finally let go, she scrambled away, crawling over Max's legs and kneeling in front of him to provide some sort of protection for her wounded hero. The young man who'd taken her picture at the prison that day picked up the suit jacket he'd tossed into the grass.

"You do good work, Miss March," he said, shrugging into his jacket.

"Who are you?"

"A friend of a friend who's looking out for you." He turned his gaze out to the water where there weren't even bubbles left to show where the car had sunk. "Dr. Wells was becoming a bit of a problem for us."

Max's big hand grazed her knee and held on, comforting her as some of his strength returned. "You're Asher's man."

"No, Detective. I'm my own man." Without any more explanation than that, the mysterious Glasses Guy climbed the hill toward a black Chrysler parked at the top. "I already called 9-1-1. An ambulance is en route.

I surely hope you don't bleed to death, Detective." He climbed inside his car and started the engine. "Ma'am. I think you'll understand that I'd rather not be here when the police arrive."

And with that, he drove away.

Rosie heard sirens in the distance and started to stand. But Max pulled her back to her knees. "Come here."

Without regard for modesty, she pulled off her T-shirt and wadded it up to stanch his wounds.

He splayed his fingers on her bare stomach and grinned. "Honey, I'm afraid I can't help you with that right now. Maybe later?"

How could he joke and flirt when she was so afraid? "Max. You're bleeding. Maybe dying. I don't want to lose you."

"Come. Here." He grabbed her and pulled her down into the grass beside him. He pressed a kiss to her temple and rubbed his grizzled cheek against hers. The sirens were getting closer. Glasses Guy hadn't lied. Help was coming. "Are you okay? Are you hurt?"

"I'm fine. You're the one who got shot. Twice."

"I'm gonna live through both. I'm a tough guy, remember?"

"Damn it, Max—"

"Rosemary March. Did you just swear? You know I don't like hearing that from you," he teased. He pulled her in for a kiss that lasted until a groan of pain forced him to come up for air. "You get under my skin, Rosie."

"Like an itchy rash?" she teased, pushing the wadded T-shirt back into place over his stomach wound.

"Like an alarm clock finally waking me up to the life I'm supposed to have. With you." So when did the tough guy learn to speak such beautiful things? Tears stung her eyes again as she found a spot where she could hug him without causing any pain. "I know I'm not the guy you expected to want you like this, and I know you weren't the woman I was looking for. Hell, I wasn't even looking."

"Neither was I."

"But we found each other."

"We're good for each other."

"I'm not an easy man to live with. I come with a lot of emotional baggage."

"And I don't?"

"You can do better than me."

Rosie shook her head, smiling. "I can't do better than a good man who loves me. A man who encourages me to be myself and to be strong and who makes me feel safer and more loved than I have ever felt in my life."

"I do love you, Rosie."

"I love you, Max." They shared another kiss until she realized the ambulance and two sheriff's cars were pulling to a stop at the top of the boat ramp.

"What are we going to do about these feelings?" Max asked.

"What do you want to do?"

"Let's give the Dinkles something to talk about."

"You're moving in upstairs?"

"And opening all the windows."

Rosie smiled. "Oh, I hope we give them plenty to talk about."

* * * * *

"You have a complicated life, Nina."

Jase opened the latch of the broken gate and ushered her through with a sweep of his hand.

"You have no idea, Jase."

He held his breath as she moved past him, her light fragrance tickling his nose. Would she tell him about her pregnancy? Open up about Simon?

She climbed the two porch steps and turned to face him.

He held her gaze, ready for her confidences. Not that he'd be sharing any of his own—revealing his identity was not part of his assignment—yet.

"You know that proposal you made over dinner?"

He blinked. Not what he'd been expecting, but he'd go with it. "About moving in with you? For your safety?"

"Yes. Still interested?"

"Sure."

"Good." She turned and shoved open the front door of the B and B. "Because I want you to move in—right here, right now."

THE PREGNANCY PLOT

BY
CAROL ERICSON

Published in Great Britain 2015
by Mills & Boon, an imprint of Harlequin (UK) Limited,
Eton House, 18-24 Paradise Road, Richmond, Surrey, TW9 1SR

© 2015 Carol Ericson

ISBN: 978-0-263-25314-6

46-0815

Harlequin (UK) Limited's policy is to use papers that are natural, renewable and recyclable products and made from wood grown in sustainable forests. The logging and manufacturing processes conform to the legal environmental regulations of the country of origin.

Printed and bound in Spain
by CPI, Barcelona

Carol Ericson lives with her husband and two sons in Southern California, home of state-of-the-art cosmetic surgery, wild freeway chases and a million amazing stories. These stories, along with hordes of virile men and feisty women, clamor for release from Carol's head. It makes for some interesting headaches until she sets them free to fulfill their destinies and her readers' fantasies. To learn more about Carol, please visit her website, www.carolericson.com, "Where romance flirts with danger."

For the LA women (and men)
of the Los Angeles Romance Authors (LARA)

Chapter One

The nurse handed her the blurry picture of her baby boy, and Nina tilted her head to the side, trying to figure out if the white, fuzzy appendage in the upper-right corner of the photo represented a foot or an arm. At just about eighteen weeks that appendage could be anything—even that which distinguished him as a boy.

The nurse smiled and flicked the edge of the ultrasound. "Well, at least if his father can't be here, you can send him his son's picture."

Nina pasted an answering smile on her face, ignoring the knife in her heart. "Yes, I'll do that."

If she could ever find her baby's father.

She hadn't wanted to get into the whole complicated story of her ex-fiancé's disappearance off the face of the earth, so she'd just told her obstetrician that her baby's father was in the military and was deployed. All good lies contained a bit of the truth.

"Make sure you stop by the front desk to make your next appointment." The nurse closed the door behind her so that Nina could get dressed.

That was another issue she hadn't discussed with her doctor yet. There wouldn't be another appointment if she decided to pull up stakes and move to Washington.

The paper crinkled as she slid off the examination

table. How had her life gotten so complicated in such a short period of time? She'd been happy with her job, happy with her fiancé and safe.

Safe? Where had that come from? She crumpled up the paper gown and shoved it into the trash can. She didn't have to dig too deeply for the answer.

She'd been feeling uneasy ever since Simon had started blowing up at the smallest issue until his ranting and raving had gotten so severe, she'd broken off their engagement over four months ago. Then he'd dropped off her radar for good. Or had he?

She squeezed into her fat jeans, making a mental note for the hundredth time that week to shop for maternity clothes.

Since her breakup with Simon, she'd had the unsettling feeling that her ex-fiancé had been stalking her—watching her, following her. She had no evidence at all to back up that suspicion, only a creeping feeling of dread. Looking over her shoulder and checking her rearview mirror had become habits for her—habits she didn't like.

Habits that gave her even more reason to leave LA for her family's bed-and-breakfast up in the Puget Sound area. The TLC that place needed since her stepfather passed away would be enough to keep her occupied.

Slipping her feet into her wedges, she hooked the strap of her purse over her shoulder. She kissed the ultrasound picture of her baby and slipped it into her purse.

She breezed into the reception area. Leaning over the counter, she said, "I need to make my next appointment."

"Of course." The receptionist's fingers raced across the keyboard of her computer. "Does this same time next month work for you, Nina?"

If the great Pacific Northwest hadn't called her home by that time. Nina peered at the calendar on the phone cupped in her hand. "Yes, and Tuesday or Wednesday of that week looks good."

"Perfect." The receptionist checked some boxes on an appointment card and held it out between two fingers.

"Thanks." Nina took the card and dropped it into her purse.

While she waited for the elevator that would take her down to the parking garage below the building, her cell phone buzzed. She glanced at the display and sighed.

Six months ago she'd been thrilled to land this job, designing the interior of a beach house in Malibu, but after Simon had gone AWOL and she'd found out she was pregnant, she had no patience for this demanding client.

She answered the call anyway. "Hello, Jennifer. Were the tiles delivered on time?"

"They arrived yesterday. I opened one of the boxes and I'm not so sure I like that yellow and blue."

Of course you don't.

The elevator doors slid open, and Nina stepped into the car, nodding at a woman holding a squirming toddler in her arms.

The woman dipped her chin while blowing a strand of hair from her face. "You need to get in your stroller now, Ben."

How did kids even move that way? He looked like a giant worm. She placed a hand on her belly. Would her baby be wiggly like that?

"Nina? I said I don't like the color."

She blinked. "If we send it back, it's going to be another two weeks, at least, before the vendor can get another shipment from Italy."

"Two weeks? I can't wait. Everything will be done by then."

"You loved the colors a month ago."

"You're right. I'll keep them."

"I'll let Fernando know the tiles are in. He and his assistant will be out tomorrow for the installation."

She ended the call at the same time the elevator stopped at the first level of the parking structure. The woman had coaxed her son into his stroller and rolled him out the door, calling over her shoulder, "Don't worry. It's all worth it."

Nina's mouth dropped open when the doors slid shut on mother and child. Had she been sending out that silent motherhood vibe?

She shifted her weight to her other foot, vowing to swap her high, wedged heels for flats any day now. She didn't need a psychiatrist to tell her that her refusal to switch up her clothes to accommodate her pregnancy was a form of denial. She absolutely wanted the baby, but the pregnancy had been a surprise, and coming on the heels of her breakup with Simon, it had been an overwhelming surprise.

But one she could handle, one she couldn't wait to handle.

The doors swooshed open on her parking level and she got a whiff of exhaust fumes. She waved her hand in front of her face. She'd definitely be breathing cleaner air if she made the move from LA to Washington, but she'd be leaving her life and her friends behind.

As she headed for her car in the far corner of the parking lot, her cell buzzed again. She held her phone up to her face in the dim light of the garage and squinted at a text from Jennifer—more doubts about the yellow tile.

Pinning her purse to her body with the inside of her elbow, she used both thumbs to text Jennifer some more encouragement. She sent the text and looked up.

"Three C?" she said to herself. She'd missed her aisle.

As she backtracked, a slow-moving car on the row above caught her attention. Unlike when she'd arrived for her appointment this afternoon, the parking garage sported plenty of empty slots. No need for that car to be rolling along at such a slow speed past vacant parking spaces.

In contrast to the speed of the car, her heart rate ticked up a few notches. She turned down the aisle where she'd parked her car and moved as fast as her shoes would allow.

Holding her key fob in front of her, she clicked it over and over just to make sure the car would be unlocked when she reached it.

She glanced over her shoulder at the other car, a black sedan, now crawling down the ramp to her level. She slid out of her shoes, grabbed them with one hand and jogged toward her car.

A woman getting into her car turned to stare at her. Nina didn't care what she looked like running to her car.

She grabbed the handle, pulled open the door and dropped onto the seat, smashing her fist against the automatic lock. The woman who'd been eyeballing her started her own car and pulled out, giving Nina full view of the end of the row.

The slow-moving sedan showed up in the aisle, and Nina cranked on her ignition. If that car decided to follow her, she'd drive straight to a police station. If the driver was Simon, he'd get the picture soon enough that, baby or no baby, she'd press charges against him for stalking if he kept up this cloak-and-dagger stuff. All he had to do was call her.

Her car's ignition clicked, but the car didn't start. She tried again, clenching her teeth against the grating sound coming from her car. She didn't need car trouble now.

She cut off the unresponsive engine, took a deep breath and turned the key one more time. Again, the engine failed to turn over.

The black car had turned around on the next level and

was heading back toward her again. A cold fear seized her. She didn't know if it was Simon or someone else in that car with the tinted windows, but she sensed a powerful evil heading in her direction.

She cupped her hands over her barely discernible belly, and a surge of protectiveness rushed through her body. She removed her key from the ignition and pressed the red panic button on the remote.

Her car alarm blared alternately with her honking horn as she slid down in her seat.

With her nose just above the steering wheel, she watched the car zoom past her.

A minute later, a man and a woman were knocking on her car window.

She buzzed down the window, and the woman poked her head inside the car. "Are you okay?"

Nina's heart slowed its gallop. "I'm fine. I…I was trying to start my car, and I hit the alarm on my remote by mistake."

No point in revealing her emotional instability to anyone else. That's all it was—pregnancy hormones running amok.

The woman stepped back. "We saw you slip down in your seat and thought you were having some kind of medical emergency."

"No. I'm fine."

The man shrugged and turned away, obviously less interested than the woman, concern still creasing her face.

"Can you start your car now?"

Nina turned the key and got the same noise. "I guess not."

"Can you get a ride?"

The man glanced at his watch.

"I have an automobile club service. I'll call them." Nina popped her door handle, since she had no intention of waiting for the tow truck in this rapidly clearing parking lot.

The woman smiled. "You take care now."

Nina slung her purse over her shoulder and trudged back to the elevator, periodically glancing over her shoulder to look out for the black sedan.

Was it just a coincidence that her car broke down at the very same time a mysterious vehicle seemed to be shadowing her in the parking structure?

Maybe, maybe not, but the scare had just sealed her fate.

She was leaving LA for Break Island, Washington, sooner rather than later.

JASE FLIPPED UP the collar of his jacket and shoved his hands into his pockets, as the ferry chugged into port. Who the hell would leave sunny Southern California for this godforsaken island in the middle of Puget Sound at this time of the year?

Crazy pregnant lady.

When Jase reached land, he ordered a cup of coffee from the window next to the ticket office. He balanced the cup on the edge of a planter and pulled out his phone.

Jack Coburn picked up on the first ring.

"Jack, I made it to Break Island. I have no idea why anyone would want to open a bed-and-breakfast on this rock. No wonder the place closed down."

Coburn cleared his throat. "Fishing, sailing, hiking, bird-watching at the sanctuary, and ferries to Vancouver and Seattle. The Moonstones B&B didn't close down for lack of business. Nina Moore's mother became ill and passed away. After her mother's death, her stepfather committed suicide."

Coburn always did his homework. Jase had known all that about Nina Moore's tragic history, but he'd been too busy arguing with Coburn about this babysitting job to really take note of her background. Sad stuff—and she didn't even know about her ex-fiancé yet.

Coburn read his thoughts. "You would've remembered all that if you hadn't been so intent on protesting the assignment. I need you focused, Bennett."

"I'm on it, boss. Protect the pregnant lady."

"We have to cover all our bases. We don't know what's going on right now or what to believe from Max Duvall's crazy stories."

"The body of Nina Moore's fiancé hasn't turned up yet, has it?"

"Nope."

"Maybe he's not even dead."

"Maybe not, but that doesn't change our mission."

"Protect the pregnant lady."

"Exactly."

Jase ended the call and squinted through the gray haze that enveloped the small town rolling out in front of him. Maybe the pregnant lady had escaped to Break Island to hide her condition from her ex-fiancé. He snorted and snatched his coffee from the planter.

Wouldn't be the first time a woman had tried to hide a pregnancy from a man.

He checked into a small motel in the center of town and returned to the office to get to work. He touched the bell on the counter, and the motel's proprietor came out from the back.

"Everything okay in your room?"

"Everything's fine." He picked up a flyer about the island's bird sanctuary and tucked it into his pocket. "Maisie, right?"

"That's right."

In true small-town fashion, Maisie had introduced herself when he checked in. "On my way in on the ferry, I noticed a B and B on the shore. It looked kind of rough but still open. Any chance the owner needs some help fixing up the place? I'm looking for a little work, and that's right up my alley."

"I don't know if Nina's looking for help, but she should be. Moonstones has been empty for a few years now and could sure use some TLC."

"Thanks, Maisie." He rapped his knuckles on the counter. "I think I'll head over there and see if I can offer Nina some TLC."

Once outside, Jase adjusted his shoulder holster beneath his blue flannel shirt. He'd fit right in with these lumberjack types.

He jogged down the steps of the motel, which sat at the end of the main street, and headed for the path that led down to the beach. He made a left turn, hugging the shoreline as he scuffed along the sandy path toward Nina's B and B. Moonstones perched on a rocky beach on the far edge of town, along with a few other beach houses. Nina must've really wanted to get away from it all.

He traipsed through the sand and clambered over some rocks to get a good view of the building before approaching it.

A tangled garden spilled over the ramshackle fence that ringed the property. One blue shutter hung by a broken hinge, revealing a crack in the window. This didn't look like a prime spot for someone expecting a baby.

But Coburn had ordered him to get close to the subject, and this ramshackle B and B offered the perfect opportunity. He wouldn't be his grandfather's disciple if he didn't know his way around a hammer and nail—even though Dad had disapproved.

He shuffled through the dry sand and crossed the road to the B and B. The battered wooden gate sagged and he pushed through to the garden in the front. Using the rusty hook, he latched the gate behind him.

This place wouldn't provide much security if someone wanted to get to Nina. He had to make sure that didn't happen.

He veered off the overgrown walkway to the front of the B and B, slogging through the knee-high weeds, and cut a path to the corner of the building. He peered around it, taking in a deck with patio furniture stacked in the corner and a fire pit crisscrossed with charred logs.

Squinting, he could almost envision a circle of guests around a roaring fire, toasting marshmallows as the waves lapped at the dock where the boats gently bobbed. Almost.

He hooked his thumb in the front pocket of his jeans and started to turn back...but the unmistakable sound of a shotgun being readied for use stopped him in his tracks.

Chapter Two

His adrenaline pulsed for two beats, as his finger twitched for his weapon. Then he took a deep breath. If one of his enemies had a gun on him, he'd already be dead.

A woman's voice barked out an order. "Put your hands in the air and turn around...slowly."

He complied and added a smile to his face for good measure.

Nina Moore held him at bay with an old shotgun that looked as if it had seen its best days during the Civil War. Her dark ponytail hung over one shoulder and she widened her stance as she leveled the barrel of the shotgun right between his eyes.

Crazy pregnant lady.

"Who the hell are you and what are you doing on my property?"

"My name's Jase Buckley and I heard you needed some help fixing up this place."

Her eyes narrowed. He couldn't quite catch their color from here, but they glittered dangerously.

"Who told you that?"

"Maisie—the woman at my motel." He'd led Maisie on, but she would at least verify that they'd had a conversation about how the owner of Moonstones might need help repairing the place. "I'm new on the island. I came here to do some writing, but I also need to earn some cash."

"Maisie, huh?" The gun slipped a little and she tapped the toe of her sneaker on the sandy ground. "I can check out your story."

"Go right ahead." He waved his hands in the air. "Can I put my arms down now?"

She loosened her grip on the shotgun and pinned it against her side. "I *could* use some help around here, but I fully intend to check you out."

"I thought Break Island was one of those friendly, small-town places." He cocked his head. "Didn't realize you could get shot going up to someone's front door."

"You didn't go up to my front door." She tipped her chin toward him. "You came around here to the side."

He jerked his thumb over his shoulder. "I was admiring the deck and the fire pit, or at least admiring what it could be."

She ran her tongue along her lower lip, her shoulders still rigid. "Yeah, I plan to fix that up...eventually."

He hadn't expected Nina to be on edge, unless she always greeted strangers with a shotgun. Had someone attempted to contact her already? What did she know about her ex-fiancé's disappearance?

"I can help you with that." He cleared his throat as his gaze swept across her lean frame, no baby bump in sight. He'd have to pretend he knew nothing of her pregnancy. "I'll be on the island for a while, and I need some gainful employment."

"What do you write?"

Shoving his hands into his pockets, he kicked at a rock on the crumbling path. "I'm a former marine, did a few tours in Afghanistan. Thought I'd write what I know, a fictional account."

Her eyes widened and her fingers curled around the butt of the shotgun. "Y-you're military?"

"Retired." He thought it best to stick as close to the

truth as possible, but his military background bothered her—must be memories of her ex-fiancé, Simon Skinner. She *had* ended it with Skinner before he disappeared. Maybe they'd had a bad breakup.

With his hands still stuffed in his pockets, he lifted his shoulders to his ears. "Just thought I had an interesting story to tell, but the book's not a bestseller yet. Hell, the book isn't even written yet. That's why I need to make some money while I figure out if this story will write itself."

"I do have a soft spot for military men." She blinked and rested one hand on her stomach. "My...my stepfather was in the navy."

And her ex-fiancé was a navy SEAL before joining Tempest as an agent...and winding up dead.

"I hope you'll give this vet a chance." He swept his arm across her property. "I can help you out here."

She puffed a breath of air from between her lips as if she'd been holding it. "Maybe. Give me a day or two to check you out, and a couple of references wouldn't hurt. Can't pay you much more than minimum wage."

"I'll get right on the references. Thanks." He pointed to the purse she'd dropped on the ground next to her before leveling the gun at his head. "Were you going out?"

"I'm going across the bay to the mainland to pick up some supplies."

"Can I help you?"

"No." She picked up the gun in her hands again and made a move toward the house.

She hadn't been joking about looking into his background first. A woman in her condition should be cautious and he was glad Nina was, unlike some women he knew, but she'd obviously brought her big-city paranoia to the small town.

As she retreated to the house, he scuffed through the

sand toward the front gate and left it open behind him. He clambered on top of a pile of rocks and faced the bay, his eyes watering at the sharp, cold breeze stinging his face.

He hadn't brought the full Bennett charm into play yet—just didn't seem right with a pregnant woman, even though he wasn't supposed to know she was expecting—but it looked as if it was going to be harder than he'd imagined getting close to Nina Moore.

And for some strange reason, he'd completely changed his mind about this assignment after meeting his quarry. He couldn't wait to get close to Nina Moore.

NINA LOCKED THE front door behind her and cursed the weeds as she slogged through them to the sagging gate. Her pulse jumped as she spied Jase on the rocks in front of the property next door. Was he waiting for her?

She'd felt such a connection to him the moment he'd turned and faced her shotgun. He had a quality that reminded her of Simon—not his looks. Simon was a good-looking guy, too, but his red hair and broad features were worlds apart from Jase's dark intensity. Both men had an air of watchful readiness about them, as if they could spring into action at any moment.

They also both shared a commanding presence, giving her the uneasy feeling that she'd do their bidding even at her own peril. All a man had to do was promise to lead and she'd follow him anywhere.

Must be the pregnancy hormones making her crazy. She shook her head and tossed her ponytail over her shoulder.

She latched the gate and veered left. Her sneakers hit the wood planks leading to the boat dock where Dad's sixteen-foot boat bobbed in the water. Keeping one eye on Jase still peering at the bay, she started the seventy-horsepower engine. It sputtered and coughed and then rumbled to life. She aimed the boat toward the line of shore she could just make out in the distance.

The salty breeze whipped the ponytail across her face, and she stuck out her tongue to catch the spray just because she felt like it. She glanced over her shoulder at Jase, still on the rocks, his figure getting smaller and smaller although he still loomed large in her mind.

It must be that inner spit and polish that gave military men their bearing, leaving the impression of invincibility. That's why Simon's behavior had been so frightening. At first she'd pegged it as post-traumatic stress disorder and had encouraged him to visit a therapist, but he'd have none of that. The same personality traits that gave him supreme control in the face of danger also led him to an impenetrable stubbornness.

She sighed and slightly shifted the course of the boat. If Simon ever wanted to be part of his son's life, he'd have to get some counseling first.

She shivered and stamped her feet—in a puddle. She looked down, gasping at the pool of water sloshing over her sneakers. The spray hadn't been that high or wild to flood the boat—not yet anyway, although a storm was on its way down from Alaska.

She skimmed the toe of her wet shoe across the bottom of the boat and more water gushed in. Bending over, she ran her fingers across the fiberglass surface, her tips tripping over the edge of some electrical tape.

"Are you kidding me?" She peeled back the tape, exposing a hole in the fiberglass the size of a quarter and getting bigger as more water gurgled into the boat.

She rose, jerking her head toward the mainland and then toward the island. Faster to go back.

She eased into a turn and started chugging back to Break Island. The boat lurched and listed as it took on more water the faster she went. When the water got ankle-high, she slowed the boat and tried to bail out with a bucket.

When the left stern started to dip, she abandoned the idea of a bailout and eyed the shoreline of the island. Even if she could swim that distance with her clothes dragging her down, the water would be freezing cold. Would her baby feel the cold?

How had this happened? She kicked the side of the boat. When she'd checked out the boat a few days ago, she thought she'd found one thing at Moonstones that still worked.

The boat limped several more yards toward Break Island, and Nina climbed onto the seat cushions and waved her arms above her head. Did she even have a beacon on this thing?

In the distance, across the water, two boats seemed to be charging hard toward her. One had come straight from the boat docks on her side of the island and the other had rounded the bend from the town side of the island. Had they actually seen her or were they just out for a boat ride across the bay?

She flapped her arms to her sides like a giant bird and jumped—bad idea. The water in the belly of the boat sloshed and the outboard motor swung to one side, lifting the other side of the boat out of the water.

She stepped off the seat and shuffled to the leeward side of the boat. A loud crack resounded and the whooshing sound of water pushing through a small opening had her grabbing the bin where Dad had stored life jackets.

Why hadn't she thought of that before? Gripping the edge of the lid, she paused, lifting her head to check on the progress of those two boats. The one from the docks by the B and B was still making a beeline toward her, while the other seemed to have disappeared. Maybe that one never saw her.

She grabbed an orange life jacket and slipped it over her head. She knew how to swim, but the flotation device would keep her afloat until her cavalry came to the rescue in case the cold water made her cramp up or her heavy clothes dragged her down into the murky water of the sound.

The boat rocked and she planted her feet on the deck beneath the water to steady herself, but the little fiberglass boat couldn't take it. One side of the boat went under and the force flung her into the icy embrace of the bay.

The cold sucked the air from her lungs for a moment, paralyzing her, and then she made a grab for the side of the capsized boat. Her hands clawed against the slippery fiberglass until she found a hold.

The hum of an outboard motor got louder and louder, and she would've yelled out to make sure the boat was going to stop but her teeth were chattering so much she couldn't get a sound past her lips.

She didn't need to. The other boat's motor cut out as it drew next to her incapacitated vessel. It floated around to her side, and a strong hand reached for her.

"Oh, my God. Are you all right, Nina?"

Tossing wet strands of hair back from her face, she looked into the dark eyes of Jase Buckley—her savior, or was he?

Chapter Three

His grip tightened around her wrists. "Are you ready? I'm going to haul you up."

With her teeth chattering, she nodded and braced her feet against the side of the boat.

Jase lifted her into the boat with ease, despite the eight extra pounds she'd packed on during her pregnancy. She glanced over her shoulder at her boat, now heavy with water, and shivered. She could've clung to the side, but she might've been there awhile if Jase and that other boat hadn't been on the sound.

"What the hell happened?" Jase shrugged out of his flannel shirt, draped it over her shoulders and tucked it around her body.

"There was a hole in the bottom and it started taking on water."

"Should we try to tow it back in?" He crouched next to a bin on the deck of the boat and tugged at the padlock securing the lid.

"I'll call the Harbor Patrol when we get back to shore. They patrol the sound and they'll bring it in for me."

"If it hasn't sunk to the bottom of the sound by then."

She hunched her shoulders against the chill snaking through her body. "It's insured if it does. Do you think we can get my purse off the boat? It's hooked onto the side."

"I'll try." He brought his boat abreast of hers, planted one foot on the ailing boat and snagged the purse. "Got it."

Safely back in her neighbors' boat, he handed the purse to her. "When was the last time you took that thing out on the water?"

"It's been a few years. I haven't been in it since I've been back. I meant to give it the once-over, but there were just so many other things to do."

"That's because you need some help." He aimed the boat toward the shoreline.

Narrowing her eyes, she sniffed through what was probably a very red nose right now. What better way to get her to trust him than by staging a rescue? How long had Jase been snooping around the B and B and her boat dock before she'd discovered him in her yard?

"You look like you're freezing."

The wind raked its fingers through Jase's chocolate-brown hair and infused his face with a ruddy glow. No pinched, red nose for him. He looked like an advertisement for some brisk aftershave.

"I am freezing. This water is not meant for a leisurely dip, especially with that storm from Alaska on its way." She rubbed the back of her hand across her nose and pressed a palm against the small rise in her belly. Hopefully, the baby was still snug and cozy.

Jase's eyes dropped to the movement and then shifted to stare at the land rushing toward them.

"Hang on. Not too much longer."

"You borrowed this boat from the Kleinschmidts next door."

"I figured they wouldn't mind if I used it in the commission of a rescue."

There it was again—pumping himself up as her savior. She crossed her arms, cupping her elbows and blowing out a long breath. She needed to relax. He *was* her savior.

Why would Simon send someone out here to do his bidding for him and why would a man like this be interested in doing that bidding?

"You're my savior because you got here faster than the other guy."

"The other guy?" His brow crinkled as he nudged the rudder.

"Another boat was headed my way from the other side of the peninsula, the town side. I think he must've turned around when he saw you had the situation covered."

"Really?" He downshifted and the boat chugged to a choppy crawl. "You'd think he would've come out anyway to make sure everything was okay."

"Maybe he didn't see me at all and continued across the sound."

"Maybe." He steered the boat back into the Kleinschmidts' dock. "Can you reach the county patrol now?"

"Probably." She dug into her bag and pulled out her phone.

Jase expertly maneuvered the boat into the dock and held out his hand to help her onto dry land. "You make that call while I secure the boat."

Turning her back to him, she placed the call, and ten minutes later, just as Jase hopped onto the wooden dock, Nina spied the red county patrol boat heading toward her disabled craft.

"Do they need you to tow that back here?"

"No. They'll secure it to my dock."

"Good." He squeezed her shoulders, still trembling beneath the blue flannel of his damp shirt. "Let's get you inside and get you something hot to drink. Coffee?"

"I don't drink coffee—anymore."

"And I only drink it first thing in the morning. Do you have some tea or hot chocolate?"

"I have some chamomile tea, if you like."

"It's not for me. It's for you." He spun her around and marched behind her, his hands lightly on the back of her shoulders.

"You're the one missing a shirt. That white T-shirt isn't enough to protect you against the harsh elements out here." Although she hadn't minded the way the thin cotton had molded to his muscles. Simon had been broader and beefier than this man with his lean muscles and patrician features. But Jase didn't come off any less capable than Simon. In fact, they both possessed a similar air of efficiency and confidence—that is until Simon changed.

Strong fingers dug into the sides of her neck. "You okay? Your back is as stiff as a board."

"Just cold." She traipsed up the two steps of the porch, escaping his touch, and fumbled for her keys. She shouldn't be getting that much pleasure out of Jase's warm touch while carrying Simon's baby.

Not that she would ever trust Simon in their child's life—at least not until he got some help for his anger issues.

What the hell had he been so angry about anyway?

The keys dropped from her shaking hands, and Jase scooped them up in one fluid movement. "Let me."

He slid the key home and pushed open the door, stepping to the side.

She ducked around him, the condition of the B and B bringing warmth to her cold cheeks. She really hadn't made much progress. It didn't help that every afternoon a slow, sneaking lethargy stole over her body.

She waved at the sitting room with its worn wood floors and blackened fireplace. "I still have a lot of work to do."

"That's what I'd heard. You change into some dry clothes." He dangled the keys from one finger. "And I'll boil some water for tea."

Snatching the keys from him, she pivoted away from him. And just like that she'd allowed another controlling male into her life.

She called over her shoulder, "Tea bags are in the cupboard to the left of the stove."

"I can handle it. Get those wet clothes off and change into something comfortable."

Nina turned, sucked in her lower lip and studied Jase's handsome face. He seemed a little too interested in getting her out of her clothes.

She dipped her head once and said, "I still have that shotgun."

His eyes widened above raised hands. "Yes, ma'am."

Tossing a strand of wet hair over her shoulder, she crossed to her separate living quarters tucked behind the staircase. She'd make it quick and get out of this flannel shirt that had Jase's fresh, manly scent in every fold.

She didn't need any more complications in her life right now.

WHEN HE HEARD a door close in the back of the house, Jase whistled through his teeth and turned toward the kitchen. That woman had a suspicious mind. Maybe it came from being pregnant…or dating a spy. A spy who had disappeared. That would do it.

A copper teapot perched on a burner, and he grabbed it by the handle and filled it with water from the tap. A couple of mugs dangled from a wooden tree. He plucked them off, reading the words printed on the white one aloud, "Number one runner."

He figured Nina for the runner, since she looked like someone in good shape, despite the pregnancy, not that a woman couldn't be pregnant and in good shape, but he hoped she wasn't out there running marathons. He banged one of the mugs on the counter with a little too much force. Hell, what did he know?

He claimed the plain, red mug with the chip on the handle for himself. Then he swung open the cupboard to the left of the range and took out the box of chamomile tea. He'd rather have a snifter of cognac to warm up, but he didn't figure Nina would have any booze on hand.

By the time the kettle whistled, Nina had returned, wedging a shoulder against the refrigerator, hugging a shapeless, red sweater around her body.

She wrinkled her nose. "You don't look too comfortable in the kitchen."

"Really?" He swung a tea bag in the air, wrapping the string around his finger. "I thought I was doing a bang-up job in here."

"Find everything okay?" She had scooped her shoulder-length, dark hair back into its ponytail, and the tilt of her head sent it swinging behind her.

"I did." He held up the runner's mug. "Is this you?"

Shoving her hands into the pockets of her jeans, she lifted her shoulder to her ears. "I ran cross-country in college."

"Impressive. Here in Washington?"

"Oregon."

"A runner's paradise—even more impressive." He poured the bubbling water over the tea bags in the cups, and the rising steam gave a much-needed homey touch to the dilapidated kitchen.

She joined him at the counter to take her mug, her shoulder brushing against his, the fuzzy softness of her sweater tickling his arm through his T-shirt. Her pale, stiff fingers curled around the handle of the mug.

What she really needed was a warm bath, but if he suggested that, she'd probably haul out that shotgun again.

"Does that fireplace in the other room work?"

"Yes, and I even have a cord of wood that my neighbor delivered—the same neighbor who owns that boat you borrowed." She tapped his mug with her fingernail. "Do you want some sugar or milk for that?"

Since he never drank tea, he didn't have a clue. "I, uh, take it black."

She wrapped her hands around the cup, closed her eyes and sniffed the steam floating up from the mug. Her long lashes created dark crescents on her cheeks, and her full lips curved into a slight smile.

He caught his breath at the simple beauty of her expression and then shook his head. Put him in the presence of a pregnant woman and his thoughts went haywire. Nina wasn't Maggie, and the baby she was carrying was Simon Skinner's, not his.

"Let's get this fire started." And he didn't mean the one that had been doing a slow burn in his belly ever since he locked his gaze onto Nina Moore.

She skirted past him, her pale cheeks sporting two red spots, as if she could read his mind.

He followed her into the great room, which must've functioned as a sitting room and gathering place for guests—when there were guests.

She gestured toward the big stone fireplace that took up half the wall. "I've already used it once, so I know it works, unlike the boat."

"Speaking of the boat." He swept aside the curtain at the front window and peered outside. "Looks like they're bringing it in, so at least they saved it from sinking."

"I'll look at it later." Nina collapsed into a recliner, facing the fireplace and folding her hands around her cup.

She looked as if she needed warming up, and even though he had a few impure thoughts about how he could do that, he placed his mug on the table beside her and crouched in front of the fireplace and got to work.

"Did I ever say thank you?"

"For?" He cupped his hand around the orange flicker as it raced across the edge of the newspaper crumpled beneath the logs.

"For rescuing me out there on the bay. Even though I wasn't in imminent danger of drowning, the water was freezing cold and…"

He held his breath. Would she mention her pregnancy now?

She coughed. "And I could've been floating out there for a while before another boat came along."

He let out his breath and prodded a log into place before rising to his feet and retrieving his tasteless tea.

He eased into a love seat at right angles to Nina's chair and the fire, crackling to life. "There was that other boat. They were probably on their way to save you when they saw me. I'm glad I could get to you faster."

She stretched her long legs in front of her, crossing her legs at the ankles. She'd gotten rid of her sodden sneakers, her feet now encased in a pair of soft red socks that matched her sweater. Her coloring played well against the red, her blue eyes a contrast to her dark hair, giving her an exotic look.

Simon Skinner had been a redhead. The baby could be an interesting combination of Mom and Dad.

Then the truth punched him in the gut. If her ex-fiancé and the father of her baby was dead, she had a right to know. They had only Max Duvall's word for that now, but once they received confirmation, he'd convince Jack Coburn that they had to tell Nina.

He didn't like it when people kept the truth from him, and he wouldn't be a party to doing that to someone else.

Of course, he was in the wrong line of work for those sentiments.

The fire danced higher, creating a wall of warmth, and Nina held her hands out toward it, wiggling her fingers.

"Are you warming up?"

"Slowly but surely." She pointed to his cup, still brimming with pale gold liquid. "You're not drinking your tea."

"I'm not the one who wound up treading water in the sound for ten minutes."

"True, but you did give up your flannel and had to cross the bay in nothing but a flimsy T-shirt." Her gaze flicked over his chest, and he resisted the urge to flex.

That glance alone did more to heat him up than ten cups of chamomile could.

She snapped her fingers as if to break the spell between them. "I hung up your shirt in the bathroom, but maybe it would dry faster in front of this fire."

She scooted forward on her chair and he held up his hand. "I'll get it. Tell me where."

"Down the hall past the staircase, through the door and the bathroom's the first room on your right. Those quarters are separate from the rest of the B and B."

He pushed up from the chair, taking his cup with him. He made a detour to the kitchen and placed it in the sink.

Nina called from the other room. "You could've asked for something stronger."

"I hate drinking alone."

She turned in her seat as he came out of the kitchen and she cocked her head. "How'd you know I wouldn't join you? You didn't ask."

"You seemed hell-bent on tea." He shrugged and ducked behind the staircase.

Idiot. He planted the heel of his hand against his forehead. If his boss could see the way he was conducting this assignment, Coburn would pull his secret agent card.

He pushed open the door to the small bathroom and snagged his shirt from the shower curtain rod.

His hand hovered at the corner of the medicine cabinet and then he abruptly turned and exited the bathroom. He was here to watch over Nina, not spy on her.

His agency didn't suspect her of any wrongdoing and she deserved her privacy.

He shook out the still-damp shirt in front of him as he returned to the great room. After he'd boarded the boat to go after Nina, he suspected he might have to go into the water after her, so he'd stashed his weapon and shoulder holster on the neighbors' boat. He hoped they didn't decide to take it out for a spin.

The fire was in its full glory, and the glow from the flames cast an aura over Nina, backlighting her dark hair as she turned toward him and giving her face a rosy sheen.

"Is it still wet?"

"A little." He dragged an ottoman in front of the fireplace and spread his shirt on top of it. "This should do the trick."

He sprawled in his chair, wedging his ankle on the opposite knee. "So what made you come out here and open a B and B?"

"I grew up here, and it seemed like a good idea to come home and try to get this place back into shape. My mom and stepdad ran it until…their health failed. That's why it's just a mess now."

"Sorry." He opened his mouth to say more, but a horn from a boat bellowed outside. "What is that? Sounds like an angry moose."

"That—" she struggled to her feet from the deep chair "—is the county rescue boat. They must be pulling my craft into the dock."

Jase snatched his warm shirt from the ottoman and stuffed his arms into the sleeves. "I'll go have a look."

"I'll join you. It's my boat." She slipped her feet into

a pair of clogs and grabbed a hoodie from a hook by the front door.

Sure enough, the big red Harbor Patrol boat had backed Nina's damaged craft against her dock.

They approached a member of the rescue team who was leaning over the side of the boat and writing something on a clipboard.

"Afternoon, folks. This your boat?"

"It's mine." Nina waved her hand. "I made the call."

"You must be Bruce and Lori's girl."

"That's right. I'm Nina Moore."

"Well, Nina Moore. I'm afraid I have some bad news for you."

Jase instinctively stepped in front of Nina. "What's the bad news?"

"This hole here?" The man jerked his thumb over his shoulder. "Someone did that on purpose."

Chapter Four

Jack Coburn had been right about this assignment and the need to watch over Skinner's ex-fianceé. Someone had Nina in his crosshairs already.

Two vertical lines formed between Nina's eyebrows, and she kicked the toe of her clog against a wooden post. "I figured it was just a matter of time."

He jerked his head up. Nina knew about Tempest?

The patrol officer tipped his hat back. "You have an idea who did this, Ms. Moore?"

"You can call me Nina, and yes. It has to be my stepsister, Lou." She swept her arm across the bay as if the mysterious Lou lurked somewhere out there on the water.

"Oh, yeah, Lou." The officer nodded in a way that made Jase feel completely out of the loop. "I remember her. Do you have any proof she did this?"

"None at all, except that someone in town mentioned they'd seen her around. So, she's back on the island."

"Watch your back, Ms.—Nina." The officer smacked the side of Nina's boat and jumped onto his own.

Jase watched the Harbor Patrol boat for a minute as it maneuvered away from the dock, and then turned to Nina. "Why would your stepsister be putting holes in your boat?"

Keeping her gaze on the retreating patrol boat, she

crossed her arms over her waist and her sweater outlined a small bump below, the first visible sign of her pregnancy—at least to him. Nina's lean runner's frame would probably take a while to show evidence of her condition, but she had to be at least four or five months along, judging by the last time she saw Skinner.

He'd seen pictures of Maggie pregnant at about the same stage as Nina, and she'd had a distinctive rounded belly, but then Maggie was smaller and more rounded in general than Nina.

When Nina swung her head around, his gaze jumped to her face.

"My stepsister, Lou, is a disturbed person. She's had some problems with drugs and alcohol, but her issues go beyond that. When her father married my mother and Mom and I came to live with them when she and I were both children, she had a fit. It only got worse from there. I knew when Dad, Bruce, left this B and B to me, she'd never let it go."

"So, you think she's bent on sabotage?" Noticing a tremble rolling through her body, he took Nina's arm. "Let's go back inside. You're still chilled from your swim in the sound."

She allowed him to steer her back toward the house. "Putting a hole in the bottom of my boat would definitely be something in Lou's repertoire."

"Is she capable of more? Would she do you physical harm? Not that plunging into the icy depths of that bay couldn't have resulted in something worse than a bad chill."

Pushing open the door, she paused on the threshold. "I don't think she'd pull out a gun and shoot me, but she'd pull stunts that could have unintended consequences—just like putting a hole in a boat."

"And I thought my family had issues." He stomped his feet on the mat at the door.

"Oh?"

He had no intention of getting personal with her and mentally gave himself a kick for even mentioning his family. He'd used his nickname and a fake last name, just in case she decided to do a little research on the internet, because it wouldn't be hard to find Jason Bennett—or his family.

"Do you want more tea?" He pointed to the flames simmering in the grate. "Looks like the fire died down."

"I'm fine." She stood in the entryway, making no move to go back to their cozy situation in front of the fire.

"Okay, I'll be heading back to my motel. Do you want me to stoke that up for you before I go?" He made a move toward the fireplace, but she placed a hand on his arm.

"I'll let it go, thanks."

He strode past her anyway. "I'll reposition those logs, so they don't roll off the grate."

He couldn't help it. Nina's pregnancy gave him an overwhelming urge to do things for her—all the things he never got to do for Maggie. He prodded the logs and then snagged Nina's mug and deposited it in the kitchen sink next to his.

Shoving his hands into his pockets, he grinned because women had told him in the past he had an irresistible grin and he needed to be irresistible right now. "Let me know when you're done checking me out and I can get to work for you around here."

"Oh, I'm done. Anyone who rescues me from drowning deserves a chance." She sized him up beneath lowered lashes. "You can start tomorrow."

"Awesome." He stuck out his hand and she gripped it. "I'll be back around eight o'clock."

Her blue eyes widened. "Make it ten."

"You got it…boss."

When he reached the curve in the road that led back to the town, he pulled his cell phone from his pocket and called Coburn.

"What do you have for me, Jase?"

"I met Nina Moore and she hired me as her handyman. I start tomorrow."

Coburn chuckled. "Must be that killer grin of yours. Is she suspicious about anything? Did she mention the father of her baby?"

"The father?" Jase glanced over his shoulder at the empty road. "She didn't even mention the baby. She's, uh, not really showing, so the subject never came up."

"She's gotta be five months along and she's not showing?"

"Yeah, your wife had twins, so I think that's a different case."

"Probably. What do I know anyway?" Coburn coughed. "You okay with this assignment?"

Jase chose to ignore Coburn's implication. Jack made it his business to know the personal histories of all Prospero agents, and sometimes Jase thought he used those histories just to test them, to mess with their minds.

"I'm never okay with babysitting assignments, Coburn, but you might be onto something here."

His boss sucked in a breath. "Oh, yeah?"

"Someone drilled a hole in Nina's boat and she discovered it while she was on the water."

"Is she okay?"

"Chilled but fine."

"You think it might be our friends at Tempest?"

"If they're trying to kill her, sinking her boat on a well-traveled bay is a long shot. Seems Nina has some crazy family members in the mix, too."

"Great. Just keep doing your job, Jase—watch Nina Moore and protect her if necessary."

"Got it, boss."

Jase ended the call and tapped the phone against his chin. He'd have no problem either watching or protecting Nina Moore. He'd do whatever it took to safeguard Nina and the baby—Simon Skinner's baby.

NINA STRIPPED OFF her clothes and turned sideways in front of the mirror as the bathtub filled with warm water. She massaged her bump with the palm of her hand and smiled. Her little guy was growing by leaps and bounds.

Had Jase noticed her pregnancy? No way. Any hint of a pregnancy would've doused those scorching looks he'd been sending her all afternoon. She'd been enjoying those looks so much she hadn't wanted them to end.

What did that say about her? Carrying another man's baby and getting hot and bothered by a stranger with a to-die-for grin. Simon had vanished from her life, but it didn't mean he didn't plan on charging back into it.

And she needed to be prepared when he did.

She stood on her tiptoes and checked the lock on the bathroom window. When the Harbor Patrol officer had told her about the hole in the boat, her suspicions had immediately turned to Lou, since any mischief connected to the B and B would have Lou written all over it.

But had Simon followed her here? He knew about the B and B, of course, even though he'd never been here. She rolled her shoulders and stepped into the warm water, inhaling the fragrant steam from the lilac bath salts.

She'd found a good doctor in town, a family practitioner rather than an ob-gyn, but Dr. Parducci had come highly rated and regarded.

She sank into the warm water, stretched out her legs

and closed her eyes, determined to relax. Dr. Parducci had told her to relax and not dwell on anything stressful.

Her eyes flew open. Like Lou. That had been the most unwelcome piece of news when she'd returned to Break Island. Had Lou known she was coming back to claim the B and B? Lou had no interest in the place, but she'd been livid when Bruce had left it to his stepdaughter instead of his daughter.

What did she expect? Her father had loved this place. Turning it over to Lou would've resulted in a quick sale and money blown on drugs, booze and a good time.

Nina closed her eyes again and swirled her hands in the silky water, willing her mind to happier thoughts.

Jase Buckley—now, there was a happy thought. Something about that man attracted her like a magnet. It could be his general drop-dead gorgeousness. She slipped farther beneath the water and blew bubbles.

Or it could be that for some reason, in some weird way he reminded her of her baby's father.

NINA ZIPPED UP her jacket to her chin and made the last turn into town. The brisk walk from the B and B into the town center had done her good. The fifteen-minute walk had cleared her head and relaxed her more than the warm bath had.

She hadn't completely shrugged off her big-city addiction, and the thought of spending a quiet evening at home just sounded like a big bore.

The locals usually liked to gather at Mandy's Café for dinner or at one of two watering holes that hadn't become tourist traps—yet. The island had changed a lot since the last time she'd really spent time here. At least the crowds had allowed Mom and Dad to run a flourishing business, but Break Island didn't offer the complete serenity she'd hoped for.

Maybe that was a good thing. The warmth and conversation that enfolded her as soon as she stepped across the threshold of Mandy's felt like a friendly hug. And she could use a few of those.

She tripped to a stop when she saw Jase Buckley at the center of a lively group in the corner. Hadn't he just arrived in town? She kept tabs on him out of the corner of her eye as she slid into a booth by the window. He must be a good writer, because he sure seemed to have the gift of the gab over there, spinning stories for an enthralled audience.

"Do you want something to drink, Nina?" Theresa Kennedy, one of her mother's old friends, tapped a pencil against her pad of paper. Theresa's family had owned Mandy's for years.

"Just water, but I'll take a cup of the chicken noodle soup right now."

"You got it. So, are you really going to fix up the old place? We could use another B and B on the island."

"I am, but I'm going to take my time, so I hope you're not in any hurry."

"It'll go faster with my help."

Theresa stepped back to allow Jase to sidle up to the table. "Are you going to help Nina get the place back on its feet?"

"Starting tomorrow."

Theresa poked Jase in the chest with the eraser end of her pencil. "I hope that doesn't cut into your writing time, Jase."

Nina raised her eyebrows. Had the guy spilled his life story all over town? Perhaps the connection she'd felt with him had been nothing more than Jase being Jase. "I'll have plenty of time, Theresa." He winked. "A man's gotta eat, too."

"Oh, go on. You could come in here and I'd feed you

anytime of the day or night. It would just be like having my son home again when he was studying for the bar. Anyway, I think it's a good idea for you to lend a hand to Nina."

"Nina needs help and I need work, so it's a perfect fit."

"Nina does need help." Theresa cocked her head to one side like one of the birds from the island's sanctuary. "But for the life of me, I still can't figure out why she abandoned her exciting life in LA for this old place."

"Sometimes we all just need a break. Maybe Nina needs a break."

"Hello." Nina waved her hands between Jase and Theresa. "I'm right here. No need to talk about me like I'm not."

Theresa clucked her tongue. "I'll get you that soup, Nina. Jase?"

"I'll take some soup, too." He patted the back of the banquette across from her. "Do you mind if I join you?"

Her gaze flicked to the table of locals still bunched together. "Is your audience going to miss you?"

"Them?" He snorted. "They're on to the next tall tale."

"And you?"

"Tall tales? I've told my share." He slipped into the booth across from her. "Did you finally warm up?"

"I did a little work around the house and then took a warm bath. That did the trick."

"Any more news about your sister?"

"Stepsister. I was going to ask around town tonight if anyone has seen her today." She rubbed her hands together when she spotted Theresa backing out of the kitchen with a cup of soup in each hand. "But not before I had some sustenance."

Theresa placed the soup in front of them, along with a basket of crackers. "Do you want to order now?"

Nina didn't have to look at the menu. "I'll have the fish-and-chips."

"I'll have the same." Jase tapped the edge of the plastic menu on the table. "And another beer, Theresa, that pale ale."

"You got it. Just water for you, Nina?"

"That's it."

When Theresa took their menus and walked away, Jase asked, "You don't mind if I have a beer, do you?"

"Why should I?" She blinked and then planted her elbows on the table. "You don't think I'm an alcoholic, do you?"

"No."

"Because I leave all the drinking in the family to my stepsister."

Jase raised a spoonful of hot soup to his lips and blew on the puddle. "Just didn't want to make you uncomfortable in case you're a rabid teetotaler."

She was no rabid teetotaler, whatever that meant, but the way Jase's lips puckered made her plenty uncomfortable. She shifted in her seat and busied herself with the wrapper on a package of crackers.

"Drink all you want. Be my guest."

"I'd like to be your guest."

Her soup went down the wrong way and she coughed. Pressing a napkin to her lips, she asked, "What?"

"You run a B and B, don't you?"

"We've established that." She sniffed and dabbed her eyes. "But you've seen the condition it's in. It's hardly ready for prime time."

"It would work out great for me—and you. I could stay in one of the rooms, do work around the place every day and get my writing done in a much better setting than my current location at The Sandpiper." He crumbled a cracker into his bowl and then dusted his hands off over a napkin. "You could pay me in room and board instead of cash. It's a win-win for both of us."

"Although I already hired you, I still want to do a background check on you." After months of being on edge, how had she allowed Jase to lure her into feelings of security already? She still needed to remain vigilant. Simon could be anywhere.

"Check away." He thanked Theresa for the beer and took a swig from the bottle. "My life's an open book."

She wished she could say the same. Keeping her pregnancy a secret from Jase and everyone else in town was silly. They'd find out soon enough. She ran a finger along the inside of her tight waistband. Like in about two days when she made the switch to maternity clothes. She'd already done a little shopping in Seattle on her way to the island.

Theresa delivered their platters of fish-and-chips and conversation came to a dead halt as they busied themselves with lemons, vinegar and tartar sauce.

Nina bit into the crispy coating of the fish and closed her eyes as the salty, tart tastes flooded her mouth.

"I think this meal alone is worth coming all the way out here for." Jase swept a French fry through a mountain of ketchup on his plate. "Is this why you returned to the old homestead?"

"Mandy's fish-and-chips?" She laughed. "Yeah, that's it."

They finished their meal and split the check. How had Jase known that's exactly how she'd wanted to handle it? If he'd insisted on paying, it would've felt too much like a date—and it already felt too much like a date.

When they hit the sidewalk, she thrust out her hand. "You're coming by tomorrow to go over the necessary repairs, right?"

"Sure." He took her hand but didn't release it. "I'll walk you to your car."

"Car?" She raised her eyebrows. "I'm not in LA anymore. I walked over here."

His grip tightened on her hand. "Really? I'll walk you home, then."

As her eyes traveled over his shoulder to take in the dark curve of the sand dunes that marked the turn toward the B and B, she said, "That's not necessary," but her voice didn't hold the conviction she'd wanted.

Would Simon track her down here? If he wanted to speak with her, he should just approach her like a normal person. But Simon hadn't been normal the past few times she'd seen him—not normal at all.

He shrugged. "I don't mind the walk."

"It *is* a nice walk."

They turned together and after two blocks the sidewalk ended in sand. He put his hand on the small of her back. "Be careful."

She appreciated Jase's solicitousness, but she didn't understand it. Why was he so attentive? It was almost as if he knew about her pregnancy.

She stole a sideways glance at his perfectly chiseled profile. *Idiot.* Maybe he did know she was pregnant. Just because she hadn't made the switch to maternity clothes yet, it didn't mean people couldn't tell. That woman in the elevator at the doctor's office knew. She was pretty sure Carl and Dora Kleinschmidt knew.

She cleared her throat. "You never did tell me why you chose Break Island for your writer's retreat."

"Do I have to explain?" He spread his arms. "It's isolated, beautiful, but has just enough tourists for some serious people-watching for inspiration."

"I thought you were writing a fictional account of your

experiences in Afghanistan—not many soldiers here to study." Unless Simon was lurking around the corner.

"They don't have to be soldiers. Human nature is human nature."

A bush rustled beside them and a gust of wind showered them with grains of sand.

Then a figure stepped onto the path in front of them and a voice came out of the night. "Home at last."

Chapter Five

Nina stiffened beside him, and Jase's own muscles coiled as he sprang in front of her, blocking her from the stranger on the path.

A low laugh gurgled from the woman's throat. "That's our Nina, always has a man to protect her."

Nina placed a hand on his arm and stepped beside him. "Are you stalking me, Lou?"

Instead of diffusing his concern, the fact that it was Nina's stepsister standing in front of them blocking their path heightened it. Lou had put a hole in Nina's boat, and even if Nina had been convinced the act wouldn't have resulted in her drowning, he didn't trust this woman anywhere near Nina.

"Stalking?" She took in the bay with a sweeping gesture. "I'm just enjoying the night like everyone else."

"Have you been working on Dad's boat by any chance?" Nina squared her shoulders and locked eyes with her stepsister, whom she topped by a good five inches. In hand-to-hand battle, he'd put his money on Nina any day—except she was pregnant.

"Moi?" Lou crossed her hands over her heart. "I haven't touched *my* dad's boat, and don't go calling him *Dad* like he's your dad or something. Your dad took off

a few months after you were born, having the good sense to dump you and Lori while he could."

"Hey." Jase curled his hands into fists and took a step forward. "Don't talk to Nina like that. I don't care who you are."

"And I don't care who *you* are." Lou put a hand on her hip, her gaze raking him from head to toe. "Who *are* you?"

"This is my…my handyman, Jase. He's going to help me fix up Moonstones."

What had Nina been about to call him? Handyman sounded so impersonal.

Lou leveled a finger at Nina. "That B and B should be mine and you know it. That's why you left it so long after my dad died. You felt guilty about inheriting it."

"We both know what would've happened to Moonstones if Dad had left it to you. Dad knew it, too. You would've sold this place so fast and used the money for God-knows-what. I can get it up and running again, and I have no problem sharing the profits with you if there are any."

"None of that matters. I don't want the piddly profits from some mom-and-pop business." Lou sliced her hand through the air a little too close to Nina's face for his comfort. "I could've used the money. You didn't need it with your stuck-up interior designing job in LA. Why did you give up all that to come back here anyway?"

Jase studied Nina's face as she formed an answer. So, her stepsister didn't know about the pregnancy, either, but he didn't blame Nina for not telling her. Lou had nut job written all over her.

In the end, Nina shrugged. "Moonstones needs some TLC. Dad and Mom loved the place."

"My dad had this dream before he met Lori, before he left my mom for her."

Nina sighed and ran her hands through her hair. "We've been over and over this, Lou. I'm sorry that happened, but it has nothing to do with us."

"It does now because Dad disinherited me for you. I always hoped Lori would die before Dad because I thought Dad would cut you out. Lori did die first, but Dad cut me out anyway." Her laugh sounded just this side of hysterical. "So, you gypped me out of my inheritance *and* my father."

"I'm sorry about that, too, Lou. They were the loves of each other's lives. You and I both know they loved each other more than they loved their daughters." Nina crossed her arms over her stomach. "Sometimes life just works out that way."

"Oh, you can be generous because you got the goods after Dad kicked off."

"Lou, baby? Lou, you out here?"

The slurred words came out of the darkness, along with a shuffling gait.

What now? As if all this family drama wasn't enough.

"Over here, Kip."

A lean man with tousled sandy hair came up from the beach, listing to the side as he scrambled up to the path. The stink of stale beer came off him in waves.

He staggered to Lou's side and draped a heavy arm across her shoulders.

"This is my stepsister, Nina, the golden child. Nina, this is Kip, my partner in crime."

Keeping her feet rooted to the ground, Nina leaned in with an outstretched hand. "Good to meet you, Kip, but Lou doesn't need a partner in crime."

Ignoring the proffered handshake, Kip hacked and spit into the sand dunes. "Just a figure of speech."

Nina nodded in Jase's direction. "And this is Jase."

Jase held up one hand. He had no intention of shaking

with Kip. The guy might topple over on him in a drunken free fall.

Nina continued to pretend this was some normal social gathering.

"Where did you and Lou meet?"

"In a bar." Kip pulled Lou in for a sloppy kiss on the side of the head.

"I meant—" Nina rolled her eyes "—what city?"

"Portland." Lou brushed a sandy lock of hair from Kip's eyes. "I've been living in Portland."

"Are you staying here now?"

"Just in town at one of the dumpy fishermen's motels." She clicked her tongue. "Don't worry, little sis. It's not going to be permanent. I have some business to settle."

Jase studied Lou and Kip side by side through narrowed eyes. The only business he could imagine these two settling is a drug deal. That, or harassing Nina.

He took Nina's arm. "We were just on our way back to Moonstones."

"And we were on our way back to the bar." Kip tugged on Lou's hand. "Come on, baby. Let's finish gettin' our drink on."

The other couple squeezed past them on the path to make their way back to the town. Once again, Jase caught a strong whiff of booze. Had Kip bathed in it?

When Kip and Lou disappeared into the night, Nina let out a long breath. "I can't believe she'd hook up with someone like that."

"Seems to me old Kip is just her type."

She pulled her jacket around her body. "Lou needs help, professional help. I don't understand people who refuse to seek therapy and medication when it's glaringly obvious to everyone around them that they need them."

"I'm not sure. I've heard the drugs flatten out your personality, and people don't like that."

"Some personalities need flattening."

"Lou sure holds a grudge, doesn't she?" A bird, probably an escapee from the sanctuary, shrieked above them and Nina jumped.

"Where's her mother?"

"Lou's mom has been through a couple of husbands already. She could be anywhere, since she pretty much washed her hands of Lou, too." She kicked at a rock with the toe of her shoe. "One thing Lou did have right is that her father left her mother for my mom."

"That's not your fault."

"Lou instinctively knew the score when she was nine years old. She hated me and my mom from the get-go."

"Nine is old enough. Did your stepfather prefer you to his own daughter?"

"Not really—he preferred my mom and my mom preferred him. I was a lot easier to deal with than Lou, and Dad knew she'd sell Moonstones as soon as she could and then drink up, snort up and shoot up the profits."

The road curved in front of the disputed B and B, and a glimmer of light from the quarter moon spilled across Nina's disabled boat.

"Lou denied sabotaging the boat."

Nina snorted. "Did you think she'd admit it? She's never fessed up to a single misdeed in her life."

"You have a complicated life, Nina." He opened the latch of the broken gate and ushered her through with a sweep of his hand.

"You have no idea, Jase."

He held his breath as she moved past him, her light fragrance tickling his nose. Would she tell him about her pregnancy? Open up about Simon?

She climbed the two porch steps and turned to face him.

He held her gaze, ready for her confidences. Not that

he'd be sharing any of his own—revealing his identity was not part of his assignment—yet.

"You know that proposal you made over dinner?"

He blinked. Not what he'd been expecting, but he'd go with it. "About moving in here?"

"Yes. Still interested?"

"Sure."

"Good." She turned and shoved open the front door of the B and B. "Because I want you to move in—right here, right now."

THE THRILL THAT rushed through his body better be for the assignment and not the woman. She'd done a one-eighty and ditched her previous reservations. Had Lou spooked her?

"Why the sudden turnaround?"

"Do you see it that way? I told you I'd consider it after doing a background check."

"And now you don't need a background check?"

"Now I've seen Lou and the company she's keeping."

"Do you really think Kip is helping her? The dude seems barely capable of a coherent thought."

"I've seen his type before. Lou's been with this type before—they egg her on and use her because they think she has some money coming. They encourage her in her wild schemes."

"He scares you?"

"They both do. Did you see his eyebrows?"

He raised one of his own. "I didn't notice."

"They were lighter than his hair."

"Is that supposed to be some sign of evil or some-thing?"

She pinched his arm. "He gave me the creeps."

"Okay, I defer to your creep meter, but if you want me

to move in tonight, I'm going to have to go back to my motel and get my stuff."

"I'll take you back in my truck. You can start some repairs tomorrow and write whenever you want."

"And run interference between you and Lou and Kip. Is that it?"

"If you don't mind."

"I don't mind at all." He came here for that express purpose—to run interference for Nina Moore—not that she knew it.

"Hold on and I'll get the keys to the truck." She left him standing at the door while she ran to the kitchen and snagged a set of keys from a hook.

The driver's-side door of the truck protested when he opened it for her. "Is there anything at Moonstones that's *not* falling apart?"

"No, and that includes the current owner." She hopped onto the seat and slammed the door.

He climbed in beside her. "If it's too much for you, Nina, why don't you go back to LA? Lou seemed to think you had it made there."

"Lou?" She adjusted her mirror. "You believe anything Lou says?"

"Does that mean you *didn't* have it made in LA?"

She bit her lip before starting and once again he expected confidences.

"I liked my job, had plenty of clients and left a lot of friends there, but this island has something…"

"A dilapidated B and B and crazy family members."

He didn't know why he was trying to encourage her to return to the big city. It would be so much harder to watch her there, and what possible excuse could he offer now for turning up in LA?

She laughed and he liked the sound. She needed to laugh more—for the baby.

"With your help, Moonstones won't be dilapidated for long and hopefully Lou will be on her way, taking her low-life companion with her."

"Once she finishes her important business."

She swung the truck onto the road leading to town, a smirk twisting her lips. "I'm afraid her important business is getting me to cough up some money."

"Will you? Have you ever?"

"I've given her a few bucks here and there, but that only seems to encourage her. Honestly, I do it out of guilt."

"Because your mom stole her dad away from her mom? That's ridiculous."

"I know it is. I just know how it feels to lose a parent." She glanced at him. "You heard Lou. My dad abandoned me and my mom when I was a baby."

"For another woman?"

"I have no clue, but my mom raised me alone until Bruce Moore came into her life." Her hands tightened on the steering wheel. "A baby needs two parents, don't you think?"

He licked his dry lips. "It's optimal."

As if sensing something in his tone, she turned to him. "Have you ever been married? I'm assuming you're not now because, well, you don't wear a ring and I can't imagine your wife being okay with you escaping for a few months to write."

"I am not now, nor have I ever been married."

"Children?"

"None that I know of." He didn't feel like talking about babies right now—hers or his.

Nina nodded once. Then she wheeled into the space in front of his motel room and threw the old truck into Park. "Do you need any help packing up?"

"It'll take me five minutes." He jumped from the truck

and five minutes later with his laptop tucked under his arm, he tossed his duffel into the back of the truck.

When he climbed into the passenger seat, Nina was texting on her cell.

"Everything okay?"

She held up the phone. "Still putting the finishing touches on a client's house in Malibu—job from hell."

"You should be able to do right by Moonstones with your expertise."

"Yeah, but I need a clean palette to work with, not a place falling down around my ears."

"That's where I come in."

It took her three tries before the engine cranked to life, and she looked over her shoulder before backing out of the space.

"How'd a soldier and a writer wind up being handy with a hammer and saw?"

"I learned everything from my grandfather. He liked working with his hands, even after..." He tugged on his ear before the truth came spilling from his lips. "Even after he got old."

He didn't need to clue in Nina that his grandfather had been a self-made millionaire and that his father had expanded the family fortunes and gone into politics. That reality wouldn't mesh with Jase Buckley's.

"Do you mind if we make a stop before heading back to the B and B? I need to pick up a couple of things."

"There's a drugstore on the main drag, a few doors down from Mandy's." She swung the truck around in a U-turn and rumbled back down the main street of town.

When she parked, he grabbed the handle of the door. "You coming with me?"

"Sure."

As they walked inside the brightly lit drugstore, the

clerk behind the register called out, "You have ten minutes until closing."

"We'll make it quick." Jase nudged Nina with his elbow. "Toothpaste."

They rounded the corner of the aisle, which gave them a straight shot to the pharmacy counter, where a couple was arguing with the pharmacist.

"I think someone else was using my driver's license."

"I don't think so, ma'am."

"God, don't call me ma'am. I'm only thirty-one."

Nina tugged on his sleeve to try to escape her stepsister's notice, but Lou caught the movement and turned.

"Nina, can you help me out?"

"Ma'am... Miss, you can't have someone buy the antihistamine for you after just trying to buy it yourself."

Lou cussed at the pharmacist and slapped the counter. "Hick town."

"C'mon, babe. Let's go back to the bar." Kip, looking more beat-up than before, wrapped an arm around Lou's waist.

"Hold on." She shrugged him off. "What are you doing back in town, Nina? I thought you were headed to Moonstones."

"Needed a few things." Nina tipped her chin toward the pharmacist, who was hastily rolling down his window.

"Why are you trying to buy antihistamines?"

"You know, runny nose." Lou pinched the bridge of her nose and sniffed.

"Antihistamines are for stuffed-up noses."

Lou plucked a tube of lip balm from a hook and put it in her pocket. "You have any room at the inn?"

"What?" Nina visibly recoiled.

"At Moonstones? Any vacancies for me and Kip to crash?"

"I...I thought you were staying here in town."

"We are, but we're running out of cash."

Jase reached his arm behind Nina and gave her hip a pinch. Surely, she could say no to her stepsister. The woman tried to drown her just this afternoon.

"I can't help you, Lou."

"Of course not. You got what was rightfully mine, and now you can't even spare a room for me."

"Jase and I were expecting to be alone."

His heart slammed against his chest. What was she playing at?

Lou narrowed her reddened eyes. "You and your handyman?"

Nina tossed back her shoulder-length hair. "I just didn't want to get you all wound up, Lou, but I'm getting sick of tiptoeing around you."

"What does that mean?" Lou's voice had taken on a dangerous edge, and Jase inched closer to Nina.

"Jase isn't my handyman. He's my fiancé."

Chapter Six

Nina wrapped her arm around Jase and gave him a squeeze. It was what she'd been wanting to do ever since he pulled her from the water anyway. Now she had an excuse.

Kip had dropped the box of condoms he'd been fidgeting with, and Lou gave it a kick with the toe of her shoe.

Nina's muscles went rigid, bracing for the explosion.

Lou's trembling lips stretched into a line and then turned up at one corner. "I'm not as surprised as you might think."

Not as surprised as Jase anyway, who hadn't uttered a sound since her announcement of their impending nuptials.

"And why is that, Lou?"

"I'd heard you were engaged, but that was through a friend of an acquaintance's second cousin or something like that, so I didn't know how true it was."

Lou had heard about Simon? Nina squared her shoulders. "Well, it's true, and we want to be alone, so you'll have to tough it out at your motel."

"I wouldn't expect anything more of you, sis."

A low sound rumbled in Jase's throat and he pulled her close. "Now that I'm going to be part of the family,

I can speak my mind. You need to stop ragging on Nina and get your life together."

"Really." Lou crossed her arms and her light-colored eyes glittered.

Even though Lou self-medicated with drugs and booze, those substances did nothing to calm her down. But Nina had Jase to protect her until Lou left the island. She hoped he understood the lie. He seemed to be taking to it like a natural.

"And we don't want to see any more damaged boats or anything like it."

Lou spun around and grabbed Kip by the arm. "Whatever. You two deserve each other, but just beware, Jase. Nina will use you and then chew you up and spit you out."

"Folks." The clerk was standing at the end of the aisle, her eyes wide. "We're closed."

Jase waved his toothpaste in the air. "I still need to buy my toothpaste."

"Hurry it up, and you two—" she wagged a finger between Lou and Kip "—you need to leave."

They left without a backward glance, Kip leaning heavily on Lou.

Aware of the cashier glancing from her face to Jase's, Nina kept her mouth shut as Jase paid for his toothpaste and they walked out of the store.

Not until they climbed into the truck and Nina cranked on the engine did Jase whistle through his teeth.

"Sorry, sorry." She put her hand on his thigh. "It wasn't just a way to get her to stop trying to wiggle into Moonstones—it was a message to her that I wasn't alone. I hope you don't mind too much. If she follows her usual pattern, she'll throw a few temper tantrums and then leave the island when she doesn't get her way, and hopefully take that creepy Kip with her."

"I'm okay with it just as long as you don't start shopping for rings."

The hand on his thigh curled into a fist and she punched him. "Don't worry."

After they returned to the B and B and she'd shown him to the one decent room and bathroom, she lay on top of her covers in a pair of flannel pj's, rubbing her belly.

The stress of seeing Lou today couldn't be good for the baby.

Had her stepsister been watching and waiting for her to return to Break Island? Did she have spies here reporting to her?

She rolled to her left side and buried her face in the pillow. Now she sounded as paranoid as Lou.

At least seeing her stepsister today convinced her that the hole in the boat was not the work of Simon. And why would it be? What did Simon have to gain from giving her a scare?

She'd escaped from LA to Break Island for relaxation and simplicity, but her problems had not only followed her, they'd multiplied.

Now she didn't have to face them alone. She had Jase Buckley on her side.

She tucked her hand beneath her cheek. She didn't even know the man. Why did he make her feel so safe? The boat rescue was only part of it. He reminded her of Simon—before the PTSD had taken control of Simon's mind—steady, strong, loyal, lethal.

Lethal? Where had that come from?

Simon had always insisted he held a boring government job developing security systems, but she'd never believed him because he traveled a lot and never discussed his work or coworkers—except that one she met, Max Duvall, who'd been as mysterious as Simon. Maybe she'd let her imagination carry her away, but she'd had a hard time believing Simon was a pencil-pushing civil servant.

Maybe if he had been, the PTSD wouldn't have destroyed him.

And Jase? Was he more than he appeared to be?

Right now he was her pretend-fiancé—and that was good enough. But shouldn't even a pretend-fiancé know that his pretend-fiancée was pregnant?

SHE WOKE UP the next morning to the sound of a saw. She shoved her feet into a pair of fuzzy slippers and scuffed across the floor to the front rooms. She peeked through the curtains at Jase sawing wood, the old fence torn down and lying in a heap.

He had shed his flannel, and his muscles bunched and flexed beneath his white T-shirt as he worked. As if sensing her scrutiny, he looked up from the fence.

No good pretending she hadn't been staring. She raised her hand and he waved back.

Tucking her robe around her body, she opened the front door and stepped onto the porch. "How long have you been at it?"

"About an hour. Did I wake you?"

"No. You've made a lot of progress. Do you want some breakfast?"

"Isn't this a bed-and-breakfast?"

"Yeah."

"Then I'd like some breakfast."

She put a hand on her hip. "It's not like you're a regular guest."

"That's right. I'm your fiancé." He picked up his saw and started attacking the next piece of wood.

She let the door slam behind her as she stepped back into the house. Brushing her hands together, she made a beeline for the kitchen. Her mom had been a great cook, but she hadn't inherited that cooking gene. If she ever got this place back on its feet, she planned to hire a chef to cook the meals for the guests.

But she had a guest now, and he had to be hungry after working for an hour on the fence.

She rustled up enough ingredients for an omelet and made some toast to go with it. She put the kettle on for tea but Jase had mentioned relying on a cup of coffee to get him going in the morning. She hadn't drunk much coffee even when she wasn't pregnant and she didn't want to pump the baby full of caffeine, so she didn't even have any instant coffee to offer him.

She poked her head out the front door. "I don't have any coffee. I can run into town and get you a cup at Logan's Coffee."

He reached for the top of a post and held up a white cup with a sleeve wrapped around it. "Beat you to it. I told you I needed a shot of caffeine in the morning to give me a jump start. Do you think I could've accomplished all this without it?"

"Impressive. Are you ready for breakfast?"

"You don't have to call me twice." Holding his cup in one hand, he stepped over a pile of debris and met her on the porch.

"Let me wash my hands and I'll be right with you."

She set the table as the water ran in the bathroom and then Jase emerged, buttoning up a different flannel from the one he wore yesterday.

She circled a finger in front of him. "Do you think a flannel shirt is the state shirt of Washington or something?"

He laughed and tugged on the collar. "If it is, it's for a good reason. It's chilly up here, and I have a feeling it's going to get worse with that storm on the way."

"It's supposed to be a monster." She sat down and broke

off a corner of toast. She'd passed the stage in her pregnancy for queasiness, but hadn't yet broken the habit of nibbling on dry toast.

"Where are you from, Jase? I detect a little bit of a New England accent."

"Really?" He selected a piece of toast from the plate as if he was picking out a new car. Then he spread a pat of butter across the surface in slow motion.

"Yeah, really. Are you from the Northeast?"

He shrugged. "Connecticut."

"And what did you do in Connecticut before your stint as a marine?

"I taught high school history for a year before enlisting and went back to that when I got out before I decided I needed to write down my experiences."

"Were they bad?"

"What? Who?" He crunched into the toast.

"Your experiences." She swirled the tea bag in the hot water, watching the ripples spread across the surface. "Did you have bad experiences during the war?"

"It was war, but it wasn't all bad and my book is mostly about that part—the not-bad part." He took a pull from his coffee cup. "How about your…stepfather? Did he talk about it much?"

"He was in Vietnam. I think it affected him deeply. He suffered from depression."

"Is that why he…?"

"Killed himself?" She took a quick slurp of tea, burning her tongue in the process. "I'm sure that contributed to it. My mom was his lifeline, so when he lost her he felt as if he'd lost everything, even his will to live."

He shook his head. "That's either a great love, or that's obsession."

"They are different, aren't they?"

"Definitely." He picked a mushroom out of his omelet

and pushed it to the side of his plate. "Have you ever had either one?"

A smile curved her lip as she resisted laying a hand on her tummy. "Yeah. How about you?"

His brown eyes darkened to black as he stared past her. "I thought I did."

"I've been there, too." She sighed and picked up her fork, aiming it at his plate. "You don't like mushrooms?"

"No."

"Sorry. I should've asked."

He brushed off her apology with a wave of his fork. "No problem. This is a good omelet with all the other stuff in it."

"What's up after the fence?"

"Thought I'd start clearing some of the weeds in the front and maybe do some repairs on that deck."

"I've got a guy lined up for the gardening, but I'd love to have that deck back online. My parents loved sitting out there in front of a fire and watching the bay."

"I can see why. It's a great spot." He shook his empty coffee cup. "Do you think our ruse was enough to get you off Lou's radar for now?"

"Maybe. Again, I apologize for the drastic measures. I just wanted to let her know that I wasn't alone, that I had someone…on my side."

"I am on your side, Nina."

"Why, Jase?" She planted her elbows on the table and rested her chin on her folded hands. "Why have you been so helpful to a total stranger?"

He cocked his head. "I think it's just the circumstances. I was there when your boat sprang a leak, and I was there again when you ran into your evil stepsister and her creepy companion. I'm not here completely out of the goodness of my heart. This is the perfect place for me to set up shop for a little while."

"Are you saying if I didn't have this B and B, you'd have let me sink in the bay?"

"I wouldn't have let anyone sink in that bay—including Lou and Kip."

"I'm just teasing. You have some natural protective instincts, just like…"

"Your stepfather?"

Her stepfather's only protective instincts had been toward his wife, but Simon had wanted to save everyone. Until he couldn't save himself.

"Yeah, my stepfather was pretty protective."

"Maybe it's a military thing."

"Yeah, a military thing."

"Are you going to be working around the B and B, or do you have other plans for the day?"

"I'd like to head across the bay today like I was trying to do yesterday, to get some supplies."

"Are you going to take the ferry?"

"I am."

"Are you going to be able to haul back everything that you need?"

"Not as much as I could with a boat, but I'll manage. The mainland provides carts for the islanders, especially now with the storm on its way."

"Do you want me to come along?"

"When do you write?"

A muscle in his jaw twitched. "I'll do some writing tonight."

"I can go it alone." She pushed back from the table and grabbed their empty plates. "You have your work cut out for you here."

"Do you need a ride to the ferry dock?"

"I was just going to drive and park, unless you think you need the truck for something."

"I might need it, if that's okay."

"Sure, I'm sorry I didn't think of it."

"That's not why I offered to drive you." He plucked the keys from the hook on the cabinet. "Never mind. It's a good enough reason."

There it was again. He'd been looking out for her. She might as well accept it and go with the flow.

When Jase pulled up in front of the dock, he reached into his pocket and pulled out a slip of paper. "You could use a few things for the yard unless your gardener had it covered, that is, if you have room in your cart."

She took the slip of paper from his fingers and dropped it into her purse. "I'm sure Brian's going to need supplies and tools for the yard. He's not really a gardener, just a dropout from U-dub, and there will be plenty of room on the cart. People do this all the time. Not everyone has a boat, believe it or not."

"I'd hate to be stuck on an island and dependent on the ferry to get off and on."

"Lots of people do it, but Mom and Dad always had a boat." She popped the door handle before Jase had a chance to hop out and get her door. He'd really go overboard if he knew she was pregnant.

Not that she minded his attentions, but if she planned to embark on single motherhood, she'd better get used to managing on her own.

He sat in the idling truck until she boarded the ferry and turned to wave. As the ferry chugged across the bay, she kept her eyes on the truck until it turned into a toy.

He'd watched her across the water, and she'd watched him. What was this connection they had? She didn't know whether to feel relieved or nervous that it didn't seem to be all one-sided.

The ferry cut through the bay, heading toward Newport. It was the closest thing Break Island had to a big city. It did have a big-box store, and that's all she needed for now.

As she walked down the gangplank, her tennis shoes squeaking on the metal, she nodded to a couple of Break Island locals waiting in line for the ferry back.

She snagged a taxi and bypassed Newport's tourist shops on the way to the working area of the city.

The driver eyed her in the rearview mirror. "On a supply run from one of the islands to get ready for the storm?"

"Break."

"That's a pretty one. My mother likes that bird sanctuary."

"Are you a local?"

"Naw. Came out here from Portland to get away from it all. You know?"

"I do know." As the big-box store came into view, she pulled some cash from her purse. "Your mom's here, too?"

"She just visits once in a while, but Break Island's her favorite because of that sanctuary."

She wished the entire island was a sanctuary. "You can just drop me in front."

"I'd offer to wait, but you're probably going to need one of the vans to get all your stuff back to the ferry."

"Yeah, I'll call in when I'm done shopping." She paid the driver and whipped out her membership card for the store as she marched up to the entrance. She grabbed a cart and maneuvered up and down the aisles, with a mind toward feeding a guest.

If Jase planned on doing physical labor all day and mental labor all night, he needed more than a vegetarian omelet for breakfast.

She'd gotten over her morning sickness and queasiness pretty quickly and could stomach just about anything now—except peanut butter. One sandwich early on in her pregnancy that hadn't gone down well had turned her off peanut butter for good.

She parked her cart in the meat aisle and hunched over the refrigerated display, evaluating the different cuts of meat. Jase looked like someone who might be picky just because of that patrician air he wore around him. His actual actions couldn't be further from a high-maintenance guy's, but he just seemed so darned perfect.

A flash of red hair caught her attention, and she jerked her head around. Two little dark-haired kids jostled for position in front of a free-sample table—no redheads in sight.

She patted her belly. Would this little one have red hair? She couldn't imagine anything cuter.

She continued to load her cart and changed lines twice to find the shortest one. Resigning herself to the wait, she hung on her cart and watched the stream of people in and out of the store.

Her heart jumped when her eyes locked on to a tall, broad man with red hair leaving the store.

She climbed on the edge of the cart and craned her neck for a better look. She shouted, "Simon."

A few people threw curious glances her way, and her cheeks warmed under their scrutiny. Calling out to him didn't make any sense, since her voice couldn't carry that far, especially with the noise level in the big warehouse.

If that were Simon, would he even turn around if he heard her? In all the weeks she'd suspected him of stalking her in LA, he'd never once attempted to make contact with her.

That's what frightened her. Why play games? Their breakup hadn't been that acrimonious, not at the end anyway. What led up to it, however…

She shivered and hugged herself.

"Miss?"

She glanced over her shoulder at the anxious face of a grandmotherly type. "Yes?"

"You can move ahead now."

She rolled her cart into the gap between her and the next cart with her heart thumping in her chest. First Lou and now Simon. Who *wouldn't* show up here in Washington?

She shook her head. There were tall men in the world with red hair, even here in Washington.

She transferred several items from her cart to the conveyor belt and left the big stuff in the basket. Once she'd checked out, she rushed to the exit and scanned the crowds of people eating in the outdoor food court area. No redheads.

She blew out a breath and shoved her cart in front of her. She'd been like this in LA, too—seeing red-haired men all over the place.

She ordered a taxi van to the dock and waited for it at the edge of the parking lot. When the yellow van arrived, the driver helped her load her supplies in the back.

"Which island are you from?"

"Break."

"Haven't been out to that one so much."

"It's quiet."

"Aren't they all?"

"Some more than others."

He hit the main drag, lined with T-shirt and trinket shops, and traffic slowed to a crawl. "Everyone over from the islands trying to stock up before the big storm hits."

"Uh-huh." Nina pressed her nose against the window, her gaze tracking back and forth along the sidewalks.

"Looking for someone?"

She peeled herself off the glass and slumped back in her seat. "No."

The driver rolled up behind a line of taxis in front of the harbor. "You need a pallet cart for this stuff?"

"Yeah, I do." She slid open the door. "Wait here and I'll grab one."

She weaved through knots of people on the wharf to claim a cart. As she dug into her pocket for the five-dollar bill that would rent the cart, someone grabbed her arm.

She spun around, her jaw clenched and her hands balled up into fists.

"Whoa!" Jase held out his hands. "I wasn't going to steal your cart."

"Jase." She swallowed. "You scared me."

"Obviously." He studied her face with his eyebrows meeting over his nose.

"What are you doing here?"

"I borrowed the Kleinschmidts' boat."

"Again? They're going to have you arrested."

"I asked them this time, and they said we could use it until yours is repaired. I figured I'd save you the hassle of lugging this stuff on a cart onto the ferry and then loading up the truck on the other side. The boat will take you practically to your doorstep."

"Great, thanks." She stuffed a still-trembling hand into her pocket. "The stuff's in the taxi."

"We'll get the cart anyway to transport it from the taxi to the boat, since I can't get the boat any closer to the ferry terminal."

She let him deal with the cart and led the way to the waiting taxi.

Jase and the driver loaded up the supplies, and after paying the driver, she helped Jase steer the cart toward the slip where he'd docked the Kleinschmidts' boat.

As she lifted a bag of fertilizer, Jase stopped her. "I'll get that."

"What *won't* you get?" He'd grabbed every item heavier than a feather out of her arms.

"Nothing." He flicked his fingers at her. "Go get the boat ready for departure and make sure this stuff is secure enough on the deck."

She saluted. "Aye, aye, Captain."

While she was mumbling about bossy men, she lifted her head to brush the hair from her face and saw the weak sun glinting off a redhead in line for the ferry.

A surge of anger thumped through her veins, and she jumped from the boat.

"Nina?" Jase called after her, but her single-mindedness drove her feet in the direction of the ferry.

Reaching the end of the line for the boat, she began pushing her way through, ignoring the comments and protests.

"Hey! Hey, you! Simon!"

As she reached the redhead and grabbed handfuls of his jacket, he jerked around.

Nina met a pair of cornflower blue eyes and stumbled back.

The man grabbed her arm. "You must be Nina Moore."

Chapter Seven

Jase reached Nina just in time to pull her away from the redheaded stranger's grasp. She collapsed against him, her face pale and her lips trembling.

The man's eyes darted to Jase's face, and he spread his hands in front of him. "Just catching her fall."

"Who is this, Nina?" Jase wrapped his arm around Nina's waist, curling it around her front.

"I…I don't know. I thought he was…someone else, but he knows my name."

The man's face turned almost the same shade as his hair as he jerked his thumb over his shoulder. "Can we talk about this somewhere else?"

"Spill it now. You're going to miss your ferry." Jase nodded toward the front of the line shuffling toward the gangplank.

"Doesn't matter. This ferry is going to Break Island. I was on my way to see Nina anyway."

Nina's body froze and she clawed at Jase's wrist. "Why? Who are you? What do you want?"

"He's right, Nina. Let's continue this conversation out of this line. We're going to start holding people up."

They jostled their way out of the line, and Jase pointed toward the Kleinschmidts' boat. "We have a boat over here."

The stranger followed them, as Nina shrank against Jase's side. Why was she so afraid of him? Just because he knew her name?

When they got to the boat, Jase balanced one foot on the pallet while still holding onto Nina. "So, who are you and what do you want with Nina?"

"Nina." The man turned to face her. "I'm Simon Skinner's brother."

Jase worked hard to keep his face impassive, clenching his teeth in the process. Now he could see it. The picture Jack had shown him of Tempest Agent Simon Skinner revealed a man with reddish hair, but in full living color, Simon's hair must be a match for this man's. "Nina?"

She huffed out a breath, as if she'd been holding it from the moment she'd confronted this man.

"Th-that's not possible. Simon had no siblings."

One corner of the man's mouth lifted. "That he knew of. Simon told you he'd been adopted, didn't he?"

"Yes." Nina had loosened her grip on Jase's wrist, although the imprint from her fingernails remained.

"That's why I'm a Kitchens, not a Skinner." He held out his hand. "Chris Kitchens."

When nobody moved to shake his hand, Kitchens dropped it. "Our mother gave us up for adoption when I was three and Simon was just a baby. Of course, he'd have no conscious memory of me, but I remembered a baby brother and when I got my stuff together I decided to find him."

Nina clasped her hands in front of her and faced Jase. "Simon Skinner was my ex-fiancé."

Jase nodded. She could interpret that any way she wanted.

Chris continued. "So, you can imagine my disappointment when I went through all the time and trouble to locate my brother only to...not locate him. I found his life to an extent, and I found you, but not much more."

"H-how did you find me?"

"I was able to track down Simon's last known address, which was an apartment in your name. A little more digging by a PI friend of mine led me to Break Island."

"I'm sorry. I can't help you, Chris. Simon and I split up months ago, and I haven't seen him since."

"Yeah, I gathered that from some of your neighbors in LA."

Jase ground his back teeth even more. If Chris and his PI friend had tracked down Nina that easily, what chance did she have against Tempest if that agency wanted to find her?

"And yet you still followed me out to Washington?" Her eyes narrowed and her spine stiffened. "Why?"

Chris shrugged his big shoulders. "I don't know. I thought maybe you'd heard from him. Maybe I just wanted to find out about my baby brother from someone who knew him well. Y-you did know Simon well, didn't you? I mean, you two were engaged."

Nina smiled a tight smile while tucking her hair behind her ear. "Of course."

Jase swallowed. You had to feel for the guy. He'd searched high and low for a brother he remembered before adoption split them apart, and now that brother was dead. And Jace couldn't even tell him. Couldn't tell Nina—not yet anyway.

"Why don't you come back with us?" He pointed to the ferry to Break Island chugging away from the dock. "I think you missed that boat."

"Sure, if—" he glanced at Nina "—if it's okay. I won't stay too long, Nina. Who knows? Maybe after talking to you, I'll be able to find Simon myself."

"Maybe." Nina's flat voice didn't offer much encouragement for that endeavor. "I'm sorry. Chris, this is Jase Buckley."

Jase shook the other man's hand. "I'm staying at the B and B and helping Nina fix up the place."

"I'd offer you a room, but I'm not ready to take on guests yet."

"No problem. I already booked a room at a motel in town." He tapped the cart. "Do you want me to return this for you?"

"Sure." Jase shoved it in his direction. "We'll get the boat ready for takeoff."

When Chris took off with the cart, Nina turned to him. "Sorry about the craziness. He looks a lot like his brother, my ex-fiancé, and I thought…"

"You thought your ex had come back for you?"

"Something like that."

"Is that something you want? I mean, do you want to get back together with Simon?"

She snapped, "No!"

He took her by the shoulders. "Did your ex hurt you, Nina? You were so freaked out about this guy, Chris."

"Simon never physically harmed me, but he could've been heading that way. I have to believe it was PTSD, but he wouldn't get help."

Chris came back into view and Nina grabbed Jase's arm and put her finger to her lips. "Chris doesn't need to know anything like that about his brother, okay? I plan to tell him only the good stuff."

"I think that's a good idea. He's gonna be heartbroken enough as it is."

Nina tilted her head and wrinkled her nose. "What do you mean?"

Jase sealed his lips and busied himself with the motor.

"Why's Chris going to be heartbroken?"

He glanced up at the big redhead barreling toward the dock. "Just that after thinking he'd found his brother, he's gone."

"Yeah, maybe he will have some luck tracking him down." She turned and waved to Chris. "Hop on board."

Jase maneuvered the boat across the water, passing the ferry at the midpoint of the trip. The brisk wind and the rumbling motor on the boat kept conversation to a minimum. All passengers seemed lost in their own thoughts anyway.

He had sized up Chris and felt comfortable enough to invite him back to Break Island with them. He was headed that way anyway, whether or not they'd extended the invitation. This way, Jase could keep an eye on him.

Nina seemed to think Chris resembled Simon enough to believe he was her ex-fiancé, so the story about him and Simon as brothers separated by adoption rang true.

Tempest wouldn't go through the trouble of finding someone who resembled Simon and then sending him out here with that story—would they?

Jase didn't know too much about Tempest. Like his agency, Prospero, Tempest was deep undercover, beneath the umbrella of the CIA but involved in missions completely off the radar.

Even Jack Coburn had only a foggy notion of Tempest's assignments. Jase hadn't given the other agency much thought at all until one of its agents, Max Duvall, had come in with wild stories about superagents and drugs and world chaos.

He gazed at the approaching shoreline of the peaceful island and snorted. Break Island was about as far removed from that world as it could be.

Missing siblings turning up unexpectedly? That, it had in spades.

As the boat eased up to the Kleinschmidts' dock, Chris jumped from the deck and started pulling the craft in.

"You know your way around a boat?" Jase tossed him the anchor rope.

"I should hope so. I spent five years in the navy."

Nina drew in a breath. "Simon was in the navy, too."

"I know that." He looped the end of the rope around the post. "That's how I was able to get some info on him."

With his back to the bay, Chris surveyed the island. "This sure is pretty. Simon spend much time here?"

"None at all. We had a busy life in LA. When he managed to get time off, we'd spend it in Hawaii, mostly."

"One of my favorite places, too." He snapped his fingers. "It's sort of like twins separated at birth, except Simon and I were two years apart."

They got the boat docked, and Chris helped him carry the supplies and groceries to Moonstones. Jase watched Nina closely, wondering if and when she planned to tell Chris he was going to be an uncle.

But so far, her lips were sealed.

Maybe Jack and Prospero had been wrong for once. He didn't doubt that his agency had discovered Nina's pregnancy, but maybe she'd lost the baby.

A knife twisted in his gut and he almost doubled over. He wiped a sudden bead of sweat from his brow with the back of his hand. He had to stop taking this whole assignment so personally. From accessing her medical records, Prospero had no indication that she'd lost the baby.

"You okay?" Chris slapped him on the back after dropping off another load of soil next to the porch.

"Low blood sugar. I haven't eaten in a while."

Nina stood on the porch, hooking her thumbs in the pockets of her jeans. "I think we all need something to eat."

"Is there someplace we can meet for dinner?" Chris

pointed to the bend in the road. "I think I'm headed that way into town. I'll check into my motel and we can meet up later."

"Mandy's. It's on the main street. You can't miss it, or ask a local. Six okay?"

"Fine with me. Thanks, Nina, for humoring me."

"I understand completely. I'm sure it's what Simon would want."

"So, where do you think he is?"

She shrugged. "He had a job with the government. They sent him places, sometimes for a long time."

"Six months?"

"I can't help you with that part of it, Chris."

"I understand. Dinner is enough. I just want to find out everything about my brother, or as much as you can tell me."

Nina joined Jase at the fence to watch Chris follow the road to town.

She murmured under her breath, "No, you don't."

"A few little white lies won't hurt. Then if he ever does find Simon, he can make his own judgments." He smacked the top of the post. "Let's put this stuff away. You can do the groceries, and I'll take care of the yard supplies. Still don't trust a store where you can buy fertilizer along with five-gallon jugs of milk."

Nina disappeared inside the house, and Jase hoisted a bag of soil onto his shoulder and walked to the back of the B and B.

He lifted his work cell phone from the inside zippered pocket of his jacket and placed a call to his boss.

"What do you have to report, Jase?"

Jack knew agents didn't use these phones for social calls.

"A twist."

"Is the subject okay?"

"The subject."

"Ah, Nina Moore."

"The subject's fine, but her ex-fiancé's long-lost brother showed up on her doorstep."

"Simon Skinner doesn't have a brother. He has no family. That's the way Tempest prefers its agents—rootless, alone."

"Skinner was adopted, right?"

"Yeah."

"Well, he had a brother who was adopted out, too. The brother is older and remembered having a younger sibling."

Jack's voice sharpened. "You're sure? Could be a Tempest ploy."

"Don't think so. Apparently, the guy's the spitting image of Simon Skinner."

"Name?"

"Chris Kitchens."

"We'll look into him."

"Nina's flaky sister made an appearance on the island, too."

"This is getting more complicated than we'd bargained for. Keep the players straight and keep the subject safe."

"I'm on it."

"You still think this is an unnecessary babysitting job?"

"I haven't seen any evidence of Tempest's interest in Nina yet."

"I had a gut feeling Tempest wasn't going to ignore Skinner's fiancée, ex or otherwise."

"I know all about your gut feelings, Jack. That's what I'm doing out here."

"It's more than a gut feeling now, Bennett."

Jase's pulse ticked up a notch. "Why is that?"

"Simon Skinner finally turned up—dead."

Chapter Eight

Nina stood on her tiptoes on the chair to shove the package of thirty-six rolls of toilet paper onto the top shelf in the storage room. She didn't need them now, but once guests started checking in on a regular basis, they'd come in handy. They'd probably come in handy once this baby started crowding her bladder, too.

A pair of strong hands clasped her around the hips. "What the hell are you doing?"

She glanced down into Jase's face, lined with worry. "I'm putting away some toilet paper."

"This chair isn't exactly steady, and if you have to go up on your tiptoes, it's not high enough."

"Okay, but it's not like I'm twenty stories high."

He took her hand. "Let me help you down."

She stepped down in front of him, facing him only inches apart. "I can't figure you out."

His dark eyes deepened to inky unfathomable depths. "What's to figure out?"

"Either you grew up with sisters and were very protective of them, or you were in a house full of boys and treated your mother like a queen." She bit the end of her finger to lighten the mood, since she could feel the tension coming off his taut body.

He cracked a smile. "Neither. I have one sister and

we fought like a couple of boxers circling each other in a ring, and everyone else treated my mother like a queen, so I was spared Her Majesty's service."

"Must be a military thing, then."

"Probably." He lifted a shoulder and stepped around her. "I'm going to clean up for dinner."

"You don't have to go, Jase." Would he really want to sit through a litany of Simon's accomplishments and virtues? "I know you have writing to do, and you've gotten precious little of that done since you've arrived on Break Island."

"I think it's a good idea if I tag along."

"Why? Do you suspect Chris of some ulterior motive?"

"Do you?"

"Why would you ask that? He looks very much like Simon. For that reason alone, his story rings true."

"Something about all of this—" his hands framed an imaginary ball "—seems off."

She swept her tongue along her dry bottom lip. "What do you mean, *off*?"

"You're a woman who ended an engagement with a man and then haven't laid eyes on that man for months. When you think you see him, your response isn't curiosity or even anger. It's fear." He put out his hand, palm forward. "Don't even deny it, Nina. I saw you. I held you. You were trembling like a petal in a rainstorm."

"I told you. Simon was suffering from PTSD. He was acting crazy before we split up. It's why we split up. He wouldn't get help, denied anything was wrong."

"Do you think he'll track you down?"

She spun away from him and grabbed the storage room doorjamb. "I'm not sure. When I was in LA, it felt like someone was watching me."

Jase sucked in a noisy breath. "Simon?"

"I don't know. I never saw anyone, could never pick out a face in the crowd, but I felt a presence."

Jase's angular features had sharpened even more. "You never told me this."

"Uh, we met yesterday, Jase. That's not something you generally spring on a stranger. It's bad enough that you got the full force of Hurricane Lou, and now my ex-fiancé's brother has come calling. I'm surprised you haven't run for the hills yet."

"That's serious stuff if you think your ex is stalking you, but why wouldn't he just approach you?"

"I don't know. I told him I wouldn't see him again until he got help. He probably hasn't gotten help."

Jase took a step toward her and threaded his fingers through hers. "It's not Simon."

She whispered, "How do you know that?"

"It just doesn't make sense." He toyed with her fingers. "I don't think he'd creep around stalking you. If anything, he'd confront you head-on. The way you describe him, he sounds like that guy."

Her nose tingled with unspent tears. Jase made her feel so good, so safe. Should she tell him now about her pregnancy? It might be the last straw to send him running for the exit, but she wanted him to know everything. She'd be making the switch to maternity clothes in the next week anyway. Much better to tell him than announce it with a maternity shirt hugging her visible baby bump.

He chucked her beneath the chin with his knuckle. "Let's go meet Chris and give him a glowing report of his brother. It's the least you can do for the guy."

She blinked and nodded, not even trying to recapture the moment between them. Jase was a nice guy, a protective guy—a hot guy—but what did she really owe him? He might find it too intimate for her to tell him about her baby as if it was some kind of special announcement. Better to mention it in an offhand way.

"I'm going to hit the shower. Meet you in the sitting room in about twenty minutes."

She allowed him to escape the storage room without embarrassing him with any more personal revelations.

She showered and shimmied into a pair of black leggings that she topped with an oversize blue sweater that hit the top of her thighs and a pair of black knee-high boots.

When she entered the sitting room, Jase turned from studying pictures on the mantel. "Your mom and stepdad look like a young couple experiencing first love."

"Yeah, and that was taken after they'd been together for ten years."

"Isn't it what every couple aspires to?"

"At the expense of their kids?" She flicked her fingers in the air. "I don't think so. You have to be a family unit first."

"Family units are not all they're cracked up to be." He slipped her keys from the hook in the kitchen. "You ready? I think we should take the truck into town and skip the late-night walk."

"Afraid of running into my crazy sister again?"

"Would you think less of me if I copped to that?"

"I'd think you had your head on straight." She winked at him.

Jase insisted on driving the truck and she let him. He parked half a block from Mandy's.

"Looks like more people in town tonight."

"I think it's the big storm."

"People are heading to the island because of the storm? You'd think they'd want to stay away."

"Once the storm starts blowing full force, there's no fishing. Most of these guys have to get their fix in before the moratorium."

"The storms pretty bad here?"

"They can be. This one's supposed to be coming down from Alaska. It can shut down the island—nothing coming, nothing going."

"Do you have a generator at Moonstones?"

"I don't have a working dishwasher at Moonstones."

"Got it."

Chris was waiting in front of Mandy's like an eager puppy dog. In that way, he resembled Simon not at all. Simon had nothing of the puppy dog about him. He had the intensity of a jungle cat, sort of like Jase.

Chris grinned and pumped their hands. "I like this island—friendly town."

"Where did you say you lived, Chris?" Nina crossed her arms low on her waist, cupping her elbows. She hoped he didn't have any plans to settle here.

"Arizona—going back there once I finish my search for my brother."

Jase got the door and held it open for her and Chris. "You're continuing your search after this?"

"Sure, why not?"

Jase caught her eye as she passed him and raised one eyebrow.

They were seated by the window again, and Jase tapped the menu. "Fish-and-chips two nights in a row?"

"Go for it. Live dangerously. It'll be good for your book."

Chris looked over the top of his menu. "You're writing a book?"

"Trying to."

"What's it about?"

"War story, fictional account."

"Were you in the service?"

"Marines."

"Ah, sorry to hear that." Chris chuckled. "Were you deployed in Iraq or Afghanistan?"

"Two tours of duty in Afghanistan."

"I'd read that book." Chris downed half his water. "From what I got out of the navy, Simon did a couple of tours in Afghanistan and then seemed to drop off the radar—just like now. Makes me wonder what he was into. The navy wouldn't tell me anything more."

"Lotta stories to be told." Jase closed the menu and dropped it to the table. "I have to go with the fish-and-chips again."

Nina took a sip of her own water, eyeing Jase over the rim of the glass. He didn't seem all that eager to talk about Simon. Maybe he should've stayed home to write, because she planned to give Chris a glowing report of his brother to make him that more anxious to find him and send him on his way.

The waitress approached their table and flipped open her pad. "You ready?"

They all ordered the fish-and-chips, and the men ordered beers. Nina stuck to water.

When the waitress left, Chris hunched over the table. "Tell me about Simon. Do you have any pictures?"

Of course she had pictures. After the breakup, her inclination had been to delete all pictures of Simon from her phone. She'd gotten rid of a few, but stopped when she found out about her pregnancy. Her child deserved to know what his father looked like, even if he never saw him or met him.

She pulled her cell from her purse and tapped her photos. She'd moved them all to a separate album. Another tap and Simon's face filled the screen, his megawatt smile and bright red hair causing a lump to form in her throat.

He'd been a good man, full of joy and ridiculous impressions. Why did he change?

She handed the phone to Chris. "That's Simon."

"Wow, we do look alike."

"You can scan through that whole album. All those pictures are of Simon."

Chris's eyes met hers. "You're not one of those exes who trashes and burns every picture? I had one of those. My girlfriend and I split up, got back together a few months later, and I'd come to find out she deleted every image of me off her phone. Then we broke up again. Are you holding on to these because you hope to get back together with Simon someday?"

Nina ignored Jase, even though she could feel his gaze focused on her like a laser beam. Was he jealous? Would she mind if he was?

"Simon and I won't be getting back together, but he was a part of my history and I'm not about to rewrite history."

"I like that attitude. Why'd you two break up, if you don't mind my asking?" Chris thanked the waitress when she placed his beer in front of him and then returned to the pictures on the cell phone.

She shrugged. "We both changed, went our different ways. It was mutual."

As he slid through each image, he peppered her with questions. She answered him with the vision of the old Simon in her head—the cheerful, fearless, protective man she'd fallen in love with, not the paranoid, angry man given over to fits of rage she'd kicked out of their house and her life.

Occasionally, Jase would lean across the table to look at a particular picture, his features sharp as if on high alert. Simon had that look about him at times, too, much more toward the end—always on edge, always expecting something to happen.

She must be drawn to that intense type, because she

had to admit it to herself, pregnant or not, she was drawn to Jase Buckley.

Their platters of deep-fried fish and golden French fries arrived just as Chris had thumbed through the last picture of Simon. He placed the phone next to her plate and patted her hand. "Thanks for that, Nina. Makes me more determined than ever to find my brother."

Jase rubbed his hands together and reached for the vinegar. "Best fish-and-chips I've ever had."

Nina threw a sharp glance in his direction. Way to break a mood.

Chris didn't seem to notice or care as he squeezed a lemon quarter all over his food. "Looks great."

As they dug in to their meals, the conversation turned to fishing and the weather.

"I understand there's a big storm heading down this way." Chris took a sip of beer and the foam clung to his red mustache. "Do you ever get cut off?"

"Cut off, blacked out, flooded—you name it."

"I should probably take off before all that happens."

"Where are you headed next?" Jase ran his fork through a glob of tartar sauce before stabbing a piece of fish.

"I think I'll go back to LA to see if I can pick up any more threads down there. That's the last place I can track him to. I appreciate the pictures and all, Nina, but I was hoping you could tell me where to find him."

"If I knew, I'd tell you." She folded her hands around her glass of water. "We broke it off. He packed up his things, took his car and left. I didn't hear one word from him after that."

"Did you have a big fight at the end? Was he distraught or suicidal?"

She shoved her glass aside. "Look, Chris. Simon was suffering from PTSD. I wasn't going to tell you because I didn't want to concern you, but if you're going to take up this search, you need to know. Simon was going off the rails. He was paranoid. I think he had delusions. People were after him. He was raging against some unseen enemy. I encouraged him to get help, but he refused. The day I gave him the ultimatum is the day he walked out."

Chris whistled. "I'm glad you told me, Nina. Why did you think you had to hide it from me?"

"Because you wanted to know your brother, and that wasn't Simon. Simon was all those things I told you about him."

"You're wrong, Nina. That was a part of Simon, too." Chris shifted his gaze to Jase's face. "Am I right, man? That was a part of him."

Jase nodded. "You're right, but maybe now's not the best time to go searching for him."

"There's no better time." Chris slapped the table. "Thanks for telling me that, Nina. It gives a whole new urgency to my quest."

"Not happy with just one guy, gotta have two?"

Nina groaned and closed her eyes briefly before meeting her sister's watery blue eyes. "I thought you'd be on your way by now, Lou."

"Kip and I are on vacation. We're going to hang out for another day or two, and you know how I love a raging storm." She wagged her finger in Nina's face. "But don't think we've given up on Moonstones. Kip's brother is an attorney in Seattle and he thinks I might have a case against you."

"Kip's brother thinks that or Kip? 'Cause Kip looks pretty out of it right now." She pointed at her sister's shadow swaying behind her.

"Whatever." Lou batted her eyelashes. "Who's this cutie?"

"This is Chris Kitchens. Chris, my sister, Louise Moore, and her friend Kip…"

"Chandler." Kip stuck out a surprisingly steady hand. "You a local?"

Nina held her breath and glanced at Jase.

"Me?" Chris crumpled up his napkin and tossed it onto his empty plate. "Naw, I just came out here to find Nina."

Lou blew a strand of dyed blond hair from her face. "Everyone wants Nina."

"Oh, no, it's not like that. I'm Simon's brother."

Nina was clenching her jaw so tightly her teeth ached.

Lou widened her eyes. "Am I supposed to know who Simon is?"

"Simon Skinner. Nina's ex-fiancé."

"Whoa-ho, girl, you work fast."

"Don't you have a joint to smoke somewhere?" Nina kicked Jase under the table, but she didn't know what she expected him to do. From the look on his face, he didn't know, either.

"What does that mean?" Chris cocked his head and ran a thumb across his mustache.

"This—" Lou poked a finger in Jase's direction "—is Nina's fiancé now, so I don't know how long ago she was engaged to your brother."

Chris's jaw hung open as he turned to Nina, his gaze darting to Jase's face. "Really?"

"Sorry, Chris." Nina pressed her fingers against her hot cheek.

"That's your business, but is what you told me about Simon's PTSD true or did you two break it off because of Jase?"

"Not at all." Jase kicked her back. "I met Nina after the breakup. It just happened fast for us."

"Wish you all the best, then." Chris reached for his wallet. "Let me pay for dinner for all your trouble today."

Jase already had cash out. "We'll get it."

"Tell you what." Chris tapped her phone. "You send

me a few of those pictures of Simon, I'll pick up dinner and we'll call it even."

"I'd be happy to." She shoved her phone across to him. "Call me from your phone so I have the number."

Kip had wandered off to the bar, but Lou hadn't given up yet. Placing a hand on Chris's shoulder, she leaned over the table. "If you want a ride back to the mainland in style, Kip and I can hook you up."

Chris looked up from placing his call to Nina's cell. "Really?"

"If the boats stop running because of this storm, Kip has a line on a helicopter."

Nina raised her eyebrows. "Kip has a helicopter?"

"I don't know about that. It probably belongs to his brother, who's a big-time lawyer. I just know because I heard him on the phone asking around for helipads on the island."

"Thank you, I'll keep your offer in mind."

Disappointed that she hadn't stirred up more trouble, Lou joined Kip at the bar, where he had a beer waiting for her. They drank them down and left before Chris even paid the bill.

When the waitress dropped off the check, Chris studied it and said, "I think they charged us for two more beers. You just had one, right?"

"Yeah."

Chris waved to the waitress. "We just had two beers at this table, and you charged us for four."

She jerked her thumb over her shoulder. "That couple who was at your table earlier? They had a couple of beers at the bar and said you were picking up the tab."

Nina rolled her eyes. "And you didn't think to check with us first?"

"Sorry, hon. They were over here."

"Chris, I'll pay for my sister's drinks."

"That's all right. Some bad blood there?"

Jase snorted. "In case you hadn't noticed, Nina's *step*-sister has some issues."

"I sure hope when Simon and I finally meet, we'll get along. I'll make sure of it."

"Good luck with that, man." He clapped Chris on the shoulder.

Nina grabbed her jacket and scooted out of the booth. If Chris ever found Simon, would he report back to him that she'd gotten engaged? How had everything gotten so complicated? She'd come out to Break Island to escape complication.

Jase opened the door of the restaurant, and as Nina stepped onto the sidewalk, droplets of rain, propelled by the wind, pelted her face. "Looks like we're getting the edge of that storm creeping in."

"You left your umbrella in the restaurant. I'll get it."

As Jase returned to the restaurant, Nina turned to Chris. "Do you plan to stick around the island?"

"Maybe for a day or two, but don't worry. I can look around on my own. You've been helpful and you didn't have to be."

"I just hope you find what you're looking for, Chris, and that you're not disappointed." She reached out to him, feeling guilty and sorry at the same time.

As he hugged her, a piercing screech came from behind. Before Nina had a chance to react, a strong force yanked on the back of her hair, dragging her from Chris's embrace.

She staggered backward, her arms flailing.

"You bitch! You have to take everything. One fiancé. Two fiancés. Are you working on your third?"

As Lou screamed in her ear, she began driving her bony knee into Nina's back.

Nina's feet scrambled on the wet sidewalk to gain

purchase, and then suddenly the threat evaporated. She turned to see Jase lifting Lou off her feet by the back of her jacket.

Lou dangled there like a scarecrow until Jase set her down with a jolt.

"Keep your hands off Nina. She's pregnant."

Chapter Nine

Everyone froze. She still had her hands splayed in front of her to ward off Lou's next attack, but she didn't have to worry.

Lou's feet were rooted to the sidewalk where Jase had dropped her, with her mouth hanging open and a wild look in her eye.

Even Chris stood as still as a statue.

How the hell did Jase know about her pregnancy? And why the hell did he choose to announce it in front of these two particular people?

Chris broke the silence first. "Is it…? Is it…?"

Nina took a shuddering breath. She couldn't handle this—not now. "No, Chris. It's not Simon's. It's the reason Jase and I decided to speed up our commitment."

She finally met Jase's eyes. Poor guy. First she'd foisted an engagement on him and now a baby. Poor guy? Her nostrils flared. How dare he spill the beans like this in the middle of the sidewalk.

Lou sank to the ground, her keening wail putting an end to any conversation. Nina shot a worried look at her stepsister crumpled on the ground, rocking back and forth.

She finally noticed Kip hugging the wall near where Lou must've launched her attack. She swept her arm toward Lou. "Help her. Lou, what's wrong?"

"A baby, a baby, a baby." Lou raised her tear-streaked face, her mascara little black rivulets down her cheeks. "I've always wanted a baby."

Lou's words sent a shower of cold fear down her back. Lou had never expressed any interest in children before. Now she wanted a baby?

Nina pushed a lock of wet hair from her face. "You need help, Lou."

"We're leaving." Jase stepped into the circle that had formed around Lou's forlorn figure. He put an arm around Nina's shoulders and held out his hand to Chris. "I hope you find peace with your brother."

Then he pointed a finger at Kip. "You'd better get her out of here unless you want to see her get locked up for being drunk in public."

Jase steered her down the street, opening the umbrella over their heads.

Nina glanced over her shoulder at both Kip and Chris helping Lou to her feet and Chris draping his jacket over her shoulders. Chris was that kind of guy, just like his brother used to be.

When they got to the truck, Jase helped her in and then blasted the heat when he started the engine. He rested his hands on the steering wheel and stared straight ahead without putting the truck in gear.

"Sorry, you know, sorry I did that."

She folded her hands across her belly. "How did you know I was pregnant?"

His hands tightened around the steering wheel. "I don't know. Little things. You didn't drink alcohol. Your silhouette when you were all wet after I pulled you from the water. You put your hands on your stomach a lot."

"Do I?" She lifted her hands from her stomach and sighed.

"I was waiting for you to tell me. I figured you'd do it

in your own time, or, you know, you don't owe me any explanations or anything."

"But why then?" She watched a droplet of water tremble on the end of a strand of hair and then fall to her thigh. "Why did you have to blurt it out at that moment—in front of Lou, in front of Chris?"

"I don't know." He pressed the heel of his hand against his forehead. "I wanted to stop Lou without physically throwing her against a wall."

"Yeah, well, picking her up by the scruff of the neck did a pretty good job of stopping her."

"She was still moving and squirming. I knew the minute I let her go she'd resume her assault on you."

"Thanks for stepping in, but I wish you hadn't let the cat out of the bag about my pregnancy."

He drummed his thumbs against the steering wheel. "Why didn't you tell Chris it was Simon's? It *is* Simon's, isn't it?"

"Of course he's Simon's."

"You're having a boy?" Jase turned toward her, but his gaze shifted over her shoulder to stare into the wet night.

"Yes, and I didn't want to tell Chris because I didn't want to complicate his life even more than it is. He's so hell-bent on finding Simon and so convinced that he's going to have some wonderful, brotherly reunion, I didn't want to dump this on him, too."

"Are you ever going to tell him?"

She patted her cell phone in her purse. "I have his info. I'll tell him later when everything settles down, and if he wants to be an uncle to the baby, that's fine. He seems like a decent guy."

His eyes locked on to hers. "You're not trying to keep this pregnancy from Simon, are you?"

"God, no. I wouldn't do that. But as you can tell from Chris's fruitless search, Simon is not an easy guy to find.

But if he is stalking me, he needs to get help before I tell him anything."

As always when she started talking about Simon, Jase's face closed down and shutters came down over his eyes. He started the truck. "Why do you think Lou went off like that?"

"Because she's unbalanced, and the way she self-medicates with booze and drugs only makes her worse. She needs a good treatment facility. Dad offered many times to pay for it, but she refused."

He checked the rearview mirror and pulled onto the street. "I think she could be a danger to you and the baby, Nina, and I think you're fooling yourself if you think her stunt with the boat and her attack tonight weren't meant to cause you physical harm."

"You're probably right." She twisted her fingers together and leaned her head against the cool glass of the window. "I came up here to Break Island to get away from the fear and the tension, and it looks like they followed me."

"Do you really think Simon is stalking you?"

She hadn't meant to harp on her suspicions, especially since Jase was taking this protectiveness thing to a whole new level.

"I don't have any reason to believe he is. When we split up, he left—no begging, no threats—it was as if he couldn't care less. I don't know why he would be stalking me, but I can't think of anyone else who would tamper with my car and lie in wait for me in a parking structure."

"What?" He slammed on the brakes in the middle of the road and the truck's back tires fishtailed.

She grabbed the dashboard. "For being an overly protective type, you should learn to drive more carefully."

"Someone tampered with your car? You didn't mention that before?"

"I'm not really sure. I had no proof, but my car had been working just fine before that and it sure seemed like there was a car following me."

"When did this happen? Right after Simon left or later?"

"Not right away. It was later, after I discovered I was pregnant. That's why I suspected Simon. I figured maybe he found out about the baby and got some weird notion in his head to start following me around—maybe to see if the baby was his."

"You never saw him?"

"Oh, I saw flashes of red hair here and there." She tugged on her earlobe. "Just like today, only today I matched the hair to a real person. In LA, I was never able to do that. I don't know."

"You don't know what?" He'd continued driving and Moonstones came into view.

"I thought the hormones were making me paranoid. At least here on Break Island, Lou really *is* after me. It's not all in my head."

"Do you believe the feelings you had in LA were all in your head?"

She planted her hands on her knees and hunched forward. "The feelings I had were real. Whether or not those feelings were based on anything real is another story. Does that make sense?"

"Yep."

They dashed through the rain, and when they stepped inside the B and B, Jase hung up the umbrella on a hook by the front door. "I'm going to get that fire going. You go get into some dry clothes, or better yet, some warm pajamas. Do you want some warm milk? Tea?"

"I'll take some tea." She turned at the hallway that led to the back of the house. "Are you always this bossy, Jase Buckley?"

"This is nothing."

She disappeared into the back, and Jase strode to the fireplace and prodded the charred wood from yesterday's fire. He hoisted a few more pieces onto the grate and tucked some kindling into the spaces.

In two minutes, he had the flames dancing across the wood and he stared into the flickers of orange and gold. How could he have been so stupid?

Straight up, he wouldn't be able to tell if a woman was pregnant any more than he'd be able to tell what she ate for dinner. He must've bluffed his way through that one, because she seemed to believe his line of bull.

If the boss could've seen his performance tonight out on that sidewalk, Coburn would've questioned his sanity.

Nina had been faster on her feet than he'd been, telling Chris that Simon wasn't the father. All he needed was for Chris Kitchens to be hanging around Nina, bringing up Simon every other minute.

Man, he felt for the guy. Waiting all this time to track down his brother only months after that brother had died. Once Prospero and the CIA could straighten things out regarding Simon Skinner's story, they'd have to notify Chris…and Nina.

Maybe he'd be long gone by then, out of Nina's life.

Had she been right about her suspicions in LA? She might believe it was Simon who'd been stalking her, but he knew that couldn't be true. Prospero had finally confirmed Max Duvall's story, and even if they never recovered Simon's body, they had no reason to doubt that Duvall had killed him in self-defense. But if not Simon, who?

Would her stepsister have gone down to LA to watch Nina? Stalking didn't seem to be Lou's style. She preferred an all-out, in-your-face attack.

Could the boss be right again? Had Tempest already

been following Nina in LA? For what purpose? She knew nothing about Simon's work.

"You're hogging all the warmth."

Still crouching in front of the fireplace and a now-blazing fire, he cranked his head around. Nina had wrapped herself in a pink robe that matched her cheeks. She'd dried her hair and it floated around her shoulders like a cloud.

"The flames can be hypnotic." He rose to his feet and stretched. "And I didn't make your tea."

"I can make my own tea."

"Sit." He pointed to the chair across from the fireplace. "I'm bossy, remember?"

"It's sweet of you to be so concerned, but I'm not going to break."

"Sweet?" He scratched his jaw. "That's the first time that adjective's ever been used to describe me."

"Oh, please." She settled into the chair and curled her long legs beneath her. "You're probably great with your nieces and nephews, too."

"Nieces and nephews? That's a laugh. My sister's the type who would eat her young." He crossed into the kitchen and started filling the kettle with water.

"Really? I'm surprised."

"You don't know my sister."

"No, I mean I'm surprised you're not an uncle. I would've thought the way you picked up on my pregnancy, you'd been around a pregnant woman before. I just assumed your sister…"

He swore under his breath. He was getting himself in deeper and deeper here. He had to stop acting so natural around Nina. This wasn't natural.

He wasn't writing a book. He didn't need to work as a handyman to make money. He hadn't recognized any signs that she was pregnant. His agency had spied on her.

"A lot of my buddies have been getting married lately and having kids. Seems like a new baby popped out every other month."

He folded his arms and leaned against the counter that separated the kitchen from the sitting room.

"I suppose these things do run in cycles." She held her hands out to the fire. "You're sure you're not married with five children at home?"

He forced a laugh and then gratefully turned toward the whistling kettle. "Seven."

"Seven what?"

"Kids."

She laughed, but it was a tight, mirthless sound. She doubted him.

He had to come clean, had to tell her about Simon— at least the part where he was dead. Coburn had wanted to verify Simon's death and parts of Max Duvall's story before releasing any information to Simon's loved ones. Nina still counted as a loved one, since Simon was the father of the baby she was carrying.

Poor little thing—no daddy from the get-go.

He poured the hot water over the tea bag and carried the cup to her, still curled up in the oversize chair.

She thanked him and winked. "You're not joining me this time?"

"I discovered I don't like hot tea."

"I have cold beer in the fridge."

"After the day I had, I'm going to take you up on that offer." He returned to the kitchen and peered into the fridge at three bottles lined up on the shelf. "Are these all local breweries?"

"I have three cases in the storage room and put one of each type in the fridge, just in case. They're all good."

He grabbed a pale ale with an interesting label and used

a bottle opener to pop the top. He settled into the love seat closest to hers, just like last night.

Only everything between them had changed.

"Don't you think it would've been a better idea to have this baby in your home city with your friends around?"

"I have friends here—a different type of friend, people who knew my parents, women who cooked for my dad during Mom's illness—the type of friend that will be here for me when the time comes."

"You don't have those kinds of friends in LA?"

"I have good friends there, friends to lunch with, meet at coffeehouses, attend concerts with, but not the kind to watch a baby in a pinch or know how to put together a crib or who know a home remedy for colic." She blew on her tea and sipped it. "Those people are here, and I need those people around me now."

"I'm sorry...sorry Simon's not in the picture."

"I'm not." She uncurled her legs and wiggled her toes. "Not the way he was acting. I didn't need another un-hinged person in my life—Lou is more than enough."

"That's for sure." He whistled between his teeth. "I couldn't believe it when I saw her take a flying leap at you. I still think you could've taken her down, pregnant or not, if she hadn't surprised you."

She rolled her eyes. "Thanks for the vote of confidence, but I'm not going to get into a brawl with my stepsister in the middle of the street."

"It makes sense that you kicked Simon out so quickly after what you've had to deal with in your own family."

She sucked in some tea and then choked on it. "I didn't kick Simon out all that quickly. I encouraged him to get help. I called a psychologist friend of mine. I called the Department of Veterans Affairs."

"What was he doing? What was he saying?"

"He'd come home from an assignment—" she circled

her finger in the air "—he traveled a lot. Worked for the government but couldn't talk about his job much. When he'd get home, he'd lock all the doors and draw the blinds. Sometimes he'd sit for days in front of the TV with a gun in his hand."

"You didn't feel threatened?"

"Not then. His anger and paranoia weren't addressed at me. He kept saying we weren't safe, that if they found out about him, they'd come and get him."

"Did he ever identify who *they* were?" He rubbed the stubble on his chin. This account sounded similar to the types of things Max Duvall had been claiming.

"He never got into it, wouldn't answer me." Hugging herself, she continued. "Then the ranting started alternating with the violence. He'd punch holes in the wall or kick a piece of furniture to pieces."

"That must've been scary, even if it wasn't aimed at you."

"That's the thing." She clasped her hands between her knees. "The last time he was home, he started going on and on about how I was next, how they wouldn't leave me alone, either."

Did Simon Skinner's ranting hold more truth than paranoia? "And that was the final straw?"

"It freaked me out. I still had no idea who he was talking about. Maybe he was talking about himself. I'd been bugging him for weeks to get help, but he refused. When I gave him an ultimatum—get help or leave—he left."

"Would you have made good on your threat?"

"I'd like to think so, but the final punch to the gut was his warning to me never to look him up or contact him again."

"You respected his wishes?"

"About not contacting him?"

"Yeah."

"Up until the time I found out I was pregnant. Then I did everything in my power to find him to tell him, even though I wasn't sure what kind of role he'd play in the baby's life."

"That makes sense."

"Not a whole lot made sense at that time, but I sort of have a theory about how it all went down."

"I'm listening."

He wasn't kidding. Jase had scooted to the edge of the deep chair, bracing his forearms against his knees and hunching forward. He'd been absorbing every detail of her story from the beginning. How was this guy even still single?

"I think Simon found out I was looking for him and why. He knew I wouldn't let him be a father to the baby unless he checked into a treatment facility or went to the VA. Not being ready for that or even believing he needed that, he decided to stalk me instead. Until yesterday when I spotted Chris Kitchens, I figured Simon had given up when I came out here. It's kind of hard to hide on a small island like this."

Jase had covered his face with his hands, digging the tips of his fingers into his thick brown hair.

"What? Do you think that's far-fetched?"

He parted his fingers and peered at her through the spaces. "I don't know, Nina. I think you should try to put Simon out of your mind right now. Concentrate on staying relaxed and happy. That's what you're here for, right? And I'm here to write and help you get this place in working order."

She rolled her shoulders back and slumped in the chair. "You're right. Simon's going to come back or he's not. Maybe Chris will have better luck."

Jase sat back and wrapped his long fingers around his

sweating bottle. He tipped the rest of the contents down his throat. "That's good stuff."

"Do you want another?"

"I'm tired enough as it is. I worked all morning on the fence, fetched you, your groceries and a total stranger who turned your world upside down, fought off a wild Tasmanian devil and let a huge cat out of the bag. I'm ready to hit the sack."

She raised her arms above her head and yawned. "When you put it that way, but you need to promise me something, Jase Buckley."

"Anything." He rose from the chair, beer bottle in hand, and then swooped down to sweep up her cup.

"You need to promise me you'll do some writing tomorrow." She pushed up from the chair and hugged the robe around her body. "I feel so guilty. You came to Break Island to write and you've been entangled in my family drama."

As he turned toward the kitchen, he shrugged. "Family drama's good for my writing."

She paused at the hallway leading back to her living area. "Thanks, Jase, for being there, for everything."

She didn't know if he heard her or not, since his only answer was the clinking of glass. She took a breath to repeat herself and then blew it out as she walked down the hallway. She could add modesty to his list of virtues.

HOURS LATER NINA woke with a start. The rain had increased through the night and drops of it pelted her window in a relentless rhythm.

She rolled to her side and squished down a pillow to see the floating green digits of the alarm clock. Three o'clock?

Groaning, she pulled the pillow over her head. Ever since her pregnancy, once she woke up like this in the early morning hours she'd had a hard time getting back to sleep.

She closed her eyes and tried some deep breathing. A gust of wind hurried the spatters of rain against her window and then blew an errant branch against the pane, where it scratched and tapped out its own Morse code.

Its message was insistent and sinister.

She bolted upright. Sinister?

With her heart pounding, she rolled from the bed and pressed her nose against the window, where trickles of rain formed a pattern on the glass. The window looked out on the deck with the fire pit, and she felt a strong force beckoning her outside.

The deck had been her parents' favorite spot. Her mother had died on that deck, wrapped in blankets and her husband's loving arms. Not wanting to defile the sanctity of the place, her stepfather had shot himself out on the water, but his presence lingered on the deck, just as her mother's did.

She shoved her feet into her clogs and dragged her robe around her body. She made a stop at her closet to retrieve Dad's shotgun—not the weapon he'd used to commit suicide—and shuffled to the front door.

Raindrops sprinkled her face, and she wiped them away as she stepped onto the porch. The clouds parted just long enough for the moon to glisten against the wet leaves before hiding it from view again and casting the ground into darkness.

Nina took the two porch steps slowly and scuffled along the gravel path that led to the side of Moonstones and the deck.

Darkness draped every inch of it. And then a burst of wind picked up the leaves on the ground and sent them dancing in the air and snatched at her robe, daring her to dance with the leaves.

The wind also shoved the clouds apart, and the moon cast a glow over the deck and the fire pit.

A formless shape huddled in one of the chairs and a shaft of fear pierced her heart. She whispered, "Mom?"

Her feet propelled her toward the deck, the clogs slogging through the mud and the hem of her robe dragging behind her.

She gripped the battered wooden railing as she navigated the three steps up to the deck. The clouds decided to play peekaboo with the moon again and bathed the deck in gloom.

She froze, afraid to take a step onto the deck with its rotten spots. As if sensing her hesitation, the wind gently swirled around her and the clouds shifted. The moon spilled its light once more on the deck and Nina picked her way across to the rattan love seat beneath her bedroom window.

She crouched beside the love seat and reached for the pile of clothing in front of her. Her fingers met flesh— cold, dead flesh.

Chapter Ten

The scream that shattered the night launched Jase from the porch. When he hit the ground, he grabbed a handful of leaves on a bush to keep from sliding into the mud. The scream had come from the side of the house, and he aimed his flashlight in that direction and followed the beam of light.

He swept the flashlight up the deck and zeroed in on Nina hunched over a piece of furniture against the wall of the house.

"Nina! Nina, are you okay?"

A pale oval turned his way, and he clambered up the steps of the deck and rushed to her side. His flashlight played over the figure slumped sideways on the love seat and lit up the face of Nina's stepsister, Lou.

Nina craned her head around to look at him, the rain mingling with the tears streaming down her face.

He set down his flashlight, away from the sad spectacle on the love seat, and hooked his hands beneath Nina's arms. "Let's go inside and call 9-1-1."

"She's dead, isn't she?"

She sure looked dead to him, and he'd seen plenty of dead people, but he pressed two fingers against the pulse in her throat to satisfy Nina. "She's gone."

"I don't... Can you see...? Is she hurt?"

"It's too hard to see anything out here, Nina. Let's allow the professionals to do their jobs." He put an arm around her. "You're shivering."

He led her back into the B and B, the flashlight showing them the way. After settling her before the fireplace, he picked up her landline and punched in 9-1-1 to report finding Lou's body.

Then he sat on the arm of Nina's chair and rubbed her back. "Do you want to get out of this wet robe? The hem's all muddy."

She untied the sash and he peeled the robe from her shoulders. She'd been wet and shivering three times in two days. That couldn't be good for the baby.

He put some water on to boil and went into his room to yank the blanket from his bed. When he returned, Nina was rocking back and forth with her hands pinned between her knees.

Dropping the blanket around her shoulders, he said, "Get warmed up. I'll bring you some tea."

When she didn't make a move, he tucked the blanket around her body, noticing for the first time a fullness to her breasts and a rounded belly beneath the filmy material of her nightgown. His desire for her surged through his veins with red-hot need and he dropped the corner of the blanket in her lap, as if it had burned his fingers.

He backed away from her and moved into the kitchen to watch the kettle on the stove. He was losing it. He'd allowed his past disappointments to get mixed up in his feelings for Nina and his job assignment. He had to pull out of this nosedive.

A revolving light from the front of the B and B splashed red light into the sitting room. "Let me do this."

Jase moved to the door, but Nina followed him, the blanket trailing behind her.

He stepped onto the porch as the EMTs were hopping

from the ambulance. He pointed to the side of the house. "She's on the deck."

Two police cars rolled up, facing the B and B, and illuminated the entire yard with white spotlights.

Two police officers approached them. The taller one spoke first. "You're Nina Moore, aren't you? Bruce and Lori's daughter? I'm Sergeant Pruitt."

"Yes, the...the body we found is my stepsister, Louise Moore." She touched Jase's arm. "This is Jase Buckley."

"Good to meet you." The sergeant nodded. "I knew Lou. She caused a bit of ruckus a few nights ago."

"Lou could do that."

"Your father did all he could for that girl." He jerked his head to the side of the house. "What happened?"

Jase answered. "We're not sure. We didn't see any visible signs of injury on the body, but it was dark."

"The body just appeared? No noises? Signs of struggle? How'd you come to find her?"

Nina tugged the blanket closed. "I woke up, and I had a bad feeling. I looked outside first but didn't see anything. Then I walked outside and found her there. I...I must've screamed, because Jase appeared almost immediately after I found Lou."

"You did scream, but I was already coming out here. I heard noises—must've been you coming outside."

"You didn't see anyone else, Ms. Moore?"

"You can call me Nina. I didn't see anyone or anything."

"Did you hear any cars or dogs barking?"

"Just the wind and the ocean, Sergeant Pruitt."

"Yep. Helluva storm coming in." The sergeant used his powerful flashlight to light a path to the deck on the side of the house.

As Nina started to follow him, Jase grabbed her hand. "Why don't you go back inside?"

"She's my sister." She shook him off and caught up to Sergeant Pruitt.

The EMTs had moved Lou's body to a gurney, while the other officer was blocking off the deck with yellow tape.

Jase squinted against the bright light. "What does it look like?"

One of the EMTs answered. "At first look, a drug overdose."

Nina gasped and drove a fist against her mouth.

Jase put his arm around her shoulders and pulled her close. "No signs of violence?"

"Not that we can tell, but we'll deliver the body to the local hospital and the coroner will want to do an autopsy."

Nina choked. "I don't understand how she got here. We left her in town earlier tonight, or rather last night."

The sergeant lifted his shoulders. "It's not a long walk."

"But if she was under the influence or drugged out…"

"Maybe the drugs didn't take full effect until she got here. We'll let the coroner figure that out, Nina, but we need to treat this as a crime scene until we know what happened."

"What does that mean?" She shivered but this time she moved in against Jase instead of pulling away.

His body reacted in all the wrong ways to the feeling of her soft curves melding against his frame.

"Just the deck. When it gets light, the crime scene investigators will come out and survey the area." The sergeant stomped his feet and rubbed his hands together. "Was she with anyone last night when you saw her?"

"Her constant companion on the island, Kip Chandler."

"Oh, yeah, I've seen him around, too."

Jase cleared his throat. "And Chris Kitchens."

"That name I don't know."

Nina tilted her head back to look Jase in the face. "She wasn't really with Chris."

"He was giving her his jacket when we left them."

"Who is this Chris Kitchens?" Pruitt took a pad of paper out of his front pocket.

"He was a visitor to the island. He was looking for his brother, someone I used to know. I couldn't help him with his brother, but we had dinner with him."

"Did he know Lou?"

"He had just met her. He was giving her his jacket because…because it had started raining."

"That's the last you saw of them? Of your stepsister?"

"Yes." Nina turned her face into Jase's arm, pressing her nose against his sweatshirt.

"Sergeant Pruitt, can we finish this inside? Nina's chilled to the bone."

"I think I'm done with my questions tonight." He lifted the tape flapping in the wind. "Stay off the deck until the crime scene techs do their investigation. I'm leaving Officer Jamison here until dawn, which—" he yanked up the sleeve of his jacket "—will be just a few hours from now."

"If you need anything else, Sergeant Pruitt, we'll both be here."

Pruitt's eyes darted from Jase's face to Nina's. "You taking in guests already?"

"Jase isn't really a guest. He's helping me fix up the place in exchange for room and board."

"You *should* fix up this place, Nina. It meant a lot to your mom and stepdad."

"Maybe that's why Lou made her way back here." Her bottom lip trembled along with her voice, and Jase gripped her arm and steered her back toward the house.

"Let us know if you need anything, Sergeant."

"It won't be until sunup, so try to get some rest. "I'm sorry for your loss, Nina."

Jase bundled her back into the B and B while the EMTs and officers were still talking over the body covered by a sheet.

"Get back to bed. I'll get the lights."

She flopped back into the chair and kicked her feet up on the ottoman. "I can't go back to sleep. Lou's still out there."

"What made you get up?"

"I don't know. I felt her presence out there. My mom died on that deck, too."

"Maybe you heard a noise that woke you up."

"That's the logical explanation, isn't it? But nothing about Lou has ever been logical. I thought she was off the hard stuff. I know she was still smoking weed, and she was an alcoholic."

"Maybe it was the booze—alcohol poisoning."

"The EMT thought it was a drug overdose."

"He guessed at that by looking at her in the dark. We'll have to wait for the autopsy."

"Maybe in the end, she was coming to me for help. When she was clearheaded, she could be so funny and warm."

"I wouldn't know. I only ever saw her as an acute danger to you."

Sighing, she rested her head against the chair's cushion. "I suppose I had been waiting for this ending for a while."

"You're still shivering." He nudged her. "Is there room in that chair for me? You need to get warm."

Her eyes widened but she scooted over and he wedged himself into the chair next to her. He repositioned himself and opened his arms so she could rest against his chest. He tugged the blanket around her more closely and she draped her legs over his thighs, burrowing halfway onto his lap.

He held her, and she nestled her cheek against his chest—right above his pounding heart.

He stroked her hair and whispered, "I'm sorry."

Her eyelashes fluttered and her lips parted as if she were ready to answer, but she emitted a soft breath instead.

He tightened his arms around her, and she drifted to sleep. He could hold her for the rest of the morning and never grow tired of watching her face, peaceful and free from worry.

Would Coburn have sent him on this assignment if he'd known the complications of Nina Moore's life? Probably. Some of those complications, namely Chris Kitchens, had deep roots in Nina's connection to Simon Skinner and Tempest.

But she knew nothing of her ex-fiancé's job and life. Tempest had to realize that, too.

He'd step back when the assignment ended. Once they figured out Tempest had no interest in Nina, he'd move on to the next assignment and she could run her B and B and raise her baby—alone.

Lots of women chose single motherhood. Hell, Maggie had insisted on it and Nina had a lot more strength than Maggie did.

After two hours of thinking too much and sleeping too little, Jase shifted his position in the chair as the gray light of dawn seeped through the drapes.

A vehicle pulled up to the house, its engine idling. Must be the crime scene guys relieving the cop standing guard at the deck.

Jase stretched his legs in front of him and slipped his arm from beneath Nina's body. She mumbled and her eyelashes fluttered against her cheeks. He repositioned her head against the cushion of the chair and sauntered to the window to peer outside.

A black van had pulled up in front of Moonstones, discharging personnel from the sliding door on the side where he could make out white letters announcing the Snohomish County Sheriff's Department.

He glanced over his shoulder at Nina, still sleeping, and pulled last night's sweatshirt over his head. Stepping out onto the porch, he walked into beads of moisture that clung to his hair. The clouds from last night continued to threaten, but the storm hadn't rolled in with its full force yet.

One of the techs from the van stopped and waved. "We're here to sift through the location where the body was found, even though the report I saw details a simple overdose."

"Are overdoses ever simple?" Jase shoved his hands into his pockets and walked down the steps.

"Suppose not. Sorry, was she a relative? A friend?"

"My friend's stepsister. She had a lot of problems, so her ending isn't a surprise."

"Still tough to deal with."

The officer from last night emerged from the side of the house, shrugging out of his poncho. "Was Ms. Moore okay last night?"

"She slept. Do you know when the coroner's office is going to release the body for burial?"

He pointed to the techs. "If these guys don't discover anything and the autopsy doesn't indicate foul play, I don't think it'll be that long. But with the storm coming?" He shrugged. "I'm sure the coroner will want to do a toxicology test, and that can take a while out here."

"Did you find anything?"

Jase turned at the sound of Nina's voice. She'd not only woken up, but she'd pulled on a pair of black leggings paired with some fuzzy boots and a down jacket that hung almost to her knees.

"We're just getting started." The lead crime scene tech

patted the black bag slung over his shoulder. "She was your stepsister?"

"Yes. Will you be able to tell how long she'd been on the deck? How long she'd been dead?"

"The autopsy will get to that. We'll look at how she got here and if there was anyone with her."

She blew on her hands and rubbed them together. "I just have a feeling she came here to see me. Maybe she knew she was dying and she wanted to tell me something."

"Between us and the coroner, we should be able to paint a picture of her last hours. I hope it gives you some closure." He joined his team on the deck.

Jase rubbed Nina's arms through the slick, puffy sleeves of her jacket. "How are you feeling?"

"I'm okay. How are you after sleeping upright in a chair all night?" She shook her finger in his face. "Don't think I don't know what you did, Jase Buckley. You watched over me in that chair when you should've just carried me to my bed and gotten a few hours of shut-eye in your own bed."

"You needed to warm up and…"

"Moonstones *does* have central heating."

"…and you needed someone to hold you."

A rush of color stained her cheeks and she twisted her ponytail around her hand. "Did you think I was falling apart?"

"Nina, you'd just found your stepsister's body, hours after she attacked you in the street. Pregnant or not, that's enough to drive anyone to the edge."

She scuffed the toe of her boot against the soft ground. "Thanks for being there. I actually fell asleep and slept through the morning, when I never thought that was going to happen."

"I owe you. You opened your B and B to me without a moment's hesitation."

"Be honest, Jase. I've been nothing but trouble for you ever since you arrived on the island."

She'd spiced up what could've been a boring assignment. He should be thanking her, but that wouldn't play.

"Like I said before, human drama is good for my writing."

"That's putting a good spin on the situation." She took a few steps toward the porch. "I'm going to stop by my sister's room at the motel after breakfast and collect her things and probably pay her bill. I also want to talk to Kip and Chris to find out what they know about last night."

"I'm sure Sergeant Pruitt is already on that."

"I'm sure he is, but that's not going to stop me from talking to those two myself."

"I'll go with you."

She kicked the porch step. "You don't need to do that, Jase. You should be here writing."

"I'm not letting you talk to a guy like Kip by yourself, especially if it gets confrontational. Besides, I write better at night than during the day."

"You're not getting any time at night, either."

"Let me worry about the book, Nina."

"Okay, at least let me cook you breakfast. Blueberry pancakes this morning. Dora Kleinschmidt from next door dropped off some fresh blueberries."

"Fresh blueberries? You don't have to twist my arm." He sprang up the steps past her and held the door open. "I'm going to take a shower and change, and then I'm going to eat pancakes."

He needed to start writing something before Nina got any more suspicious—either that or come clean.

Once he did that, any connection between them would fizzle and die. And he wasn't ready for that.

About an hour and a half later, his belly full of the best damned blueberry pancakes he'd had since his family's

French chef had quit in a huff, he drove Nina in her truck into town and pulled up in front of the police station.

"I hope they can tell me something." She grabbed the handle of the door before the truck even came to a stop.

"Don't get your hopes up. It's been less than twenty-four hours. The crime scene investigators just finished up minutes before we left, and I'm sure the coroner hasn't even started the autopsy yet."

"Okay, you just threw cold water on all my expectations."

He met her at the station door and opened it for her, gesturing her through. The small station had an old-fashioned feel with a counter in the front and enclosed offices beyond that. Vinyl furniture dotted the waiting room.

The officer at the counter glanced up when they walked in, and then her eyebrows jumped to her hairline. "You're Nina Moore, aren't you?"

"Yes. I remember you."

"Nancy Yallop. I used to work patrol when you and your mom first moved to the island." She shook her head. "Such a shame about Louise. Bruce was always worried she'd meet some fate like that."

"I know he was."

"Are you going to call her mother, Inez?"

"I'm hoping to find her number among Lou's stuff." Nina tapped the counter. "Is Sergeant Pruitt in? I know it's early, but I thought he might have some news about Lou."

"Sarge isn't in, but the chief is, and I'm sure he'd like to talk to you." She flicked her fingers at the waiting room. "You can have a seat, but I don't think he's going to be that long."

Officer Yallop disappeared into one of the offices in the back and returned with a smile. "The chief will be out in a minute. Coffee?"

"No, thanks." Nina turned to face him. "Do you want another cup?"

"I'm fine."

"You definitely want to stay away from caffeine. I cut it out for both of mine just to be on the safe side," Officer Yallop said.

Nina spun around, folding her arms over her middle. She'd shed her jacket when they walked into the overheated station. She still sported a pair of black leggings, but her red sweater hugged her body, outlining a distinct baby bump.

Officer Yallop said, "I…I'm sorry. You *are* pregnant, aren't you?"

"I am, but I've just started showing recently, so I'm not used to the attention yet."

"Whew." The officer wiped the back of her hand across her brow. "For a minute there I thought it was foot-in-mouth time, but you're so slim otherwise I didn't think I was mistaken."

The chief came out from the back, bouncing on his toes with each step. His gait could be compensation for his short stature, but what the chief lacked in height he made up in muscle.

"Ms. Moore? I'm Chief Hazlett. Sorry for your loss. I came to the island after your stepfather…passed away, but I did hear some stories about Louise Moore."

"Nice to meet you, Chief. This is Jase Buckley." She extended her hand over the counter. "My stepsister was very troubled."

The chief shook hands with Jase, too, and invited them behind the counter. "Let's talk about this further in my office, although I don't have much to tell you yet."

Nina's shoulders slumped as she followed the chief toward the back of the building, and Jase rubbed the space between her shoulder blades.

"Have a seat." He pointed to two leather chairs across from his desk. The chief's office obviously got the bulk of the furniture allowance in this place.

The chief proceeded to tell them a whole bunch of nothing about the case, except that they didn't find any evidence of foul play—no wounds on Lou's body, no evidence that she'd been dumped on the deck by another party. They'd have to wait for the toxicology report for more details regarding the substances and their quantity in her body.

"What about her companions from last night?" Nina had folded her hands in her lap and her white knuckles stood out against the black of her leggings.

"Can't locate either one of them."

Nina shot a look at Jase, her mouth forming an O. "What does that mean? I told Sergeant Pruitt last night they were all staying in the same motel—The Sandpiper."

"We got that info and even checked out her room, but the men aren't there now."

Jase hunched forward. "The two men checked out?"

"Kitchens did an automated checkout from the TV in the room around midnight and the other guy—" he checked his notes "—Kip Chandler, didn't bother checking out, but the room was in Lou's name. Chandler wasn't at the motel this morning."

Nina perched on the edge of the chair. "I'm going to head over there now and pack up Lou's things and probably settle her bill."

The chief waited until Nina stood up before pushing back from his desk and extending his hand. "We'll keep you posted on your stepsister's autopsy, Ms. Moore, but right now it looks like an unfortunate overdose."

"Of what?" She planted her hands on his desk and leaned forward. "Can they tell yet?"

"Probably heroin."

Nina crossed her hands over her heart and Jase placed a hand on her back.

"I really thought she'd kicked that stuff."

"Once it has you in its grip—" the chief shrugged "—it's a tough monkey to shake."

Jase shook the chief's hand and guided Nina out of his office. They waved to Officer Yallop and landed on the sidewalk in front of the station.

"That's so odd." Nina worried her bottom lip between her teeth. "Didn't Chris say he was going to stick around the island for a day or two?"

"Maybe he decided to get out before the storm hit. He seemed kind of worried about it."

"Kip was Lou's shadow. Why would he disappear?"

"That one's easier." Jase fished the keys to the truck from his pocket. "He was shooting up with Lou, found out what happened and took off."

"Maybe we'll find some answers at The Sandpiper." She waved her phone in the air. "And I'm going to call Chris to find out what happened after we left last night and see if he knows about Lou."

He opened the passenger side of the truck for her, and by the time he climbed into the driver's seat, she was on her cell phone.

She started speaking. "Hi, Chris. This is Nina Moore. I was wondering if you'd heard about my stepsister before you left the island. She OD'd early this morning and passed away. I wanted to find out what went down last night after Jase and I left. Give me a call when you get a chance."

He pulled away from the curb. "If he checked out of The Sandpiper at midnight and left the island, how would he know about Lou?"

"Maybe he heard something from a local. If he's off the island, he got a private boat to take him to the mainland, because the ferries don't start running until five in the morning."

"That didn't occur to me. Why would he check out of his motel at midnight if there was no place for him to go?"

"Like I said, maybe he made arrangements for a private party to take him across. Lots of people on the island make extra money by ferrying people across."

He drove the short mile to The Sandpiper and swung into a parking space in front of the office.

As soon as they walked in, the motel's manager came from behind the counter. "I was so sorry to hear about Lou, Nina. That girl had her problems, didn't she?"

"She did, Maisie. I know she owed you for the room, so I'll take care of that."

"Well, I don't know how things work when someone's, uh, deceased, but Lou put the room on a credit card. I was just going to charge the card."

"Lou had a credit card? I'll figure it out with her mother, then…when I track her down."

"Good luck with that." She held up her index finger. "I'll get you a key card for the room. Housekeeping hasn't been in there yet since the cops left."

Jase cleared his throat. "You haven't seen Lou's friend, have you?"

"The skinny guy with the shaggy blond hair?" Maisie wrinkled her nose. "No. The cops, Gus Pruitt, already asked me about him. When Gus came by to tell me the news about Lou, we went to the room together, but Kip had cleared out already."

Maisie slid a card across the counter toward Nina, and Nina peeled it from the Formica top. "Thanks, Maisie."

They found Lou's room and Nina slid the card into the slot. She hesitated at the threshold.

"Let me." He stepped around her and pushed open the door.

The smell of stale pizza and cigarettes permeated the room, and he propped open the door so they could breathe. "I guess they ignored the no-smoking rule."

"Lou ignored a lot of rules." Nina moved into the room with folded arms and hunched shoulders as if expecting to find another dead body.

She nudged a pizza box on the floor with the toe of her boot. "I suppose I'll start with the bathroom."

Jase picked up one of the boxes they'd thrown in the back of the truck. "Let me get the stuff from the bathroom and you can pack up her clothes."

"I don't think she ever unpacked." She pointed to an open suitcase in the corner of the room, its contents spilling over the sides.

"Check the drawers and closet, just in case." He left her to Lou's clothes and stepped into the bathroom. It reeked of cigarettes and the slightly sweet smell of marijuana.

Did the two of them think they could hide their drug use by holing up in the bathroom? Maybe this is where they shot up, too.

He kicked at two towels bunched up on the floor and then crouched to run his hand across the terry cloth. Both damp. Had they both showered last night before going out or had Kip taken a quick shower early this morning after waking up alone?

A little bottle of motel shampoo lay on its side in the shower caddy next to a bar of soap. A toothbrush, small tube of toothpaste and spray can of deodorant were scattered on the counter next to the sink. A see-through toiletry bag hung on a hook on the back of the door.

He got up close to the door and peered into the bag. If he thought he'd find a syringe in there, the face cream, hair gel and dental floss just quashed that hope. Junkies used dental floss?

He dumped everything in the trash can and joined Nina

in the bedroom. She'd moved the suitcase to the bed and had tucked the clothes back inside.

Throwing up her hands, she said, "I didn't find anything in here out of the ordinary, but I guess the cops already knew that, which is why they let us in."

"Nothing in the bathroom. If she took the fatal overdose here in this room, there's no evidence of it now."

"Maybe Kip cleaned up when he took his stuff and left." She stood in the middle of the floor with her hands on her hips. "I guess that's everything—oops—except these jeans on the back of the chair."

She took two steps to the chair and plucked the jeans from it. She swung them through the air and a piece of paper fluttered to the carpet. She stooped to sweep it up.

"What's that?" Jase flipped back the covers of the bed in case Nina hadn't thought to do it. Nothing.

"It's a cocktail napkin from Mandy's."

"If you want to toss it on top of this pizza box, I'll take all the trash out to the Dumpster container I saw around the corner." Jase picked up the edge of the box, vowing to swear off pepperoni pizza for the next year.

"Okay." She shook out the napkin. "There's writing on it."

"Anything important?"

"I don't think so. Just one word." She tugged on each side of the white square.

"What?"

"Tempest."

Chapter Eleven

The room spun. He gripped the pizza box, crushing the cardboard. "What did you say?"

Holding up the napkin, she waved it in the air. "Tempest. You know, like the Shakespeare play, or I guess that was *The Tempest*. Or maybe it means tempest in a teapot or she's referring to the oncoming storm."

"Is it Lou's handwriting?"

"As far as I can tell." She crumpled the napkin in her fist and chucked it at the pizza box, still clutched in his hand.

He dipped to catch the balled-up napkin on top of the box, amazed at the steadiness of his hands when his mind was racing in a million different directions. "I'll take this out. Anything else need to go in the Dumpster container?"

"Was there anything in the bathroom?"

"Just used toiletries. I put them in the trash can. Housekeeping can get rid of it when they clean the room."

"Nothing else in here. I'll locate Lou's mother, Inez, and see if she wants Lou's clothes and the contents of her purse. I'm guessing Inez will come out and handle Lou's apartment in Portland."

"I'll take this stuff out while you give the room a once-over."

As Nina pulled out the drawer of the nightstand, Jase

headed for the door, holding the pizza box as if it were a silver platter and the crumpled napkin a bottle of nitro-glycerine.

The napkin with Simon's agency printed on it in Lou's pocket certainly did have an explosive quality about it. Why the hell had Lou written *Tempest* on that napkin? What did she know about Tempest? She hadn't even known Simon.

Had Chris Kitchens mentioned Tempest to Lou? His step faltered on the way to the Dumpster container. Was Chris Kitchens really Simon's brother? They'd had only his word for it.

That, and a striking resemblance.

This afternoon, he'd request a background on Kitchens that he should've requested before allowing him anywhere near Nina. He'd done that for Kip Chandler already and he'd checked out as a small-time thief and junkie from Seattle whose brother the attorney had gotten out of a few scrapes.

When he reached the Dumpster container, he smoothed out the napkin on top of the cardboard, folded it and slipped it into his pocket. Lou had heard that name from someone—and he planned to find out from whom.

By the time he returned to the motel room, Nina had zipped up Lou's bag and parked it next to the door.

"I think that's everything. The police have her purse at the station, and…and I guess I can pick up her clothes from the hospital, where they took her for the autopsy."

He wedged a finger beneath the chin she'd dropped to her chest. "Are you okay? I know you and Lou had a difficult relationship, but she was your stepsister, your father's daughter."

Her chin quivered and one tear rolled down her smooth skin. "Maybe she's at peace now. It's all I can hope for."

He caught the tear on the edge of his thumb. "I'm sorry

it was so hard, but it doesn't sound as if Lou could've had a normal relationship with anyone."

"She couldn't. Maybe she even scared away Kip."

"I don't think Kip was as out of it as he pretended to be."

"Really? Why do you say that?"

"I don't know." He yanked up the handle of Lou's suitcase and tipped it on its wheels. "Something about his eyes—too sharp to be totally wasted."

Tilting her head, she pulled open the door. "So, what was he doing with Lou?"

"Beats the hell outta me." He rolled the bag through the door. "Maybe Lou talked up the B and B to him, told him it was hers. He thought she had some money coming and tagged along to Break Island. When it became clear to him that she didn't have a shot at Moonstones and was into heavier stuff than he was, he hightailed it out of here."

"I have no clue. Lou always seemed to run with an entourage—big or small. She accused me of collecting men to take care of me, but she did the same. I guess we were both affected by playing second fiddle to our parents' great love."

"Lou must've had issues before her parents' divorce and her father's remarriage to your mom."

"I did, too."

Jase hoisted Lou's suitcase into the back of the truck and hooked his thumb in his belt loop. "Your father's abandonment?"

"It's hard growing up without a dad." She folded her hands across her belly. "And here I am about to do the same thing to my child."

"Hey." He took her by the shoulders. "Through no fault of your own. You split up with Simon before you knew you were pregnant, right?"

She nodded.

"You tried to reach him, right?"

"Maybe not hard enough."

"There's no way you were going to find him."

"What?" Her forehead furrowed.

"I mean, if he didn't want to be found, you weren't going to find him." The napkin from Lou's jeans burned a hole in his pocket. Had Simon somehow reached out to Lou before he was killed?

"Simon knew about Lou, didn't he?"

"Knew about her but had never met her. When he started…acting weird, I told him I'd witnessed firsthand what could happen when mental illness went untreated. He'd heard all the stories about Lou. Why do you ask?"

He steered her toward the passenger side of the truck. "Just that—just wondering if he knew you'd dealt with erratic behavior before."

"Oh, yeah. He knew."

As he pulled away from The Sandpiper, he made a right turn and Nina put her hand on his arm. "Where are you going?"

"I want to head down to the harbor and see if anyone gave Chris a ride back to the mainland. If not, he checked out of The Sandpiper after midnight and waited around for about five hours for the next ferry out of here, which makes no sense at all."

Nina wrinkled her nose. "You don't think Pruitt and Chief Hazlett already checked that out?"

"I think Pruitt and the chief believe Lou's death was a simple overdose. Case closed. This is a small-town department and they don't have the resources to run around checking out possible leads on a hunch."

"What are you saying, Jase? Do you think Chris had something to do with Lou's death? Why? What possible motive could Chris have had for killing a woman he'd just met?"

Tempest. Why had Lou written that word? What did Chris Kitchens know about his brother's work and eventual breakdown?

He squeezed her knee. "That thought didn't occur to you?"

Nina plowed her fingers through her hair. "I don't know what to think, Jase. As far as I know, Lou hadn't been using H for years. Of course, it doesn't mean she didn't try it again. Maybe that's why it killed her. She'd been used to a certain amount but her body couldn't handle that anymore after being clean."

"Could be. I just need to satisfy my curiosity."

And to protect Nina.

After driving through town, he swung the truck into the parking lot for the wharf, busy with fishing boats and the tourist ferry that hopped from island to island. "Where are the private boats?"

She tapped the glass. "On the far side by the bait shop."

He parked and Nina was out of the truck in a flash. Did she half hope that Lou's death wasn't an accidental overdose? Maybe she was afraid that Lou had taken her own life, just as her father had done, and felt guilty that her stepsister might have done it because of her pregnancy.

And she didn't even know about Tempest.

He trailed after her as she marched up to a man working on his powerful-looking Wellcraft boat.

Nina balanced one foot on the boat and his heart skipped a beat. Then he took a long breath of salty air. He couldn't wrap Nina in cotton. Despite all the stress swirling around her, she was taking care of herself.

She called out to the man, who still hadn't seen her. "Good morning. Can I ask you a question?"

The man looked up from his work and pushed his cap back on his head, squinting at her with his already squinty eyes. "Yes, ma'am?"

"Do you take people to the mainland?"

He took her in and then shifted his gaze to Jase. "Depends on who's asking, a potential customer or the state transportation agency."

"Oh, I'm not—" she flung her arm back at Jase "—we're not from any agency. I just want to know if you took a friend of mine to the mainland earlier this morning—like really early."

He dropped his shoulders and adjusted his cap again. "I took a couple over about two hours ago. That's it."

"Okay, thanks." She backed off the boat.

His voice stopped her. "You might check with Steve down that way. He's the one with the Hewescraft aluminum boat about three slips over. I overheard him in the coffee shop this morning complaining about an early morning fare."

"Thanks."

Jase took her arm as if to steady her on the bumpy metal of the gangplank.

"Even if Steve did take Chris over this morning, what does it prove, Jase?"

"It proves that he left the island instead of checking out of the motel and then hanging around for a few hours to wait for the ferry, which makes no sense."

"Whether he hung around or left immediately, it doesn't necessarily implicate him in or exonerate him from Lou's death."

"Once that autopsy report comes back, it could."

He slowed his steps. "Maybe we should let the cops do their job." Or Prospero. The less Nina was directly involved in the destruction Tempest left in its wake, the better. She didn't need the added stress of investigating Lou's death.

She stopped and widened her stance, just in case he thought she was about to topple over. "Jase, you're not my protector. You're supposed to be fixing my B and B, not me."

He should've investigated this on his own. His lids fell half-mast over his eyes and his mouth hardened for a split second. "You don't need to prove anything here. Lou treated you badly until the very end."

"She was my stepfather's daughter. I owe it to Bruce to figure out what happened."

Stepping back, he gestured her toward the boat. "Have at it, Nancy Drew."

She brushed past him, rolling her eyes. Controlling and high-handed, just like Simon.

The next boat owner—Steve—was working on his engine when they walked up. She had to wave to get his attention over the roar of the motor.

He cut the engine and wiped his hands on a greasy cloth he had sitting on the deck behind him. "Do you need a ride to the mainland? It's a good thing you're gettin' while the gettin's good. Once that monster storm hits, there will be no crossing this sound."

"Actually, we're not. I live on the island. Do you know Moonstones?"

"I know Bruce Moore's daughter was found there this morning—dead. OD'd just like we all expected her to one day."

"Lou Moore was my stepsister."

He scratched his grizzled jaw. "Sorry, young lady. You must be the other daughter. If it's not a ride you're after, what can I do for you?"

Jase wedged a foot against the boat. "We'd like some information about your early fare this morning."

Steve uttered a curse and spat into the water. "I didn't have a fare this morning. I got a call from a guy after midnight wanting a ride over, told him I'd meet him here, and he never showed up."

"Did you call him back?"

"I sure did. He wouldn't pick up. I thought maybe someone poached my ride, but if they did, nobody's fessing up to it."

Nina reached for her phone and cupped it in her hand. "Do you still have the number on your phone? I just want to see if it's my friend. I thought he was leaving the island last night. If he didn't, I might have to take him over today."

"Why don't you just call him?"

"I tried." She shrugged. "Same result as you. He won't pick up or his phone's dead or something. Do you mind?"

"Nope." He chuckled. "In fact, if you're an angry girlfriend, the guy deserves it."

He reached for his cell phone sitting on a deck bin and tapped the screen. "Here it is. You ready?"

She displayed Chris's number and nodded. He read off the exact number on her display, and her heart somersaulted.

"That's not his number. Thanks anyway."

He saluted and went back to work.

She pivoted and stepped off the gangplank onto the sidewalk that led to the parking lot.

"Are we done interrogating people for the day?"

She tapped her phone against her chin. "That was Chris's number."

Jase raised his brows. "Why'd you lie to Steve?"

"I didn't want to get into any long discussion with him. Why would Chris try to get off the island after checking out of the motel and then change his mind?"

"I don't know, Nina. Maybe we should just leave this alone. I need to get back to my laptop."

She covered her mouth with her hand. "Of course you do. Sorry for dragging you all over town when you have work to do."

"I was happy to do it, and I think I was the one doing the dragging."

When they got back into the truck, he started the engine and turned to her. "I have a question for you."

She formed a cross with two fingers and held them in front of her face. "Don't ask me why I'm running around, trying to figure out Lou's last hours on earth."

"I'm not. I wasn't." Stretching his arms in front of him, he clasped the steering wheel. "You know those jeans you found on the back of the chair in Lou's motel room?"

"Yeah?"

"Was she wearing those jeans when we saw her earlier in the night?"

A clothing question. She blinked. "I don't think so. No. The jeans she had on the last time I saw her had metal studs along the back pockets, and those are the jeans she had on when she died."

He pulled out of the parking lot and turned down the road toward the other side of town, toward Moonstones.

She studied his profile, which gave away nothing. "Why are you asking about Lou's jeans?"

"Just curious about the piece of paper in the pocket."

"The piece of paper?" She wrinkled her nose, trying to remember the word. Snapping her fingers, she said, "Tempest."

"That's right." He paused for two beats. "Does it mean anything to you?"

"No. Should it?"

"You never heard it before?"

"Well, yeah, I've heard the word before, but not in any context related to Lou, except that she created a tempest wherever she went."

Jase narrowed his eyes and drilled the road ahead. "Creating trouble everywhere."

"That was Lou." Her fidgeting fingers pleated the hem of her shirt. Were they even discussing Lou anymore?

He blew out a breath that turned into a whistle. "She won't be causing any trouble now."

When they returned to Moonstones, all Nina's curiosity and energy had been overtaken by a leaden lethargy.

Jase had brought Lou's suitcase into the house and Nina wheeled it into the corner, swallowing a lump in her throat.

"Are you going to write?"

"Do you need anything before I do?"

"I'm going to take a nap. Now that I've gotten over most of the nausea, the thing that bothers me most about this pregnancy is how it saps my energy in the middle of the day sometimes."

"You hardly had any sleep last night, so I wouldn't blame it on the pregnancy."

"That's true." She stopped at the corner of the staircase. "Do you need anything before I drift off to dreamland?"

"I'm good." He turned toward the guest rooms on the other side of the sitting room.

"Jase?"

He stopped and answered without turning around. "Yeah?"

"Thanks for everything…I mean last night, for holding me. I don't think I would've fallen asleep on my own."

His back stiffened but still he didn't turn around. "It was…nothing. No problem. Glad I was here to help."

He continued across the room and she didn't stop him.

It was nothing. He'd said so. He just had one of those take-charge kinds of personalities—just like Simon—and what better way to indulge it than with a pregnant woman?

Why would he be remotely attracted to a woman carrying another man's baby? Especially a man she'd admitted was half out of his mind. As if she hadn't dragged Jase

Buckley into enough crazy. If she didn't watch it, he'd change his war story into a story about a crazy family starring drugs, suicide and demented ex-fiancés.

She clicked the bedroom door shut behind her and sat on the edge of the bed to pull off her boots.

Her eyes flicked to the window. Why had Lou come here to die? Maybe she'd shot up on the deck. That would be just like her to defile the place where Mom had died and that was so special to their parents.

But if she had injected a syringe full of heroin into her veins on the deck of Moonstones, she hadn't been alone. The CSI team hadn't found any drug paraphernalia on the deck, so someone would've had to remove it.

Is that what Chris had been doing while waiting for the morning ferry? Or is that why Kip had disappeared?

She rolled over and punched her pillow. Maybe Kip and Chris and Simon were all in the same place.

And they could all stay there as far as she was concerned.

NINA AWOKE WITH a start and a pounding heart. She ran her tongue along the inside of her dry mouth, dread thudding through her veins.

The last time she'd been startled awake, her stepsister had turned up dead on the deck outside.

She sat up and scooted to the edge of the bed, her head cocked, listening for...whatever. She eased forward to peer through the drapes at the window and a glorious pink-and-orange sky greeted her. The calm before the storm.

She glanced at the clock. She'd slept away the afternoon. Hopefully, Jase had gotten some work done.

She rubbed her eyes and crossed the room. Still on alert, she pushed open her bedroom door and walked down the hallway that connected her rooms to the rest of the B and B.

She opened the door at the end of the hall and heard the clicking of a keyboard.

"Jase?"

"I'm here. Did you sleep well?"

She massaged the back of her neck and entered the sitting room, where Jase had set up shop near the window. She sauntered across the room, approaching him from behind, but if she'd hoped to catch a glimpse of his book, he disappointed her by minimizing his active window.

"Are you one of those writers who won't share his work in progress?"

"I don't know if I'm one of those writers. It's all new to me. I don't even know if it's any good." He drummed his thumbs on the edge of the keyboard. "You slept for a long time. Do you feel better?"

"Not about Lou's death, but in general I do."

"Hungry?"

She yawned. "I suppose I am, but I'm not up for cooking."

"And you don't want to taste my cooking. I can pick something up—just not pizza."

"What's the matter with pizza?" She bumped her forehead with the heel of her hand as she remembered the stale-pizza smell from Lou's motel room. "No pizza. There's a Chinese place that delivers."

"Sounds good."

"I already have the number saved to my cell phone." Still yawning, she shuffled to the front door, where she'd hung her purse on a hook, and retrieved her phone.

The display showed two text messages—one from her demanding client in LA and one from a friend asking if she was still alive.

As she responded to her friend's message, a third buzzed

through. She recognized Chris Kitchens's phone number and waved the phone at Jase. "Finally, a message from Chris."

"What's it say?"

She held the phone to her face and peered at the words as she read them aloud. "'Leave the island. Your life is in danger.'"

Chapter Twelve

Jase's heart slammed against his chest. Why would Chris be warning Nina?

She looked up from the display, her face drained of all color. "He found Simon."

"Wait. What?" He ran a hand over his face. His mind had been traveling a completely different course, but Nina had reached a logical conclusion...for her.

"He doesn't say that in the message, does he?" He thrust out his hand and she dropped the phone in his palm as if she couldn't get rid of it fast enough.

The message stated only what Nina had read aloud. "He doesn't mention Simon."

"What else could it be? Lou's dead and she never posed a grave threat to me."

"Yeah, you keep saying that."

"She doesn't pose a threat now." She pointed to the phone in his hand. "But someone does—and that someone has to be Simon."

It couldn't be Simon, but he couldn't tell her that—not yet.

"Text him back." He held out the phone to her. "Ask him where he is, who's threatening you."

"It has to be Simon." She took the phone from him and flicked it with her finger. "That's the connection with Chris."

"Your stepsister just turned up dead and Chris was one of the last people to see her alive. Maybe this has something to do with Lou. You have no idea what Lou could've been into."

He shoved his hand into his pocket, toying with the corner of the napkin. While Nina had slept, he called Jack with this latest development. Jack had theorized that Tempest had somehow contacted Lou, even if she didn't know who and what they were.

If so, Jase's job had just gotten more serious than protecting Nina from crazy family members, and he'd have to somehow back down from his personal involvement or risk putting her in danger.

"Text him, Nina. Find out what he knows."

She sat down on the edge of a bar stool and texted with her thumbs.

She stared at her phone for almost a minute and then set it down on the counter and slid off the stool. "Done. Maybe he'll respond with some information I can actually use instead of some vague warning."

Jase massaged his temples. He didn't like any of this. First Lou and now Chris—two people seemingly unconnected to the threat that Tempest could be posing to Nina—now all somehow related.

"You're worried, aren't you?"

"Huh?" He dropped his hands. He had to stop telegraphing his emotions to her and put on his poker face. "It's a text message from a guy you barely know. Maybe he's referring to the big storm on its way. He seemed spooked by it."

She pursed her lips and tapped her toe. "You can't be serious."

"We won't know what he means until he communicates more. In the meantime, you have your shotgun and you have me." And his Glock 23 pistol.

She widened her eyes. "Do you think it'll come to that? Do you think Simon would come here and try something?"

Simon again.

"Why would Simon want to hurt you if he knows you're carrying his baby?"

She covered her stomach with both hands. "I don't know. He changed. If his own brother is warning me against..."

"Hang on." Jase sliced a hand through the air. "We don't know anything yet. Don't jump to conclusions."

Totally wrong conclusions, since a dead man didn't pose a threat to anyone—neither did a dead woman. Since both Simon and Lou could be ruled out, why did Chris believe Nina's life was in danger?

"You're right." She tucked her hair behind one ear. "I'm going to order that Chinese food. Any requests?"

"Anything is fine with me."

"Spicy?"

"The spicier, the better, but—" he made a vague circle in the air in the general direction of her midsection "—can you handle spicy?"

"Oh, yeah. I think this kid's going to be born with steam coming out of his ears with the amount of spicy food I've been putting away." She swept her phone from the counter, glanced at the display once and tapped a few buttons.

After she placed the order, she tipped her chin toward his laptop set up by the window. "Did you get much writing done this afternoon?"

"Yeah."

Writing a report and sending an encrypted email to his boss regarding Chris Kitchens definitely counted as writing.

"You can try to get in a little more before dinner arrives. I'm going to wash my face and change out of these crumpled clothes."

When he heard the click of the door to the back rooms, Jase made a beeline to Nina's cell phone, which she'd left on the kitchen counter.

He scrolled through the text messages until he saw Chris's ominous words. He committed the phone number to memory and then returned to his laptop, where he brought up his email. Then he sent a request to Prospero's tech unit to track the phone and tagged it as urgent.

While he was at it, he created a document file on his desktop and called it *Book*. What else? He typed in a chapter heading and added a few lines—not that he didn't trust Nina, but natural curiosity might lead her to snoop around his laptop—just in case she got past his password. At least she'd see a file on his desktop and he had something to work on if she kept insisting that he write.

He kept the laptop powered on in case someone at Prospero got back to him regarding Chris's cell. Then he retrieved a beer from the fridge.

"Can you please get me a glass of sparkling water? I'll set the table."

Nina had appeared looking fresh-faced and casual in a pair of black yoga pants and a soft, rose-colored T-shirt that gently hugged the swell of her belly. Her beauty made his heart skip a beat...or two.

He set down his bottle of beer before it slipped from his hand. "You mean we're not just eating out of the cartons?"

"This is *not* the edge of civilization despite your belief to the contrary."

"I'm not accusing Washingtonians of being barbarians. I like eating Chinese out of the carton."

She looked up from arranging place mats on the table, her head cocked. "I never would've had you pegged as that type."

"The type to eat out of a carton?" He laughed. "Is that a type? I thought everyone did that."

"You know, the cold-pizza-and-beer-in-the-morning type. The brush-your-teeth-with-your-finger type."

"Whoa!" He filled a glass with ice and poured flavored sparkling water over the cubes. "Let's not get crazy. I always use a toothbrush, but I've had a few cold-pizza breakfasts in my day. Did you think I ate pizza on fine china with silverware?"

She folded a napkin and placed it on one side of the place mat. "You seem cultured to me, not quite comfortable in your flannel shirts and work boots."

He stomped his feet. "I'm okay in my work boots, and I detest the ballet."

"You're from Connecticut, aren't you? Prep school. Ivy League. Lacrosse."

He took a gulp of beer. She had him pegged. "I never played lacrosse."

"A guy like you, marines, you must've gone in as an officer."

"I did. Intelligence."

"And you went to an Ivy League school?"

"Yale." Might as well tell the truth where he could.

She snapped her fingers. "Utensils, please."

He yanked open a drawer and collected a couple of forks and knives. "Did you order soup, too?"

"Hot-and-sour." She reached across the peninsula for the utensils. "You must have some good stories for your book."

"Yep."

The doorbell saved him from any other personal revelations. "I'll get it."

He approached the front door from the side and leaned to the right to peek through the peephole. A young, pimply dude shifted from side to side on the porch.

"We have delivery." He swung open the door and took the food from the delivery guy while digging in his pocket for cash.

He turned and almost bumped into Nina.

"You didn't have to pay for that. I'll get half."

"I haven't done enough work around here to earn my keep. Let me get dinner."

They popped open the cartons and shoveled the steaming food onto their plates. One spoonful of the soup cleared his sinuses.

"That baby of yours is in for a treat."

"He should have an international palate the way I've been eating."

"Have you picked out any names yet?"

"I've been thinking about William, Will for short. Do you think everyone will call him Bill or Billy?"

"Not if he calls himself Will. I trained everyone to call me Jase."

As soon as the words left his lips, he stuffed his mouth with food, hoping Nina would let them slide. No such luck.

"Your name's not Jase? It's short for Jason?"

"Yeah." He waved his fork in the air. "Too many of those where I grew up."

Would she now try to find Jason Buckley on the internet? It still wouldn't lead her to Jason or Jase Bennett. The lives of Prospero agents were not for public consumption in search engines.

What had she discovered about Simon Skinner? Since both agencies were black ops under the umbrella of the CIA, he had to believe Tempest agents had the same protections, maybe more. Prospero hadn't been able to uncover anything about Max Duvall when he'd contacted them—not until they'd requested his records from the CIA.

"Jase suits you better than Jason."

For the rest of their dinner, he turned the talk away

from his background and his real name to the baby. Nina had her worries about raising this baby on her own, but her excitement and joy about the pregnancy bubbled over despite everything.

Her happiness flowed into him and filled that hole left by Maggie and her selfishness. He ignored the red flags and soaked in the joy emanating from Nina.

As they cleaned up, Nina got a phone call from Lou's mother. She took the call in the back rooms, and Jase flipped open his laptop to check his mail.

The techies hadn't let him down. He clicked on the email and scanned the contents. The department had been able to triangulate the location of Chris's phone—he was still on the island.

What the hell was this guy's game? Had he somehow made contact with his brother, Simon, before Simon's death? Maybe Simon had sent Chris on a quest to track down Nina. Maybe the whole aw-shucks-I-just-wanna-find-my-brother shtick was an act. Was Chris here on Simon's orders? For what purpose?

Jack hadn't gotten back to him yet with a full dossier on Chris Kitchens. He should've never let the guy get anywhere near Nina without it. She didn't owe Kitchens anything.

"Whew, I'm glad that's over with." Nina walked into the room, pressing a hand to her heart. "Inez took Lou's death pretty hard."

"You didn't expect her to?" He closed out of his email.

"It's hard to tell with Inez. She's going to take care of Lou's apartment in Portland, and I'm going to ship Lou's things to her there."

"And the funeral?"

"Once the coroner gets the toxicology report and releases the body, I'm going to send her to Portland—to her mother." She swiped a tear from her cheek. "Lou was never happy on this island once her father married my mother."

"It doesn't sound like Lou was ever happy."

"Some people are like that."

"But not you."

"I try." She rubbed her nose. "Why do you say that?"

"You have a lot going on right now and you still have a great attitude, a great attitude about your pregnancy."

"I always wanted children and I thought Simon was the one, but life doesn't always turn out the way you plan it."

"That's for sure." He reached across the table and picked up his bottle and her glass. "Do you want more sparkling water? A cup of tea?"

"More water, please. That food made me thirsty. Are you having another beer?"

"No." He cocked his head. "Is that your phone buzzing? Mine's not set to buzz."

She dived for her phone charging on the kitchen counter and touched the display. "It's another message from Chris."

"Does he give any more details about this threat?"

She looked up from the phone, her tongue darting from her mouth. "He wants to meet me. He must still be on the island."

He put on his surprised look—raised eyebrows and open mouth. "I'll be damned. What does he say?"

She held the phone in front of her. "Meet me at the wharf in town at ten o'clock. I'll tell you what I know. Then get me off this island."

"Why can't he tell you in his text or, better yet, call you?"

"It sounds like he needs a way off Break Island and wants to make sure I provide that way."

"I don't like it, Nina. Tell him I'll go in your place."

"Jase..."

"Tell him." He jabbed a finger in the air. "You're not putting yourself or your baby in jeopardy for this guy."

She texted Chris back and held the phone cupped in her hand, waiting for a response.

Jase's muscles tensed, his breath short.

Nina's phone buzzed and she shook her head. "He said he doesn't trust you. He doesn't trust anyone. It has to be me."

"I'm coming with you, and don't even ask him if that's okay."

Her thumbs danced across her phone's screen, and again she waited for the answering buzz. Even so, she jumped when it sounded off. She blew out a breath.

"He wants us to take a boat to the town harbor. He'll tell me what's going on when we're on the way to the mainland."

"We still have the arrangement with the Kleinschmidts. We can use their boat."

She glanced at her display again. "We have just over an hour."

He traced a line down the side of her arm. "Are you sure you want to do this? He can find his own way back to the mainland."

"I have to know. I have to know if Simon is out there and what he wants from me." She held the phone to her chest with both hands. "I told you, I sensed he was stalking me in LA. I just want to find out what he hopes to gain by this behavior."

Spreading his hands, he said, "It might not be about Simon at all. It might have something to do with Lou. Maybe you were right about her death—maybe Kip Chandler had something to do with it."

"That's just it, Jase. They all headed back to the same motel together, so Chris may have heard something, or seen something with Lou and Kip, that I need to know.

Something that may not mean a lot to the police, but would mean a heck of a lot to me." She placed her hand over his, still on her arm. "I have to meet Chris to find out."

Her skin against his felt soft and warm but electrifying. Did she feel it, too? He looked into her blue eyes and caught an answering spark.

Jerking his head to the side, he broke the connection. This was wrong on so many levels he couldn't even begin to count them. "We'll come prepared."

She paused for two beats, and when she responded, her voice had a hoarse edge. "I can't exactly bring my shotgun."

She felt it, too, this thing between them, and she didn't even know who he was. It was all a lie.

He turned from her and grabbed his backpack, which was hanging over the back of the chair at the desk. He reached for his weapon. "I don't want to freak you out, but I'm bringing this."

When he faced her holding his Glock pistol, barrel down, her eyebrows shot up.

"Why do you have that?"

"I'm a former marine. I have a conceal-and-carry permit. It's all legal."

"None of that answers the question I asked."

He parked the gun next to his laptop. "Sure it does. I'm an ex-marine. Carrying is second nature to me."

"Okay, so you'll be the one with the gun this time. Just don't shoot anybody." She formed her fingers into a gun and pulled the trigger. "I'm going to change into something warmer."

Jase snagged his own jacket from the hook by the front door and shoved his weapon into the pocket. He'd leave the pocket zipped—until they got to the town wharf. He didn't know what to expect from Chris Kitchens, but he wasn't going to take any chances—not with Nina's life and not with Will's.

His child had been a boy, too, until Maggie carelessly ended his life. He hadn't even gotten used to the idea of being a father before it was all over in the blink of an eye. He hadn't been able to protect his son, but he sure as hell could protect Nina's.

She came from the back wearing jeans, a bulky green sweater and deck shoes. She pointed to his jacket. "Do you want something waterproof? The water's getting choppy out there and it still might rain."

He glanced down at his down jacket in his hands. "This isn't waterproof?"

"That may be waterproof for Connecticut rain, but not for a storm on the water in the sound." She flung open the door of the closet in the foyer and pulled out a black full-length slicker. "Bruce wasn't as tall as you, but this will cover most of what needs to be covered."

He pulled on the coat, which hung just past his knees and rode up his wrists, but it was roomy enough. "This'll do."

"Let's go see about that boat."

"I'll go see about the boat. You wait here. Have some hot tea."

"Anyone ever tell you that you are bossy, Buckley?"

"All the time."

He prepped the boat for departure and returned to find Nina rinsing out a cup in the sink.

"I took your advice and had some tea. Now I'm unstoppable."

"You're not unstoppable, so don't even think about doing anything dumb."

She wedged a hand on her hip. "What exactly do you think I'm going to do, take Chris down?"

"I hope it doesn't come to that."

"Do you think it would be better if I showed up alone?"

"Absolutely not. Didn't we already discuss this? I'm not going to allow you to put yourself in danger. I'm not going to allow you to put Will in danger."

By the way Nina's mouth hung open, he realized he'd stepped over the line—way over the line.

"Hold on there, Papa Bear. I didn't mean I'd actually show up by myself. You'd be there, just hidden away."

The heat clawed up his chest, disguised by the double layer of clothing he'd piled on.

"Sorry I overreacted. Maybe it's my imagination working overtime, but I don't trust Chris Kitchens as far as I can drop-kick him." If Jack would get back to him on Kitchens's background, he might be going into this meeting a little less twitchy.

She tilted her head, and her ponytail swung over her shoulder. "I appreciate your concern, but I'm not going to do anything to harm my baby. In fact, I'm doing this to protect him. If Chris has information about some threat to me, I want to know about it."

"Fair enough." He pulled his weapon from his down jacket and held it up. "And if Chris Kitchens is the actual threat, I'll know about that soon enough."

"Okay, then. Is the boat ready to go?"

"All set."

She locked up Moonstones, and they crossed the dark yard to the Kleinschmidts' boat.

He gunned the motor and flicked on the spotlights, which illuminated the lapping water. The trip to the town wharf couldn't be more than ten minutes, but judging from the choppy water, it would be a rough ten minutes.

"Do you get seasick?"

"No, do you? This ain't like sailing on some calm bay, preppy boy."

He laughed, and the wind snatched the sound and

rolled it over the waves. "Okay, pioneer girl of the Pacific Northwest. Did you fly up from LA or come over in a covered wagon?"

She punched him in the side, which he barely felt.

The boat chugged into the water, which slapped its sides, sending salty spray into the air. The mist clung to his eyelashes and moistened his lips, where he licked it off.

The ten-minute trip turned into fifteen as he negotiated the waves, riding them up and down. As the lights from the wharf grew brighter, he reduced his speed and shouted, "Is it very busy this time of night?"

"No, but I expect it to be busier than usual as people try to make their way off the island before the storm hits."

"Why do you suppose Chris isn't among them? Why does he need a ride from you?"

"I don't know. Maybe he figures out on the water is the safest place to warn me."

He aimed the boat toward an empty slip and crawled into the harbor. Streetlamps every fifty feet or so cast a glow on the boats bobbing in their slips.

"Chris better be keeping an eye out for us, because I'm not going to let you wander around looking for him and I sure as hell am not going to, either."

"He's the one who set this up."

He pulled into the slip, and as the boat bumped the boat dock bumpers, he tossed a rope to Nina. "Are we supposed to pay for the slip?"

"Not if we're doing a quick in-and-out."

"I guess that depends on Chris."

Jase left on the boat's lights to create a circle of illumination on the wooden walkway fronting the boats. He didn't want any surprises from Kitchens.

A boat started several slips over and they both turned to look.

"Where is this guy?"

"Are you jumpy or what?" Nina sat on the storage bin. "We just got here."

Jase felt for the gun in the pocket of the mackinaw. Definitely jumpy. "I thought he was in a big hurry to leave the island. Maybe he got a ride on Kip's helicopter."

Nina snorted. Then she put down the boat's stepladder and climbed over. Glancing one way and then the other, she called out softly, "Chris?"

Jase vaulted over the side of the boat to join her, his feet landing with a clang on the gangplank that echoed in the night. He shoved his hand into his pocket and gripped his gun.

Something didn't smell right, and he didn't mean the fishy odor that permeated the air. Had that even been Kitchens texting Nina? Anyone with access to his phone could be sending her messages.

Someone halfway down the line of boats shouted.

Nina's head jerked up. "What was that?"

"Someone yelling down there."

The voice rose again and a few boats turned on their spotlights.

"What do you think is going on?"

"I have no idea." But he had an uneasy feeling in his gut.

A man burst out of the bait shop and started running toward the lights.

Nina took two steps toward the commotion. "Jase."

Something about the men's shouts chilled his blood. Nina must've heard it, too.

She took two more steps.

"Wait, Nina."

"I heard... I heard..." Her shoes pounded against the damp wood as she ran toward the agitated knot of people at the water's edge.

He had no choice but to follow her, his weapon banging

against his thigh. He reached her before she reached the clutch of people, all talking and pointing at once.

They approached the group together and Jase asked, "What's going on?"

The boater they'd talked to earlier that day pointed at the brackish water lapping against the side of his boat. "It looks like...I don't know, something."

Jase grabbed the flashlight from him and crouched on the silver gangplank, leaning forward as the beam of light played over the water.

Something floated out from beneath the gangplank and everyone behind him gasped and jumped back.

It was something all right—it was Chris Kitchens's dead body.

Chapter Thirteen

Nina stumbled against Jase, almost falling over him. "It's Chris."

"You know this guy?" The man from the bait shop squatted next to Jase.

The boater snapped his fingers. "Is that the one you were asking about this morning? The ex-boyfriend?"

Three pairs of eyes drilled into her. She put her hands over her face. This was getting crazy and she couldn't even keep her own lies straight.

"Yes. No. I didn't say he was my boyfriend."

Jase refocused the flashlight on the group. "We do know this man, however. Has someone called 9-1-1 yet?"

Thank God for Jase taking charge. She was finding it hard to even stand up.

Steve, the boater from earlier in the day, scratched his chin. "Hell, I didn't even know if it was really a body or not. I thought I saw a face in the water. Scared the hell out of me."

The bait shop owner held up his phone. "I got it."

While he made the call, Nina tried to catch Jase's eye, but he was busy trying to haul in the body—Chris.

"I think he's stuck on something beneath the slip."

"Maybe we should just let the professionals handle this."

"Bubbles!" Jase flattened out on his belly and scooted closer to Chris's floating head. "I saw bubbles. He's not dead."

Jase shed her stepfather's coat and slid into the black water as Nina screamed his name.

"I'll be damned." The boater dropped to his knees and aimed the flashlight where Jase had disappeared.

Nina released a breath when Jase popped up again, keeping Chris's head above the surface.

Jase coughed and shook wet hair from his eyes. "His leg is pinned. Hold him up while I release him."

Steve leaned forward and hooked his arms beneath Chris's armpits while Jase dived down again.

Nina wrapped her arms around her body to stop the shivering, but it wasn't the cold that was causing it.

Sirens wailed and the emergency vehicles lit up the pier.

Finally, Jase rose from the murky depths and the rest of Chris's body floated to the surface.

The EMTs did the rest as they hauled Chris from the water. They pumped his chest.

"Is he alive?" She hovered on the outside of the circle of EMTs working on Chris.

A cop stepped in front of her. "Ma'am, you're going to have to give them room."

She spun around and grabbed Jase, soaking wet and freezing cold to the touch. "What were you thinking, jumping in that water?"

"He was alive, Nina. I saw bubbles at the surface of the water."

"That could've been anything."

"She has a point there. There're all kinds of things bubbling in that water." The bait shop owner shook his head. "He sure looked like a goner to me."

A police officer approached them with a pad of paper in one hand. "I'm Officer Franklin. Who discovered him?"

Steve raised his hand. "That's my boat. I was going to ready her for a trip to the mainland when I saw something white floating beside her."

"He yelled out and I'm parked right next door." The other boat owner thrust his thumb over his shoulder. "I came over to see what all the commotion was about. I saw Ned step out of his shop and called him over, and then these two showed up."

The cop wagged his finger between her and Jase. "And what were you two doing out here?"

Jase poked her in the small of her back. "Nina's stepsister died earlier this morning. I was just taking her back to this side of the island because she left something in her sister's motel room."

"Oh, yeah." Franklin tapped his chin with the eraser of his pencil. "Louise Moore. Sorry for your loss, ma'am, but couldn't you two just walk from the dune side of the island?"

"We had the boat out anyway."

Nina nodded, marveling at the easy lies that sprang to Jase's lips. She supposed it was best the cops didn't know they'd come here to meet Chris, but wouldn't they discover that anyway once they checked out his cell phone and saw his texts to her number?

The EMTs pulled a white sheet over Chris's face, and Nina swayed. Jase caught her around the waist.

"Is he gone?"

The EMTs strapped Chris's body to the gurney. "He's gone."

The cop circled his pencil in the air. "Does anyone know who he is?"

Would Jase lie about this, too?

He cleared his throat. "His name is Chris Kitchens.

He's related to a friend of Ms. Moore's. We met him for the first time yesterday and figured he'd left the island today."

Steve shoved a toothpick between his lips. "This isn't the boyfriend?"

"Boyfriend?" Nina ran her tongue along her bottom lip. "I think you misunderstood. He's related to an ex-boyfriend."

"Does anyone know next of kin?"

Ned was already heading for his bait shop and Steve shrugged his shoulders. "Don't know a thing about him."

"Like I said, we just met him yesterday. He was looking for his brother, whom he hadn't seen since they were both adopted over twenty years ago." Jase draped the mackinaw over his shoulders. "We couldn't help him."

"Anyone plan on leaving the island anytime soon?"

Nina rubbed her eyes as the EMTs began loading Chris's body into the back of the ambulance. "I live here now, not going anywhere."

"Just in case." Franklin put away his notepad. "We'll see what the autopsy turns up. Could be he took a wrong turn, fell into the water, hit his head and drowned."

Nina doubted that scenario, but unless she wanted to spend the rest of the night at the police station, she'd keep her mouth shut.

"If it's okay, I'm going to get him home before icicles start forming on the end of his nose." She took Jase's arm and pulled him toward the parking lot.

He resisted. "The boat."

"You're not going back on the water. We'll get a taxi back and fetch the boat tomorrow morning."

Officer Franklin spoke up. "I'll give you two a ride back. Moonstones, right?"

"That's it." Everyone here already knew her business. She wouldn't be surprised if the officer knew about Chris's contact with her stepsister before she OD'd. "Did you find Chris's phone?"

"Just his wallet, no phone. Maybe it fell in the water."

Even more reason to keep quiet about her connection to Chris, since the police department wouldn't discover anything without that phone.

Jase's teeth chattered on and off during the ride back to the B and B, so she threaded her fingers through his and squeezed his hand every time a chill claimed his body.

He leaned forward and spoke through the mesh separating the front seat from the back. "Sorry I'm getting water all over your backseat."

"That's okay. It's seen a lot worse."

Franklin wheeled his patrol car in front of Moonstones. "Are you two going to be okay?"

"As soon as I dry off and warm up, I'll be fine. Damn, I could've sworn he still had breath in him."

"Tough break. We'll be in touch."

They scrambled from the car and Nina ran ahead of Jase to open the front door. "Why is it every time we come back here, one of us is all wet?"

"It's an island."

She shoved him from behind. "Go get some warm, dry clothes on and I'll get the fire started—then we talk."

He planted his feet on the floor. "Sit down and relax. I'll start the fire when I come back. In the meantime, crank on the furnace. I'm going to hop in the shower for a few minutes first."

She didn't argue with him, since he'd somehow come to the conclusion that pregnancy sapped a woman's strength and energy—and reason, come to think of it.

She sat meekly on the edge of the chair, and as soon as she heard his door shut, she crouched before the fireplace and lit the kindling. Jase had already stacked the logs in the grate.

Fanning the fire to life, she stared into the depths of the flames. What had just happened? Chris had been the one to warn her and he'd wound up dead. No way was that a coincidence.

Would Simon kill his own brother? What did Chris mean to Simon anyway? They'd grown up apart. They were strangers despite Chris's romanticized vision of finding his little brother.

She'd listen to Jase's conclusions before jumping to any of her own. He seemed to discount Simon's involvement so quickly. Maybe he just couldn't imagine a man wanting to harm his own child. Jase seemed quite taken with hers.

She rubbed her belly and then ducked behind the bar to nab her stepfather's good cognac. Tea wouldn't cut it for Jase. She filled the bottom of a bowl-shaped snifter with the golden liquid and brought it to the table by the fire. Her gaze shifted to Jase's laptop.

For a writer, he sure didn't do much writing. Of course, he was living out a real-life drama with her and her problems. Maybe he was putting all this in his book.

She ran her fingers along the seamed closure of the laptop and snatched her hand back when she heard Jase emerge from his room.

"That hot shower felt good." He sauntered into the room, dark gray sweats covering his long legs and a white T-shirt hugging the muscles she'd always suspected of hiding beneath his bulky flannels.

He caught her stare. "I'm sorry. Were you expecting a smoking jacket or silk pajamas?"

She lifted the glass of cognac. "Would've gone nicely with this cognac."

"How'd you know I'd enjoy a glass of the good stuff?"

She swirled the liquid in the glass before handing it to him. "Just a guess."

He took the snifter from her, brushing her fingers in

the process, before sinking into the love seat. "I see you got the fire going anyway."

"It wasn't hard or taxing, believe it or not."

He stretched out his long legs. "Feels good."

"Don't ignore the elephant in the room." She dropped to the floor in front of his chair and hugged her knees to her chest, or at least as close as she could get them to her chest. "What happened to Chris?"

"He drowned." Jase took a sip of the cognac and watched her over the rim of the snifter.

"Someone killed him before he could warn me."

Jase's eyes flickered but he didn't jump into a denial—which scared the hell out of her.

"When I pulled him out of the water, it looked like he had an abrasion on the side of his head, but that could've happened when he fell into the water."

"Who falls off a gangplank into the water?"

"It was dark out there. Steve's boat's in the shadows."

"Just who are you trying to convince?" She rested her chin on her knees. "It's Simon."

"You think he'd kill his own brother?"

She clicked her tongue. "He didn't know Chris. He never mentioned having a brother to me once. He never discussed his birth family. As far as Simon was concerned, the people who adopted him were his parents and he had no siblings."

The amber liquid in Jase's glass sloshed from side to side as another chill rolled through his body.

"Scoot over." She hopped to her feet. "You're still not completely warmed up. You're going to catch a chill."

He shifted to the side of the love seat and patted the other cushion. "Be my guest."

She settled beside him and her body flushed with warmth as she remembered falling asleep in his arms the other night.

Maybe tonight he'd fall asleep in her arms.

He cupped his glass with two hands. "Have you ever reported Simon? Gotten a restraining order against him?"

"How can you get a restraining order against a ghost?"

His body stiffened. "What does that mean?"

He really was still chilled to the bone. She pressed her hands against his shoulders, pushing him forward. Then she began kneading the tight muscles between his shoulder blades with her knuckles.

"What I mean is I've never seen Simon. I haven't seen him since the day he walked out of our place." She skimmed her hands down his back, feeling the smooth flesh beneath his thin T-shirt. "I've sensed his presence or at least a presence, but you can't get a restraining order against a presence."

His muscles bunched into even tighter knots beneath her fingers.

"You're going to be sore tomorrow morning if you don't relax your muscles. You must still be chilled." She tapped his glass with her fingernail. "Drink up and have another."

He tossed back the drink and set the glass on the table with a clink. "If there is someone out there stalking you, I don't want to be drunk when he comes to your door."

She tucked her feet beneath her body and leaned against Jase's arm. "I'd put my money on you drunk or sober, Jase Buckley."

He sucked in a breath as if about to make an announcement but kissed her mouth instead.

The nutty taste of the cognac on his lips was almost enough to make *her* drunk. She melted against him, her soft breasts pressing against his rock-hard biceps.

He scooped a hand through his damp hair. "I'm sorry. I shouldn't have done that."

"Why not?" She rubbed her cheek against his shoulder.

"I've been wanting you to kiss me for the longest time. Is that... I mean, do you?" She huffed out a breath. "I'm carrying another man's baby."

He stroked her back. "And that man is gone...a ghost."

"The pregnancy was a mistake."

"Shh." He pressed two fingers against her lips. "Don't ever say that."

"I don't mean I'm upset about it or don't want my baby. I do—with all my heart. I just wanted to explain to you how it happened."

The corner of his mouth quirked into a lopsided grin. "I understand the basics."

"I mean—" she dug her fingernails into his upper arm "—how it happened with Simon, since we were having problems. The night the baby was conceived was a last-ditch effort on my part, one last attempt to reach Simon and bring him back to me."

"It didn't work."

"Sadly, no." Her bottom lip quivered. "But I have Will, and I'm glad I do. I'll never allow him to feel anything but loved and wanted, because he is."

"I believe that." He traced her lips with the tip of his finger. "I can tell you'll be a great mom."

"But first I need to keep Will safe, even if that means protecting him from his father."

"Are you going to leave the island?"

"I came here to get away, as a sanctuary, but Simon knew about Moonstones. Maybe I need to escape to a place where Simon can't reach me."

"I might be able to help you with that."

A thrill raced along her spine. Was he saying he wanted to continue their relationship?

A knock on the door made the thrill turn into a chill and she instinctively grabbed Jase's hand.

He squeezed her fingers. "Stay put."

He pushed out of the chair and stalked up to the front door. He placed his eye to the peephole. "It's Officer Franklin."

"Do you think they discovered anything yet?" She rose from the chair.

"Too soon." He opened the door. "Officer Franklin. Can we help you with anything else?"

"No, but I can help Ms. Moore."

Nina peered over Jase's shoulder. "How?"

The officer reached into his pocket and pulled out her cell phone. "You left this in the backseat of my squad car. I figured it was yours instead of Mr. Buckley's because of the pink polka-dotted case, but correct me if I'm wrong."

She held out her hand, wiggling her fingers. "It's mine. Thanks."

"No problem."

Jase asked, "Any word on Chris Kitchens?"

"Not yet. We'll keep you posted."

"Good night and thanks." Nina held up her phone. She meandered back to the love seat, hoping she and Jase could take up where they'd left off, since he'd just hinted at some kind of future for them. Her phone beeped at her.

"What was that?"

"My cell phone telling me I need to charge it." Changing course, she walked toward the kitchen to plug in the phone. She slid her finger across the display to unlock it and her pulse ticked up. "I have another text message from Chris."

Jase materialized by her side. "What does it say?"

She tapped her phone and read the message. "'I'm here. Meet—'" she shrugged "—and then gibberish."

"Gibberish?"

"Some letters and numbers."

"That's weird. Let me see it."

She handed the cell to him. "He must've sent that right

before he fell into the water or whatever happened. Look at the time."

Jase had the phone practically to his nose, and the knuckles of the hand clutching the phone were white.

Her heart skittered in her chest. "Jase, what is it?"

"The gibberish?" He turned the phone toward her. "He was typing *Tempest*."

Chapter Fourteen

"Tempest?" Nina's face registered complete and utter confusion, and then she snapped and pointed her finger at the same time. "The piece of paper in Lou's pocket. That had *tempest* written on it, too."

"That's right." The dread was pounding through his veins so relentlessly he could barely hear his own voice. He held out the phone and tapped the message. "Look, it's a *T*, 3, *N*, *P*, 3, *S*, *T*. He was definitely trying to type *Tempest*—in a hurry."

"What the hell is that all about? What does *tempest* mean? Have people started running around calling big storms tempests all of a sudden?"

"I…" He held out his hands and then clasped them together. "I'm not sure, but for both Lou and Chris to refer to Tempest and then both wind up dead, whatever it is it's not good."

"And what does it have to do with me? Do you think that's why Kip disappeared? Did we all unwittingly run across something that put us in danger?"

She was definitely on the right track. But what had Lou and Chris discovered about Tempest that Nina hadn't? The name still meant nothing to her. If the agents of Tempest were going after her to keep her quiet, they were wasting their resources. Why expend this much effort going after a dead agent's ex-fiancée to the point of killing people in the way?

It didn't make any sense.

He'd been on the verge of telling her everything, but without getting clearance from Coburn he'd be breaking all kinds of rules and maybe putting other lives in danger.

He was here to protect Nina, and that's exactly what he planned to do—whether or not she knew the reason.

"I think we need to find Kip."

"Unlike Chris, he's probably left the island by now. After hearing about Lou and Chris, I doubt Kip's going to want to be found. Who knows? Maybe his brother really does have a helicopter. He didn't strike me as the type to stick around and warn others."

"Not like Chris." She threw back her ponytail and marched to the closed door of her office.

"What are you going to do?"

"I'm going to do an internet search on *tempest*. Maybe it has some meaning we're not aware of. Maybe it's a new synthetic drug or something."

He slipped past her and stood in front of the office door, and not because he was afraid she'd find out something about the covert agency Tempest. She never would.

"It's late. You need to get some sleep. Will's had enough excitement for one day."

She reached out, her fingertips skimming the white cotton covering his chest. "Thanks for worrying about us. I'm sure you never bargained for any of this when you came to this quiet island to work."

He hadn't—not Tempest's interest in her and certainly not his own interest in her.

Tapping his head, he said, "It's all fodder for the book."

"Am I going to turn up as some crazy pregnant lady in your book?"

"You'll be the intrepid heroine." He stroked her cheek

with the back of his hand, getting lost in the blue depths of her eyes.

"Jase." She caught his hand. "Can you come into my room and talk to me while I fall asleep? I'm not sure—I just don't want to be alone right now."

"Absolutely." He brought her hand to his lips and pressed a kiss against her palm. "Get ready for bed and I'll close up shop here."

"Thanks." She spun around and headed for the back rooms.

He needed to check for any messages from Jack. He didn't have any confidential information on this computer, but he could still send messages to and receive messages from Jack. Standing over his laptop on the desk by the window, he entered his password to unlock it and then jumped as he felt a warm breath on the back of his neck.

"Sorry." Nina put a steadying hand on his arm. "I just came out to tell you not to bother with the dishes. I'll load them in the dishwasher tomorrow morning."

"Got it."

As she floated to the back of the house on her silent, stocking feet, he checked his email and then powered down the computer.

He rinsed his glass, checked the locks, turned off the lights and retrieved his Glock pistol from the mackinaw and shoved it into the pocket of his baggy sweatpants.

If he was watching over Nina tonight, he'd do so locked and loaded.

By the time he reached her room, she had changed into a pair of flannel pajamas with pink bunnies scattered across a field of white, puffy clouds.

If he'd expected her to get her sexy on, she'd just dashed those hopes.

She fluffed up a pillow against her headboard. "I'm pretty tired, but I appreciate the company."

He sat on the foot of her bed. "Are you cold? Get under the covers."

She plucked at her pajamas. "With these on? These pajamas are like wearing a blanket."

She lay on top of the bedspread and pulled a pillow beneath her head. Patting the bed, she said, "You can join me. I don't bite."

"That's a relief." But it wasn't the biting he was worried about. He was worried about the way she smelled like a field of wildflowers after a spring shower. He was worried about the way her dark hair cascaded down her back like a silky waterfall. He was worried about taking this woman, pregnant with another man's child, and claiming her as his own.

Pushing it all aside, he stretched out on the bed behind her. He slipped his weapon under the bed and rolled onto his back, staring at the ceiling.

She emitted a soft sigh as she curled an arm beneath the pillow. "Are you close with your family? Your parents? Your sister?"

She remembered he had a sister? He decided to tell the truth for once. "Not particularly. My parents didn't approve of my enlistment and I didn't approve of their disapproval."

"What did they want for you? Family business?"

Nina didn't miss a thing. How'd Simon manage to keep her in the dark for so long? "Yeah, something like that."

Of course, she didn't have to know that his family's business was politics and that she'd probably seen his father bloviating on national TV a time or two.

"Jase?"

"Yeah?" Here it came, more questions and more lies.

"Why *are* you so protective of me…and Will? Most guys would be doing an about-face if they had to deal with a pregnant woman."

He didn't have to lie about this, did he? He owed her some truthfulness.

"I was in a similar situation to yours a few years ago. My girlfriend and I had been discussing marriage, but things didn't work out."

"You broke up?"

"Yeah, and like you, Maggie found out she was pregnant after the breakup."

She rolled onto her back, her head falling to the side to study his profile. "B-but you told me you didn't have children."

"I don't." The pain that sliced through his gut surprised him. "Maggie lost the baby in her fourth month—just about where you are now."

She sucked in a quick breath. "I'm so sorry."

"It was her fault."

"Sometimes these things happen." She traced one of the bunnies with her fingertip. "I thank God every day that my pregnancy is progressing without any issues."

"At least you're not out there rock climbing."

"Rock climbing? Maggie was rock climbing going into her second trimester?"

His jaw tightened and he tried to keep the bitterness from his tone. "Can you believe that? She fell, broke her arm and lost the baby—our baby. Do you wanna know the kicker?"

She took his hand and whispered, "What?"

"I never even knew she was pregnant. She didn't tell me. I heard about the accident when I came back from an…from a trip."

"That's so unfair." She laced her fingers through his. "Is that why you jumped on me about whether or not I told Simon?"

"I guess so."

"And that's why you care so much about Will."

"It's not just Will I care about, Nina." He shifted to his side and wound a lock of her hair around his finger.

As she met his eyes, she parted her lips and he kissed her. The minty taste of her toothpaste was as sweet as honey.

"Jase, I don't know where this can go."

"Let's not worry about that right now." He touched her bottom lip with the pad of his thumb. "Go to sleep."

She turned on her right side and he pulled her lush body against his. His arm curved around her waist and his hand naturally cupped the swell of her belly.

If Tempest wanted to come after Nina, they could try but they'd have to go through him first.

NINA AWOKE ALONE in the bed. All night she'd been aware of Jase's comforting presence next to her. She'd nestled against him and felt his arms tighten around her in response.

His story about losing the baby he never knew existed had tugged at her heartstrings. It explained so much about his attitude toward her. In protecting her and Will, he hoped to make up for his missed chances with his own unborn child.

Was that the basis of his attraction, too? Once she had her baby, would Jase find another pregnant woman to nurture? It sounded crazy, but the pull of filling emotional voids in your life was strong.

She should know. Having never had a protective father figure in her life, she'd always been attracted to take-charge guys. She and Jase were a match made in psychological, subconscious heaven.

Sighing, she pushed back the covers. Jase had tucked her into bed later, but he never joined her beneath the sheets. Was he afraid of igniting the flame that kindled between them?

She was the one who had stopped the kiss last night. She wanted to know him better, find out what really made him tick. She wanted to read his book.

She tumbled out of bed and crept into the B and B's living area. Jase had flung open the drapes at the front window, allowing the gray, misty light to filter into the room.

Her breath fogged the glass as she leaned in close. She wiped a streak through it with her fist and peered outside.

It had rained again last night, harder than ever. The storm was still toying with them. Maybe it would bypass Break Island altogether.

Dressed in his Pacific Northwest uniform, Jase was leaning against a fence post he'd repaired and talking on his phone.

She didn't see him make many phone calls. His family must still be holding a grudge for his shunning of the family business, which he'd never gotten around to explaining to her. It was probably plastics or something equally staid and boring. Jase wouldn't do staid and boring—hence his stint as a marine.

He thrust his arm out to the side and waved it in the air. Maybe he was talking to his estranged family.

She shuffled into the kitchen and poured herself a glass of orange juice. Holding her breath, she glanced at her fully charged phone. No more messages from the dead.

Of course, Chris hadn't been dead when he sent that message—not yet anyway—and she hadn't forgotten about the mysterious code word. *Tempest.*

She charged toward her office and retrieved her laptop. When she powered it on, she groaned at the blue screen mocking her. She'd been having problems with her computer ever since she moved here. The tech guy on the mainland told her it might happen again, and if it did, she'd need to bring it back. No chance of that now.

Her gaze darted to the side where Jase's laptop glowed invitingly. No blue screens there. She strolled toward the invitation.

He did have password protection, but she'd seen him enter it last night—Semper Fi—all lowercase and no spaces. How could she forget that?

Resting her fingers on the keyboard, she watched Jase outside, still on the phone. He wouldn't mind if she looked up *tempest* on his laptop, would he?

She was surprised he hadn't jumped on that himself. He'd seemed more intrigued by the word that linked Lou and Chris than she was. She knew he'd been up early this morning to retrieve the Kleinschmidts' boat, so maybe he had already looked it up and didn't tell her because he hadn't found anything.

She launched his web browser, which automatically displayed a search engine. She entered the word *tempest*.

The expected and the unexpected popped up—references to Shakespeare's play, a dictionary definition of the word, a video game and even an actress's name. She continued to page through the findings, but didn't discover anything ominous about the word—no new drug, nothing illegal, no secret society.

What had it meant to Lou and then Chris? Was it something that had signed their death warrants? Would it sign hers?

She bit her lip and switched to her email provider. Scrolling through her email, she deleted the junk and saved the queries from her website for estimates. Getting Moonstones up and running was going to take longer than she expected. She might as well see if she could pick up a few decorating jobs in the meantime, even if it meant a few quick trips down to LA.

She patted her stomach. She'd be good to fly for the next few months.

She closed out of everything and zeroed in on a file called *Book* on Jase's desktop. Could it be that easy?

She hunched over the table to look out the window. Jase had ended his call, but was busy measuring from one post to another.

Feeling guilty and sneaky, but very excited, she double-clicked on the file. It opened and her mouth opened with it.

One sentence glared back at her and sent a chill up her spine. She whispered the words. "'It was a dark and stormy night and a tempest was headed for Break Island.'"

With her hand trembling, she closed out of the file and slammed the laptop shut and then remembered that he'd left it open. She opened it again with a sinking feeling. She hadn't made any changes to the file, but would the computer record that someone had opened it?

Too late now.

She raised her eyes to Jase working in her yard. Who was he? That couldn't be his entire book, could it? She felt like the wife in that scary movie with Jack Nicholson when she'd read pages and pages of the same phrase over and over again in her husband's tome.

A shattering noise from the front yard made her jump back from the window. Jase had split a cord of wood with an ax. Jack Nicholson's character in the movie had an ax, too.

Crossing her arms, she backed away from the computer and the window. She retreated to the kitchen, her eyes flicking toward the laptop. Maybe that file didn't represent his book. Maybe his book was in a folder somewhere else.

She hadn't even checked when he'd last saved the file. Maybe he was just playing with a new idea based on all the stuff going on since his arrival on the island. The sentence itself was a joke, not a serious attempt at writing.

She paced while hugging herself, the flannel pajamas no longer warm enough. She'd snooped and paid the price.

If she confronted him about it, she'd have to admit she'd accessed his laptop on the sly. If she didn't confront him, she'd have to continue to suspect his motives—and his sanity—just as with Simon.

She heard him stomping his boots on the porch and took the best course of action. She retreated to the rooms in the back and cranked on the shower. After locking the door.

The warm water calmed her nerves. She hadn't stumbled on his book. Jase Buckley didn't pose any threat to her. He'd saved her on the water and had been there for her when Lou had attacked her and then wound up dead on the deck. He'd come to her defense when he thought Chris Kitchens meant to do her harm and then had insisted on accompanying her when Chris texted her his warnings.

Jase was one of the good guys.

She finished her shower and dressed in the bathroom. When she entered the sitting room, Jase turned from staring out the window, his hand resting on his open laptop.

Keeping her eyes pinned to his face, she asked, "Did you get a lot of work done this morning? The fence is looking pretty good."

"What?"

"The fence." He knew. He knew she'd been snooping.

"Oh, yeah. Coming along, and I picked up the boat." He swung his head back toward the window. "Did you have breakfast? I was kind of hoping for more blueberry pancakes."

"I was…busy."

He turned to face her, his gaze raking her from head to toe. "Taking a shower? You must've slept in. That's good. Did you sleep well?"

"Yes, because…" She closed her eyes and dragged her fingers through her damp hair. "I went onto your laptop."

His eyebrows jumped. "I have a password."

"I saw you enter your password last night before I went to bed."

"Why did you use my computer?"

His soft voice made her swallow. "M-mine is corrupted and I wanted to search for *tempest*."

"Did you find it?"

"I found— No, I didn't find out anything about that word." She twisted her fingers in front of her. "I found your book. *Is* that your book?"

"That's it."

His flat admission sent adrenaline surging through her body and she flung her arms out to her sides and took a step back. "I don't understand."

"I'm not Jase Buckley, Nina, and I'm not a writer. I'm Jase Bennett and I'm an agent for an undercover ops organization—just like Simon was."

Chapter Fifteen

Her arms fell to her sides. She took another step back. Why did she attract the lunatics? She'd had this man in her bed, in her heart.

She folded her arms over her baby bump. No wonder he'd reminded her of Simon. Two sides of the same crazy coin. Jase had done a much better job of disguising his madness, though.

"Jase, I think you'd better leave now."

His dark eyes widened and he threw back his head and laughed.

She jumped.

"I thought you'd be angry with me, maybe throw something at me—but you just think I'm crazy."

"I don't think that." She shook her head back and forth, her hair whipping from side to side. "Not at all. But I think it's time you left and did your covert ops stuff somewhere else."

He reached behind his back. She ducked.

The look on his face gave her pause—gave her hope. He held his hands in front of him, clutching a thumb drive. "Don't be afraid, Nina. I know it sounds crazy to you, but it's the truth. I would've told you sooner, but I wasn't supposed to reveal my identity to you or tell you what was going on until…until a later date. But with everything going on—Lou, Chris, Tempest—we need to tell you."

"Don't be afraid? You ask me not to be afraid and then bring up Lou and Chris?" She jabbed her finger at him. "What's that?"

"Proof." He pulled out the chair in front of the laptop. "It's proof that everything I'm saying is true. Have a seat. I don't bite."

He'd used the same phrase she'd used on him last night when inviting him to join her in bed. Was it deliberate? She studied his face, and his mouth turned up at one corner.

A little bit of tension seeped from between her shoulder blades and she walked to the chair. She sat on the corner of it, gripping the edge of the table.

Jase leaned over her to insert the thumb drive into the side of the laptop, and her shoulders stiffened.

"Sorry about this." He moved the cursor to the Book file and deleted it. "It was my attempt to add some humor to our situation."

"Our situation."

"You're not in this alone, Nina. I've always been on your side."

A man this sincere couldn't be a whack job, could he? But the alternative he was proposing wasn't much better.

He opened the thumb drive, which was populated with multiple folders. "I'm really not supposed to be sharing this with you, but you deserve to know what's going on and I've kept you in the dark long enough."

He double-clicked on a folder, and she held her breath. If this folder contained more of his bizarre attempts at writing a book, she was ready to sprint.

Instead, a photo of her on the phone and getting into her car on the street in front of her LA condo filled the computer screen. She jerked her head to the side. "How did you get this?"

He clicked the mouse and another picture of her appeared and another and another, all going about her daily business.

She gasped, half out of her chair. "You were following me in LA?"

"Not me personally. I don't do surveillance like this."

The photos were professional, taken with a high-powered telephoto lens. There's no way she wouldn't have noticed someone that close taking a picture of her. But maybe she sensed the scrutiny.

"What *do* you do?"

"I'm on the personal security end. My job right now is to protect targets."

"I'm a target? Why?"

He closed out her personal photo album and opened another folder. Some sort of document or report flashed on the screen with Simon's picture prominently displayed in the middle.

She covered her mouth with one hand. "You knew all about Simon."

He tapped the monitor. "Probably more than you did. Simon Skinner was a covert ops agent, like me, but for a different agency."

Her eyes scanned details of Simon's life, including a map pinpointing his locations over the past few years.

She squinted at the red dots. She knew he'd traveled a lot for his so-called government security job, but she had no idea he'd traveled to Yemen, Beijing, Libya.

She slumped back in her chair. Jase couldn't be just a garden-variety nut job with all this info and high tech at his fingertips, but that meant he was telling the truth. She didn't know which frightened her more.

"When you say covert ops agency, do you mean the CIA?"

"Both of our agencies are offshoots of the CIA. The average citizen has never heard the names and is unaware of our activities."

"Who *is* aware of your activities?"

"It's on a need-to-know basis—sometimes the military, sometimes the CIA, sometimes the president."

"Only *sometimes* for the president?"

"Do you believe me now? The book was just a cover to take me to Break Island."

"Why are you here? Just because I'm Simon Skinner's ex-fiancée? Was I right all along? Is he the one stalking me? And because he's one of these secret agents, you guys had to get involved?"

"It's more complicated than that, Nina. It's Tempest."

She slammed her palms down on each side of the laptop. "What's Tempest? What is it? You know, don't you? That's why you got so freaked out when I showed you that slip of paper from Lou's pocket."

His broad chest expanded as he filled his lungs with air. When he'd released the last bit of breath, he double-clicked another folder. An image of dark, swirling clouds took over the screen and an unaccountable feeling of dread thrummed through her system.

"Simon worked for Tempest. It's one of the covert ops agencies I was talking about."

"Then it is Simon following me. He has something to do with the deaths of Lou and Chris. That's why they knew about Tempest."

"It's not Simon, Nina."

"How do you know that? How can you be so sure?"

"Nina." He crouched beside her chair and took both of

her hands in his, still rough with dirt from his work outside. "Simon's dead."

"No." Her belly flip-flopped. "He can't be dead."

"He is. I'm sorry, Nina. I'm sorry I couldn't tell you before. It's been hell listening to you voice your suspicions about him, knowing all the time how false they were."

She snatched her hands away from his. "You're lying."

"I'm not lying, Nina."

A laugh bubbled up from her throat and she jumped up from the chair, knocking it over. "Because you've been so honest about everything else?"

"I had no choice in the matter. We're talking national security issues."

She drove a thumb into her chest. "I have something to do with national security?"

"You do now."

She paced away from him, her hands settling on her stomach. "How did he die? When did he die?"

He ran his hands across his face and for the first time she noticed the deep lines on both sides of his tight mouth. "I'm telling you this because he was your fiancé, because you're carrying his baby and because your life may be in danger because of that."

Her heart fluttered in her chest and for a brief moment she wanted to run away and pull the covers over her head, but this was Will's father, a story she might well have to tell her son someday.

"What happened to him? Is it related to his PTSD?"

"It's related to his behavior but Simon didn't have PTSD."

"What did he have? Why did he go off the deep end like that?"

"He'd been drugged, programmed, and in trying to break free from the mind control, he lost his mind."

Her body swayed as if she was on the deck of a sailboat, and Jase was immediately at her side. "Sit down. Do you need some water?"

He led her to the love seat where they'd been so close last night in front of the fire. And all along he'd known these terrible truths about Simon, her baby's father.

She sank into the cushion, and Jase returned with two glasses of water. She downed half of hers with one gulp.

"Are you telling me that Tempest did that to him?"

"Not just to Simon. We have reason to believe that Tempest had all of its agents on the same program. They're still on it. Simon was one of the strong ones. They could never completely control him, and when he and another agent figured out what Tempest was doing to them, they went rogue."

"Another agent?"

"He's the one who came in from the field and told us this story. We had plenty of reasons to doubt him, but everything he's claimed has checked out."

"Max Duvall."

His hand jerked and he spilled his water all over the front of his flannel shirt. "How do you know that name?"

"I met him once. He came to our condo when our relationship was on the precipice. Simon introduced him as a coworker and then they went outside to talk."

"That's the agent."

She nodded. "You still haven't told me what happened to Simon."

He looked away and cleared his throat.

"It's bad, isn't it?"

"He died, Nina. He died as a result of what those bastards did to him. He died trying to break free from the yoke of servitude that Tempest imposed on him."

"Why is Tempest doing this to its agents?"

"According to Duvall, Tempest is creating a cadre of

superagents—strong, invincible, impervious to pain, devoid of conscience."

"That's crazy." She dipped her fingers in her water glass and rubbed her temples with the cool moisture. "It's like science fiction."

"That's why it took a while to verify Duvall's story."

"But why me? Why did you land on my doorstep?"

Jase wiped his hands on the seat of his pants. "I told you. I'm the protector. I came here to watch over you."

"Why would Tempest care about me? Simon told me nothing about his work. I obviously didn't even know the name of his agency."

"We're not sure. My boss had an intuition about you and sent me out here."

"To pose as a writer-handyman."

"That's right."

"And it seems that your boss's intuition was correct. Tempest is here. Tempest is watching me. Tempest was watching me in LA. You both were. No wonder I felt stalked."

"I don't know how they contacted Lou and I don't know how Chris found out about them, but it's clear they had a hand in their deaths." He scratched the stubble on his chin. "And your boat accident."

"What?" She choked on her last sip of water. "The boat?"

"The first day I met you. We both assumed Lou was responsible for damaging your boat, but she never admitted it. Why not? She'd admitted everything else."

"You think Tempest put a hole in my boat?"

"Yeah."

"For what purpose?"

"To scare you, put you on edge. They don't know you or this area. Maybe they thought that would be enough to drown you, but if they wanted to kill you, I think they would've done so by now."

She pushed up from the love seat. "That's a lovely thought. What now?"

"I need to get you out of here, off this island. My agency can offer you refuge."

"I think it's a little too late for that."

"Why do you say that?"

As if to punctuate her point, a flash of lightning lit up the room and a rumble of thunder shook the floor.

"Nobody's getting off this island."

Chapter Sixteen

Jase flung open the front door and stepped onto the porch. The dark clouds that had been threatening from a distance all morning had moved in swiftly to envelop the island. A gust of wind slammed against the house, ripping off the shutter that had been hanging by a thread.

Backing up, he stepped over the threshold and clicked the door shut on the encroaching storm. "That came in fast."

"Not really," Nina called from the kitchen, where she'd put on the kettle for hot water. "The weather guy on TV has been forecasting it all week. All the signs were there."

He strode to the kitchen. "Why don't you sit down? You've had a huge shock this morning. If you give me directions, I can try to replicate those pancakes from yesterday."

She kept her back to him and hunched her shoulders as she braced her hands against the stove. "You can stop now, Jason Bennett."

Uh-oh. He had a feeling he'd been experiencing the calm before the storm when he told her about Simon and Tempest...and his own deception.

He wedged his shoulder against the wall. "Stop what? And everyone calls me Jase anyway."

She snorted. "At least that wasn't a lie."

"I thought you understood why I had to lie." Folding his arms, he dug his fingers into his biceps.

"Of course." She flicked her fingers in the air. "National security."

"We didn't have all the facts, Nina."

The whistle on the kettle blew, piercing the thick air between them. She grabbed the handle and dumped the boiling water over her tea bag in the cup and then jumped back as drops of water must've splashed up and scalded her wrist.

He shrugged off the wall and then stopped as she turned with her cup in hand, her blue eyes blazing. "You can stay here because it's going to start pouring rain in the next thirty minutes, but you don't have to pretend to care about me and the baby anymore."

"Pretend? There was no pretense on my part."

Biting her lip, she moved away from the stove and squeezed past him, holding her steaming cup aloft. She stopped at her office door and turned. "Was there ever really a pregnant girlfriend? A baby lost?"

His stomach dropped. "Good God, Nina. Do you really think I'd lie about that?"

"I think you'd lie about anything to do your job, which was get close to me and find out what I knew about Tempest."

"Tempest?" He ran a hand along his jaw. "We didn't think you knew anything about Tempest. It was always just about protecting you, making sure Tempest didn't come after you."

"I know. I got that part and now that I know all about Tempest and…and Simon, you can just do your job. You don't have to fake affection for me or my baby."

"Nina…"

The office door slammed and then shook for good measure.

He shoved his hands into his pockets and kicked at the leg of a chair. If it had been up to him, he would've told her when Lou died and she found that piece of paper in her stepsister's pocket, but Coburn had just given him the okay to tell her. The tremor in her voice and her glistening eyes told him she felt more hurt than angry.

Maybe he should've never gotten personal. Would she be this upset if he'd remained the handyman? Now she believed he'd held her and kissed her just to fake her out and let him in.

She couldn't be more wrong.

The wind howled outside and he felt like howling along with it.

He hunched over the counter, surveying the kitchen and weighing his options. Cereal. Instant oatmeal if she had it.

He glanced at the office door, firmly closed in his face. He'd look for it himself.

He grabbed a bowl from the cupboard and almost dropped it when someone started banging on the front door.

He shoved his weapon in the back of his waistband and put his eye to the peephole. Mr. Kleinschmidt, the single piece of gray hair on his head standing straight up, swayed on the porch.

Jase inched open the door so that it wouldn't be snatched from his grasp. "Mr. Kleinschmidt, what are you doing out here? You look ready to blow away."

He braced a gnarled hand on the post. "Like my boat?"

"Your boat?" The wind blew the rain sideways and soaked Mr. Kleinschmidt's jacket. Jase grabbed his arm and pulled him inside. "What about your boat?"

Nina had wandered in from the sealed fortress of her office, her eyes wide. "What's going on? The storm has really picked up, hasn't it?"

"It snatched my boat right from the dock." Mr. Kleinschmidt ran a hand over his wet face.

"How did that happen? It was tied up." Jase stalked to the window to peek outside. The Kleinschmidts' boat had, indeed, vacated the dock.

"That's what I was going to ask you. We haven't taken it out since you brought it back early this morning. Did you secure it?"

"Of course."

"Did you see the boat out on the water, Carl?"

"It's gone, Nina."

She shot a gaze toward Jase. "Maybe someone stole it, maybe someone desperate to get to the mainland."

"We may have been desperate to get to the mainland. I think we just lost our last chance."

"Is the Harbor Patrol still letting boats cross?"

"I think this morning would've been our last opportunity."

Jase spread his hands. "I'm sorry, Mr. Kleinschmidt. I don't know what could've happened."

But he had a hollow feeling in the pit of his stomach. He had no doubt someone from Tempest was on the island and could even be responsible for the theft of the Kleinschmidts' boat. This agent had made contact with both Lou and Chris somehow. What he couldn't quite grasp is what he and Tempest wanted with Nina.

If the agency wanted her dead, she'd be dead. They could've targeted her in LA before Prospero even had her in its sights, before he'd taken up the job of protecting her.

And if they'd taken the trouble of punching a hole in Nina's boat, they could've just as easily packed it with explosives. He clenched his teeth and took a shuddering breath.

"Were you and Mrs. Kleinschmidt planning on evacuating the island?"

"Not now." Mr. Kleinschmidt tugged his damp jacket around him. "You know, Nina, the water's getting pretty high out there. The Harbor Patrol just might tell us coastal folks to move to higher ground."

"Would they do that?" Jase turned to Nina, whose pale face caused knots to form in his gut. Had the missing boat raised her suspicions, too?

Maybe he should've kept his secrets. He could've explained away the Book file, made a joke of it. He had enough legitimate reasons to protect her that had nothing to do with Tempest. She'd been buying his story up until this point. Now she was needlessly worried about something out of her control…but not out of his.

She twisted a lock of hair around her finger. "It happened once when I was a teenager. Am I remembering that right, Carl?"

"It was about ten years ago, and I think this monster storm has that one beat."

An evacuation would definitely complicate things. Jase asked, "How does the Harbor Patrol notify you if there's an evacuation?"

Mr. Kleinschmidt scratched his chin. "If they can't get out on the water, they'll come door-to-door and you'd better obey or they'll come down on you with fines. Maybe Dora and I can ride with you in the truck if it comes to that, Nina."

"Of course we'll give you and Dora a lift, Carl, and I'm sorry about the boat. I don't understand what could've happened. Do you think the wind was strong enough to snap the rope?"

"It might be in an hour or two, but it wasn't that bad this morning."

"Maybe the Harbor Patrol will find it on the bay."

"Maybe. You two take care now. Dora's going to want to help you out with the baby, Nina. She's been after me to move to California to be closer to the grandkids, so she can use yours as a substitute in the meantime."

So, she hadn't been fooling the Kleinschmidts at all. "That would be lovely. Do you need Jase to help you get back home?"

He waved them off. "Naw."

"I wanna have a look at the bay anyway. I'll walk back with you." Jase grabbed the mackinaw from last night and winked at Nina.

As soon as he stepped onto the porch, the rain lashed his face. He grabbed on to Mr. Kleinschmidt's arm, and the older man listed to the side.

He kept a firm grip on Mr. Kleinschmidt all the way to his front door, where his wife was hovering.

Then he turned toward their boat dock. The water churned and gurgled. Waves formed and crashed against the beach, the wind carrying the salty spray inland.

Even the current force of the water and wind weren't enough to rip a boat from its moorings. Either someone had untied it with the intent of letting it get carried away, or someone had stolen it.

And he hadn't noticed a thing. There was a lot he hadn't noticed since falling under the spell of Nina Moore.

He crouched and studied the area around the dock. Indentations from footprints crisscrossed the dirt and sand. They could belong to anyone.

He returned to Moonstones, and the closed office door. What was she doing in there? Her computer didn't even work.

He sat at his own computer and stared out the window at the darkening sky, which made the afternoon look like midnight.

He brought up his email and clicked on one from Jack. He'd sent a minidossier on Chris Kitchens and the guy was legit—dead but legit. So how had he run afoul of Tempest?

If Break Island had truly been a small town, without all the tourists and the mainlanders coming and going, it would've been a hell of a lot easier to zero in on a stranger. As it was, Nina didn't know half of the people she ran into on a daily basis.

A few hours later, after no communication from Nina, no food and an increasing deluge outside, the table lamp flickered and died. His laptop made a buzzing noise and went black.

Nina flew out of the office. "We lost power."

"Flashlights? Candles? You already mentioned you didn't have a generator."

"I'm not even sure about candles."

They both jumped when a voice boomed from a loud-speaker outside.

"This is the Snohomish County Sheriff's Department calling for an evacuation. Leave your homes on the coast and head over the dunes into town."

"The Kleinschmidts." Nina made for the front door and barreled down the porch.

By the time Jase joined her, she was already hanging on the door of the sheriff's truck and turned at his approach. "There's an evacuation center in the school gym. The school sits on a hill behind the main street."

"I've seen it."

The sheriff jerked his thumb over his shoulder. "You folks need to get going. The water's rising and churning and we're expecting some big waves and flooding. The road's going to be washed out for sure by the end of the day, and then you'll be completely cut off."

"Maybe the storm will level this place and I can start from scratch." Nina tossed her head back toward Moonstones.

"You might get your wish, but you don't want to be inside when it happens."

"We need to pick up the neighbors." Jase gestured to the Kleinschmidts' house.

"Yeah, the old guy opened the front door and waved. They heard us."

"We'll get going, then." Jase smacked the roof of the vehicle. "Thanks."

As Nina picked her way over the soggy ground to the Kleinschmidts' house, Jase held her arm whether she liked it or not.

Mr. Kleinschmidt swung open the door before they took their first step onto the porch.

"I heard, I heard. This storm's coming in like a son of a bitch."

"Carl?"

"It's Nina and her friend."

"Her fiancé?" Dora Kleinschmidt joined her husband at the door, carrying enough jackets to outfit a small army.

The fiancé and pregnancy story must've spread far and wide, because Mrs. Kleinschmidt studied him from behind a pair of thick glasses that magnified her eyes to scary proportions.

"Dora, this is Jason…Buckley—my fiancé."

Jase returned Mrs. Kleinschmidt's surprisingly strong grip. "Call me Jase. Everyone calls me Jase."

"Okay, enough with the introductions. You'll have hours to grill him at the school gym, Dora." Mr. Kleinschmidt took an armful of jackets from his wife.

Nina held up her finger. "Wait here. We'll get the rest of our stuff and drive the truck up to your gate."

They returned to the B and B and Nina collected a few items while Jase packed up his laptop and his weapon and stuffed them into a backpack.

Before she locked up, Nina paused on the threshold and gazed into the sitting room. "I almost do hope the place is destroyed. I need a fresh start."

He took the keys from her hand. "I'll drive."

They picked up Carl and Dora and crawled along the road to town with the rain falling so fast and furious the windshield wipers couldn't keep up.

They hit a little traffic jam winding onto the main street as other coastal residents had gotten the same directive from the sheriff's department.

As Jase pulled into a packed parking lot, he said, "I'll drop you all off at the entrance to the gym and then park the truck."

By the time he parked and slogged his way back through the school parking lot to the gym, Nina and the Kleinschmidts had claimed one corner of a few low bleacher rows.

Jase shed his jacket and hung it over a bleacher railing. "At least they keep it warm in here."

Mr. Kleinschmidt snorted. "With all these bodies in here it's going to get plenty warm."

"The Emersons are over by the coffee." Mrs. Kleinschmidt placed a hand on Nina's arm. "Do you mind if we leave you to say hello, Nina? I'm sure you two would like some time alone anyway."

"Of course not. It looks like they're getting a card game going, too. You might as well enjoy yourself."

Mrs. Kleinschmidt patted her arm. "You have this big, strong man to look out for you now."

Nina managed a tight smile.

When the Kleinschmidts crossed the room to join the card game, Jase puffed out a breath. "Thanks for not blowing my cover."

"What am I supposed to say? 'Jason Bennett is actually a spy for some black ops agency. Oh, and my ex-fiancé was one, too.'"

"I told you a lot more than you needed to know, Nina."

She rounded on him, her nostrils flaring. "You didn't

tell me nearly enough, Jase—you or Simon. I sensed the two of you were alike from the minute I met you."

"What do you want to know, Nina?"

"I want to know what that agency did to Simon. What kinds of things did they make him do? What happened to him at the end? Are they just drugging agents or are they up to something else?"

He pinched the bridge of his nose and squeezed his eyes shut. "Definitely something else."

She straddled the bleacher bench and dug her fingernails into his thigh. "Tell me, Jase. I'm having Simon's baby. We deserve to know."

He blew out a long breath. Jack Coburn didn't have to know everything. "I told you there was drugging and mind control going on. What Tempest hoped to accomplish, what we've heard anyway, is that Tempest has created a sort of superagent—strong, fearless, impervious to pain and impervious to their consciences. They sent them on assignments and then erased all memory of those assignments from their minds."

She covered her mouth, her blue eyes swimming with tears. "That's what they did to Simon?"

He took her hands and smoothed his thumb across her knuckles. "I'm sorry."

She disengaged one hand and clutched her belly. "The baby. Simon must've been on these drugs when I conceived."

"Yeah, it had been going on for over a year." He drew his brows over his nose, an unnamed dread forming in his gut. "What are you getting at, Nina?"

"What if those drugs had some effect on Will? What if my baby is in danger?"

Chapter Seventeen

"No." He placed both hands on her stomach, as if he could prevent any harm to Will. "Everything's fine, isn't it? I mean, you've had ultrasounds and an amniocentesis and all that?"

"I've had a few ultrasounds. I'm not old enough to warrant an amnio, but I need one now."

She needed to stop this line of thought. He couldn't handle another lost baby. Will had to be okay.

He took her face between his hands. "Will's fine. Everything's going to be fine. When this storm is over, I'm going to take you away from here, someplace safe. We'll get the best doctors in the world to look after you."

"So, you *do* think something might be wrong."

"Not at all."

She blinked. Then her eyes widened and she whispered, "You'll never guess who's coming up behind you."

He dropped his hands and craned his head over his shoulder.

Kip Chandler, as scruffy as ever, stopped a few feet away and raised his hand in a peace sign. "Okay to approach, man?"

Jase swung his leg over the bench and turned to face him. "You have a lot of people looking for you."

Kip scooped his dishwater-blond hair back from his

forehead. "I figured that. I've already checked in with the cops. Told them I couldn't handle the heat after…after." He dipped his head, cupping a hand over his eyes.

Hunching forward, Jase asked, "So, you knew what had happened to Lou before you took off?"

"I told her to slow down, and then I left. I heard later that she probably OD'd."

Nina crooked her finger at him. "Tell us what happened that night. Do you know about Chris, the redhead we were with?"

He plopped on the floor beside them, crossing his legs. "I heard. Even more reason for me to lay low."

"Why are you still on the island?" Jase narrowed his eyes. He'd have to check with the chief to make sure he knew Kip was back. He didn't trust the guy. "We figured you'd taken off."

"I wanted to. I didn't have the dough. I've been hiding out. There are a lot of places to hide out on this island."

"Did you have anything to do with Lou's death?" Nina crossed her arms, and Jase was almost grateful to Kip for getting Nina's mind off the baby.

"No way. We'd had a few and we smoked a blunt, shared it with Red. I didn't know Lou had any of the hard stuff. Red left and Lou and I crashed at the motel. I woke up alone, heard what happened and went underground. I can't afford to have cops sniffing around me."

"Do you know where Lou got the hard stuff? The EMTs thought it might be heroin."

Nina was like a dog with a bone.

Kip held up a pair of dirty hands. "I have no clue. Maybe Red had it. He didn't seem to be any stranger to the drug culture."

One of the volunteers came by with some bottles of water. "Anyone thirsty? It's going to be a long night. We're putting out sandwiches in a few minutes, too."

"Thanks. We'll have two waters." Jase picked up two bottles with one hand.

"Make that three." Kip snatched one from the tray.

Jase rolled his eyes at Nina. He sure as hell hoped Kip didn't plan to camp out with them all night. To discourage him, Jase reached for his backpack and pulled out his laptop.

Kip leveled a finger at the computer. "You working on your book?"

Who told him about the book? Jase slid a glance at Nina, who ignored him while she twisted off the cap from her bottle of water. "Yeah."

"I got some stories for you, man."

"I'm sure you do, Kip, but this one's about my experiences in Afghanistan." Jase lowered himself to the floor, stretched his legs in front of him and leaned against the bottom of the bleachers.

After several minutes of Nina grilling Kip about Lou, she raised her head. "They're putting some food out. Do you want me to get you something?"

Jase lifted his laptop. "I'll get it."

Nina had already jumped to her feet. "You're all settled. I need to stretch my legs, anyway."

A sudden fear gripped the back of his neck. "Don't go outside."

"Why would I do that? The storm's coming at us in full force."

Kip rose to his feet. "I could use some food, but I'd better wash my hands first."

"The bathrooms are through those doors by where the food is set up."

Kip ambled after Nina across the gym and Jase kept his eye on both of them. Kip hadn't had any serious offenses on his rap sheet, but the dude was no angel.

Nina returned first with four wrapped sandwiches, two

bags of chips and a couple of apples. "It's not Mandy's fish-and-chips, but the sandwiches look pretty good."

Jase took a paper plate from her, unwrapped two sandwiches and put them on the plate. He chugged some water and put the bottle on the floor next to the plate.

Kip came back, munching on an apple. "I already wolfed down one sandwich. My meals have been a little sketchy, so that hit the spot.

"Are you going to read us any of your book?" Kip came in close to Jase and leaned over his laptop. Then his foot hit Jase's bottle of water and it fell across his plate, soaking his sandwiches.

"Sorry, man." Kip jumped back from the puddle. "Let me get you some paper towels and a couple more sandwiches."

"That's all right." Jase scooted away from the water on the floor. Were they ever going to get rid of this guy?

As if reading his thoughts or maybe just his expression, Kip said, "No, really. I'll drop off your sandwiches and go find a place to hole up in here and get some sleep. I'm hoping the ferry will be giving free rides back to the mainland tomorrow or whenever this storm lets up."

Jase watched Kip cross the room and turned to Nina. "What do you think about Kip's story?"

"I'm not sure. You?"

He tapped his wrist. "He had his sleeves rolled up, so I glanced at his arms and he doesn't have any track marks or anything. Plus, he looks too buff to be into those hard drugs."

"Kip? Buff?"

"He had his sweatshirt unzipped, too, and he's got some muscle there."

"If you say so."

He didn't want her worrying about any of this. Brushing her cheek with one knuckle, he whispered, "How are you doing?"

"I'm doing just fine, but if you think I've forgotten about what those drugs could've been doing to my baby, you're wrong."

"Nina."

"I told you, Jase. You don't have to pretend to care about us anymore."

"And I told you…"

"Sandwiches." Kip handed Jase two wrapped sandwiches on a plate. "I also picked up a blanket, so I'm going to try to get some shut-eye."

Kip wandered away, the blanket pinned between his arm and the side of his body.

Nina heaved a sigh. "Let's just leave this alone, Jase. I'm not embarrassed to admit that I felt something for you, but now I realize it was all fake."

"I was here under false pretenses, but that has nothing to do with how I feel about you."

She put down her sandwich. "And how is that? Protective because it's your job? Protective because Maggie lost your baby?"

He put a finger to her lips and then replaced it with his own lips.

She resisted his attempts at a kiss by sealing her lips, but when he ran a hand along her throat and cupped one full breast in his palm, she sighed and her lips softened beneath his.

He deepened the kiss until she made squeaking noises.

He pulled away. "You don't like that?"

"I like it a lot, but we're in the middle of a gym with hundreds of other evacuees."

He picked up his sandwich and took a huge bite, his appetite surging back. "Nobody noticed a thing—besides, aren't we engaged?"

She nibbled on the edge of her sandwich. "One kiss is not going to make me forget that you lied to me and kept Simon's death from me."

"I know, Nina, but look at it this way. Simon was in the same line of work, and he kept it all from you. He lied to you every day. He had to. He did it to keep you safe."

She sniffled and ripped a piece of crust from her bread. "He didn't do a very good job, did he?"

"He did his best." He demolished the rest of his sandwich and finished off his second one, too.

She held up a blanket. "Unless they also plan to show a movie tonight, I'm going to try to get some sleep."

"I'll put my laptop on the bench." He patted his lap. "Put your head here and tuck that blanket around you."

"Aren't you sleeping?"

He gazed around the gym, cluttered with people, some he'd seen before in the shops and businesses and along the wharf and some he'd never laid eyes on in his life.

"I'm going to stay awake, keep watch."

She spread out one blanket on the polished wood and curled up on her side, resting her head on his thighs.

He tugged the other blanket around her and whispered, "When you wake up, this will all be over. The storm will pass."

THE THUNDER BOOMED, shaking the floor beneath him. Jase blinked as cold water splashed on his face. His stomach turned.

He opened his eyes and tried to focus on the ceiling. Where was he?

Several drops of water hit him and rolled down his cheeks. He gagged as his gut churned.

The gym. They had been evacuated to the school gym. God, he felt nauseous. He dropped his chin to his chest, his neck stiff and sore, his mouth dry—until it wasn't.

He rubbed the back of his neck, and several more drops of water splashed onto his head. He looked up into the recesses of the ceiling. The roof of the gym must have a leak.

As his mouth watered, he brought his knees to his chest. He was going to vomit. Was it the sandwiches? Was Nina sick, too?

He glanced down, but Nina was gone. His head jerked up and he scanned the darkened gym. Shapes huddled around the floor of the gym, a few flashlights and penlights punctuated the gloom and low conversations hummed in the night.

Where did Nina go? He knew pregnant women had to pee a lot, so maybe she'd headed to the restroom.

That's where he needed to be if his stomach wouldn't stop roiling and churning. He didn't want to throw up on the gym floor.

He stretched and reached for his almost-empty bottle of water and nearly knocked it over when his laptop beeped at him. The screen saver flashed and flickered, and he brushed his fingers across the touchpad to wake it up and log in.

A red square pulsated on the display, indicating he had an urgent message. He clicked on it, and an email from Coburn popped up on the screen.

He read the message once. He read the message twice.

Kip Chandler's body was found in a garbage dump. He'd been dead for two weeks. The man calling himself Kip Chandler is an imposter. I repeat. Kip Chandler is an imposter.

Chapter Eighteen

The cold rain lashed her face and the wind plucked at her ponytail, yanking strands loose and plastering them against her wet cheeks. "Where are you taking me? We can't go anywhere in this storm."

The man with Kip pressed the barrel of his gun against the small of her back. "Stop talking."

She threw a beseeching glance at Kip, walking by her side, gripping her arm. "Where are we going, Kip? What's this all about?"

She didn't want to show her hand and mention Simon or Tempest. "Is this about Lou? The cops aren't even looking for you. They've written it off as a drug overdose."

"Do be quiet, Nina. This bloke isn't kidding. He really wants you to shut up and he has no sense of humor."

Just as it had when she'd first heard it, Kip's English accent jolted her. Who the hell was he and how had he hooked up with Lou? Why had he hooked up with Lou?

She shook the rain from her face and shivered. She knew why—to get to her.

"Wh-what did you do to Jase? He wasn't just sleeping, was he?"

"I drugged his sandwiches."

The robot prodding her with the gun grunted. "Enough to kill him?"

"It should be."

Nina choked on a sob.

"You just never know with those bloody Prospero agents, do you?"

"Do you want me to make sure?"

"Maybe later. We need to get her to the warehouse."

"Warehouse?" The only warehouses she knew about were located on the pier. "Why are we going to a warehouse?"

Kip had grown tired of her, and the man with the gun had no intention of answering her questions.

She should've never gone off so willingly with Kip from the gym. With Jase sleeping soundly, Kip explained that he had more info about Lou and Chris but he suspected Jase of being an undercover cop.

Nothing she told Kip, or whoever he was, could convince him otherwise, so she'd left the gym with him only to be met by the goon with the gun.

The drugging of Jase terrified her but made sense. He wouldn't have abandoned his job by falling asleep. He wouldn't have abandoned her.

She said a silent prayer that someone would notice him and try to wake him. She felt sure that once awake, Jase would do anything to fight the effects of the drug.

She glanced at Kip, his shaggy hair slicked back to reveal sharp features. What did Tempest want with her? As Jase said, they could've killed her long ago. Kip and his henchman could've killed her outside the gym. Instead, they were marching her to some warehouse.

For what purpose? Torture? Would they try to find out what Simon had told her? They'd be sorely disappointed. She knew nothing.

She placed her hand on her tummy and patted, sending soothing vibes to Will.

"Don't worry about your baby, Nina. We're not going to hurt him."

Bitter bile rose in her throat and she spit it out, aiming for Kip's shoes. Even the fact that these people knew about her baby terrified her.

After relentlessly fighting the wind and slogging through puddles of water, they came upon the wharf. She'd been right about the warehouse.

Is this where Kip had been hiding out for the past few days?

The boats moored in their slips thrashed and bucked like wild horses in a stable. The row of abandoned warehouses huddled beyond the bait shop and they trudged toward them.

When they reached the last one, Kip produced a key for the shiny new lock and pulled the door open. He pushed her through first and she stumbled in the darkness.

"Be careful." He caught her arm and steadied her.

"That's a little ridiculous—coming from you."

He clicked his tongue. "We're here to take care of you, Nina, until the next stage of your journey."

Her wet flesh turned icy cold. What the hell was he talking about? "I don't understand any of this. Who are you? Is this some plan of Lou's?"

"That junkie?" He brushed his hands together. "She was just a means to an end—you. I have to say she proved to be more loyal to you than I expected. When I tried to convince her to get close enough to you so that I could kidnap you, she refused. Even after I offered her money. Of course, I would've taken that money back once I killed her, but she didn't know that."

Nina's throat burned with tears. "You killed her."

"I offered her some smack and she took it."

"And Chris Kitchens? What happened to him?"

"He snooped where he shouldn't have snooped, but you already knew that about him—nosy, intrusive."

He flipped on a lamp powered by a generator and she gasped and stepped back.

"What is all this?" Her gaze darted around the room, where Kip had created a cozy enclave—a bed, space heaters, a platter of cheese and fruit, a carafe of orange juice and one of milk.

"We're here to take care of you, Nina. I believe the storm will abate enough tomorrow morning so that we can leave."

Her heart slammed against her rib cage. "Leave? Where are we going?"

"To a secure location where we can nurture your baby until he's born."

Her knees buckled but Kip caught her. "You see? You need care."

"What are you? Who are you?"

"Let's get you settled."

She wrenched away from him. "I don't want to get settled here and I'm not going anywhere with you."

The guard dog loomed over her, brandishing his gun.

"You'll do what I say, Nina, or Zeke will make your life miserable."

Eyeing Zeke's gun and expressionless face, she asked, "What do you want me to do?"

"That's so much better for everyone." He plucked at the sleeve of her wet jacket. "Get out of these wet clothes and change into the nightgown across the bed."

She crossed her arms. "I'm not taking my clothes off."

"We're not here to molest you." He snapped his fingers, and Zeke yanked off her jacket. "Now, you can undress yourself and get into that nightgown or Zeke can undress you and perhaps accidently molest you."

She swallowed hard and then crept toward the bed. "Keep your backs turned toward me."

"So you can run off or do something equally stupid?" He followed her to the bed and cranked on all the space heaters. "I don't think so."

"I don't…"

One look from Kip and Zeke started stalking toward her.

"Okay, okay." She toed off her boots and peeled her wet socks from her feet. She rolled down her leggings and then turned her back as she pulled her sweater over her head. Wearing just her underwear, she reached for the nightgown.

"Everything." Kip threw a towel at her back. "Remove all your clothing. It's damp and we don't want you taking a chill."

With her underwear still in place, she toweled off. She kept the towel around her waist and slipped the nightgown over her head. Then she dropped the towel and shimmied out of her panties and bra.

Kip scooped up all her clothing and laid it out in front of one of the space heaters. "You can have your clothes back tomorrow morning or whenever we get out of here."

"How are you leaving the island? Do you have a boat?"

He ignored her while he hovered over the food.

She perched on the edge of the bed. "Are you going to tell me what's going on now?"

He poured a glass of milk and selected cheese and fruit to arrange on another plate. "Have your snack and we'll talk."

She took the plate from him and balanced it on her lap. This whole situation was creeping her out.

"Your prenatal vitamin." He shook a big white pill onto her plate.

"I already take them."

"Take these."

With trembling fingers she picked up the vitamin, or whatever it was, and dropped it onto her tongue. She took a sip of milk and lodged the pill in her cheek.

Before she could blink an eyelash, Zeke was in front of her, shoving his thick fingers into her mouth. He found the pill and held it up to Kip. Then he smacked her across the face.

Her head whipped to the side as Kip swore.

"Control yourself, Zeke." Kip handed her another vitamin. "Swallow the pill, Nina. They're just prenatal vitamins."

With her eyes watering, she gulped down the pill. "Why are you doing this?"

Kip poured himself a glass of juice. "Because you're carrying Simon Skinner's baby."

She shook her head. "I don't understand."

"Simon worked for us. I know you know that now because Jase Bennett told you. You also know Simon Skinner is dead. He went berserk in a lab and was killed by one of our other agents."

Nina covered her mouth with her hand. Jase had never told her how it happened.

"Simon Skinner was very special to us—until he rebelled." He rolled the glass between his hands. "He was one of our superagents, conditioned, prepped and primed—like Zeke here. Elite."

"It put him over the edge of madness."

"Only because he stopped taking the medication that made him special—but not before he impregnated you."

Her hands cupped her belly beneath the soft flannel of the nightgown. She and Jase had been following the wrong path. Tempest didn't believe the drugs Simon was taking were going to hurt her baby—just the opposite.

"What are you saying?"

"I can see by your face that you already understand, Nina. We believe your baby is genetically predisposed to all the qualities we want in an agent."

"That's crazy."

"Is it?" He nodded toward Zeke. "Let's take Zeke. He's a man, but a reconstituted one. He's special—stronger, heightened senses, oblivious to pain—perfect for our purposes, as your baby will be."

She stood up suddenly and the plate of food crashed to the floor. "You're not getting anywhere near my baby."

"We already are, Nina. We have him. He's ours and you're ours for the next…four months. We'll pamper you, make sure you have the best of everything, make sure the baby has the best of everything. Your position will be quite enviable."

"And once I've given birth?"

"A baby needs his mother. Breast-feeding is the best start to life, and your breast milk will be very special, Nina."

Nausea swept through her body and she broke into a cold sweat. These people were insane. They really believed they could turn her baby into some kind of superbaby they could groom into the perfect agent.

"I'm not going to be a party to this insanity."

"You no longer have a choice in the matter. Once this storm clears, we're going to whisk you away to a very secure and secret location. Nobody will be able to find us—not Jase Bennett, not fifty Prospero agents, not Jack Coburn himself."

Kip took a turn around the room, his face illuminated with an almost religious zeal. "Think of it, Nina. Your boy will be the first, our test subject. Once we meet with success, our agents can impregnate other strong women like you. Our superagents have no problem in that area at all—our special formula, T-101, makes them especially potent and virile. Didn't you find that with Simon?"

Lou's craziness didn't hold a candle to this guy's. She couldn't allow him to take her off the island. Once they left Break Island, it would be over for her, for Will. Their drugs would probably kill him.

She swooped down and grabbed a shard of glass from the plate and ran for the door of the warehouse. But Zeke was at the door before she got there and twisted her hand until she dropped the glass.

He lifted her in his arms as she beat against his chest and face, but she might as well have been fighting against a slab of granite. He deposited her back on the bed and held her while Kip secured her arms and legs with leather straps lined with sheepskin.

Looking down at her, Kip clicked his tongue. "I don't know why you have to make this so difficult. You belong to us now. Your son belongs to us. And there's not a damned thing Jase Bennett can do about it."

Chapter Nineteen

Jase shoved his fingers down his throat once more and vomited the last of the poison from his system. If that ceiling hadn't been leaking above him, waking him up with cold water on his face, he'd be out cold. Then he would've regurgitated in his sleep and choked on his own vomit. That's how it worked.

Kip, or whoever the hell he was, would be free and clear to remove Nina from the island, to kidnap her. He was convinced that's what Tempest wanted. Otherwise, Kip would've poisoned Nina's sandwich, too.

What did they want with her? What did they want with her baby?

Someone flushed a urinal. "You okay in there?"

"Yeah, just puking my guts out. I'll live."

"Hope it wasn't those sandwiches."

No, just *his* sandwiches.

He waited for the other man to leave the bathroom, and then he staggered to his feet, wiping his mouth with the back of his hand. He grabbed a wad of toilet paper and blew his nose.

He pushed out of the stall and hunched over the sink. He cranked on the cold water and splashed his face, filling his mouth and then rinsing and spitting over and over.

Gripping the edge of the porcelain, he leaned into the

wavy mirror. The distorted image that peered back at him matched the way he felt.

He headed back into the gym and grabbed two bottles of water. He downed the first one and twisted off the cap to the second. Almost all of the evacuees were sleeping while the storm raged outside.

Kip couldn't have left the island with Nina, even though it had been hours since Jase passed out. A boat would've never lasted out on that sound.

He sidled up next to a window, boarded over with plywood, and put his eye to the crack between the pieces of wood. The wind had died down a little and the blackness had faded to graphite gray.

A few more hours and dawn would break over the island. The storm would be on its way out. Would the Harbor Patrol allow boats to leave for the mainland?

Would Kip be foolish enough to launch a boat from the wharf, where anyone could see him? Where he could see him?

If Kip thought his poisoned sandwiches had been successful, he wouldn't be looking for Jase, but how would you get an unwilling pregnant woman onto a boat in the light of day?

Even if Kip knocked out Nina, drugged her, he'd have to carry her onto the boat. Too many people in this town knew Nina for Kip to get away with that.

He could take her from her own boat dock at Moonstones. Maybe he'd taken her back to Moonstones and they were there now waiting for the storm to pass. If Kip thought he'd killed his adversary, he wouldn't be worried about him showing up. He wouldn't be concerned about the Kleinschmidts stopping him, and there was no one else.

Jase felt a flare of hope. That made sense. Kip would take her to Moonstones, where he had a boat waiting for them—maybe even the Kleinschmidts' boat, which he'd stolen earlier.

His gaze traveled around the gym. He had to get out of here. He had to rescue Nina and Will.

Keeping close to the walls of the gym, he crossed to the other side where double doors led to a causeway connecting the gym to the rest of the school. The organizers of the evacuation had wanted everyone to stay out of the school, but nobody saw him as he slipped out one of the doors.

Rivers of water rushed down the causeway and swirled around the drains and vents that couldn't accommodate the deluge. Jase waded through the flood and turned the corner toward the parking lot. No cars had floated away, but nothing was drivable, either, as the water had reached as high as the wheel wells of the cars.

Had Kip and Nina walked out of here? They must have, unless Kip had stored a rowboat nearby.

He half walked, half slipped and slid down the hill to the main street, where windows had been boarded up and sandbags bunched up against the doors. The ankle-deep water slowed his progress, and when he got to the path that led to the other side of the dunes, he found a river of mud and sand.

He slogged through it all, one step at a time, convinced he'd find Nina at Moonstones.

The wind stopped howling for ten seconds and a streak of light pierced the horizon. Instead of filling him with encouragement, the abatement of the storm filled him with a terrible urgency. As soon as the storm broke and the dawn awakened, Kip would whisk Nina off the island.

If that happened, he would never find her. He'd never hold her again. He'd never have a chance to make love to her. He'd never look into her baby's face.

He pushed on, battling the water and the wind and his own guilt for allowing her to be snatched away from him.

When Moonstones appeared, not much worse for wear than before the storm, he almost dropped to his knees. Instead, he hunched forward, the sand dunes concealing him from prying eyes at the windows of the B and B.

He approached Moonstones from the deck side, where the bedraggled yellow crime scene tape flapped in the wind. Tempest had planned this abduction months ago. Kip Chandler had been targeted and murdered, his identity stolen, and then the fake Kip had insinuated himself into Lou Moore's life with booze and weed. It must've been laughably easy. Kip had probably convinced Lou to visit Nina for one more try at Moonstones, told her stories about his attorney brother and how he'd get the place back for her.

Tempest had found Nina's weak spot and had gone in for the kill. Literally. What had poor Lou discovered about Kip at the end? What had Chris discovered? If Chris had gotten wind that Kip knew anything about Simon, he would've done anything to get to the truth—even put himself in mortal danger.

From the deck, Jase peered out at the sound. His stomach dipped when he didn't see any boats at Nina's or the Kleinschmidts' docks. Nina's boat was still sitting on the trailer by the shed in the back.

Holding his gun in front of him, he slipped around to the front and peeked in the windows. Everything was as they'd left it yesterday.

He circled the entire house but found no evidence that anyone was there now or had been there since they'd evacuated.

He dug Nina's spare key from the dirt in the flowerpot on the porch and opened the door, his weapon still ready.

He didn't need it. The B and B was empty. Kip hadn't taken Nina here. He didn't plan to haul her away on a boat.

Sinking to the arm of the love seat, Jase massaged

his temples. Could it really be as simple as waiting and watching at the wharf?

It might not be that simple. Kip could be in disguise. He could conceal Nina in a trunk. His gut rolled again, but it had nothing to do with the poison that had already left his system.

What resources did Kip have on the island? He knew nobody. The police considered him a person of interest. He'd been posing as a drunk his entire time on the island, hanging out with Lou, telling her tall tales about helicopters.

His pulse leaped. Kip hadn't told Lou about the helicopter. She'd overheard him on the phone asking about a helipad on the island. Maybe Lou's habit of eavesdropping got her killed.

He rushed to the window and looked at the sky over the sound. He'd seen an orange rescue helicopter over the bay before. There had to be a helipad on the island.

And Kip had been inquiring about one because he planned to leave the island by helicopter—with Nina.

He holstered his gun and waded into the yard. The force of the water had knocked down the fence he'd been working on for Nina. That could be fixed, but once Nina boarded that helicopter and left Break Island, she'd be in Tempest's clutches—and that couldn't be fixed.

Jase didn't have time to slog through two feet of water all the way back to town. He made his way to the shed on the other side of the B and B, where Nina kept a rowboat. That was the only way anyone was going to be maneuvering the streets for the next few days.

The water made it impossible for him to open the door of the shed, so he grabbed the ax he'd been using the day before and hacked through the wooden door. The water rushed into the shed and he followed it.

The boat was hanging from two hooks and he lifted it

down and plopped it on top of the water. He unhooked two oars from the inside of the boat and floated out of the shed.

Rowing back to town went a lot faster than wading, but the light of another gloomy day had started to seep through the clouds. The streets were still deserted, although he spotted a rescue vehicle, its orange light revolving on its roof.

He rowed toward the vehicle. County workers were in the back of the truck, tossing sandbags over the side.

Jase yelled to them, "Hey, do you know where there's a helipad on the island?"

They shrugged and shook their heads, but one guy pointed across the street. "Jeff probably knows."

Digging his oars into the water, Jase maneuvered toward Jeff, who was knocking on the door of a business.

"Are you Jeff?"

The man turned around. "What are you doing out here?"

"I'm trying to find someone. The guys back there said you might know where a helipad is on the island."

"Sure I do, but I hope you're not thinking of taking a helicopter off the island. Even though the tail end of this storm is riding through, the air is still unstable."

"No, no, I'm not, but that's where my friend is."

"The only helipad I know about is on top of one of the old warehouse buildings at the end of the pier at the town wharf. It's past Ned's Bait Shop. You can't miss it. The other warehouses have peaked roofs and this one's is flat and higher than the rest."

"Thanks." Jase had never rowed as a sport, but if he had, this stint would win him a gold medal.

By the time he hit the pier, he didn't need the boat anymore. The water here had already receded, although it had left many of the boats in the slips at odd angles or lodged on top of the gangplanks beside the slips.

He stashed the boat by the bait shop and rounded the corner of a tall abandoned building behind it. When he looked toward the end of the pier and the warehouses huddled there, his heart stammered in his chest.

A yellow Bell helicopter was stationed on top of the last warehouse, its blades already spinning.

Of course, Kip would want an early start before boat and foot traffic swarmed the wharf.

Jase dropped his backpack and sloughed off his jacket. Clutching his Glock pistol, he ran toward the warehouses. She hadn't left yet. She hadn't left yet.

People emerged onto the roof and Jase dived against the side of the first warehouse. He had to maintain the element of surprise.

He darted to the next warehouse, looking skyward. He caught a glimpse of three people on the roof—Nina was one of them. So, Kip had help.

He launched himself at the fourth and final warehouse. When he reached the door, he found it locked with a brand-new padlock. With the butt of his gun, he broke off the lock and burst into the warehouse.

Kip hadn't left any backup personnel, but what he saw on the floor of the warehouse made his jaw drop—a bed, food, all the comforts of home. At least Kip hadn't hung Nina from the ceiling by her wrists, but the fact that he'd taken such good care of her scared the hell out of him.

The thwacking of the blades on the roof grew louder. He knew that sound—liftoff.

A set of stairs led to the roof, and Jase took them two at a time. He thrust the heels of his hands against the board covering the opening to the roof and scrambled through it, landing on his hands and knees in a puddle of water.

Nina was already in the chopper, and her eyes widened as she spotted him. Kip had one foot on the step and one on the roof.

Jase shot him.

Kip spun around and his dirty-blond hair fell over his eyes, making him look like the old Kip. He clawed at his waistband, most likely reaching for his weapon.

But the chopper pilot must've had his own orders because he lifted off the roof of the warehouse.

Jase heard Nina's scream merge with the whine of the helicopter as it took off, Kip dangling from the doorway.

She couldn't go any farther or higher or she'd be lost to him forever. He waved his hands over his head and yelled, "Jump! Jump over the water!"

Would she do it? Could he even ask her to? She could lose her baby, but if she went with Tempest, she would lose him anyway.

Jase waved his arms again and pointed down. Would she understand? Did she know what she had to do?

The helicopter lurched over the water, weighed down by Kip hanging on to the stands. It hadn't gained much height yet.

She had to do it. Now.

As the chopper cleared the boats, Nina stepped over Kip, hugged herself and dropped into thin air.

Epilogue

Her eyes flew open and she convulsively clutched at the white sheets. A large, warm hand covered one of hers and she looked into the dark chocolate eyes of her baby's new father.

Jase brought her hand to his lips and pressed them against her palm. "Did you have another nightmare?"

"It wasn't so bad this time. I was falling out of a plane, but I landed on a puffy white cloud."

"That's a lot better than landing in a freezing-cold, choppy bay."

"Not something I want to repeat anytime soon."

"Not many people could've done it." He threaded his fingers through hers. "You were incredibly brave."

"I'm not so sure about that, given the alternative. The prospect of becoming a breeder for Tempest was not something I was relishing." She shivered despite the warmth of the room and Jase's touch. "How did they think they could get away with that?"

"They almost did." He chafed her hand between his. "Tempest's leader calls himself Caliban, and he's certifiable. We have a dire situation on our hands."

"Do you know... Did they ever find Kip's body?"

"Yes. Technically, he drowned."

"Who was he?"

He lifted a shoulder. "A Tempest agent we haven't identified yet."

"He killed Lou and Chris." Her bottom lip quivered. "They must've found out something about him that night they were all together."

"Kip's not the kind of guy to leave loose ends."

She smoothed the sheet over her belly and pressed her hand against her burgeoning bump. Holding her breath, she waited to feel some movement, some sign that Will was okay, not that she'd been feeling him move before her jump into the bay.

Jase traced her hand. "He's going to be okay."

"I'm scared."

"I know. Me, too."

"Are we ready to see what's what?" Dr. Day bustled into the room followed by a nurse with a cart.

"I don't feel any movement."

"You're not quite five months, so that's not so unusual. Everything looks good from the outside. Now let's see about the inside." Dr. Day folded the sheet down and lifted Nina's top to expose her abdomen.

She snapped on a pair of gloves, flicked on the ultrasound and held up a tube of jelly. "This is going to be a little cold and I know you're trying to stay warm, so I apologize in advance."

As the doctor spread the jelly over her bump, Jase squeezed her hand.

Dr. Day applied the paddle and circled her belly. "Ah, there he is."

Nina's head had rolled to the side and she was staring at the image so hard her eyes burned. "Is he okay? Can you tell? Is he moving?"

"Looks fine to me." She winked at Jase. "Do you want to hear the heartbeat, Dad?"

"He's not…" Nina's eyes flew to Jase's face, but he just grinned.

"Of course I want to hear his heartbeat."

The *thump, thump* echoed in Nina's own heart and her eyes brimmed with tears. "He's okay."

"I told you he would be." Jase leaned over and kissed her mouth. "A little jump from a chopper isn't enough to deter him. Maybe he'll be a navy SEAL or something."

"Stop." She poked his thigh as a tear trailed from her eye into her ear. "I'm hoping he'll be an accountant."

Dr. Day clicked a button. "I just took his picture." She plucked a few tissues from the box on the tray and wiped the jelly from Nina's abdomen.

"I'll have the nurse bring by the picture." Dr. Day stopped at the door. "I understand you'll be leaving the base here at Kitsap. Just let me know where you wind up so I can send your file on to your next ob-gyn."

Jase cleared his throat. "Doc, that information is classified. We'll be taking Nina's file with us when we leave in a few days."

"Understood, Lieutenant Bennett."

"Haven't heard that in a while."

"Former Lieutenant Bennett." She waved and shut the door behind her.

"You're not even going to tell me where I'm headed, are you?"

He pushed back from his chair and sat on the edge of her bed. "As long as Tempest is out there, you and Will are in danger. Prospero will protect you until it's safe."

"When will that be, Jase? You don't even know who Caliban is. You don't even know his endgame."

"We'll find him, Nina. We'll figure it out."

"You?" She pleated the folds of the sheet. "You, personally?"

"Just like surveillance, hunting down Caliban is not my job, either. I thought I told you what my job was."

"Personal security?"

"Otherwise known as babysitting."

"And who are you babysitting this time? Some Saudi princess? A sexy German spy?"

He slipped his hands beneath her top and caressed her belly. "Naw, just a crazy pregnant lady."

She grabbed his wrist. "You'll be with me in the secret location?"

"I'm going to be right with you all the way, Nina. I'll even be there in the delivery room and beyond, if you'll have me."

"Oh, I'll have you, Jason Bennett, but we're a package deal."

"I wouldn't have it any other way."

* * * * *

715_ST16

MILLS & BOON®

It's Got to be Perfect

IT'S GOT
TO BE
Perfect

UNCORRECTED
PROOF COPY

HALEY HILL

* cover in development

When Ellie Rigby throws her three-carat engagement ring into the gutter, she is certain of only one thing. She has yet to know true love!

Fed up with disastrous internet dates and conflicting advice from her friends, Ellie decides to take matters into her own hands. Starting a dating agency, Ellie becomes an expert in love. Well, that is until a match with one of her clients, charming, infuriating Nick, has her questioning everything she's ever thought about love…

Order yours today at
www.millsandboon.co.uk

MILLS & BOON®
INTRIGUE
Romantic Suspense

A SEDUCTIVE COMBINATION OF DANGER AND DESIRE